NO LONGER
THE PROPERTY OF
BOYNTON BEACH
CITY LIBRARY

Search for the Descendants of Christ

A Novel

by James Cary

Anrald Press
Boynton Beach, Florida

This is a work of fiction. Names, characters, places and incidents either are the product of the author's imagination, or are used fictitiously and any resemblance to actual persons, living or dead, businesses, companies, events, or locales is entirely coincidental.

Copyright © 2004 by James Cary

All Rights Reserved. No part of this publication may be reproduced, scanned, or transmitted in any form or by any means, electronic or mechanical, including photocopy, recording or any other information storage and retrieval system, without prior permission in writing from the publisher. Request for permission should be addressed to:

Anrald Press
P.O. Box 233
Boynton Beach, FL 33425

James Cary
    Seeds: Search for the Descendants of Christ

Cover Design: ©Julie Malear

Library of Congress Control Number: 2004111309
ISBN: 0-9760826-0-8
Anrald Press

Also by James Cary

Japan Today: Reluctant Ally

Tanks and Armor in Modern Warfare

To Ruth Fauver Dunlap Cary

and the brood she reared, alone and afraid:

> Doug
>
> Clint
>
> Ruth
>
> Jim

Acknowledgment

Three years ago, I joined a south Florida writers group, seeking constructive criticism of the chapters in this book as they slowly emerged from my research.

I am deeply in debt to all members of this organization. Their suggestions and reactions have helped me shape the final manuscript and move it toward a higher level of expression than I might otherwise have achieved.

So, with a dip of my computer, I particularly would like to salute Julie Malear, Monika Conroy, Bob Kerpel and Mariane Kulich for their extraordinary efforts in my behalf, and express my thanks to Ginger Curry, Ben Peck, Tom Collins, Lou Ruf, Diane Warner, Mary Yuhas, Millicent Brady and the others who have come and gone. You are the best.

James Cary

Author's Note

This is a work of fiction based on history. The Xth Legion tiles do exist. So do Mary's Well and Joseph's Cave. There are fingerprints on the Isaiah Scroll. The Copper Scroll is an inventory of gold and silver stolen from the Second Temple and Qumran and then buried in the desert. The evidence that Christ had brothers and sisters is in the Bible and other authenticated writings. The deaths of James and Symeon, the Roman siege of Jerusalem and the Xth Legion's destruction of Qumran are taken in part from selected available documentation. The flight of the Holy Family to a place called Cochaba, although its location is unknown, is supported by the fragmentary sources described. And the alleged relationship between Christ, the early Christians and the Essenes, while presented in imaginary scenes, does reflect a current trend in research that is slowly unraveling the most fascinating chapter yet in the history of Christian origins.
J.C.

Part One

Plowing

Chapter I

Tom Shannon paused at the bottom of the stone steps, heart racing.

Before him was a dirt-walled chamber crowded with tourists. Pale ceiling lights cast an amber glow over their heads and shoulders as they strolled from display case to display case, examining artifacts from the first century A.D., found at the site. Off to one side a uniformed attendant wandered in small circles, hands clasped behind his back.

Tom, twenty-six, tall and muscular, a stray lock of black hair spilling across his forehead, pulled in a deep breath, detected a faint musty odor, felt the moist air prickling skin on the back of his hands. He exhaled through puffed cheeks, trying to calm down, although certain he was on the brink of a major discovery, crucial to his research and of great importance to the world.

He shifted his gaze to the left wall. There. That's where he should find what he was looking for. Somewhere in that sandy-brown mass, draped in shadow -- and mystery too. It seemed dark, brooding, almost menacing, an overwhelming presence dominating the room.

Tom's six-foot two body went rigid and his fists clenched with barely controlled excitement. Was it possible? Could whatever is concealed there have survived for nearly two thousand years? Something that had been handled by---

He shook his head, trying to clear his mind; almost shocked he dared harbor such an idea. With a trembling hand he pushed that stray lock back into place and sighed, frustrated by having to deal with a subject as controversial as this cave beneath the Church of St. Joseph in the ancient city of Nazareth.

He kept wondering: *What will I find?* He had no idea, no clue suggesting what it might be. All he had were those twenty words -- a broken sentence from a fragment of an ancient scroll found decades ago among Christian records in the city of Tiberius, ten miles to the northeast. It said: "And then he came to his home and selected a ledge midway of the long wall. There he placed a--- "

He placed a what? The sentence ended abruptly, lopped off by deterioration of the scroll, yet so tantalizingly reproduced in the photographic copy, and translation from Aramaic, he had obtained from archives of the Smithsonian Institution in Washington, D.C.

Tom took another deep breath, fighting his impatience. *Damn! How I hate this uncertainty. But I'm sure of one thing. When I find whatever's hidden here, I'm not going to turn it over to officials at this cave or the Israeli government. No way! That would entangle me in red tape up to my eyeballs. I'd never get the answers I need, particularly the identity of the "he," the person who left the mysterious something here, the person cited in the scroll.*

Tom approached the wall, turned and checked his position. He was out of the attendant's line of sight. The nearest tourist was halfway across the room. Good. He faced the wall again, dark eyes squinting in the poor light. He ran a hand over the smooth-clay surface, trying to detect any aberration that might indicate a ledge had been there at one time. It felt cold, grainy, yet, somehow, warm, too. *That's crazy. How could it be cold and warm at the same time? My imagination is running wild.*

He stepped back, stared at the critical segment, attempting mentally to break it into sections and inspect each in detail. Then he placed both hands flat against the wall. Again he thought he felt heat, pulsing up through the cold, clammy earth. The wall seemed almost alive.

Tom continued his inspection. After ten minutes, he knew

the task was hopeless. His information was provocative. It conjured images of naked bodies hanging from crosses...shepherds tending their flocks...a brilliant star lighting the night...a bearded, robed man riding into a walled city on the back of a donkey -- but it was too vague to suggest what he should do next.

Exasperated, he turned toward the center of the room.

On the far side, an unshaven, dark-complexioned man with tangled black hair, was staring at him. Tom froze. *Is the guy watching me? I saw him when I came in, and our eyes met twice later. Strange. Each time the man looked away. But watching me? I must be getting paranoid. Still...*

Tom walked over to a rack filled with pamphlets near the attendant's desk, trying not to attract attention. He selected *History of St. Joseph's Cave,* with a painting of the church on the cover, paid the four shekels price stamped in one corner, then returned to the wall, thumbing the pages. He stopped when he came to a photograph and description of the chamber which said:

The Church of St. Joseph is built over two subterranean caverns scraped out of the side of a hill. Archaeological exploration indicates the caverns, known popularly as Joseph's Cave, were once a carpenter's workshop.

We know that the Virgin Mary and her husband, Joseph the Carpenter, lived in this vicinity. Such information and other indications have led to the conclusion this was their residence. When you enter these caves you are on hallowed ground -- the boyhood home of Jesus of Nazareth.

Tom snorted, upset anyone would write with such certainty about a subject that was far from accepted by Biblical scholars. Joseph's home could have been any place -- not necessarily this cave -- within walking distance of Mary's Well, the only source of water in the area. Tom's education in world history at the University of Michigan had made him skeptical of such assumptions. He searched the pamphlet in vain for a citation that might support the claim, then, in disgust, slammed the side of his fist against the wall.

Just as quickly he regretted it. *Damn! Got to watch my temper. Hope no one saw me.* He spun around. No one was looking his way, and the attendant was busy ushering out a group of visitors.

Tom breathed easier, tried to weigh his options, his spirits, so high a few minutes ago, now sinking rapidly. *Should I keep trying to find that elusive something -- whatever it is -- left in the cave centuries ago, or should I continue on to Jerusalem, my next stop? Damn, I can't give up now, but what choice do I have?*

Mulling these thoughts, he riffled through more pages of the pamphlet, looking for additional information that might help him reach a decision. Gradually he became aware of a strange new sensation. Something cold was touching his right foot. He looked down. A tiny avalanche of silt, pouring from the place on the wall where his fist landed, had collected in a conical heap and overflowed into his low-cut loafer.

Startled, Tom jerked the foot away, then stood on tiptoe to take a closer look. The dirt was coming from a small hole, about the size of a quarter, above his right shoulder.

What in heaven's name have I done? Should I get out of here before someone notices and accuses me of damaging an historical site?

He edged away from the wall. Of all the freakish things. What would happen next? *But damn it, I can't leave. I still think something of great importance is hidden in this cave...the scroll says...*

An idea exploded in his mind, starting a train of logic. He stopped, whirled around.

The scroll said whatever was hidden in the cave was left on a ledge of the long wall. That was the wall directly in front of him.

It also said it was left on a ledge *midway* of the long wall. He stared, measuring the wall visually. As nearly as he could tell the hole he had made was almost centered.

What else?

The hole is just above eye level. That's exactly where a

ledge used by adults would be.

His excitement returned.

Could a ledge, at one time, have been where the hole is now, that hole staring at him like some kind of evil eye? Could the ledge gradually have collapsed, losing its original form, but leaving a hollow area behind? Then, over the centuries could that dirt, and dust from the air, have collected, been pasted down by the moisture in the air, and sealed the hollow area into the wall?

No, that's too made up, too far fetched. One of those easy assumptions I detest. Then it hit him.

Oh damn! Oh Goddamn! The wall is right! The centered location's right! The height is right! The moisture in the air is right. A confluence of four factors, a coming together that couldn't have occurred entirely by happenstance. They were almost the beginning of a scientific proof. At least they had enough logical substance to improve the odds considerably. And if something actually is hidden here, wouldn't that be proof this is the ledge? My God, it could be! No matter how unlikely, this could be it! And if so, that something could have been touched...held by...! Stop it, Tom! Calm down! My God, I'm talking to myself!

He looked around, tried to act more like a professional historian.

The last few tourists were drifting out, talking, laughing, snapping leather cases around cameras they had been using a few minutes before. Some stragglers remained, including that unshaven guy, again looking Tom's way and conversing with the attendant.

A few more cameras flashed, then ceased. The attendant began picking up crumpled, discarded film wrappings, not looking at Tom in his dim part of the cave. The unshaven man had disappeared, too, and the flow of dirt from the wall had stopped.

Tom poked a finger into the hole. He felt empty space and more dust. He moved closer, stood on tiptoe to get better leverage, inserted two fingers this time. His fingertips scraped something hard and flat.

He worked the object toward the opening. The aperture was too small to permit passage. Tom looked over his shoulder at the center of the room. The caretaker was busy straightening the rack of publications.

Tom rose higher on his toes, grunted, pushed on sides of the hole and increased its size by moving an inserted finger in a circular motion. This time he hooked the object in the crook of his index finger and pulled it into the opening. Gripping it between thumb and finger, he pulled again. It fell to the floor, landing in the silt below, a dirty, white rectangle of porcelain-like material, about two inches wide, a quarter of an inch thick and perhaps four inches long.

Now the attendant was looking his way. Tom dropped his pamphlet over the object. He turned his back to the attendant, bent down, lifted the object into the palm of his right hand, picked up the pamphlet with his left and swept the object into his right pants pocket as he stood up. He swung his foot to scatter the dust, then smiled at the attendant and dropped a dollar bill into a donation box on his way out.

Tom mounted the steps, moved swiftly up the passageway, through the church and into the fresh warm air and crowds outside. He didn't relax until he reached his little, rented, Mercedes sports car. Seated behind the wheel, he took the object from his pocket and examined it, despite scores of people streaming by who could see what he was doing. It was caked with dirt, and what appeared to be beeswax or tallow on one side. He scraped the crust away with his thumb, then fished a handkerchief from a back pocket and rubbed. He spat on the object and rubbed again.

A series of hard, arched ridges appeared. He turned the object and repeated the scrubbing. An image, apparently centuries old, emerged, tinted faintly in green and black.

Tom rubbed more vigorously, then stared in astonishment at the small, decorated tile in his hand.

"It can't be," he said aloud. *Not here. And why would anyone leave this on a ledge in Joseph's Cave?*

Pleased, nevertheless, he started the engine and whirled the car around into the traffic flow on the other side of the road. An onrushing truck, horn blaring, swept by, missing the Mercedes by inches.

Tom was too elated to notice. He turned left at Casa Nova Street, then half right onto Paul VI Road, accelerating rapidly as he headed south on the modern, blacktop highway to Jerusalem, seventy-five miles away, his mind awash with the amazing happenings of the day.

Last night he had flown from New York into Israel's Ben Gurion Airport, where he rented the car, and drove through the early morning darkness to Nazareth, bathed by the gentle breezes of mid-June streaming through the window. He had arrived in time to keep a nine a.m. appointment with Dr. Aaron Levy, the bearded curator of the Nazareth Museum. "Samuel Ben Ashod is the best authority I could find for the purpose you described in your letters," Dr. Levy had assured him. "I asked him to call you at your hotel."

At mid-morning Tom had visited Mary's Well, deep in the bowels of the Greek Orthodox Church of St. Gabriel, its lofty spire topped by a cross stabbing the sky. He had stood before the well's swiftly flowing artesian waters, mouth open, sensing almost palpable vibrations from the past, aware this was the site where Mary, mother of the man millions considered the son of God, had filled water vessels so long ago.

From there, basking in the warm, shirt sleeve weather, he had hiked down the slanted street to the Church of St. Joseph -- and his startling discovery.

Tom shook his head almost in disbelief. *Boy, what a day!* He checked traffic in both directions, then gunned the car. In his rearview mirror, he saw a large, black sedan pull onto the road behind him. It remained there all the way to Jerusalem.

Chapter II

Ninety minutes later Tom checked into a spacious room in the King David Hotel, overlooking the Hinnom Valley and the white-walled Old City of Jerusalem. He unpacked, made two telephone calls, stripped and posed momentarily before a mirror to flex his muscles -- abs, biceps, pecs -- and practice his best smile, white teeth flashing in a tanned face. Satisfied, he showered, shaved, and was dressed in a white sport shirt, cream-colored slacks and brown shoes when Dr. Abraham Nizer knocked.

"Dr. Abe," he almost shouted, pulling open the door and embracing his former professor of Middle Eastern history. "It's so good to see you. You don't look a day older."

"Tom, Tom, bless my soul," beamed the stubby little man, as always attired in a rumpled black suit, bow tie and scuffed, black shoes. He hugged Tom affectionately, then hurried into the room. "Thought I'd never see you again. How long has it been, five years? You know, I haven't had a student who asked as many questions as you did, since you left."

Tom laughed, showing dimples in both cheeks, his black eyes sparkling. "I still remember your seminar on Jewish history. I learned more there than I'd ever learned before in my life."

Dr. Abe settled into a chair, his bearded face wreathed in smiles, his black Homburg still precisely in place. "You look well," he said. "Trimmer. Been out in the sun, too, I see.

Understand you're teaching. What are you doing about your doctorate?"

"Working on it, doing research. Speaking of that, I have something I want you to look at." Tom picked up the tile from a nearby table and handed it to him.

Dr. Nizer turned the tile over in his hand, studied it, lines converging around his eyes and mouth. "Where did you get this?"

"Is it what I think it is?" Tom deliberately avoided answering Dr. Abe's question.

The professor leaned toward the late-afternoon light, streaming in through the picture window. He examined the ridges on the back and the image on the front. "Exactly what do you think it is?" He was frowning.

Tom pushed back that stray lock. "You know as well as I do what I think it is. Look at that Roman number ten and that galley and boar painting in the background. That's the emblem of the Roman Xth Legion that garrisoned Jerusalem in the first century A.D., and this looks like a miniature of the tiles they used to identify buildings the legion constructed."

"It could be a fake, too. A real one hasn't been found in quite a while."

"Isn't there a way to determine if it's authentic?" Tom tried to make his voice sound casual. He didn't want to reveal too much, even to Dr. Abe, fearing the professor might think Tom's research was too unorthodox to pursue.

Dr. Abe looked skeptical, his mouth down at the corners. "Yes, we can check its age and other details. I guess you realize that if it's genuine it will be worth some money. There's a lucrative underground traffic in Holy Land antiquities these days."

Tom's eyebrows rose. "I didn't know that."

"Yes. Some Bedouin Arabs have made a killing scavenging fragments of scrolls and other relics from caves near those where the original Dead Sea Scrolls were found. Both collectors and archaeologists are bidding up the price."

Dr. Abe rose to his full five foot height, a chunky man whose unimpressive exterior, Tom knew, concealed one of the finest minds in Israel. "Have to go, Tom. That other appointment I told you about, but I'll get back to you. And, speaking of the Dead Sea Scrolls, I have time tomorrow for that run-through you requested on the phone. Why don't we meet at the Shrine of the Book, where they are on display, say nine o'clock?"

"Sounds great. As usual, I'll have questions."

Dr. Nizer paused, peered over spectacles riding the lower half of a broad nose. "I'm glad you called. I would have been very disappointed if you hadn't."

Tom squeezed the professor's hand, smiling, towering over him. "Soon as my schedule's set let's have dinner, Dr. Abe."

The door closed behind the strange, little figure. Tom waited for the footsteps to fade then donned a brown sports jacket and descended to the hotel lobby.

* * *

As Tom entered the elevator, a shadowy figure appeared in the hall and glanced in both directions. The dark complexioned man, his face covered with a three-day beard, walked quickly to Tom's room. He fumbled with the lock, inserting small angled picks, then opened the door. Ten minutes later he emerged, a disgusted look on his face. *Damn, he must have given it to that old man.*

* * *

Tom settled into a chair near a lobby window. He gazed at the gathering darkness outside, his mind drifting back to that second phone call -- to Fran Brown, an American girl working for the Catholic Church in Jerusalem, and former classmate in Dr. Abe's courses at Hebrew University. He winced, thought he had put their shattered romance behind him. Then she had answered...that same hesitant, feminine voice.

"Oh, Tom, is it really you? I got your letter. Yes, I can make it. Seven? Fine." She sounded friendly, a little uncertain but friendly, and that was reassuring, considering, not until that letter, had he apologized for his conduct the day they parted. An image of their break-up rose in his mind.

Tom and Fran had entered the courtyard of the Church of

Tom and Fran had entered the courtyard of the Church of the Holy Sepulchur in the Old City of Jerusalem, purported site of Christ's tomb. It was dusk. Tom moved close to her, smelling her feminine sweetness, took her in his arms. She raised her head, eyes closed, lips parted. He kissed her tenderly, her body crushed against him, then kissed her again, more passionately. His right hand slipped down across her buttocks, pressing her tightly against him. Breathing heavily, he moved the hand to fondle a breast.

"Tom, no," she whispered.

He didn't stop. He kissed her again, this time roughly and the roving hand went down between her legs. She struggled to get out of his grasp.

"Stop it, Tom. You're hurting me. I'm not going to let you act like this. I'm not that kind of girl." She spun away.

"Fran, let's go to my place," Tom said hoarsely. "I want you, Fran. God how I want you." He increased the pressure of his left arm, trying to bring her body up against him again.

Fran resisted obviously frightened. Tom grabbed her left hand and tugged her toward the courtyard entrance. "Come on, Fran. Let's go. We can have dinner at my apartment."

"No," she said, "I won't be treated this way. I'm not a piece of meat in a butcher shop. I wasn't brought up to act like this. It just isn't right."

"Oh, don't be such a prude. We're young and should enjoy ourselves. It's only sex. What could be more natural? What are you afraid of?"

She recoiled at his use of the word, "afraid," her face suddenly strained.

Tom looked at her more closely. "I believe you are afraid. I think you're frigid. All that Catholic indoctrination you've had. They taught you to be afraid of physical love. They've convinced you it's evil. You're frozen inside."

Tom was sorry the second he said it. Fran came apart before his eyes. He sensed he had stated something she feared deeply and was unwilling to admit, even to herself. She collapsed

blubbering and pounding on his chest with her fists.
"*I am not frigid,*" *she had screamed.* "*I'm not. You're an animal and I never want to see you again. You're a spoiled child. You think you can have any woman you want. Well, you can't have me!*"

A sudden burst of light outside the window interrupted his mind drift. Shadows dissolved and the white walls of the Old City suddenly stood, shimmering and glowing, on the next ridge, etched against an ebony sky.

Tom gasped. He had forgotten that one of the first improvements former mayor Tony Kollek made after Israeli forces captured the Old City in 1967, was to place floodlights around the perimeter. The lights came on at dusk, unveiling a scene from the Bible -- white domes, towers and crenelated walls floating in a sea of darkness.

At that moment a slim, dark-haired girl entered the lobby. Recognition lighted her face.

"Tom!" She rushed toward him, arms extended.

He leaped to his feet, heart thumping, hugged and swung her off the ground, then kissed her and released his embrace.

"Fran! Damn, it's good to see you. It's been so long."

She laughed. Both leaned back, holding hands, gazing into the other's eyes. "Too long, for such a dear friend."

Tom frowned, swallowed. That word stabbed like a knife. "I was sort of hoping..." His voiced trailed off. "I think about you a lot, Fran, especially lately." He looked away.

"Oh, come now, let's not dig up the painful past."

They sat on a nearby couch, Tom drinking in her beauty.

Fran Brown was twenty-five, a statuesque five feet seven inches tall. Cascading chestnut hair framed an oval face with large brown eyes, exquisitely cut nose and overly full lips. She had sucked the lower lip into her mouth now and was biting down gently, apparently aware his eyes were devouring the outline of her breasts beneath a pink silk dress, pulled in around her tiny waist. He wished she wouldn't wear pink. It affected him

Fran blushed, placed a finger under his chin, raised his

head until their eyes met. She kissed him on the forehead. "Haven't changed much, have you?" She edged away.

"I'm sorry, Fran." He was embarrassed. "I didn't mean to be so obvious."

Her face brightened as she shifted mood. "What about that dinner you promised on the phone?"

"Right." Tom grinned. "I've got reservations at the Gondola. As I recall, it has the best Italian food in town."

They rode in his rental car and ten minutes later were at a table in a dark corner of the restaurant, a flickering candle between them. They talked and laughed, sipped a rich red wine, consumed huge plates of spaghetti and spicy slivers of veal swimming in dark sauce, and relived the good times they had shared.

"I'll never forget that picnic when Dr. Abe wandered into the woods and came running back pursued by a swarm of bees." Fran convulsed with laughter. "People took off in all directions."

Tom laughed too, a little too loudly. The wine had mellowed his world. "And the time we put that dead snake in the middle of the trail, all coiled up, and Dr. Abe stepped on it during one of our field trips. He nearly jumped out of his pants."

They laughed again.

"Dr. Abe's irascible, pompous and sometimes ridiculous, but I admire him," Tom said. "He's truly a brilliant teacher."

"You were his star pupil. How did you get that way? You weren't that serious about other things."

Tom hesitated. The sequence that had brought him to Dr. Abe's classroom flashed through his mind: A high school teacher who made him see history as a magnificent story of human progress toward becoming more rational and humane. His cum laude graduation from college as a history major. Joint ownership in $50,000 worth of stock his father gave him as a reward. Finally his subsequent decision to do a year of postgraduate study at Hebrew University, where he met Fran.

"Guess Dr. Abe and I just like history," he said, then changed the subject. "Are you still working for the Society for the Preservation of the Faith?"

"Yes. I conduct tours for visiting Roman Catholics, help them learn about Jerusalem. It's very satisfying."

They lapsed into silence. Tom felt nostalgic. Fran, aglow from the wine, clung to his hand under the table. Tom tipped the last drops from the bottle into their glasses, then summoned the waiter and paid the bill. Ten minutes later, he escorted Fran up a dark walkway to the door of her apartment.

She turned. "Thank you, Tom. The evening was everything I'd hoped for."

Tom pulled her close, her body melting against him. He felt a surge of desire and tilted her face up to his. Fran turned her head as their lips were about to meet. He had to kiss her on the cheek.

"Goodnight, Tom," she whispered, gently pushing him away. "And if you were serious about me joining you and Dr. Abe tomorrow, I'd like to. I take Catholic groups to the Shrine and could benefit from hearing what an expert says about the Scrolls."

Tom felt that old frustration. One moment she was warm, affectionate. Then that icy curtain descended and she was back to her rigid, controlled self, behind some kind of protective barrier.

"I'd like that, Fran, and I'm sure Dr. Abe won't mind."

Fran leaned forward, kissed him on the cheek, then turned and left him standing there.

* * *

Back in his hotel room, Tom lay on the bed, his brown, muscular body clad only in white jockey shorts. He gazed out the window at a full moon projecting an elongated rectangle of light onto the wall and ceiling. That ache inside was still there. Seeing her hadn't helped.

We're so different, he thought. How can I be rational about most things and so illogical about her? Why am I so dissatisfied with my life? Losing Fran was part of it, he knew. So were the scars of his childhood.

He thought of his father, "Tough Tom" Sr., and the warm,

early years in Detroit: the tired parent rushing home from his construction job, bouncing "Little Tom," an only child, on a knee before hurrying off to night school; the coveted law degree that followed, a job on the legal staff of the Ford Motor Company, and slow climb out of poverty, guided by stock purchases, based on tips from business associates.

Tom particularly remembered standing outside the family walkup near Cass Park, when he was six, his toys packed in a large box being loaded onto a truck. "Where are we going, Daddy?" he asked.

"To a new house, son. You'll like it there."

They moved into a tree-shaded home in Grosse Pointe, and acquired a white Continental convertible. Every weekday morning after that, "Tough Tom," a cigar clamped in his strong white teeth, fired up the car, gunned the motor, came careening out of their driveway, then raced down Interstate 94, horn blaring, demanding everybody get out of his way until he turned off to his office in Dearborn.

Tom also remembered mornings when he awakened and couldn't find his father. He rushed from room to room, calling, "Daddy! Daddy!" But Daddy was in New York, serving on the boards of three corporations.

Tom turned on his back. His mother's face rose before him.

Tony -- her name was Antoinette -- worked to help finance her husband's education, only to be rewarded with his long absences and obsession with money. She took refuge in bridge games and afternoon cocktails at the Detroit Country Club.

Tom, left alone after school, would stand in front of a mirror, trying to imitate his father. "Get out of my way!" he would tell an imaginary playmate, then give him a shove, or say, "Give me that!" and grab the friend's ice cream cone.

Tom looked out the window, thinking.

The year in Israel had been the best of his life, he decided -- until the breakup with Fran. The ensuing five at home the worst. He taught at Wayne State University in Detroit, stagnating mentally until one day he stumbled upon a quotation from the Bible in a history book and lightning flashed in his mind. He checked, found other references, and soon had major research underway.

That became his project, his strange, secret project. He decided the subject matter was too inflammatory to discuss with anyone until he was certain his findings could be supported by documentation fellow historians would accept.

With diligent digging, he found supporting data in records obtained from American universities and libraries as far away as California. As the project grew in importance, his dissatisfaction with the rest of his life suddenly reached a climax. Six weeks ago, he had answered his office phone and heard an ominous inquiry.

"Is this Thomas Shannon Jr.?"

"Yes."

"This is Officer Jack Conrad. We've been unable to reach your father. Is your mother's name Antoinette Shannon?"

"Yes."

"She's been in an accident. Her car ran off the road. Could you come to Emergency at Bon Secours Hospital immediately?"

Tom, shocked, had swallowed, choked, asked in a hoarse whisper, "How...how serious is she, officer?"

"She's unconscious, apparently had been drinking, was going at least seventy. Please hurry."

Tom had rushed to the hospital and sat by her bed, head down, holding her hand, struggling to control his grief. He felt her fingers move and looked up. She was staring at him, eyes damp with tears. Her hand came up, gently stroked his head. "My poor, Tom," she whispered. "I've made such a mess of things...Wish...could do...over... but...but...too late ...Promise....take care...your father."

Tom broke down, weeping, wailing. "Mother...Oh, my God, Mother. Don't go. I love you so...please...please hang on...We'll get you well..."

She smiled faintly, closed her eyes and died peacefully. He was still holding her hand.

Three days later, he sat by her open casket in Campbell's Funeral Home, his father weeping nearby. He saw more than a beloved parent lying there. He saw a tragedy. Her life had ended without meaning. She had been a loving wife and mother, but had never tapped the great potential Tom sensed was dammed up inside her. She had drifted without purpose or direction in her final years, just as he was doing.

That's when he asked for six month's leave, packed his research notes, wrote advance letters, and flew to Israel to pursue his project, the one thing that seemed right in his life.

Tom gazed at the reflection of the window, now covering the far wall. So he was here and his feelings about Fran were still confused. How could she affect him so deeply? She abjectly accepted all the religious myths in the Bible. He found many of them repugnant, based on emotion with little or no basis in fact. His training as a scholar made him question claims of magic and miracles. Finally, he turned over, closed his eyes and slept.

* * *

Across town, Fran, too, was awake in bed, pondering the re-entry of Tom into her life. *Why am I so attracted to him? He doesn't go to church, is contemptuous of my religion, has tried repeatedly to seduce me. Each time I feel a surge of desire, then revulsion.*

And, as always, when she thought of sex, her father's face appeared before her, shock registering in his watery blue eyes, just as it had that awful day years before when she was five years old.

Fran and three other children were playing in the garage of her home in Burbank, California. "I'll be the doctor," *the little boy had announced.* "Lie down here."

The doctor had looked into their mouths, ears, eyes, noses, listened to their hearts, then pulled down Fran's panties, declaring, "Let's see if there's any thing wrong here."

That's when her father had showed up. "Nice girls don't do that," he had told her after a severe spanking.

Fran also thought about the morality pounded into her in

Fran also thought about the morality pounded into her in Burbank's Catholic schools, those imperatives for girls -- chastity, obedience, prayer, modesty and humility.

So deep was the impact, she had wanted to become a nun, but the Mother Superior of a convent in Santa Barbara told her: "You're not prepared for a life of seclusion. I can't approve your application" Fran came away with a sense of guilt. She wouldn't be devoting her life to God. So when offered a chance to work for the Church in Jerusalem she had accepted, thinking that the next best thing, particularly when assured she could continue her education there.

Fran sat up, hair tumbling over white shoulders. She pounded the pillow with her fist. "Darn you, Tom. You've caused me so much pain. I'd like to beat on you; beat, beat and beat some more." She struck the pillow again and again, then stopped abruptly, lifted and kissed it tenderly. "Oh, Tom, Tom, what am I going to do about you...?"

Suddenly she sat up straighter. *And now there's Derek. I almost forgot about him I've got to let Tom, know...and...and...I guess tomorrow would be as good a time as any.*

Chapter III

The next morning Tom ate breakfast in the hotel coffee shop then settled into a chair in the lobby to read the English-language *Jerusalem Post* while waiting for Fran. The lead story was an investigative report about the spreading tentacles of a New York crime syndicate that had infiltrated Israel, beginning in 1964. Police believed the organization had branched out from prostitution, drugs and loan-sharking, and was involved in a rash of strong-arm robberies of wealthy tourists, and trafficking in historical artifacts.

Tom was deep into a sidebar about a police task force formed to battle this upsurge in crime when Fran rushed in. She was wearing a lavender and white pants suit, one hand fiddling with a gold locket around her neck.

"Good morning," Tom said, scrambling to his feet. "Did you -- "

"Tom," she interrupted, watching the entrance. "I've asked a friend to join us today. Hope you don't mind."

"Why no, I -- "

"He's from London. A professor, an excellent one too. He should be here shortly. Oh I see him now."

A tall man wearing a Harris Tweed jacket, contrasting gabardine slacks and brown knit tie, entered the main door. He spotted Fran, and headed their way.

"Good morning, my dear," he said, pecking her on the

cheek and grasping her hands. "I must say, you look simply smashing today."

Fran, blushing, turned toward Tom. "This is Derek Frost, Tom, a professor of English history and literature at Hebrew University. He has helped on our church tours and is interested in the Dead Sea scrolls, so I invited him to come with us. Derek, Tom Shannon."

"Oh, glad you could make it." Tom tried to conceal his surprise. "Nice to meet you." He extended his hand.

"Same here, old boy." Derek looked off into space and sounded bored, but the strength of his grip startled Tom. He reminded Tom of movie actor Roger Moore. Had wavy brown hair, dark gray eyes, sharply chiseled features and an impressive physique. At six foot three, he was an inch taller than Tom, of more muscular build -- and smelled of tobacco and lavender aftershave.

"Well, we should get started," Tom said after an awkward pause.

They crowded into his rented Mercedes. Derek in the small back seat took a pipe from his pocket, tamped in tobacco with his left thumb, and filled the automobile with smoke. Tom, half choking, rolled his window down, trying not to be too obvious.

He drove south on King David Street, east on Jabotinsky then right on Herzog. Moments later they approached the white dome of the Shrine of the Book, modeled after the ceramic lid of the container in which the Dead Sea Scrolls were found. Tom parked the car, and led Fran and Derek down a sunken corridor into the Shrine's circular, partly underground, central chamber. Vertical display cases lined the circumference, each with glass windows and a scroll inside. Tom looked around, felt cold fingers ascending his spine. He was in the presence of giant monuments of history, and, as always on such occasions, was filled with awe. He felt like a pygmy surrounded by giants, but shook off the spell.

"Dr. Abe said he might be late," he said. "He suggested, while waiting, we read up on how the scrolls were discovered."

They moved from case to case, perusing sequential segments of a story that had begun in February, 1947. A Bedouin shepherd, Muhammed adh-Dhib, while searching for a lost goat, entered a cave in a dry wash known as Wady Qumran near the Dead Sea. Inside, he found what he described as "stinking" rolls of inscribed parchment, wrapped in linen, protruding from broken ceramic jars. He carried them into the sunlight, then, on foot, to Bethlehem, where they were purchased by antiquities dealers.

One dealer showed part of a scroll to E.L. Sukenik, professor of archaeology at Jerusalem's Hebrew University. Sukenik recognized the writing as pre-Christian Hebrew, but his efforts to purchase the documents were interrupted by the 1947-48 Arab-Israeli war. Undaunted, he made a dangerous second trip to Bethlehem -- by that time behind Arab lines -- and bought three of the scrolls from the same dealer. Four other scrolls turned up seven years later in New York City. The Israeli government obtained them for $250,000.

Eleven scrolls, comprising six distinct compositions, were eventually recovered, including *The War of the Sons of Light with the Sons of Darkness*; *The Thanksgiving Psalms,* and a complete text of the Old Testament book of *Isaiah.*

Tom finished reading just as Dr. Abe came bustling in, peering at a gold watch fished out of a vest pocket and muttering, "Five minutes late. No way to start a day." He looked up. His eyebrows went up. "Oh, Dr. Frost, Tom told me Fran would be with us. I didn't know we would have the pleasure of your company also. How nice. Let's begin."

The little professor moved to the central pedestal. "Let's start with Isaiah, the most important of the scrolls."

"Why is it the most important?" Tom noticed as he asked that Derek was holding Fran's hand.

"It's at least a thousand years older than any complete book of the Bible in Hebrew ever found before," Dr. Abe said, "and several hundred years older than any translation from Aramaic, Greek, Latin or any other language."

He continued in a louder voice.

"There were three main groups in the Kingdom of Judah, as this part of Palestine was known at that time.-- the Pharisees who wanted to make Judaic law the guide for all duties; the Sadducees who controlled both the Temple and the ruling religious body, called the Sanhedrin, and the Essenes.

"The Essenes were fundamentalists who had religious differences with the other two groups. They broke away from the mainstream of Jewish life and established a settlement at Qumran, near the Dead Sea, apparently in the second century B.C. Essene scribes at Qumran copied the scrolls from earlier documents about 100 B.C. and placed them in the cave where they were found, near the settlement.

Tom, anxious to ask several questions, shifted his weight from leg to leg, but didn't interrupt.

Dr. Abe droned on. "The Essenes established an isolated, monastic society, in their desert setting, yet always believed that one day they would return to Jerusalem, rebuild the Temple and lead the Jewish people back to proper ways of worshipping God."

"That doesn't explain why this scroll is the most important," Tom interrupted.

"Well, Tom, It gives us a chance to compare Isaiah, as it was known more than two thousand years ago, with more recent copies. It differs in many respects."

"But this isn't the original Isaiah, is it?"

"No. The Isaiah manuscript found among the Dead Sea Scrolls was a copy made at Qumran. What you are looking at is a copy of that copy, carefully reproduced on leather by skilled craftsmen. The manuscript found by the Bedouin shepherd is over there." Dr. Abe motioned toward a glass case to the left of the entrance. "At first it was on display here where this duplicate is, but light darkened the parchment and faded the ink, so it was moved to a more protected case. Now, let's look at the one found at Wady Qumran."

They walked the few steps. Again Tom was overwhelmed. He could see four pages of the ancient manuscript through the tinted glass that protected it from sunlight. *To think that...more than two millennia ago...before Christ walked the shores of Galilee, before there was a Sermon on the Mount, before there was an America, a France or Germany...when Athens and Sparta were major powers...a bearded scribe clad in a white robe, sat down at a stone desk in Qumran, picked up a pen and copied...my God...copied words...four centuries older than the scribe was...written by an ancient Hebrew prophet...words with a vision of righteousness and justice that still resonates today...*Tom gulped, wrenched his mind back to the present. Dr. Abe was talking again:

"If you examine the pages visible through this window, you'll see the scribe made parallel lines across the parchment, then hung letters from them. When he made a mistake, he inserted the words he had omitted.

"Then look over here. See the stitches? This Isaiah was written on seventeen sheets of leather, sewn together, making a document almost twenty-four feet long. We call it parchment, but it is the skin of a sheep or goat prepared to be written on, like paper."

Dr. Abe paused to dab his brow with a handkerchief.

Tom glanced from the manuscript to the professor then back. It was time for a question vital to his research.

"You were one of the scholars who examined this scroll immediately after it was found?"

Dr. Abe nodded.

"What's on the back of it?"

The professor frowned. "Nothing. Why do you ask?"

"I've read there are smudges there."

"Well, yes, there are. So what?"

"I'm trying to clarify what those smudges are and how they got there."

Derek and Fran moved closer, still holding hands. Fran was listening closely. Derek looked bored.

"Why, how should I know what they are," Dr. Abe replied. "Just smudges, probably made by the sweaty fingers of people who have handled the scroll in the past."

"Could they be fingerprints?"

Dr. Abe looked startled. "Well, yes, they...actually...well of course they're fingerprints, hundreds and hundreds of them, one on top of another. Why do you want to know?"

"It would be interesting if we knew whose prints are there."

"I'm certain we'll never find out. Any more questions?"

"What progress is being made in analyzing the scrolls?" Fran asked.

"Some. All have been released for study, and one recent translation describes the execution of a Messiah-like leader, demonstrating ancient Jews shared the Christian belief in the slaying of a Messiah sent to save them, their world and their souls. The translation says this Messiah suffered 'piercings' and 'wounds.' This strengthens the possibility of a connection between early Christians and the author of the scroll, most likely an Essene. But don't ask me who this Messiah was. He predated Christ because the scrolls were written before the Christian era began."

"Wow!" Tom said. "We already knew the scrolls showed similarities in the ceremonies and religious practices of the Essenes and early Christians. Now this. It seems to link them even more closely than before."

"Don't jump to too many conclusions," Dr. Abe warned.

Fran stared at Tom, mouth slightly open. "You surprise me, Tom. All this interest in early Christianity. You've always been such a skeptic, the great irreconcilable agnostic."

Derek removed the pipe from his mouth. "Are you really an agnostic, old boy?" He sounded as if that were beyond belief.

"Oh, he just talks that way, Derek," Fran hastily added. "He likes to make people think he is a man of pure reason. He's as much a Christian as you and I are."

"I'm pretty much an agnostic," Tom acknowledged.

Dr. Abe looked at his watch. "Must be on my way. Nice to see all of you." He rushed out the entrance, leaving as abruptly as he had arrived.

Tom looked at Frost and extended his hand. "Nice meeting you, Derek. Be happy to drive you wherever you want, or back to the hotel."

Frost ignored Tom's hand. "Oh, no, old boy. I'll take a cab. An appointment I have to keep." He turned toward Fran, planting a kiss on her cheek. "I'll call you, my dear."

Tom and Fran, standing together outside, watched his taxi disappear down the street, Derek peering back at them through the rear window, waving, pipe in hand.

Tom thought about the Englishman as he drove Fran toward the King David. He had questions, but was almost afraid to ask them. Not until they pulled into the hotel parking area did he summon the courage.

"I guess I wasn't prepared for Derek, Fran. I realize it's none of my business, but is something going on between you two?"

Fran bit down on her lower lip, gently placed a hand on his arm. Her eyes sought his, then she looked away. "You were gone...I didn't hear from you. He was here. He's so mature... reassuring...religious. He sort of reminds me of my father. He's asked me to marry him, Tom. I'm very fond of him, but haven't decided anything." She pulled her hand away. "Oh, darn, I'm making a mess of this. I honestly don't know my own mind."

Tom weighed her words. At least she had doubts. "Fran, look, I'm supposed to meet Dr. Abe at my hotel room tonight. I'd like you to be there. Why not drop by about five o'clock. I'll buy you some dinner, then we can hear what he has to say."

She studied him. "Okay, why not. Don't want to turn down a free meal -- with such outstanding company."
* * *

At that moment a meeting was taking place at the Club Tomcat in the basement of a small, downtown hotel. A dark-skinned man, right hand rubbing his unshaved face, was standing before six seated men in rumpled business suits, ties loosened. The man was agitated and spoke with a New York accent.

"I don't know what the guy got from the cave, but it wasn't that scroll the attendant told us might be hidden there. It was small and solid. I could tell 'cause I tailed him back to his car and watched. He kept staring at it, kept turning it. Man, he was really taken. I was going to jump him, right there, or on the road back to Jerusalem, but there were too many people around, too much traffic, too many witnesses. So I slipped into his hotel room last night, but found nothing. Whatever it was, he must of given it to that old guy he met with. I don't think it's such hot stuff anyway. Doubt we could get much more'n twenty 'r thirty grand for it."

Total silence greeted his statement. The six continued to stare at the man, scowling, tension building. He shuffled his feet, swallowed, began to sweat.

A slight, balding man at the center of the seated group, his eyes cold, pale-blue, studied his employee. He whispered something to the fat, dark-haired man on his right. The subordinate spoke.

"That cave was your responsibility, Schwartz. Excuses aren't acceptable. You know we had been told something very valuable, probably a scroll, was concealed there. You blew a chance for us to make some dough. We're taking you off that detail and assigning you to the hit team working over them high-tone places. The boss is unhappy with you, so don't screw up again. Got it?"

Schwartz, perspiration drenching his face, looked relieved. "Okay. You won't have no more problems with me." He knew the punishment could have been a lot worse.

Chapter IV

Dr. Abe knocked on Tom's door precisely at seven o'clock. He came bustling in, nodded to Fran and fished the tile out of his briefcase. "It"s authentic," he said, handing it to Tom. "We used a fast dating process. It's from the first century, and the image and Xth Legion marking are correct in every detail. Now where did you get it?"

Tom pumped a fist in the air. "Great!"

He examined the tile, ran his fingers over the grainy surface. It had been thoroughly cleaned. He passed it to Fran seated in a chair nearby, then moved to the window to gaze at the hotel veranda below, and the illuminated Old City beyond. Tom was framing his response to Dr. Abe's question when Fran broke in.

"Why it's one of those emblems of the Roman Tenth Legion," she said, "but frankly I haven't seen one quite like this before."

"It *is* the emblem of the Tenth Legion," Dr. Abe said, settling into a chair across from Fran. "Whenever the Legion built permanent structures they imprinted the Tenth's logo, if I can call it that, on some of the bricks or tiles used in the construction. This, however, looks more like a model, a miniature, rather than one of the actual tiles used in a building. Now, Tom, no more evasions. I want to know where you found it."

Tom turned back toward the room, drew in a deep breath,

let it out through puffed cheeks, glanced at the professor. "I'm afraid my answer will raise some unanswerable questions, Dr. Abe, but here goes." He paused. "As you know a number of Tenth Legion tiles have been found near Jerusalem, often by farmers plowing in their fields. None recently, however."

Dr. Nizer nodded.

"I found this one in Nazareth."

"In Nazareth?" Dr. Abe came out of his chair. "There's never been one found there before. Where in Nazareth?"

"In Joseph's Cave in the old part of the city."

"Joseph's Cave! You know there's no proof Joseph had anything to do with that hole in the ground. What connection could this tile have with Joseph, even if the cave was his home?" Dr. Abe's voice was rising, his face flushed.

"Since these emblems have never been found in Nazareth but have been found near Jerusalem, I think it was taken there by Joseph or Mary, or someone else in the family."

"That's pretty far-fetched, Tom," Dr. Abe snorted, his face a deepening pink. "You haven't got any evidence. All you've done is make a wild guess."

The stubby little professor sat down, sputtering. "You of all people. You were always so full of questions and doubts. Don't you remember anything I taught you about the scientific method?"

Tom knew the emotion would pass. The professor's choleric nature was always pumping adrenalin into his body. Exasperation was as normal to him as breathing.

"I'm basing my opinion on more than an assumption," Tom said. "Did you notice those curved lines on the back?"

Dr. Abe grabbed the tile from Fran's hand. He turned it over, ran his thumb over the ridges, then looked up.

"I think that's a fingerprint of a family member, and the fingerprint became calcified and was preserved."

Dr. Abe squinted at the tile again, then pulled a magnifying glass out of his pocket and examined the ridges closely, tilting the tile at different angles. When he put the glass down, the taut lines around his mouth had relaxed somewhat.

"Perhaps it is a fingerprint." His voice was subdued. "I hadn't thought of that, and it is scientifically possible that an imprint from a human finger could leave an oily outline which could collect dust and then become hardened, or calcified, as you suggest. But even if it is a human fingerprint that doesn't mean it's the fingerprint of Joseph or Mary, or any of their kin."

He began to laugh, bending over, hugging his waist, collapsing in the chair. "Even if it were Joseph's or Mary's fingerprint, you could never prove it. We Jews don't have their prints on file. Not even Interpol does." By this time the little professor was in near hysterics over his joke.

Tom winced. Dr. Abe's sense of humor hadn't improved. He waited for the final spasm of laughter to pass. The professor was wiping his eyes as Tom began again.

"But there may be a way to establish a relationship with another fingerprint, one that could be the same or similar and could be traced...perhaps to Christ."

Dr. Abe froze in place, body rigid and straight. Fran stared at Tom.

"Surely you're not trying to connect this tile and the smudges on the Isaiah Scroll?" Dr. Abe asked.

"Why not? I have a theory -- "

"Oh, twaddle your theory. Tom, you really are exasperating."

"Now just a minute," Tom said, slamming a hand on a nearby table. "What I'm suggesting is not that irrational."

Dr. Abe lapsed into silence. Fran, fascinated, said nothing.

Tom took a deep breath. "You acknowledge those smudges on the back of the Isaiah Scroll are fingerprints, and that this is a fingerprint on this tile, don't you?" He waved the tile at Dr. Abe.

"I suppose so."

"What was it Jesus read from in the synagogue at Nazareth when he preached there? One reference is Luke, Chapter Four, verses sixteen through nineteen."

Fran began to recite. "'And he came to Nazareth, where he had been brought up, and according to his custom, he entered the synagogue on the Sabbath and stood up to read. And the volume of Isaiah, the prophet, was handed to him...'"

"He read from an Isaiah scroll."

"So?" Dr. Abe waved an arm. "There's no reason to think the Isaiah scroll found near the Dead Sea was ever at the synagogue in Nazareth." He sounded angry again.

"I haven't said it was," Tom replied. "But I think it's quite possible it might have been."

Dr. Abe's face was beet red, now, cheeks puffed out. He looked like he was about to explode.

"How many texts of Isaiah were in existence at that time?" Tom jabbed a finger at the professor.

"Scores I suppose. Most communities had scribes who could have made copies."

"Actually most communities had scribes who spoke only Aramaic, not Hebrew," Tom said. "The only significant number who could have transcribed such a massive Hebrew document into Aramaic -- the language most Jews spoke after returning from the Babylonian captivity -- would have been among the educated classes in Jerusalem, or in Qumran, where there were scribes versed in the Hebrew language. Personally, I doubt if there were more than ten or fifteen Hebrew texts of Isaiah in existence when Jesus spoke in the synagogue, maybe less. After all, only about two hundred thousand Jews lived in the area at that time."

By his silence Dr. Abe signaled Tom had made a point.

"Furthermore," Tom continued, "it seems logical the Essenes, who had deep differences with the Temple priests, would have been in contact with, and sought the support of, other groups that opposed the Temple leadership. Most certainly the people in Nazareth would fit into that category."

"Why do you say that?"

"The Temple leaders ridiculed people from Nazareth, thought they were country bumpkins, mocked the way they talked, didn't like the Greek influence there, a holdover from

Alexander the Great armies passing through in the third century B.C. They didn't think people from Galilee, where Nazareth is located, were entirely Jewish."

Dr. Abe was considerably subdued. He studied Tom a moment. "As I understand it, your argument is?"

There was a sudden loud noise outside the room, something being dragged across the carpeted floor, a tinkle of broken glass and a muffled oath.

Tom, startled, whirled around, rushed to the door and jerked it open. Two men in coveralls bearing King David Hotel patches were standing there, mouths open, one with a foot on a stepladder, the other reaching down to pick up fragments of shattered glass on the floor.

"Sorry, sir," the nearest man said. "We were changing bulbs in the hall lights. I lost my balance...one got away from me. Hope we didn't disturb you." He looked flustered.

Tom, with Fran and Dr. Abe peering over his shoulder, exhaled slowly. "No, just startled us." He closed the door and slowly returned to the room, deep in thought, right hand rubbing his chin.

"That was a surprise. Scared me," Fran said, sitting down.

"Gave me a start too," Dr. Abe admitted. He dropped into a chair.

Tom looked at Fran. "I guess I overreacted also, but for a good reason. When I returned from our dinner last night, Fran, several of my belongings seemed out of place. I had a feeling someone had searched the room. And when I was at Joseph's Cave yesterday I felt like I was under observation there also. A big black sedan even followed me all the way back to Jerusalem. Now this." Tom felt icy fingers running up his spine. He couldn't help wondering, *What the hell is going on?*

Chapter V

Tom pondered these thoughts several moments, then shrugged, dismissing his concerns, decided he could be over reacting. He looked up. Let's see, where were we? Oh, yes, Dr. Abe, you were about to comment on what I said about the number of Isaiah texts in use during the first century."

"Yes, I was trying to summarize your reasoning -- that there were only a relatively few such texts in Hebrew, that most or all of them had to come from Jerusalem or Qumran, that the Essenes at Qumran very likely had contact with Jews in Nazareth because both disliked the Temple priests, and all this enhanced the possibility the Isaiah Jesus read from in the synagogue came from Qumran."

"Precisely," Tom said, smiling.

"I'd say you've lowered the odds against that possibility but you still haven't established a relationship between the fingerprints on the scroll and the one on the tile."

Tom looked relieved. "I agree. That's the reason I need some blown-up, high-fidelity photographs of the fingerprints on the back of the Isaiah scroll to see if there is a print there that matches the print on the tile. Can you help me?"

Dr. Abe's mouth dropped open.

"Photograph the...fingerprints?" He sounded incredulous.

"Yes. Don't they remove and examine the scroll periodically to see if there's deterioration? Couldn't you be present and request photos be made at that time?"

"I guess I could. I can't promise anything but I'll see what I can do."

Fran stared at Tom, asked hesitantly, "Tom, what's going on? All these questions about religion. Does this have something to do with why you're in Israel?"

Tom again moved to the window and gazed at the illuminated Old City, shimmering in the darkness below. He turned, looked at Fran. "I wanted to see both you and Dr. Abe, Fran. That's part of the reason I'm here. I'm also trying to complete some research on the First Century A.D. I started in Detroit. I hope to use the results in my doctor's dissertation. Something important for the whole world began here about that time, maybe the ability of an advanced society to live by law and moral principle, rather than force. In any event, I've been studying the origins of Christianity. And although I don't believe many Christian myths, the research seems to fill a psychological need. It compensates for something lacking in my life. I don't want to go any further than that right now."

Tom paused, uncertain how much more he should reveal about his project. "I realize I'm not being as responsive as you would like." He added, searching the faces of Dr. Abe and Fran. "But bear with me a little longer. I should be able to explain more fully soon."

"Well, I must go," Dr. Abe said, picking up his briefcase.

Fran stood up, too, and recovered her purse from the chair where she had been sitting. "I can't wait for the next installment in this who-done-it," she said, laughing.

"Me too," Dr. Abe said. "What is the meaning of the mysterious tile? How did it get to Nazareth? Does it -- "

"All right, you two," Tom said, grinning, as he escorted them to the door. "I have my reasons for what I'm doing."

He watched as they disappeared down the hall, then went to bed. An hour later he suddenly sat up, a startled look on his face.

There was no hallway light outside his door, therefore no

light bulb to change. So what were those two men doing? Could they have been looking in over the transom...and listening? But why? Now he was really concerned. Those icy fingers returned to his spine.

It was another two hours before he could settle down enough to sleep.

* * *

Later that night, Derek Frost returned to his apartment at Hebrew University. He closed the door behind him and leaned against it, eyes tightly shut, recalling the disturbing experiences of the day.

The taxi he had taken from the Shrine of the Book let him off at the same downtown hotel where the syndicate's council had reprimanded Schwartz. Derek had strolled into the Club Tomcat in the basement, loosened his tie and settled into an empty chair at a felt-covered table, lighted his pipe and nodded to the other players, saying, "Deal, I feel lucky today."

A man in a checked suit, smoking a large cigar, strolled over. "You better be, professor," he whispered in Derek's ear. "You're overdue in more ways than one." He blew smoke in Derek's face, then resumed his seat.

Now Derek, eight hours later, couldn't believe how much he had lost -- again.

Chapter VI

Derek had no classes the next day, a Thursday, so slept until two o'clock in his faculty apartment. Then, clad in robe, rumpled pajamas and slippers, his worries of the night before put aside, he brewed a pot of tea and made toast. He was spreading it with marmalade when the phone rang.

He cradled the receiver against an ear, using a knife to scrape more marmalade from the nearly empty jar while answering.

"Good afternoon. Frost here."

Heavy breathing, then that voice: "Like I suggested yesterday, professor, the people I work for are getting impatient. You'll have to come up with a lot of money soon or that twenty thousand dollars you owe is going to grow. Then some bad things are going to happen. Think about it." The line went dead.

Derek suddenly felt cold. He stumbled to the kitchen table and dropped into a chair, his face drained of color. He understood all too well, the threat shrouded in what he had heard, and asked himself: *How in God's name am I going to get out of this?*

He pulled in a deep breath, exhaled slowly, trying to remember how he had handled similar problems in the past. *Those bounced checks in Monte Carlo. Wouldn't want to tangle with those people again. Finally borrowed enough to hold them off, then sneaked out of town.*

That psychiatrist in London was no pushover either. His

bill collectors hounded me, demanding payment for all those sessions. He claimed that voice I heard, urging me on when I gambled, was dangerous. Said I needed treatment, but he was wrong. I'm doing fine -- or was.

Derek raked a hand through his thick brown hair, saw his sagging face reflected in a cabinet mirror. This time he had no place to borrow, had exhausted all normal sources of credit, had nowhere to run. And he'd never been threatened with violence before.

He dropped his head into trembling hands. His tongue circled a parched upper lip. *Why was I so stupid?*

He knew the answer. That feeling he was bound to win, that voice shouting, "One more hand will do it...Go! Go!" The gambler's belief a pot of gold was waiting to be taken.

Derek rose and paced the apartment's cluttered living room, brushing past piles of books, magazines and unfiled newspaper clippings. *Why didn't I suspect that quick offer of a loan by the man who had just called, that cigar-smoker who kept hovering around the poker table? "Four-fingers Guzik" they called him because of the peculiar way he held a deck of cards.*

"If you're having difficulties, professor," he had said, *"I can get you some cash. Now I'm in debt to loan sharks who keep hiking the interest on me.*"

Derek didn't know much about Guzik, but assumed he was part of the criminal syndicate now operating in Israel, according to a story in the *Jerusalem Post* yesterday. The newspaper reported that a man named "Doc" Steiner was the first to arrive, then in 1967 Max Cochrain and Frank Reuter, top lieutenants of syndicate boss Meyer Bernstein. In 1970 Al Mendez and a "Jimmy Brown Eyes" something-or-other appeared. Finally, Bernstein showed up.

Derek sat down, reached for the tobacco pouch and pipe in the pocket of his robe. A nicotine-stained thumb packed the aromatic mixture into the ash-encrusted bowl. He didn't hear the flip of the lighter or hissing spurt of flame that fired the tobacco into a glowing ember. As the smoke curled up around his face he began the reasoning process that had made him a top scholar.

Point one: I have to devise a repayment plan quickly.

Derek shifted in the chair, puffing steadily, sending up clouds of smoke.

Point two: Fran. She told me she has $15,000 in a savings account, an inheritance from a maiden aunt. If she accepts my marriage proposal I could use her money to relieve the pressure. Then we could slip away to the States, and I could, hopefully, take that teaching job I've applied for at the Massachusetts Institute of Technology.

Derek walked to the room's lone window, gazed at the campus walkway below, jammed with students hurrying to and from classes. He puffed slowly, pipe in his right hand, a wisp of smoke curling up from the bowl.

A vision of Fran rose before him: soulful eyes filled with self-doubt; burnished, red-brown hair; parted lips; lush, ripe body; innocent mind. What a beautiful, fragile, little bird.

"But she hasn't accepted," he muttered. *I'll have to seek a quick, favorable decision.*

Derek, still pondering, removed the pipe from his mouth, right elbow braced in the palm of his left hand.

Point three: Tom. He knew about Tom and Fran's prior romance, assumed it was over, but could tell she had lingering affection for the American.

Tom is danger, could upset my plans. Besides he irritates me. He's undisciplined, nonconformist, disorganized. His hair needs combing. He violates proper standards of dress and manners, and his posturing as an agnostic is simply not acceptable.

Derek began to feel better. He fumbled through stereo records in a wall cabinet, selected Rachmaninoff's Concerto No. 2 in C Minor. The rich, spaced chords of Artur Rubinstein's piano rendition, slowly increasing in volume, floated through the apartment. The orchestra joined in, then the moaning, soaring strings took over, with the piano bursting through again and again in brilliant, crashing accents.

Derek headed for the shower where he hummed his way through the first movement and was toweling off when the second began.

He definitely felt better now, knew what to do. Fran was the key. And to succeed with her he had to get Tom out of the way.

Derek decided: *It'll be no contest. I'm handsome, urbane, educated at Cambridge, have deep, Anglican, religious convictions and am thinking of converting to Catholicism, a move that would please Fran. I would be a credit to her as a husband. Tom, on the other hand, apparently treats her religion with contempt, judging from what Fran says.*

Derek tightened his necktie, gazed fondly at his image in the mirror and decided: *Tom is a moral inferior. It's time we had a talk.*

He dialed the King David, then Fran's office. "I want to talk to Tom about the Isaiah Scroll," he told her. "His hotel says he left word he wouldn't be back until late afternoon. Any idea where I might find him?"

"He said he was going to the Israel Museum sometime today. It's next to the Shrine of the Book. You might try there."

* * *

Tom emerged from the museum, squinting into the late afternoon sun as he looked down the walkway toward the Valley of the Cross-and the Old City of Jerusalem. *Spent more time than I intended,* he thought, noticing the sun's distance above the horizon. *Got to prepare for that trip tomorrow.*

He stopped, shaded his eyes, focused on a tall, familiar figure approaching from the parking area. Derek. *What's he doing here?* Tom waited, uncertain whether the Englishman would come his way or enter the adjoining Shrine of the Book. Derek turned toward the museum.

"I say, old boy, there you are," Derek said, catching sight of him. "Fran told me you might be here. I've been wanting to talk to you and thought this a good time."

Tom nodded coolly. "Why don't we move over to the

bench under those trees," he suggested, motioning, "away from the crowd and out of the sun." He started walking, wondering what was on Derek's mind. He didn't like the Englishman, felt he was arrogant and patronizing, reeked of tobacco and had an annoying habit of pulling on his ear and looking away when talking.

Derek, striding beside him, pulled at that ear. "Might as well get to the point."

Tom stopped, turned, waiting expectantly.

"You probably don't realize it, old boy, but your arrival here has been upsetting to Fran. I've asked her to marry me and have every reason to believe she will accept. I think it would be better if you didn't see her any more."

Tom felt a rush of blood to his face. Muscles in his arms and back tensed. "I don't think Fran would agree with that." He bit off the words. "Furthermore, you can damn well rest assured I'll see Fran whenever I feel like it, and as often as I feel like it. Do I make myself clear?"

Tom planted his feet, faced the Englishman, only a few steps from the trees.

"No need to get abusive, old boy," Derek said, looking away and again tugging that ear, "but you aren't in her class, you know. You've led a dissolute life and should go back to it before you harm Fran any more than you have."

"You silly asshole," Tom said, dropping the last vestige of courtesy, "it's none of your business how I live. And quit calling me 'old boy.' And for God's sake stop pulling on your ear and go wash that tobacco stink off your body."

Derek glared, face red. He shifted weight to his right foot, balled his right hand into a fist, swung a hard right to Tom's chin,

Tom reeled backward and tumbled to the ground near the tree, but came up quickly. He charged, tackled Derek just above the knees. They went down in a heap, flailing arms and tangled legs, grunting and gasping, Tom on top.

Tom crashed a right hook off Derek's cheekbone and was

following with a left when propelled backward by Derek's legs, doubled under him. Again he landed near the tree.

Tom heard shouting and saw people running in their direction. A uniformed museum guard hauled him to his feet. Two other guards grabbed a puffing, red-faced Derek, hair dangling over his eyes.

"Enough! You act like child," the largest guard shouted in heavily accented English, stepping between them. He addressed Tom. "You hurt?" Not waiting for an answer, he turned to Derek. "You hurt?"

Tom managed a choked, "I'm okay." He brushed dirt off his pants and tucked in his shirttail. Derek nodded too.

The guard, hands on hips, looked from one to the other then elevated his shoulders, grimaced, raised and moved his hands horizontally in front of him, palms up. "No big deal, I guess, as Americans say. Go now. You first." He pointed at Tom.

Tom brushed his clothes and checked his pockets to make certain he still had his car keys. He nodded to the guard then walked slowly toward the parking lot with as much dignity as he could muster. Moments later he drove away, Derek staring angrily after him.

A huge bearded man, his hair a tangle of black strands, [up] from his stooped position as Tom approached.

"Can you tell me where I can find the Ben Ashod farm?" [he asked.]

The man eyed him several moments, then, in a cadenced [tone] Tom assumed was Yiddish, addressed the woman next [to him. S]he was slight, sunburned, looked frazzled and weary, but [...] and tough.

"Samuel's farm is beyond that next hill," she said in [E]nglish. "Pass the bridge and take the first road to the left. [You can]'t miss it." The distinctly British accent and expression [made hi]m wonder what fateful life sequence had brought her to [this place.]

[H]e thanked her, returned to the car and made the turn onto [the] road that disappeared over the next hillock. Beyond, he [saw] it rising, falling, twisting, toward a rocky bluff ahead. [Ju]st then the road topped a rise. Spread before him, in a [v]alley was a rich carpet of green -- wheat in its exuberant [heal]ty and teeming, voraciously drinking in, storing energy [from] sun above and damp earth below, with Mount Gilboa [rising] in the background.

[To]m drove slowly, bumping and bouncing, over the rock-[y ro]adway, until he reached a house where converging hills [and p]oplar trees lined a bordering stream.

[He] stopped, stepped down from the car, looked around. [It] was ancient -- thatched roof, thick stone walls, dirt clay [visib]le through a gaping door. A cow in an attached corral [chewed] a mouthful of hay, soft brown eyes watching him. He [smelled] heavy, fecund odor of barnyard and pasture. No one [in sigh]t.

["He]llo!" he shouted.

["He]llo!" the echo came back faintly from the nearby hills.

[Ag]ain.

["He]llo!"

[Ag]ain the echo, then silence.

Chapter VII

The road to Jericho rushed at Tom in a swiftly expanding ribbon of black, raced by and imploded behind him to normal size. He increased pressure on the accelerator. The little Mercedes leaped forward, cleaving the morning air, its motor humming a song of focused power.

Tom was excited. He had virtually forgotten yesterday's fight with Derek, except when reminded by a twinge of pain from the bruise on his chin. Instead he thought about the telephone call he had received yesterday just before going to the Israel Museum.

"This is Samuel Ben Ashod," the caller had said, his voice cracking. "I had a letter from Dr. Levy of the Nazareth Museum last week. He said you wanted to talk to me and gave me your number. I have information that will interest you, but I can't discuss it on the phone."

Directions to his farm followed: "Take Route One out of Jerusalem, go north from Jericho to the road junction just south of Beit Shean, then west two kilometers. Ask anyone in the fields there the location of Old Samuel's place. Everybody knows me."

Now, following those instructions, Tom was on his way to meet a man who was an authority on the oral tradition in Jewish history, and might know more about the beginnings of Christianity than any other person in the world.

Tom's mind snapped back to his driving.

He swept through Bethany, an eruption of ancient buildings and a modern, roadside Catholi

More bleak villages followed.

Suddenly the road coiled into a t down from two thousand five hundred three hundred below. Tom's ears popp pressure.

The road straightened, turned no He raced through a desert relieved on Bedouin tent on the horizon.

Shattered buildings appeared c their broken walls thrusting toward th prayer. Tom winced. Palestinian refug Israeli war in 1948 had settled here, homes again when more fighting broke

Again the scenery changed -- before him, rich with hanging, succule dates, dusty and splashed with sunshir

The emerald jewel of fruited desert returned, a tortured domain, l man.

Tom pondered this contrast - desert, side by side. He thought: Remove water and death returns. potential had to be embedded in tl charge, and a death potential had charge.

A life potential and a death p way. Life waiting to be victorious and courage were applied. Death v were removed. He sensed there wa didn't know what it was.

Forty minutes later Tom re Beit Shean. He wheeled left, wa kilometers and pulled off to the si bordering field where a work crew

"Mr. Shannon?" a voice asked behind him.

Tom whirled, goose bumps prickling his arms. Standing behind him was a man who looked as if he had been lifted from the Bible, then outfitted in modern work clothes. His hair was a matted tangle of gray, heaped up and sprouting in all directions. It continued down the sides of an eroded, triangular face, ending in an equally tangled, pointed beard that gave a satanic cast to a large hooked nose, wrinkled skin, and huge bushy eyebrows over pale blue eyes. The man was stooped, spare, but towering in stature, perhaps six foot four, clad in dirty blue overalls and heavy work shoes.

"Oh," Tom said, "I didn't hear...see you. Are you Mr. Ben Ashod?"

"Yes, I assume you're Mr. Shannon?"

Tom nodded.

The man's voice was deep and clear. Not much like the almost cackling voice he had heard on the phone, yet there was a vague similarity. Tom wondered if there were times when the cracked voice prevailed and the underlying Biblical appearance of the man was in ascendancy, other times when the modern, clear voice was dominant, befitting a man dressed like an American farmer.

"Thank you for coming so promptly," Samuel said. "Please join me in the shade by the house. We can talk there. Would you like some buttermilk?"

He pulled two rickety chairs from a shed, brushed dust from the seats and set them on hard, packed ground where a large pine cast deep, cool shade. Samuel disappeared into the house and returned bearing two overflowing mugs of pungently fresh buttermilk.

Tom was amazed at the refreshing coolness of the drink.

"Mr. Ben Ashod."

The old man raised a hand. "Please, call me Samuel."

"Samuel," Tom said, "a number of months ago while still in the United States, I read a news story about a study stating there were people living near Nazareth who were descended from families that had resided in the area for centuries. It spoke of an oral tradition in these families in which stories from ancient times were passed from generation to generation by word of mouth. I wrote to Dr. Levy, who was quoted in the story, asking his assistance in arranging a meeting with someone from such a family. I explained this might help me complete some research I had underway. He wrote back, said he had only evaluated the study, and had little contact with the participants, but would do what he could. Upon my arrival in Nazareth he gave me your name and said you would call, which you did."

Samuel, listening intently, became more and more agitated as Tom talked. He opened and closed his mouth, jerked a hand through his hair, then slammed a fist on the arm of his chair.

"I guess he told you I was crazy, too, didn't he!" Samuel exploded, this time in the cracked, ancient voice Tom had heard on the telephone. "Told you I was some kind of crank. They're a bunch of bastards at that museum. Just like those professors in Jerusalem, those so-called Biblical scholars. They think if something isn't written it has to be wrong."

Samuel gulped air and continued, wheezing and gasping, eyes flashing. "I'm a scribe. My father, my father's father, and fathers in our family back in time were all scribes. Scribes were among the most learned and respected people in ancient times. We wrote letters for people, made copies of documents and studied language, history and philosophy. But that respect doesn't exist anymore."

Samuel was on his feet. He stabbed a finger at Tom, almost shouting, pulling in short breaths. "Those bastards!" The finger was now aloft. "I have as many college degrees as any of them, and know far more than they do about people who lived here a long time ago. I can tell you stories from any age going back to Alexander the Great in the third century B.C."

Samuel sat down, breathing heavily, phlegm rattling in his throat.

Tom was startled by the almost maniacal fury of the man. "Please, Samuel, no one said you were crazy. Dr. Levy said you were highly educated, that scholars had tried to tape and study your stories, but you wouldn't permit it."

Samuel was only partly mollified. "I'm not parting with those stories until I get the right price. I'm an old man. My health is failing. I need money to get through the remaining years. I certainly can't make enough from this farm to survive."

"If I paid you, would you allow me to record what you know, particularly information from the first century A.D.?"

"How much?"

"Say six American dollars per hour. You could make a couple of hundred dollars in a few days."

"No, I couldn't. Dictating five hours a day, it would take me seven days to earn two hundred and ten dollars."

Tom was surprised by the accuracy and swift calculation. "How about seven dollars an hour with a bonus of three hundred dollars if I'm satisfied with what you give me?"

Tom saw a quick flash of interest in Samuel's eyes. His eyebrows knitted into a "V" over the bridge of his nose. He licked his lips nervously, and struck a closed right fist into the palm of his left hand. His left leg came off the ground then back down. Tom assumed these were signs of avarice.

"We might strike a bargain," Samuel said, "if you'll make that bonus a thousand dollars and meet one other condition."

"What's that?"

"I have a document," Samuel said. "My grandfather started it. My father worked on it too. From time to time I've added to it. That, with what I can provide verbally, will give you as complete an account of Biblical times as I can put together."

Samuel paused, lowered his voice. "It might even tell you where to look for King Solomon's gold mines -- or some other treasure just as valuable. So if you pay me five thousand dollars more, I'll let you photograph the document, and I won't reveal its contents to anyone else." Samuel's eyes were blazing, his face flushed.

"Five dollars an hour, plus a thousand dollar bonus, plus five thousand dollars to photograph a document I haven't seen!"

Tom shook his head. "I haven't got that kind of money -- and I'm not certain what you are saying about King Solomon's mines."

"Something just as valuable." One side of Samuel's face and most of his mouth converged on one closed eye in an exaggerated wink. "I know a lot about old Jewish treasures. Besides, I know you can get the money. All you Americans are rich." A tinge of contempt crept into his voice.

Tom studied the crafty old man, weighing what he had heard. "I need information on particular persons who lived in the Nazareth area many centuries ago. How do I know you could supply that?"

"If they lived there, I'll know about them. I'll even know who their descendants are."

Tom's mouth dropped open. It was as if Samuel had read his mind. He sat in silence, staring at him. Samuel stared back, unblinking.

"Okay," Tom finally said. "I'll see what I can do about raising the money. I'll get back to you as soon as I can."

On the way home he stopped at a pay telephone in Jericho and called Fran. She answered immediately. "Tom! Where are you? I've been trying to reach you all day. What's this about you and Derek having a fight? He told me you became insulting and attacked him when you happened to meet at the Israel Museum."

"That's not the way it -- "

"I'm upset with you, forcing a gentleman like Derek to defend himself. Are you hurt? Derek had a huge bruise on the left side of his face, and said his knees were sore."

"Fran, I'm all right. I don't have time to explain."

"Where are you? You sound like you're at the bottom of a well."

"I'm calling from Jericho. I'll explain later. Look, I'd like for you and Dr. Abe to have dinner with me tonight. Please make a reservation at the Hump of the Camel in the Old City for eight o'clock. I'll meet you there. I have some things I want to tell you."

There was a long pause. "Okay. I'll call Dr. Abe , but why

can't
you -- "
    "I'll see you at eight, Fran," he interrupted and hung up.

Chapter VIII

The flickering candle on the table contorted their faces into blobs of light and shadow and sent grotesque images dancing along the wall.

Tom pushed back his chair, glanced around the dimly lighted restaurant. "That was some meal, Dr. Abe. Glad I let you do the ordering. And this wine is superb. I didn't know the Israelis made a white with such body and flavor." He passed the glass beneath his nose, savoring the bouquet, then fell silent. The pause lengthened.

So far Tom's conversation had been small talk, including his version of the fight with Derek, but he knew the time had come to reveal his purpose in asking them to join him. He glanced at Fran, seated between him and the professor. She was watching him expectantly. Dr. Abe also. Tom pulled in a deep breath.

"I promised I would tell you why I'm in Israel as soon as I could and I'm ready to do so now." He paused, glanced at both of them. "I guess I should begin with my departure five years ago."

He sipped some wine, refilled his glass.

"Fran and I had just broken up. I was upset, especially with myself, and after I returned to the States became increasingly dissatisfied with my life. I overdid everything."

Tom's eyes met Fran's. She blushed, looked away.

"I began to drink too much, partied with girls too much. The only satisfaction I got was from reading and I overdid that, too. I read far into the night, history mostly, particularly on the Holy Land, picking up where I had left off here."

Tom sighed, poured more wine for Fran and Dr. Abe.

"One day about a year and a half ago I was plowing through *Caesar and Christ,* a book by historian Will Durant, and came across a passage describing the reaction of people in Nazareth after hearing Jesus speak there. 'Where did he get this wisdom, and the power to do these wonders?' they asked. 'Is he not the carpenter's son? Is not his mother named Mary, and are not his brothers named James, Joseph, Simon and Jude? And do not his sisters live here among us?'"

Fran drew in a short, sharp breath but said nothing.

Tom continued. "I had never heard Jesus had brothers and sisters. I checked the footnote. To my amazement the quotation was from two of the Gospels, Matthew thirteen, verse fifty-five and Mark six, verse two."

"The Catholic Church doesn't think that means biological brothers and sisters," Fran said.

Tom nodded, but went on. "That passage meant that if Jesus had brothers and sisters then Mary did not remain a virgin all her life as many Christians contend, since there was only one case of claimed virgin birth in the family. It also raised a question: What happened to those brothers and sisters?"

Tom motioned to the bartender and pointed to their empty wine bottle. The man brought another, popped the cork and filled their glasses. Tom took a sip and continued. "My curiosity was aroused so I looked further. To my amazement I discovered ten other references to the brothers and sisters in the Bible, plus more extensive accounts about them in the works of such early writers as Hegesippus, Eusebius and Helvidius.

"For example, John seven, verses one through ten, speaks of Jesus' brothers and the disciples, saying, 'As the Jewish feast of Tabernacles was close at hand, his brothers said to him you should leave this district and go to Judea so that your disciples there may see the great things you are doing. Surely no one can hope to be in the public eye if he works in seclusion. If you really are doing such things as these, show yourself to the world. For even his brothers had no faith in him.'

"Then in Matthew and Mark there's an anecdote about Jesus addressing a crowd in a building when his mother and brothers appear outside. Someone told him, saying: 'Behold, thy mother and thy brethren are standing outside seeking thee.' But he answered and said to him who told him, 'Who is my mother and who are my brethren?' And stretching forth his hand toward his disciples said, 'Behold my mother and my brethren! For whosoever does the will of my Father in heaven, he is my brother and sister and mother.'"

Dr. Abe held up a hand. "Wait a moment, Tom, I want to make some notes." He extracted a pad and ballpoint pen from his jacket. Fran, face drawn, remained silent.

Tom tented his fingers, looked off into space. "There is also Acts, Chapter One, verse fourteen. It tells of Jesus and his disciples being in an upstairs room in Jerusalem. The disciples are listed by name. Then it says: 'All these were constantly in prayer together, and with them a group including Mary, the Mother of Jesus, and his brothers.'

"Now this is important because it makes a distinction between the disciples and members of his family. Since names of three of his brothers and of three disciples -- James, Jude or Judas, and Simon -- are identical, there has been speculation the brothers might also have been disciples. This indicates they were not."

Tom looked down, gathering his thoughts, then up.

"I should point out, like Fran indicated earlier, some authorities believe these references are to half brothers and sisters fathered by Joseph, Mary's husband, in an earlier marriage. Still others contend they are cousins. Papias, a second-century bishop at Heirapolis, was probably the first to present that argument, and Clement of Alexandria has been interpreted as believing Jesus' brothers were either stepbrothers or cousins. Similar beliefs can be found in Epiphanius and Jerome, an early translator of the Gospels."

Tom took a deep breath, looked directly at Fran. "But

other authorities don't agree. Among the most impressive are Hegesippus -- I mentioned him before -- a Jewish Christian who wrote a five-book set of memoirs about 180 A.D., and Eusebius, bishop of Caesarea, who is often called the "Father of Church History." He lived and wrote in the fourth century. He was a historian and philosopher. Both left little doubt they thought Jesus' brothers and sisters were precisely that, and so did Helvidius."

Tom paused, looked at the ceiling, deliberately offering an opening for Fran or Dr. Abe to comment.

* * *

Twelve blocks away at the dingy headquarters of the Police Anti-racketeering Task Force, Inspector Shlomo Kahane, seated at a desk, relit his pipe and studied the map on the wall in front of him. It was studded with red pins, each marking the site of a major robbery. In an irregular pattern, the pins marched across the map's twisting streets and avenues, the most recent one emerging from contours of Mount Zion outside the southwestern corner of the Old City.

"What do you think, Lieutenant," he asked the officer next to him.

"I think the next time they'll hit inside the walls, probably somewhere in the Christian Quarter."

"I think you're right." Kahane shook his head in disbelief, his pipe now in his right hand. "They almost seem to signal where they'll strike. At least they point in a particular direction."

Lieutenant David Kline nodded. "They've feinted toward one place a couple of times, then gone to another, but they always end up close to where we expected. It's almost as if they were baiting us, then demonstrating they can pull off a job right under our noses."

"I know, damn it," Kahane growled. "They're the most elusive bastards I've ever encountered. I can't prove it, but I know the syndicate is masterminding their operations, and, so help me, I'm going to nail every one of them if it takes to my dying day."

Kahane pushed his short, stocky body up from the chair

and closed the folder on his desk containing the criminal record of the gang.

"How many intelligence people do we have out tonight Lieutenant?"

"About a dozen undercover, six of them inside the walls. Nothing stirring so far. The assault team is in the ready room and squad cars are outside the garage."

"Good. We'll go in on foot if we have to go into the Old City. Can't put any cars in there. The streets are too narrow. Keep prodding our guys. Don't let anyone get comfortable. These characters strike in unexpected ways. Meantime, I'm going to catch some sleep on the cot in my office. Call me if there are developments."

* * *

The pause ended, Tom looked down from the ceiling, glanced at Fran. Her face was flushed. She looked like she was about to explode.

"I feel like I've just had a lecture on agnosticism," she said. "Why are you trying to impose your strange beliefs on us?"

Tom turned toward Dr. Abe, awaiting his reaction.

"That's an impressive array of citations you've put together, Tom. I knew about the New Testament references to Jesus having brothers and sisters, of course, but never have heard them presented with other sources in such comprehensive fashion before."

Fran glared at Dr. Abe, ready to do battle. The professor raised his hands defensively, palms out. "As you know, Fran, the New Testament is not religion to me. It's literature and a type of history. I'm just commenting on Tom's research."

Tom nodded. "I didn't bring this up to offend you, Fran. I think you'll understand in a few minutes why I've said these things. But let me make a few more points.

"Christ was the oldest child in his family. James was next. I don't know the order of birth after James. But the important thing to remember is that not only did Christ have brothers and sisters but some of them married. I refer you to Corinthians,

Chapter Nine, verse five, in which Paul complains: 'Have I no right to take a Christian wife...like the rest of the apostles and the Lord's brothers...?'

"There is also documentation that at least one of the brothers had children. Hegesippus, a little more than a hundred years after Jesus was crucified, reported the Roman Emperor Domitian (A.D.51-96) had Roman authorities question two grandsons of Jesus' brother, Jude. The grandsons were named James and Sokker. Domitian wanted to determine whether the grandsons were plotting a rebellion like the disastrous Jewish uprising of 67-70 A.D. That means Jude had at least one son, or one daughter and that son or daughter had James and Sokker.

"And to round out the family I should mention Mary's husband, Joseph, had a brother named Clopus, spelled C-l-e-o-p-i-s by Luke. Clopus and his wife Mary had a son named Simeon, or Simon, and a daughter named Susanna, who was betrothed to James.

"To all this a few more family names can be added. The parents of Mary, Jesus' mother, were Saint Anne and Joachim. There may have been another daughter named Salome, who would have been Mary's sister, and even possibly a brother, Joseph of Arimathea, who, you may recall, knew Jesus as a boy, according to the Gospel of Luke, and was instrumental in recovering and burying Jesus' body after he was crucified.

"Another relative is a possible first, second or more removed cousin of Mary named Elizabeth, married to Zachariah. Their son was John the Baptist, who would have been a distant cousin of Jesus'."

Tom paused, thinking.

"Oh, yes, two other persons should be mentioned. One is Joseph's father, identified in Matthew as Jacob, and in Luke as Eli or Heli. The other is a more distant relative, a man named Conon, spelled with a C or a K, who claimed in the third century to be a descendant of the Holy Family, but whose exact descent is not known.

"Finally, one of the apocryphal books of the Bible says the

names of two of Jesus' sisters were Assia and Lydia. That is a doubtful source, but the names could be correct. There may have been other sisters, too. That quote listing the brothers by name does not specify how many sisters were in the family.

"So that brings me to my main point. Jesus was a member of a large family and the brothers and sisters of that family had children, and those children had children, perhaps up to and into the modern era."

Tom drew in a lungful of air and blew it out nervously.

"Well, Fran, Dr. Abe, that's the reason I'm in Israel. I'm trying to find those descendants of Jesus."

Chapter IX

Dr. Abe was on his feet, face registering total disbelief.

Fran was frozen rigid in her chair. A low gasp escaped her lips, then a muttered, "My God in heaven."

"That's sheer insanity," Dr. Abe said, leaning across the table. "How could you possibly track down the descendants of Jesus?"

"I said I was going to try, and there is a good reason I may succeed."

"And what might that be?" The professor sat down, pulled a white handkerchief from a hip pocket to mop his face.

"Because they exist. Somewhere in the world, most likely here in Israel, there are persons who are descended from Jesus and we ought to find them."

"It's possible they exist," Dr. Abe said, "but there is no way you could identify them."

Fran was making rasping, scraping noises, trying to clear her throat. "My God, Tom, I don't know when I've been more astounded. You of all people. The great agnostic, embarking on a religious quest like this."

"Not religious, Fran, historical. I'm hoping I can determine what happened to members of Christ's family and where their descendants are now. I hope to use the results in my doctor's dissertation -- "

Fran interrupted with a wave of her hand. "The premise on

which your project rests is fallacious. There couldn't have been any biological relationship between Jesus and any brothers and sisters or their descendants. Jesus was a creation of the Holy Spirit. Mary was only the vessel used to carry out God's purpose. Joseph provided no physical inheritance that would link Christ to anyone else. The Gospels make that clear."

Tom shook his head. "Actually, the Gospels are quite contradictory, Fran. Take the two presumed requirements for being the Messiah -- a virgin birth and descent from the House of David. The virgin birth idea springs from a passage in Isaiah stating, 'Behold a virgin shall be with child and shall bring forth a son and they shall call his name Emanuel,' a word equivalent to Messiah. But only Matthew and Luke have the story of the virgin birth. Mark and John do not.

"Then Matthew turns around and makes a great deal of Jesus' biological descent from David through his father, Joseph, thus fulfilling the second requirement. That makes no sense. If Jesus was a product of a virgin birth then there could not have been any biological relationship between him and the House of David or any other relatives, as Fran says. But if he was descended from David, that is if his physical inheritance was from the House of David, then there could not have been a virgin birth. They can't have it both ways."

Tom took a sip of wine. "Even Paul, the evangelist who spread Christianity around the Mediterranean world after Christ's death, indicated Jesus was born of a normal, physical union, and therefore would have been biologically related to his family. In his Epistle to the Romans, Paul said Jesus was the Son of God on a metaphysical plane, through his resurrection from the dead, but was 'made of the seed of David according to the flesh.' That sounds like a normal conception and birth took place and his divinity began after and because of the resurrection."

Tom loosened his tie and gazed around the restaurant. Other patrons lingered at a dozen tables. Beyond them the bartender leaned on the polished counter in front of his array of bottles, thumbing a girlie magazine, waiting for drink orders.

Tom paused, took in a deep breath.

* * *

Lieutenant Kline bent over Inspector Kahane, snoring loudly on the cot in his office.

"Inspector! Inspector! You better come take a look."

Kahane opened his eyes, gazed vacantly around the darkened room, finally focused on Kline. "What's that? You have something?"

He came fully awake, sat up, reached for his jacket on a nearby chair, then followed Kline into the task force operations center. There, sipping a cup of coffee, he read a message phoned in by Jacob Nevis, his most skilled undercover operative: "Have tailed two suspects for an hour. Both armed. Seem to be checking several places, including Hump of the Camel and the Disciples restaurants. Most attention on latter. Still outside there. Watching."

"Hah," Kahane said, slamming a fist into his left palm, "sounds like what we're looking for. Have two more men join Nevis. Tell them to report every fifteen minutes, and alert the assault group. I'll stand by here."

* * *

Tom exhaled, ready to resume.

"Even the place of Jesus' birth is debatable," he said, looking directly at Fran. "Only Matthew and Luke say Jesus was born in Bethlehem. John and Mark both indicate he was born in Nazareth, was reared there and spent most of his life there. But since there was an expectation the Messiah would come from Bethlehem it's possible the story of Jesus being born there was added to strengthen the claim Jesus was the Messiah."

"That just about does it," Fran said, banging her hand on the table. "First you attack Mary's virginity. Now you want to wipe out the Bethlehem Christmas story." She was close to tears, her voice taut and shrill.

"Look, Fran," Tom said, "I have my principles too. To me it's unforgivable for anyone, deliberately, to record or teach something that is untrue -- and that applies in spades to early

Christian authorities just as much as it does to anyone today. Furthermore, I think Christ's story would stand up very well on its own if it could be stripped of distortions. It would be more believable, not so filled with mysticism and magic. If I can contribute to making it more truthful I intend to do so."

Dr. Abe brought his open palms together in silent, simulated applause. "Hear, hear," he said, almost under his breath.

Fran bit her lower lip. Tears welled in her eyes. Then she buried her face in her hands and wept, shoulders heaving. Tom sat stiffly by, showing no sympathy. Finally the sobbing stopped. She looked up. A few dabs of her handkerchief to her eyes and she was under control again.

"Sorry. I lost control, but my religion means a lot to me. I don't like having people chip at its foundations."

Tom nodded, relaxed. "Okay, Fran, I understand. I didn't intend to hurt your feelings, but this is as important to me as your religion is to you."

Dr. Abe riffled through the notes on his pad, the exasperation he had expressed earlier apparently swept away by interest in what Tom was saying.

"I'm not sure I got all the relationships you mentioned, Tom. Could we go over that again?"

"I'll draw a family-tree for you." Tom borrowed a page from the professor's pad and drew vertical and horizontal lines leading to names arranged at different levels. "Remember, it all began with Abraham."

Fran leaned over from her chair to watch. When Tom finished he held the paper close to the flickering candle so all three could see it clearly. It showed:

Insert Genealogy Chart

Dr. Abe studied the drawing. "Have you learned any more that doesn't show here."

"A little. Collectively the family was known as 'The Heirs,' indicating it may have been viewed as a dynasty. After the crucifixion, James, the oldest surviving brother, became the first bishop of Christ's followers, the world's first Christian community. I showed that on the drawing. He was stoned and beaten to death in 62 A.D. There are persistent rumors that the ossuary, that is the stone box, in which James' bones were kept, still exists and will surface some day.

"My research indicates Jude went to Persia and was killed on Mount Ararat, where Noah's Ark was supposed to have come to rest. I could find nothing on what happened to the other two brothers, Joseph and Simon, and very little on the sisters, Assia and Lydia.

"Symeon, the son of Clopas, brother of Joseph the father, succeeded James as bishop of these first Christians. He was crucified by the Romans, allegedly at the age of a hundred and twenty, and was succeeded in turn by bishops, named Justus, Zaccheus, Tobias, Benjamin, Joseph and Judas. I don't know if any of them were family members.

"Because of his longevity, Symeon apparently lived into the second century A.D., as did James and Sokker, the two grandsons of Jude. They survived into the reign of Trajan, the Roman emperor from A.D. 57 to A.D. 117."

Dr. Abe shifted in his chair as Tom continued.

"After that we have only fragmentary reports about one further descendant, the man named Conon. He was executed in Pamphylia on the Greek Mediterranean coast about 250 A.D. We don't know which family member he, supposedly, was descended from, but he did exist. A grotto honoring him as a martyr was established in the third century and is now incorporated in the Church of the Annunciation in Nazareth, his home."

Tom looked off into space, thinking.

"He may have been more significant than we know. He and some unnamed descendants of Christ reportedly built what have been called 'synagogues of a special type' in Galilee in the third century, construction that continued into the fifth century. It seems reasonable to believe those 'synagogues' were early Christian churches."

Tom took a deep breath. "Summing up, I was able to trace Christ's descendants into the third century. Then the curtain drops, except for the conjectured activities of Conan in building Christian-like synagogues. I found nothing more that has usable documentation, yet it is inconceivable the story ended there."

Tom stopped abruptly. He looked to the left as a sudden movement caught his eye. The bartender had jumped to his feet, knocking over a bottle on the counter. He was staring at the entrance.

Four men, faces hidden by ski masks, were there, holding assault rifles across their chests. The largest motioned and two of the intruders glided down one side of the room and took up positions along the back wall, pointing their guns at the customers, while the leader advanced toward the bar. The fourth man remained where he was, guarding the door.

Tom froze in place, heart pounding, eyes following the intruders' movements. He immediately thought of the news story he had read about such bandits while sitting in the lobby of the King David Hotel.

The room, buzzing with conversation moments before, fell silent; everyone aware now that armed men were present and their leader was at the bar. The intruder said something to the bartender then jabbed a finger several times at the top of the counter and turned toward the customers.

"Up! Up! All of you get up and empty your pockets," he ordered, first in Hebrew, then in English. "Lay all money, all your jewelry, all watches on the table in front of you. Do as you're told and nobody will get hurt."

The bartender pushed a key, opening the cash register. The ringing sound echoed in the dimly lit room. He removed stacks of bills and placed them on the counter, still wet from the overturned bottle.

First one diner, then another, rose and deposited billfolds and valuables in front of them. No one spoke. The big man swept the cash on the counter into a black bag, then faced the room.

"Hands on your head," he ordered, again in Hebrew and English, waving a pistol. "We'll search each of you as we come by."

Everyone was standing now except Tom.. He hesitated. Spotting him, the masked intruder at the bar advanced, shouting," Get up, Yankee bastard!"

Tom, angered by the epithet, rose slowly, wondering what in his appearance showed he was American. Across the table, Dr. Abe, his face chalk white, stood stiffly, fingers interlaced atop his balding head. Fran, also up, fingers joined on her head, whimpered, "Oh my God, Oh my God."

The man grabbed Tom by the shoulder, spun him around and was balling a fist to hit him in the face when Tom kicked him in the groin. He saw the sudden sickness in the eyes glaring at him through openings in the ski mask. The man reeled backward, bent over, groaning, gasping. "I'll kill you. Nobody..."

Tom shoved the man's gun aside with his left hand, then grabbed his ski mask and jerked hard. The bandit, pulled off balance, reeled to one side. Tom pulled hard again. The bandit staggered in the opposite direction.

The man shouted something in Hebrew.

Tom knew the two men at the back wall were rushing toward him. Fran, mouth open, eyes wide with fear, scrambled frantically to get out of the way. She screamed. "Tom, be careful!"

At the same moment, Tom heard gunfire outside, then distant shouting. He gave the facemask a massive tug and stuck out his foot. The bandit crashed to the floor as the mask came off in Tom's hand and the gun fell near Tom's foot. Tom had a glimpse of a dark, unshaved face and a head of unkempt, black hair before the man turned and shouted again in Hebrew,

He grabbed the bag of loot, leaving the valuables uncollected on the tables, and raced for the door, the others following. They disappeared as quickly as they had come, everyone in the room staring open-mouthed after them.

"There they go!"

The shout, from outside, was muffled by distance. There was another burst of gunfire, then the sound of men running. Finally silence.

Inside the restaurant the customers, in various stages of collapse, erupted in loud, excited conversations, some standing, some leaning on the tables, others collapsing into chairs, holding their heads, trying to overcome shock, all breathing hard.

"Heavens, Tom, you took an awful chance," Fran said, her voice quavering. "You've got to watch your temper." She sat down.

Dr. Abe, also seated now, mopped his face with his handkerchief and muttered, "I'm getting too old for this."

The bartender's booming voice overrode the chaos in the room. "Please, please be seated, everyone, resume your dinners. We called the police from the kitchen. They've been stalking this gang for weeks. I'm sure they'll catch them. A free bottle of wine for everyone. Please, you're safe now."

Tom, Fran and Dr. Abe did calm down, slowly, gradually. Tom poured each of them a full glass from the new bottle that had just arrived. He consumed most of his in one gulp. Dr. Abe did likewise and Fran took several long sips. They looked at each other, slowly recovering.

"Well, we might as well continue," Dr. Abe said. "I'm anxious to hear the rest of Tom's story."

Fran, still pale and visibly shaken, didn't object. Tom mustered a weak smile, tried to gather his thoughts. "Let's see, where was I? Oh, yes, I believe I said I had traced the descendants into the third century then hit a wall."

"So what's next?" Dr. Abe asked.

"I keep thinking about two lost records that may have contained additional information about the family."

"What records?"

"One, called 'The Logia,' was a collection of Aramaic

sayings of Jesus apparently compiled by Matthew. The other is known as the 'Q Document,' a name taken from the German word 'Quelle' which means source. The existence of the 'Q Document' is indicated by the fact that Matthew and Luke both had access to information for their gospels not available to Mark."

Fran looked puzzled. "If both are lost how can you make use of them?"

Tom poured more wine. "Through the oral tradition, I hope. Both of those records were taken from that tradition -- the practice of passing on knowledge of past events by word of mouth. If I can gain access to that oral record -- "

"How?" Dr. Abe demanded.

Tom told them of reading the newspaper report about families living near Nazareth who still used the oral tradition, of his correspondence with the Nazareth Museum and the offer by Old Samuel to let him record his stories and photocopy the manuscript he, his father and grandfather had prepared. The problem now was raising money.

Dr. Abe nodded as Tom was speaking. "We know all about Old Samuel at the University," he said. "He's hopelessly confused."

"He didn't seem completely stable to me either when I talked to him," Tom said. "At one point he hinted he might tell me the location of King Solomon's gold mines, or some equally valuable treasure recorded on a scroll recently found and now being translated."

Dr. Abe sighed. "We've tried to work with him. We were interested in that document too, but Samuel would never allow us to examine it. He insisted on payment first." Dr. Abe looked weary. "Samuel was once a brilliant scholar, and I believe somewhere in that disordered mind there is information of historical -- "

Dr. Abe stopped, stared at the door, where a stocky, uniformed policeman had appeared, pushing a disheveled, dark-haired man, wrists handcuffed behind him. Two more police officers followed.

"Please let me have your attention," the stocky one announced. "I'm Inspector Kahane. I need your help. You had a robbery here tonight. We caught this man. His name is Schwartz. We believe he is one of those who participated. The others escaped while we were watching another restaurant. Can any of you identify him?" He shoved the handcuffed man further into the room.

Tom recognized the prisoner immediately as the one he had stripped of his mask. He stood up. "I can, Inspector. He was the leader. I got a good look at his face."

The handcuffed man glared at Tom but said nothing.

"Good," Kahane said. He motioned Tom to come to the bar, wrote down Tom's name, address and telephone number and asked him to come to police headquarters the next day to provide a sworn statement. The police left and Tom returned to his table.

"I know Inspector Kahane," Dr. Abe said. "Guess he didn't see me." All three of them were silent a moment, then Dr. Abe returned to their original conversation. "One thing is missing in your plans, Tom. How will you identify members of Jesus' family if you do find them?"

"There may be a way, maybe two ways."

Dr. Abe looked skeptical.

"There's that fingerprint."

"Oh, that again."

"Let me theorize a moment," Tom said. He waited, collecting his thoughts. "Obviously I didn't know about the tile and its fingerprint before I came here, although I did know about the prints on the Isaiah scroll. The tile was a fortuitous discovery with a fingerprint that gave me a long shot at an association with Jesus' family I lacked before.

"Just suppose -- I'm speculating -- the fingerprint on the tile and some prints on the Isaiah text are identical or very similar, and it could be established the print on the tile was made by Jesus, or some other family member. Then, by association, we would have reason to believe the Isaiah Dead Sea scroll was the one Christ read from in the synagogue at Nazareth -- or handled elsewhere. We could also theorize that any person with a fingerprint pattern closely resembling those on the scroll and tile might be a descendant of Christ."

"That's preposterous," Dr. Abe said. "Everyone's prints are different."

"I don't believe that. Why should this one physical characteristic be different from other inherited physical characteristics?"

"I don't know," Dr. Abe said. "What's your other way of identifying descendants?"

I'm hoping Samuel may name some of them for me and tell me where they live."

"I wouldn't count on it," Dr. Abe said, rising.

The restaurant was deserted and the bartender was eyeing them with increasing irritation, glancing at his watch, then in their direction.

"Tom, I want to think about it, but maybe I can scrape up some school money to help in your research. In the meantime, I have an early class tomorrow and must get home. Thanks to both of you for a stimulating evening." He laughed ruefully. "Far more stimulating than I wanted."

Dr. Abe recovered his coat and hat from a closet. He started toward the door, then turned. "Oh, I made inquires about photographing the fingerprints on the Isaiah scroll. I think it can be arranged. The next examination is late this month. Do you intend to do the work yourself?"

"No," Tom said, "I'll have to hire a professional. Can you recommend one?"

"I know a young student named Sharon Ausch who is an excellent photographer and needs the work," Dr. Abe said.

He turned again to leave, then stopped once more. "Come to think of it she's also good at translating Hebrew and can type. If you buy that document, and make recordings, you may want her to translate and type for you. I don't think you could do any better."

Dr. Abe left. Tom and Fran departed shortly afterward.

Chapter X

The phone in Tom's hotel room rang at two o'clock the next afternoon. He answered, nodded as he listened, kept repeating, "Okay, Okay," then hurried over to Dr. Abe's office. He sat down, looked up, pushing that stray lock of hair into place, and told the professor: "Thanks for arranging the interview."

Dr. Abe glanced at his watch. "She should be here soon."

She was, arriving moments later, pausing in the doorway.

Dr. Abe rose. "Come in, Sharon. Tom Shannon, this is Sharon Ausch, the student I told you about. I've explained the type of work we'll be doing, and she's interested." He looked at his watch again. "I've some errands to run. I'll be gone at least an hour, so you two can talk " He rushed out, muttering his usual complaint about being behind schedule.

Sharon was about five feet three; had a short, sturdy body; black doe-like eyes and a round face, framed by dark brown curls. Tom smiled, motioned toward a chair." Sit down, Sharon. Tell me about yourself." He wanted to put her at ease.

She sat, looked down, placed a worn briefcase by her feet. "There's not a lot to tell, Mr. Shannon. I'm twenty, the youngest of four children raised on a farm near Haifa. I have two brothers in that area, and a sister in Tel Aviv. My parents are dead. I've been studying Hebrew and Hebrew literature for three years, and learned typing and photography to make money on the side."

She reached for the briefcase, extracted a handful of photographs. "These are campus scenes I took for the yearbook. As for my Hebrew, I've gotten straight A's. I should be able to handle any translation problems we encounter. I can get a copy of my grade transcript if you want to see it."

"That won't be necessary." Tom returned the photos after a quick look. "I think you will work out fine. I can offer you six dollars an hour and employment for six or seven weeks. Will that be okay?" She accepted eagerly.

They talked some more. Tom, as always with pretty girls, smiled a lot, making certain he showed his even, white teeth -- teeth like his father's. He explained the work in more detail, then added: "Oh, yes, there's no electricity where we're going. You better bring a battery operated lap-top and printer, and I'll provide a battery powered tape recorder."

"I'd prefer to use a typewriter, if you don't mind, Mr. Shannon. I've never used a computer or word processor."

Tom nodded. "Okay, that's fine." He. got up, extended his hand.

Sharon rose too. "Oh," she exclaimed, grabbing at the photos in her lap as they spilled on the floor.

"I'll get them," Tom said, bending down. His shoulder brushed hers. She blushed, drew back as if jolted by electricity, then stood up, looking flustered.

"By the way," Tom said, handing the photos to her, "call me Tom. I'll telephone you with departure details, but pack a suitcase and be ready to leave on a few hours notice. We should get to Samuel's farm as soon as we can."

They drove the seventy-five miles in a two-car convoy the next day, Tom leading in his rented Mercedes, piled high with camping gear and supplies, Dr. Abe and Sharon following in the professor's ancient Fiat. They met with Samuel, agreed on terms and made a down payment with money taken from Tom's bank account and research funds Dr. Abe talked a university trustee into releasing.

By nightfall, they had three tents pitched -- lined up ten

yards apart in front of Samuel's sagging residence -- and supper bubbling in a frying pan over an open campfire.

Tom stretched out in a folding chair and gazed at the flames. "This is the most relaxed I've been in weeks. That beef stew about ready, Dr. Abe?"

"Coming up." The professor spooned the meat and gravy onto three plates, atop huge hunks of bread. They ate slowly, talking little, washing the food down with cold water from the nearby stream.

A half hour later Tom rose, stretched, yawned. "I'm bushed. I'm going to bed."

They were up at dawn. After a breakfast of coffee, toast and packaged, preserved milk on cereal, they joined Samuel under the large pine beside his house. Again Tom was struck by the fierce intensity in the man's eyes, his tangled hair and stooped, towering body.

"Start with a general description of the tension between the Romans and Jews in the first century A. D., Samuel," Tom said, "We can get more detail after I'm certain our tape recorder is operating satisfactorily."

They had several false starts that day, and the next, but gradually settled into a routine, each session going better than the one before. Then a new problem arose. Dr. Abe made a quick trip to Beit Shean, where he checked with his office by phone, and came racing back. He jumped out of his car and rushed up to Tom, seated at a card table in front of his tent.

"Damn it," he exploded. "I told my staff not to let anyone know where I was, but they did anyway. Now I've got to return and complete a report just when we are beginning to make good progress."

The professor was a study in dishevelment. He was wearing a big, floppy, khaki hat, pulled down almost to his eyebrows, forcing him to tilt his head back and peer out from under the brim through spectacles balanced precariously on the end of his nose. A large safari jacket sagged halfway to his knees. The sleeves were rolled in messy lumps to make room for his short arms to reach open air, while khaki pants hung down over the tops of haphazardly laced boots, knickerbocker style.

Tom could contain himself no longer. He grinned, then shook his head in amazement. "You look like a sawed-off, Jewish Teddy Roosevelt, Dr. Abe. Where did you get that outfit?"

"Never mind where I got it," he sputtered. "Didn't you hear what I said? I've got to return to Jerusalem. The university president is demanding I prepare a report on this term's program for a department meeting later this week."

"Do you think Sharon and I can handle the interviews?"

Dr. Abe paced back and forth, one hand pulling on his beard. "I think so. Every evening I suggest you have Sharon give you a summary, in English, of what Samuel said that day. For some reason he accepts our requests and questions in English, but answers only in Hebrew. Using the summary, you can prepare instructions to give Samuel the next morning. Have him review what he left unclear, expand where necessary, and force him into new ground."

Tom pondered a moment. "A daily summary is a good idea. I'm lost after we tell Samuel what we want. Once he starts answering I'm out of it."

Dr. Abe nodded. "Sometimes I am too. Part of his language is archaic. The pronunciation throws me."

Tom had been jotting notes on a yellow pad from books scattered across the tabletop. He shoved them aside.

"Any idea when you'll return?" He tilted back in his chair, arms clasped behind his head.

"Perhaps by the weekend." Dr. Abe frowned, glanced at his watch. "I've got to pack and get out of here. The session went well this morning. Samuel is resting inside the house. These tapings exhaust him, but he'll be up and moving soon. I'm sorry about this interruption, Tom, but with luck we won't be seriously delayed."

Tom thought about that as Dr. Abe entered his tent, twenty yards away. Despite initial difficulties the sessions had, indeed, gone better than expected. Every morning they joined Samuel under the pine near his house and discussed what they wanted to cover that day. Then Samuel would lean back in an old, faded reclining chair, hauled from his shed, close his eyes and begin to speak. Under Dr. Abe's guidance, this had produced steady progress. Now Tom was losing the most experienced member of his team.

Dr. Abe emerged, lugging a battered suitcase. Simultaneously the flap on Sharon's tent parted and she came out, sighted the suitcase and looked questioningly at Tom.

"Dr. Abe has been called back to the University. I'll fill you in later."

Sharon's eyebrows went up, but she had no comment.

"Have to hurry," Dr. Abe said. "I don't like driving these roads at night, and I haven't got much daylight left." He glanced at the brilliant sun dropping toward the hills behind Samuel's house, the rays, like shattered silver, slanting off poplars lining the nearby stream.

Sharon walked quickly after Dr. Abe as he struggled to heave the suitcase into the trunk of his sedan. Dressed in breeches, laced boots and khaki shirt, she appeared at home in camping attire, walking with an athletic, masculine stride.

"Here, let me help." She shoved aside a tire jack and pushed the suitcase into a corner of the trunk.

Dr. Abe removed his floppy hat and mopped his brow with a rolled-up sleeve. "That does it." He turned toward Sharon. "I've told Tom it might be helpful if you prepared a daily summary in English after each taping session and he agrees."

Sharon nodded. "Sounds like a good idea."

Tom held out his hand. "Dr. Abe, hurry back. Your guidance and support are needed. I couldn't have gotten this off the ground without your help."

"Nonsense. Besides, I've enjoyed myself."

He turned and jumped into the car. The engine sputtered and caught, then burst into a great roar, rising and falling as Dr. Abe pumped the accelerator. With a spinning of tires, and grinding of gears, the car suddenly lurched ahead, bouncing and clattering down the rocky road to the main highway. Dr. Abe's arm shot out the open driver's window in a farewell wave, then he was swallowed in dust raised by the careening vehicle.

Tom laughed. "God help the driver who gets in his way."

"Yeah," Sharon added, smiling, "Israel's only unguided missile."

Tom returned to his card table. Sharon joined him a short time later. They sat side by side, going over the single-spaced summary she placed in front of him, pointing with and moving a pencil, clasped loosely in her right hand, back and forth across the page,

"We have some trouble here, and again here." The pencil moved. "We need more detail. How about asking him who these people are, where they lived and what they did?"

"Sounds good," Tom said. "And let's push him about what happened in Jerusalem immediately after the crucifixion."

Sharon agreed and returned to her typewriter.

Tom glanced at the setting sun, entered his tent, donned sandals and swimming trunks, then, carrying a beach towel, walked down the dirt path behind Samuel's house -- and entered another world. The fetid smell of barnyard, and the squalor of Samuel's dwelling faded behind him. A verdant garden landscape opened before him -- a quiet pool, framed and shaded by stately poplars, and fed by a rushing stream. The water entered over a rocky waterfall off to one side, and departed; gurgling and murmuring to itself, around a rocky bend fifty yards downstream.

Tom dropped his towel on the grassy bank. He scrambled onto a rock and hit the water in a low-angled dive. He came up, tossed his hair in a circular motion toward the back of his head and blinked water from his eyes. Shivering from the cold shock, he struck out for the waterfall on the far side, then settled into a rhythmic, Australian crawl, gliding back and forth, stretching and pulling muscles until air was pumping steadily through his lungs and fatigue made his arms and legs ache.

He pulled himself out of the water, gasping, toweled off, then laid down in the shade of a tree close to the waterfall to enjoy the gathering twilight.

A sense of well-being engulfed him. He liked what he was doing. He liked having a goal in life. He liked doing something that had not been done before. He liked the tedious work of the tapings and the magnificent relaxation at day's end, swimming in this idyllic pool.

He was beginning to love people too. That was something he hadn't always been capable of. He loved Dr. Abe, admired him, knew he was a friend whose irascible nature masked a natural generosity, a man who enjoyed giving more than receiving.

Then there was Fran. A vision of her floated before him. Large, limpid brown eyes, slightly tilted nose, high cheekbones, tumbling, red-brown hair, ripe body. How could he have been so stupid. He had caused the confrontation that shattered their relationship.

Tom's reverie drifted into troubled sleep. He dreamed of Fran and awoke with a start, feeling cold and clammy, face drenched with perspiration. He struggled to his feet and dived into the pool. A couple of laps in the icy water should clear his mind.

Halfway to the other side he become aware of another presence. Sharon, eyes big as saucers, was treading water in the center of the pond. Although the twilight had deepened, he could see she was nude. Her breasts and upper body were visible, the rest of her obscured by undulating, refracted light.

"Where...where...did you come from?" she stammered. "I...I didn't know you were here."

Tom was just as startled as she was. "My God, Sharon... "

"I didn't have a suit, " she said. "I thought you were in your tent. A swim seemed like a good idea...so I... "

"Stay where you are. I'll get out and give you some privacy,"

Tom couldn't resist taking a final look at the fullness of her exposed upper body. She blushed and turned away. He swam to the bank, picked up his towel and waved before starting up the path. She watched with large, round eyes.

They ate in silence that night, consuming vegetable soup Tom heated over the fire. He could sense a tension between them that hadn't been there before.

"I hope you're not embarrassed by what happened out there in the waterfall pool," Tom finally said. "It was just one of those things." He laughed nervously. "But I must say you were a magnificent sight."

The attempted humor fell flat. Sharon, eyes on her food, spoke softly. "Don't make fun of me, Tom. I'm no prude. You can't be if you're brought up on a farm with a father and brothers in the house, and then later work in a *kibbutz*. I've seen men before, but for some reason this time I'm embarrassed. Maybe I didn't realize how muscular you are. Maybe it's because you're so...so...Nordic, not hairy like some men. Anyway, I've suddenly realized we're out in the country, unescorted. Neither of us has been particularly aware of the other's sex. Now we are. So let's keep our emotions under control and our relationship professional."

Tom watched her face freeze into a mask.

"Okay, Sharon," he said, a smile spreading across his face, "but I didn't know you were having trouble keeping your emotions under control."

"Did I say that?" she asked, startled.

"Not really. I'm playing with words." He felt a rising surge of physical attraction. The male predator in him couldn't resist toying with her discomfort.

"Okay so you want to keep it professional." He got up, looked down at her and winked. "But that's going to be difficult, having seen such a sexy, round bottom."

"Why, you didn't see..." She started and stopped. "You only saw..." Her hands went up to her breasts, then she drew them away, realizing what she had done. "Oh, Tom, stop it. You're flustering me." She was embarrassed.

Tom reached down, took her hand, pulled her to her feet. Her soup slipped off her lap onto the ground. He took her in his arms, kissed her on the lips, then turned and went into his tent.

He had intended it as light, sexually oriented play, but the feel of her hard, young body against his sent his blood racing. Sharon, equally aroused, stared after him as he entered his tent.

That night Tom tried to read by the light of a gasoline lantern, but was restless. He turned it off and tried to sleep. After an hour of tossing, he dragged his cot into the open air.

A full moon hung in the sky overhead, bathing the camp in pale, silvery light, seeming to cast a spell over all it touched. Tom laid down on his back, clad only in white jockey shorts. He was sprawled there, hands behind his head, listening to frogs croaking in the stream, when she came to him, out of the shadows.

She was wearing cheap, rayon pajamas that accentuated the full, curving outline of her legs and breasts. He moved over and she laiy beside him. He pressed her body against his, running his right hand up and down her back. Slowly he worked the hand up under the pajama blouse and caressed her breasts. She gasped. He pulled the blouse off over her head and kissed her gently. His tongue found a round, cherry red, erect nipple and she moaned.

Both stripped off their remaining clothing and made love, passionately, violently, while the moon looked down on the longest running, repeating drama in history -- a man and a woman sharing the passion in which life begins, the passion in which a man attempts to prove he is a man, the passion in which a woman proves she is a woman, the passion that leads to resurrection and rebirth of self in another life.

* * *

Back in Jerusalem, in the office of the Club Tomcat, the five members of the Syndicate's council were lined up in front of Meyer Bernstein, standing behind his desk. They looked very uncomfortable as Bernstein eyed them contemptuously.

"I can't believe it," he said, his voice dripping with sarcasm. "Where did we get such schmucks. First they almost fall off a ladder and drop a light bulb at the King David, messing up a spy operation. Then Schwartz gets caught during that restaurant heist. What have you got to say for yourselves?"

"We did get what we needed at the hotel," Doc Steiner

ventured.

"Yeah? Explain it to me. I must be kind of dumb."

Steiner gulped, apparently sorry he had offered an opinion. "Well, Marty got a good look into the room and listened for several minutes before that bulb slipped out of his hand."

"Yeah! What the hell good is that."

"He found out what the American got in Nazareth -- his name is Shannon -- was one of those Roman building tiles. It's worth a few grand, but far less than a scroll from that cave would be. Like Schwartz said, the American definitely didn't find a scroll. So if one's there, it's still there, somewhere."

"That doesn't help much," Bernstein shouted, his fist slamming the desk. "That Shannon guy's onto something. He was looking for something when he went there, and he knew where to look. Who knows where he'll look next. I have a hunch he'll go back, but he could try elsewhere, too. I want him watched. You got that? He leveled a long index finger at the group, his face now a deep red.

"Got it," Steiner said.

"And tell Schwartz he'll lose his balls if he goes for any deal with the cops."

"Got it," Steiner said.

"And get somebody to beat the hell out of Marty and the other yokel who messed up the hotel deal. We can't permit that kind of foul up."

"Got it," Steiner said.

"Okay, now get the hell out of here."

The five left as fast as they could get out the door.

Chapter XI

Derek parked his car in front of Fran's apartment. He sat there tense and uncertain, rehearsing what he wanted to say to her. It had taken him more than a week to get this far, so the words had to be right.

There'll never be a better time, he told himself. *That letter from the Massachusetts Institute of Technology, received yesterday, and the two hundred dollars I paid on my gambling debt -- hopefully buying me a little time -- make this the proper moment. I've got to talk to her now.*

He pulled in a breath and got out of the car, a dozen red roses in one hand, a box of chocolates in the other. He rang the bell, heard Fran approaching, the scraping of wood across the threshold as she opened the door. Then she was there, her mouth forming an oval of surprise.

"Derek! And oh my, roses! I adore roses! And candy too! This must indeed be a special occasion, like you said on the phone. Come in, let me get these flowers in some water." She hurried into the kitchen, emerging moments later with the roses in a vase. She breathed deeply, savoring their fragrance as she placed them on the table.

"I have good news, my dear," Derek blurted before she could settle into a chair. "I received this yesterday." He extracted the MIT letter from his tweed jacket and handed it to her.

Fran scanned it, found the key sentences: "We can offer

you a visiting professorship in English history at sixty thousand dollars a year beginning this fall...will need your acceptance or rejection by next month...Sincerely, Lawrence Geoffrey Smith, dean Liberal Arts Studies."

"Oh, Derek, that's wonderful," Fran said, face beaming. "MIT is one of the best schools in America." She hugged him, kissed him on the cheek. "Congratulations."

Derek smiled, relieved. Her enthusiasm was all he had hoped for.

"I'm happy, too, old girl, and must make plans. Really, Fran, it's time for a decision on my marriage proposal. I think we should marry right away and make the trip to America our honeymoon. You know I love you, and will always be proud of you. You'll be an invaluable adjunct to my career."

Fran blanched, took a quick breath, settled into a chair, bit down on her lower lip. "Oh my," she said, softly. "You're right of course. It is time. You're entitled...but I'm so uncertain. I...I...really don't know my own mind. And then there's Tom, of course."

"Tom!" Derek felt his face flush, couldn't help almost shouting. "What has *he* got to do with it? He's not worthy of you, Fran. He's not even a Christian. Really, you should sever relations with that pagan!"

Fran drew back, visibly startled by Derek's anger. "I admit he's self-centered, impulsive, and rather intense at times, but he can be thoughtful, too, and is doing impressive research. You shouldn't be so critical."

"What kind of research?" Derek snapped, sensing a renewed threat from the American.

Fran hesitated. "Well, he's at a farm near Beit Shean, conducting exhaustive interviews with a man who is an expert on the oral tradition in Jewish history."

"Why? What's left to learn about Jewish history? It's the best documented ethnic story in the world."

"Perhaps, but I wouldn't be so quick to belittle what he's doing, Derek. He may be uncovering things never revealed before. The man he's interviewing says he can even tell Tom the location of King Solomon's gold mines, or some other treasure just as valuable, recorded on a previously, undisclosed scroll."

Fran clamped a hand over her mouth, as if she had revealed more than she intended.

"King Solomon's mines!" Derek laughed. "They're a myth. As for the rest, what could he possibly hope to discover?"

"I'm not sure he would want me to discuss specifics, but I've come this far...Oh, I suppose it can't do any harm, but keep this to yourself."

Derek listened with astonishment as Fran described Tom's efforts to track down the descendants of Christ.

"That's blasphemous," he exploded. "The fool's attacking the foundations of Christianity -- the virgin birth, Mary's perpetual virginity. It's the work of Satan. God damn that meddling bastard!"

Derek slammed his fist on the table, upsetting the roses.

Fran blanched. There was an awkward pause. She picked up the flowers and wiped off the table while Derek sat stiffly in his chair, muttering to himself.

"That's a little strong," Fran said in a small voice. "I've known Tom for years. He's highly intelligent and an idealist in his own way. I've heard him say many times that rejection of what human intelligence demonstrates to be the truth is the same as rejecting God. It is a refusal to accept the fruit of the capability that God gave us to find the truth. That, he says, is true blasphemy."

"Blasphemy!" Derek shouted. "What does that agnostic know about blasphemy? He's a dangerous, mixed-up child. You've got to make a clean break with him, Fran. I insist upon it. Go to that damned farm. Tell him you're going to marry me. Get rid of him once and for all."

He stopped, realizing he had gone too far. This was not in the script he'd rehearsed. He pulled on his ear and muttered, half to himself, "Blasphemy indeed."

Fran sat stiffly erect in her chair, obviously shocked by

Derek's outburst, hands clasped in her lap. She watched as he tried to regain control.

He finally spoke. "I'm sorry, Fran. I shouldn't have become so agitated, but that imposter irritates me."

Another awkward pause followed, then Derek rose, forced a weak smile. "I have a class tonight and must go, but I would appreciate it if you would give me your answer soon, my dear."

Fran rose with him. He kissed her on the cheek, whispering again, "Soon, please."

"I know," she said. "I'll try."

* * *

After Derek left, Fran sat very still, collecting her thoughts. What was she to do? Derek was everything she had always wanted in a husband -- handsome, compatible, religious, possessed of a brilliant mind and now had an excellent job offer.

But he seemed so tense lately, so demanding. And what did he mean she would be an adjunct to his career? She wasn't an adjunct to anyone. She was her own person. And if she married she would have to step out from behind the protective barriers she had erected to avoid pain, to avoid the new and untried. That made her uneasy. She would have to assume a new role in life. She lifted a hand, saw it was trembling.

And like she had said, there's Tom. He had wanted her to join him, Dr. Abe and Sharon when they went to Samuel's farm, said it would give them a chance to talk out their problems. That was thoughtful, something they had never tried before. When she said she couldn't get away, he showed her a map, pinpointing where they would be if she changed her mind.

I can't just walk away from him, she told herself. *I owe him more than that. Perhaps I should do as Derek suggests, go see him, try to clarify my own feelings so I can make the right decision. On the other hand what right has Derek to insist I do anything?*

Fran pondered Derek's demand as she prepared a light supper and bathed. It was while she was sitting in her living room afterward, clad in a pink robe, one bobbing leg crossed over the other as she did her nails, that she decided.

Why not drive to Samuel's farm tomorrow? It was a Saturday. Her office was closed. She knew the way. She could leave after lunch and be there in time to have a long talk with Tom. Yes, why not?

Decision made, she went to bed and slept soundly.

Chapter XII

Sharon arose early the morning after they made love, a Saturday, and started a fire in the, rock-circled area they used for cooking. She perked a pot of coffee atop the wire grill Tom had placed there and was preparing to scramble eggs when he joined her.

"Morning." He rubbed his eyes, poured himself a mug of coffee and took a sip. "The food working out all right?"

"Fine. The eggs you purchased from Samuel are fresher than I expected. We have enough utensils. The canned goods and bread are stored over there." She nodded toward a box between two of the tents. "I'll have some toast ready soon."

Tom nodded, finished his coffee and ducked into his tent. He emerged moments later and headed for the stream, carrying soap and towel.

"Don't be long," Sharon called after him. "Breakfast is almost ready."

They sat at the card table Tom had used as a desk the day before. He ate quickly, washing his food down with coffee. Sharon looked up every few moments, expecting him to say something about their love making of the night before. He didn't mention it, leaving her puzzled and uncertain.

She felt more uncertain when he rose after the meal and returned to his tent without mentioning the subject. He seemed withdrawn, totally engrossed in his own thoughts. Not until they joined Samuel under the big pine at eight o'clock did he become animated and enthusiastic.

"Start right after the crucifixion, Samuel," Tom said. "What happened to Jesus' family? Which ones besides Mary were in Jerusalem? Were the others in Nazareth?"

Samuel leaned back in his dilapidated chair, gazing at the branches above him. His eyes closed. He seemed to be sleeping until the words came -- at first in bursts of two and three, then finally in a torrent, sentence atop sentence, amid guttural sounds, gasping for air, jerky body movements and facial contortions.

Tom switched on the tape recorder at the first sign of response, then sat transfixed, apparently as amazed as she was by the performance, although both had seen it before.

Sharon edged her chair closer, concerned. She didn't understand some of Samuel's ancient Hebrew, but relaxed when the words evolved into forms she knew.

Samuel continued for three hours, then stopped, saying, "Amen," the signal he would say no more that day. He dropped into a deep sleep. They let him rest there while they sat down at the card table and ate peanut butter sandwiches for lunch.

"What he said was amazing, Tom. He described a scene of utter chaos in Jerusalem. I'm not certain whether this was immediately after the crucifixion or later when the Romans attacked the city. When we get it organized, you're going to have a story that's never been fully told before."

Tom nodded enthusiastically. "We're getting more than I dared hope for."

After lunch Sharon went to her tent to translate and transcribe the newest recordings and prepare the daily summary while Tom drove to Beit Shean to purchase supplies. Alone and frustrated, she found her mental processes moving on two tracks. On the upper, more conscious one, she was all business, filling the tent with the clatter of the typewriter keys as she raced through the tapes, reviewing, shaping and pounding Samuel's words into an understandable composition. On a lower, less conscious level, her mind was fantasizing, conjuring visions of new liaisons with

Tom, seeing his naked body thrashing violently against hers, moving swiftly toward a climax.

Sharon got up, walked aimlessly about the tent. She took deep breaths, tried to refocus her thoughts. Under control, she returned to the typewriter. In seconds, the tent was filled with the clatter of pounding keys again. Then, slowly, her concentration faded and her mind drifted, conjuring new erotic images, forming new questions.

Why is he so distant? He must know I would like to continue the relationship. But I can't be the instigator again -- or can I? She paced the tent until control returned. By late afternoon she was tired and frustrated, her mind in turmoil. Then she heard Tom calling.

"Sharon! Sharon!"

She stepped outside. Tom was standing there, holding a one-piece woman's black bathing suit in his right hand and pages of the most recent transcript in his left.

"Found this in Beit Shean today," he said, handing her the suit. "Thought you might like to have it."

"Oh, thank you."

"By the way, did Samuel really say this?" He pointed at several paragraphs. "I had no idea this was the way Christ's family got out of the city. The detail is incredible." There was a touch of awe in his voice.

"He not only said it but repeated it, providing new information each time. Then today he added that once family members got through the Roman lines they gathered in Pella. I'm hoping tomorrow he'll tell us where they went from there."

Sharon watched Tom retreat to his tent, then emerge in swimming trunks moments later, headed for the waterfall pool. She rushed back to her typewriter. Ten minutes later, she donned her new swimsuit and hurried to the pool, hoping to join Tom, but he was gone. She swam until sunset, then approached his tent, calling his name.

"Come on in, Sharon,," he answered.

She entered, found him standing next to his cot, one hand

holding down the top of his swim trunks, examining red marks extending down his stomach to his lower abdomen.

"Oh," she said, startled by his near nudity, then stopped and stared. "What have you done to yourself? You're hurt. Here, let me put some salve on it." She bustled around, looking for the first aid kit Tom kept on makeshift shelves behind his cot.

"Dove deeper than I intended," he said, grimacing. "Scraped myself on a rock. Dumb me." He let the trunks snap back into place.

"I'll take care of it." Sharon advanced with the salve in hand.

"You better not, " he said, laughing, "Considering where it is."

"Don't be silly. Of course I'll dress it for you."

She dabbed salve on the exposed stomach area. "Hold still. I want to rub it in." She worked over the red marks then looked at the scrapes extending below his waistline. "Okay, Tom, open up." Her voice softened and she tilted her head coquettishly. "It's not as if I haven't seen you in your swimming suit before."

She pulled the trunks away from his body and worked her fingers, smeared with salve, below the waistband.

Tom gasped. "Sharon -- "

She pushed her fingers lower still, then worked the salve almost to his groin. She saw rising passion film his eyes. His mouth fell open. His trunks began to swell, looking as if they would burst.

Sharon loosened the shoulder straps on her bathing suit, allowing it to drop to her waist, exposing her still-damp breasts. Breathing heavily, she moved closer to him, then rose to tip toe, left hand cupped beneath her right breast, thrusting it upward toward him.

She was vaguely aware of the sound of a car pulling into the campground outside, the sputter of a motor dying, and someone calling, "Tom! Tom! Where are you?"

She looked up as Fran entered the tent, stopped and blinked, staring, trying to adjust her eyes to the dim light.

"Fran -- " Tom began his eyes huge and staring. "In God's name how -- ?"

An agonized "Oh my God!" escaped Fran's lips. Her hands flew up to her face. She wheeled and ran.

Tom ran after her. "Fran! Wait! Wait! Let me explain! It's not what you think."

Sharon followed.

The motor of Fran's car burst into life. The vehicle careened out of the darkness toward Tom. The headlamps came on, flooding the scene with two bouncing cones of light. Tom stood in the road, waving his arms wildly.

The car swerved, careened over some bushes, bounced back onto the road and disappeared in a slowly diminishing mass of light and sound, hurtling through the night toward the main highway.

Sharon was frozen in place, watching, horrified.

Tom, likewise, stood paralyzed, gazing after Fran. He lowered his head, shaking it slowly in disbelief, then turned and staggered back into his tent in a state of collapse. "My God! My God!" he repeated over and over aloud, weeping in frustrated rage. Not until early morning did he fall into a troubled sleep.

Sharon, even more upset, also retreated to her tent, and wept through much of the night.

* * *

Tom felt like he was in a trance over the next several days, functioning by rote, going through the motions of a normal routine. He managed to continue the interviews with Samuel, pose questions and seek answers, but beneath the surface, he was in agony. He had returned to Israel hoping to revive his romance with Fran. Instead, he had caused a rupture worse than the first one. He grieved, unable to understand how he had made such a mess of his life. How did this happen? How could I do this to Fran? To Sharon? To myself? On and on. He was filled with pain, recrimination, and despair.

Slowly, a new resolve emerged from his self-pity and sorrow. I have to get on with my project. That's all I have left. He threw himself into the task with frenzied energy, while simultaneously treating Sharon with cool correctness and pounding his body into a hard, muscular machine with increasingly long swims every evening until he was totally exhausted.

The days flew by faster and faster. Dr. Abe returned on a sun-splashed Friday, two weeks after departure. By that time the neatly-spaced pages pouring out of Sharon's typewriter were stacked in a growing pile on a shelf in Tom's tent, most of them unread. Un-transcribed reels of recordings also accumulated in her tent.

"I'm falling further and further behind everyday," she lamented. "I can't keep up no matter how hard I try."

Tom placed a hand on her shoulder, a curled finger under her chin and lifted until their eyes met. "You're doing an outstanding job, Sharon. I want you to know how much I appreciate it. Please don't be discouraged. No one could possibly stay on a current basis, with all Samuel says." He backed away, wanting to avoid any closer contact.

Tom spot-checked the translations, did some editing, wrote questions in the margins, pinned notes to some sheets, and returned them to Sharon. She would check the required tape and write a clarification.

Dr. Abe helped also, conferring with Sharon or Samuel as necessary, then carrying the reworked version back to Tom.

By the end of the twenty-ninth day, Tom felt they had completed their mission. Cleanup sessions with Samuel would be needed later, and there was still the document Samuel had promised they could photograph. "Not yet! Not yet!" he would say when Tom asked about it. Then one afternoon, he had Tom, Dr. Abe and Sharon join him under the pine. "I have the document here," he said, pointing to a rusty metal box on his lap. "Do you have the money we agreed upon?"

"I can have it here in a couple of hours," Tom replied.

"All right please do so tomorrow. In the meantime, let's go ahead." Samuel turned to Dr. Abe. "If I remember correctly you were among the professors present when I tried to sell this document to the University some years ago."

It was the first time Samuel had indicated he knew he and Dr. Abe had previously met. It startled the professor.

"There was nothing I could do, Samuel," Dr. Abe said. "The University was not in a position to buy something after just cursory examination."

Samuel shook his head, spilling gray hair across his forehead. "Nevertheless, you of all people should have known the value of what I have here, the accumulated knowledge of a family of scribes extending back centuries in time. But that is in the past. I am getting old and must make certain this document is preserved and recorded. I believe what it says, plus the information I have given you orally, will be a complete account of what I know about the first century A.D." He tapped the box. "You helped me finish what I was unable to finish on my own. I suggest you photograph the document, then return it. I want the original to be buried with me."

Samuel inserted a key in the rusty lock, and tried to turn it. It didn't budge. He pounded the lock with the heel of his hand. After several attempts, and a few drops of oil, the lock began to rotate. There was a click and Samuel lifted the corroded lid.

Then, eyes shining as if sighting an old friend for the first time in years, he pulled out a long, irregularly creased paper, page after page, glued together end to end, parts of it covered with green fungus, some with edges eaten away.

Samuel kept pulling. The paper kept emerging.

"You have to remember, this was buried under this tree through the 1947-48 Arab-Israeli war." He nodded toward the pine. "Arabs swept over this area. I had to flee. They looted everything of value in the house, but didn't find this."

Samuel set the box on the ground and continued lifting the document until the tattered end came into sight. Dr. Abe moved over to help. Together they collapsed it into something approximating the accordion-like folds it was in before, and slipped it into a plastic packet Dr. Abe obtained from his tent.

Samuel stared at each of them, finally fixing his gaze on Tom. "The document I have just shown you contains information about a copper scroll discovered several years ago in one of the caves at Qumran. No announcement was made at the time, but sources I won't name have confirmed to me that this report is correct. The scroll was sent to London to be cut open and translated. Drop-copies of this translation, as it progresses, are delivered to Hebrew University in Jerusalem."

Samuel coughed. Spasms wracked his body, but he continued. "Unlike most scrolls, this one does not involve religion. It is a record of gold and silver buried during the Roman invasion of 67-70 A.D."

Samuel paused to catch his breath.

"Most of the gold accumulated from the annual, half shekel tax the Temple levied on all Jews. Zealots, leaders of the fight against Rome, confiscated it when they seized control of the Temple during the hostilities, then transferred it to Qumran. There it was combined with gold acquired by the Essenes. When the Romans closed in, the Zealots buried the gold at numerous locations, and recorded the sites on two copper plates. The plates were rolled up and placed in one of the Qumran caves. It is these copper rolls, or scrolls, that have been found.

"I think I have identified two of the burial sites. I appeal to you. Find this treasure. You can have half, but I want the other half. I feel it should be mine. I was tracking it long before the copper scrolls were found."

He paused, sighed. "Our sessions are almost over now. I have enjoyed working with you, but I am exhausted and need an extended rest. I wish all of you well." Samuel rose and shuffled through the doorway of his dirt-floored home to lie down.

The next day Tom drove to Beit Shean, obtained and paid Samuel the five thousand dollars he had promised for the document. Tom, Dr. Abe and Sharon packed and departed. Ten days later, Sharon brought the last of the transcribed tapings to Tom's room at the King David, including a photocopy and translation of Samuel's document.

"With Dr. Abe's help, we cleaned it up and brought out the faded writing before making the copy," she said, staring at her work with visible pride. "By the way, Tom, I'm scheduled to photograph the back of the Isaiah Scroll next week. They won't give me much time. I'll have to single out the best fingerprints I can find, take some close-ups and several over-all shots.

"If necessary, we can isolate a particular print later and blow it up for better visibility. I should have those photos, plus photos of the print on the tile, ready by next Friday or Saturday. Will that be all right?"

"That will be fine, Sharon." Tom nodded toward the stack of typewritten pages she had placed on a nearby table. "I've got plenty of reading to do in the meantime. I want to get through all of the transcriptions tonight. I can hardly wait to read the full version of everything Samuel told us."

That night, with all the lights off in his room except the reading lamp beside the overstuffed chair, Tom picked up the first page. Silence and darkness enveloped him. He read on and on, lost in a strange world that arose out of the words passing before his eyes.

After a time it seemed the shadows around him turned to mist and there were voices speaking and forms moving in the void, a babble of voices, at first far away, inchoate and blurred, then nearer and nearer until they spoke and moved with form and precision, thrusting insistently into his mind.

There were shouts and the sound of running feet, and for a fleeting moment, the mists and darkness were swept aside and the ancient, white-walled city of Jerusalem rose starkly and vividly before him. Equally suddenly, the darkness returned, but there was a difference. He had been transported, across the ages, into a long dead world.

Part Two

Sowing

Chapter XIII

Dawn. A man stands atop the Temple wall, etched against the brightening sky. He raises a great ram's horn to his lips. Three times the shofur's mournful blast breaks the stillness. As echoes die in the surrounding hills, a new trumpet raises a plaintive peal a short distance away, the cock's crow call of the Roman garrison in Fortress Antonia, overlooking and abutting the Temple grounds, summoning soldiers there to another day of duty.

There is movement in the darkness.

Below the fortress, people mill in the shadows, forming two groups around a man who stands, arms upraised, on a small platform. Slowly the sun lifts above the horizon, piercing the darkness with a thousand golden lances. The man's arms descend, striking a hymnal chord of human voices from the choir in front of him, to the wailing accompaniment of a reed pipe orchestra in the background.

Another day has begun in Jerusalem.

Already moneychangers are setting up tables in the Court of the Gentiles and the first pilgrims of the day are filtering through the gates. In the lower city, merchants are stirring too, and nearby, in the Valley of the Cheese makers, redolent wares are being placed on tables for purchase by the day's first buyers.

In the nearby countryside, the day is well advanced. The first meal has been completed and cooking fires stoked. Carts creak along rutted paths leading to wheat and barley fields, past gracefully swaying young girls returning from the village well with water jugs on their heads.

As the sun climbs higher, roads converging on Jerusalem fill with people en route to worship, to sell their wares, to buy, to beg, to stroll with friends. As each tops his own sector of ground to gaze on the city for the first time that day, it is the Temple, rising in majestic splendor, one hundred sixty feet against the sky, that fills his vision.

There it stands like frozen music, its polished white stone walls shimmering and glowing in the sunlight. From the roof, golden spires, flashing and blurring, thrust toward heaven. Sunbursts of fractured light splash off golden plates adorning the sides, while a golden vine spreads delicate tendrils above the entrance of a magnificent porch. There, too, a concave mirror of gold reflects the rays of dawn into the Temple, revealing two golden chains hanging from beams of the porch.

This architectural celebration of the Jewish reverence for God stands on an historic site. Here Solomon, son of David, raised the first Temple, only to have it destroyed in 586 B.C. by Nebuchadnezzar and his invading Babylonians, who carried the Jews into captivity. Released fifty-three years later, the Jews built an interim, makeshift Temple on the same ground. It was used until Herod the Great, a master builder, replaced it with a Temple greater than any ever before conceived.

From every corner of the kingdom, Herod assembled skilled craftsmen. When construction began in 20 B.C. ten thousand workers -- their numbers later to grow to eighteen thousand -- swarmed over the partly flattened summit of the pear-shaped ridge called Moriah, using materials assembled from many parts of the known world. From the quarries of Palestine came blocks of limestone; from Lebanon great, aromatic timbers of cedar; from the mines of Solomon, gold and silver; from Rome, magnificent slabs of marble.

As the Second Temple emerged, the ground on which it stood was extended outward over rocky escarpments, crevices and gullies on the descending slopes of the site. Foundations were sunk to bedrock. Then, block by block, new retaining walls rose until a thirty five acre platform was locked in place, filled with debris and paved with stone.

Around the perimeter Corinthian columns marched in files pierced by six gates, enclosing concentric, restricted areas.

Outermost was the Court of the Gentiles. It was here the money changers plied their profitable trade, selling Temple coins to purchase animals for sacrifice.

Non-Jews had to stop here.

Next was the Court of the Women. Jewish women could enter but go no further, while Jewish men, passing through an entrance called the Corinthian Gate, could proceed into the court of the Israelites.

At one end of this court loomed the great, blood-stained Temple altar in the entryway to the Court of the Priests, open only to the clergy.

Still further, into the interior, were two sanctuaries, first the Holy, then, in an empty room partitioned by a double, multicolored tapestry, the Holy of Holies. Only the High Priest could enter this final and most sacred of Temple areas, and could do so only once a year -- on the Day of Atonement.

It was to this Temple, and to the first of these sanctuaries, that James, the second son of Joseph the Carpenter and his wife, Mary, came to pray at dawn of a new day in the year 62 A.D.

A tangled mass of gray-black hair tumbled over the shoulders of the kneeling man. He seemed frozen in place, hands clasped beneath his chin, head bowed, craggy bearded features immobile. Slowly the massive, leonine countenance lifted. The lips began to move.

"Forgive us, Father. The children of Israel are wicked and sinful. I fear a catastrophe is coming. The Temple priests have forgotten your teachings. They killed your messenger, my brother, Jesus. When he died, they ignored the storm and the great earthquake that tore open this very ground, and ripped the sacred tapestry that hangs in the Holy of Holies beyond this room. Nor did they heed the meaning of the resurrection.

"Now, filled with suspicion, they watch every move of his followers because our numbers grow daily, and they know not what to do. Forgive them. I ask it in your name." The rumbling voice ceased. James rose.

He was a towering, unkempt man, well over six feet tall. The sage Hegesippus wrote of him: "He drank no wine nor strong drink, nor did he eat flesh. No razor went upon his head. He did not anoint himself with oil and he did not go to the baths. He alone was allowed to enter into the sanctuary, for he did not wear wool but linen. He used to enter the Temple and be found kneeling and praying for forgiveness for the people so that his knees grew hard like a camel's because of his constant worship of God. So for his excessive righteousness he was called the Just."

He was James the Just, brother of Jesus of Nazareth and bishop of the world's first Christian community. He was the holiest of men, held in awe by thousands. They knew he was of the House of David and that his older brother, the one some said was the Messiah, had been crucified, had reportedly risen from the dead, then disappeared after consulting with his followers for forty days.

James lived outside the walls of the city with his Mother, Mary, his brothers Joseph, Simon and Jude, and his sisters, Assia and Lydia. It was toward that humble dwelling that he began to walk, attired in a white, toga-like robe, head held high, eyes flashing, a hand raised and moving in benediction to the crowd that gathered ahead of him. People, babbling and shouting, swirled around him as he passed through the Court of the Gentiles.

"Hosanna to the just one! Blessed are you, oh holy one!" voices shouted.

James passed through the double gate in the Royal Portico, turned right and walked down a slope of the Tyropoeon Valley. He turned right at the foot of the decline and made his way to a tiny inn on Mount Zion, where his family had rented a room.

Jude was waiting. "Come brother, you must eat. We have a little cheese and bread, and we need to talk."

James sat at a small table, Jude watching him. Jude was slighter, shorter than James, precise and quick in his movements, neater in his dress. His features were small, eyes black and darting. A neatly trimmed beard, shaped to a point below his chin, partly covered the unusually white skin of his face.

"How did it go today?"

James sighed. "Every day the situation grows more difficult. It's not just the Temple priests watching us, it's the Zealots too. Those madmen are plotting a revolt against Rome. They whisper their plans to anyone who will listen. The priests' sense there will be an uprising, and are afraid we will undermine their power. They want to stop us and no doubt will try soon."

James finished his meager meal, rose slowly, plucked writing materials from a shelf across the room and returned to the table. He closed his eyes, his mind drifting back in time. Images appeared from that terrible day twenty-nine years ago.

James had journeyed to Jerusalem to make purchases for the family farm and try to locate his older brother. He arrived late at night, obtained lodging in a crowded inn and overslept the next day.

He awakened suddenly. There was a commotion in the street outside his window. Then he dozed and slept for several more hours. When he awoke again a strange silence gripped the city. The sky outside was dark and he could hear thunder rumbling in the distance.

"What's happening?" he asked a boy racing by the window. The youth pointed toward a hill ahead and kept running.

James dressed and rushed after him. He shoved and pushed through a crowd milling outside the western gate to the city. He looked up. The sky was almost black, but he could make out the high ground called Calvary rising in front of him. A long tongue of lightning flickered down from the clouds, lighting the horizon. James reeled back in horror. On the low hill before him, etched against the sky, three men hung from crosses, his brother, Jesus, head rolling in agony, on the center cross.

As James stared, a flaming bolt shattered against

Calvary's slope and thunder shook the ground. The air smelled of fire. Raindrops, whipped by rising wind, spattered his forehead. He turned and ran. His brother, his strange, eccentric brother, who had deserted their family to wander the countryside and preach of the coming Kingdom of God, was dying on a cross in Jerusalem. Such a disgrace. James ran and ran and lost track of time.

He remembered wandering and babbling to himself, plunging into a stream, gleaning wheat from a field. He slept that night, and the next, in the desert and wandered in circles during the day. When he awoke the following morning on the outskirts of Jerusalem his head was clear, the countryside tranquil and shrouded in fog. Then, out of the mists, a white-robed figure approached.

"James, James, you do not know me?" The voice seemed familiar but far away.

"Dear God," James muttered, his voice quavering, "What is going on." He dropped to his knees, filled with terror.

The figure extended a hand to comfort him. Through a fold in the robe, James saw a gaping body wound. The figure spoke again, the voice hollow and detached.

"Come, my brother. There is work to be done. You must contact my disciples. Tell them to go to Galilee and await me there. Go now and prepare the way."

James, quaking with fear, shut his eyes and prayed. When he opened them the figure was gone. He was alone in a silent, peaceful glen, still draped in a veil of fog.

Since that day, the doubts James had harbored of his brother's sanity, the anger he had directed against him because he was not contributing to the upkeep of the family, had disappeared. The vision outside Jerusalem had convinced him he must do as his brother commanded: "Go and prepare the way" He had been doing that ever since -- spreading the teachings of Jesus.

James passed a hand over his eyes, shook his head to clear his mind. He smoothed the papyrus roll in front of him, then lifted a quill and dipped it in ink. Slowly, meticuously, he added words to those he had written there on previous days, expressing the ethical values Jesus had left behind. He, his brothers and sisters, and his Mother were now the caretakers of those values. It was their mission to pass on what they knew. James wrote:

"What will it profit, my brethren, if a man says he has faith but does not have works? Can faith save him? Just as the body without the spirit is dead, so faith also without works is dead." The words continued to flow. "Come now, you rich, weep and howl over your miseries...your riches have rotted and your garments have become moth-eaten."

He concluded with an appeal to be patient in awaiting the new coming of the Lord Jesus, the anointed one, the one the Greeks called "Christos," their word for Messiah, a designation later combined with his first name into the lasting appellation, Jesus Christ.

Late in the day, James put down his pen and left for the Temple to worship again. He was weary, feeling all of his fifty-eight years. When he returned, his brothers and the three disciples who remained in Jerusalem -- Andrew, John and Thaddeus -- were waiting for him.

Jude approached, smiling. "I have good news."

James stopped, eyebrows up. He could use some good news.

"Two messages for you, the first from Peter."

James sat down, waiting to hear more. He missed his old comrade, his genial nature, quick smile, white teeth flashing in a tanned, black-bearded countenance.

"He is spreading the faith in Caesaria," Jude continued. "Says he has baptized a Roman officer named Cornelius of Caesaria, our first gentile convert, using rules we adopted in 49 A.D. -- that the applicant abstain from eating animals that have been strangled or offered as sacrifices, that he remain chaste and not eat blood."

"What else did Peter say?"

"That he will extend his travels to Rome."

"The second message -- "

"It's from Paul."

James' face went blank with surprise, his thoughts flashing back to the story of Paul's conversion. Originally a Hebrew Zealot, Paul had led a mob in the fatal stoning of Stephen, one of the early Christian elders, then had been stricken blind while traveling to Damascus, only to regain his sight after a vision and claimed conversation with the spirit of Christ. Now he was the most enthusiastic of Christian evangelists who had completed three successful journeys around the Mediterranean basin, establishing Christian communities. And Paul's letters to those new Christians had become major documents illuminating Christian beliefs.

James pulled in a deep breath. "Paul? ...It's hard to believe. Think I last saw him in 60 A.D. just before he was arrested by the Romans here in Jerusalem for repeatedly stating in Jewish synagogues that Christ was the Messiah." The claim infuriated the Temple priests. They demanded the Romans restrain Paul and they did. He disappeared. "So where is he now?"

"In Rome, taken there under guard and awaiting trial, but says he is allowed a great deal of personal freedom. His message was delayed, carried here on a vessel that was shipwrecked en route."

James was of two minds about Paul. He admired his eloquence, his volcanic energy, his skill in convincing others that Jesus was the Messiah, but he harbored doubts -- and anger -- about what Paul was saying. He thought Paul had gone beyond the teachings of Jesus, was inserting new doctrines that he claimed came from private conversations with the spirit of Jesus. He also feared Paul was presenting Christianity as a new religion, not as a movement within the Hebrew faith.

James sighed, tried to think of other things. His eyes swept the room, took in the depleted group, led them in prayer, then spoke:.

"All of you are aware the Temple priests fear our growing numbers. Immediately after the crucifixion and resurrection of our savior, Jesus, there were only one hundred twenty of us in

Jerusalem -- the twelve disciples; seventy followers from Galilee; my Mother, brothers and sisters; Mary Magdalene, Martha and Lazarus and other converts from Bethany, and a few Judaic followers, including John Mark and his mother. Now there are thousands. People are listening to us. We must not lose this opportunity to win new converts, although it is increasingly dangerous to seek them. I recommend that we abandon mass meetings, talk only to small groups, answer questions quietly then move away if the Temple guards approach."

This was agreed upon. The participants departed.

That night James slept fitfully, overwhelmed by a sense of impending disaster. The next morning that feeling became reality. Temple guards surrounded him as he entered the Court of the Gentiles. The officer in charge stepped forward, waved a parchment.

"I have a warrant directing you to appear before the Sanhedrin. Come with me, please."

James shuddered. He knew his life was in danger. He had been summoned by the seventy-member body of priests, elders and scribes who ruled all religious life in Judea, a summons that could lead to personal disaster.

Chapter XIV

Sharon felt the letdown as soon as the door to Tom's room closed behind her. The feeling grew as she waited, first for the elevator, then for a bus outside the King David. By the time that ancient vehicle came rattling down the street, and she pushed through standing passengers to a seat in the rear, she was thoroughly depressed.

The recording, translating, organizing and typing of Samuel's knowledge of biblical times had dominated her life for weeks, kept her driving ahead with energy and singleness of purpose. Now that was gone.

She felt lost, deflated, empty, and had almost worked herself out of a job. She still had to photograph the fingerprints on the Isaiah scroll and the tile, and would be involved in cleanup interviews with Samuel, but once that was done, she would be unemployed.

Then there was Tom. He hadn't said a word to her of a personal nature when she delivered the final, full translation of the Samuel tapings. He had been polite but detached. Hadn't even asked how she was, whether she was tired after completing such a demanding assignment. Nothing. He was so involved in his research, he had shut out everything and everyone around him, including her.

Sharon breathed in the cool night air blowing through the bus window, and closed her eyes. When she opened them again, lights of the downtown area had disappeared behind her. Darkness, relieved by an occasional corner streetlamp, had taken over, matching her deepening depression.

What was she to do? She had to get a regular job before the savings she had accumulated working for Tom, dissipated. So far she had only one lead. An English history professor had stopped her in the liberal arts building several days ago to ask if she would do some typing for him. He said he had heard she was skilled and reliable. She had smiled, gave him the number of the pay phone in her apartment building and the address, but hadn't heard from him.

That deepened her sense of drift. She felt terribly alone. Her brothers in Haifa and sister in Tel Aviv had neither the time nor energy to be concerned about her. No one cared whether she was well or got an education. Well, maybe Tom cared a little. He could be warm and considerate at times, whenever he could get his mind off his project, but had been distant since that terrible scene at the camp when Fran showed up and caught them almost in a sexual embrace.

Sharon snorted in disgust, sat up straighter. That woman. Such a goodie-goodie. What in God's name, did Tom see in her? I would be a better companion for him, even a better wife --

Sharon shivered with anticipatory delight, just from allowing herself to think of such a remote possibility. Then she returned to reality, gazing at the darkness outside the bus and the new moon peeping over the horizon. She felt like that cliché of the poor, little girl with her face against the candy store window. She had been allowed inside for a time, had tasted the sweeter things of life, but was about to be pushed out again. No job. No love. No Tom.

Sharon was so deep in thought she almost missed her stop. At the last moment, she rushed forward and swung down from the step as the bus pulled away. She paused in the darkness, took in the depressing scene. A streetlight cast a pale glow over the corner where she was standing. She could hear the laughter of children off in the distance, playing some nighttime game, and smell the dank odor of frying fish and garbage permeating the air.

Her gloom increased when she mounted the rickety stairs of her building, unlocked the door of her apartment, and turned on the lone overhead light. A desolate scene greeted her -- a battered, wooden chair, an unmade bed, a kitchen table littered with dishes and her typewriter, half-buried in discarded paper.

Her stomach churned. She wasn't the neatest person under normal circumstances, having been raised on a farm where what you took out of the fields was what counted, not how well you kept your house. But the debris, built up in the final, frantic surge to complete the Samuel tapes, was too much even for her.

She dumped the dishes in the sink, setting up a clatter. She picked up loose paper on the table and jammed it into a garbage receptacle. She reached for a broom and began to sweep, then dropped it and returned to picking up more paper.

Her hand brushed a neat stack of transcribed pages beside the typewriter. Suddenly she remembered the conspiratorial idea she had toyed with earlier in the day. As she typed that last section of the manuscript, fleshing it out with new material, she had thought: Why not leave it out, not include it in the finished version she would take to Tom. The section it would replace was not that much different, just a few words and phrases on each page affecting the tenor, not the substance, of the report. Tom wouldn't know the difference. Then, if for some reason she needed to see him again, she would have a reason for doing so. She could pretend the omission was an oversight.

Should she put the plan into action? She pondered, feeling guilty. *On the other hand why not?* She was certain now she had to let Tom know her feelings about him. She felt better as she headed for the pay phone downstairs.

Chapter XV

The Sanhedrin members arrived in small groups, taking seats on three semicircular tiers in the dimly lit Chamber of Hewn Stone. Halfway up the far wall, a blazing torch sent demon-like shadows dancing across the ceiling while decaying bits of flesh and dried blood from the Temple altar next door filled the air with a nauseating stench. Cattle, goats, sheep, doves and other animals were sacrificed there.

The black-robed High Priest, Ananus, his long, gray beard swaying with every step, appeared last. Slowly, pontifically, he settled into his seat in the center of the first row. Next to him on each side sat the oldest priests. Lesser priests and scribes filled the second and third rows.

Ananus looked bored. He raised his right hand, signaling a guard to bring James in from an antechamber off to one side. Like a great mangy lion, the aged Christian leader shuffled forward, eyes blazing through the matted hair that tumbled over his face.

The room became silent as Ananus spoke.

"You are the one known as James the Just?"

James' reply rumbled up from the depths of his huge, hairy body. "I am."

"You are the brother of the Galilean carpenter who thought he was the Messiah and was crucified."

Snickers rippled through the chamber.

"I am the brother of Jesus of Nazareth who was crucified."

"You come to the Temple daily to pray, and crowds follow wherever you go?"

"I pray at the Temple twice daily, and those who want to know the teachings of Jesus do approach and ask questions."

"We find this disturbing to the peace. You must restrain people from asking about your brother and believing he was the Messiah. I direct that you go to the Pinnacle of the Temple and tell the people not to stray after Jesus. They will believe you and do as you say."

James pulled his huge, hairy body erect, towering over those seated in front of him. One hand brushed tangled locks from his face. Fire seemed to leap from his eyes. Priests in the front row drew back.

"How dare you speak in this fashion of the Son of Man," he hissed, "How...Dare...You!" He shouted, pausing between each of the last three words.

"Take him and see he does as I say," Ananus ordered.

Temple guards fell in around James. Four priests joined them. The group moved through the Court of the Israelites and Court of the Women into the Court of the Gentiles. A crowd was waiting there for James to reappear.

""What happened? Are you all right, Just One?" someone shouted. "Why are those priests with you?"

James halted and raised a hand. "Do not be afraid. No matter what happens, remember what I have taught you. And listen to me closely for I will address you soon."

The priests and guards exchanged smiles, apparently assuming the Christian had capitulated, was going to do as Ananus directed. Others in the crowd sensed something was very wrong, the disciple, Thaddeus, among them. He whispered to a companion. "Summon the brothers and sisters, and ask all available followers to come immediately."

The messenger dashed away as the procession marched to the southeast corner of the platform. The group, moving slowly, mounted steps leading to a broad platform at the top of the juncture of the southern and eastern perimeter columns -- two guards in front, then two priests, then James, two more priests and four more guards. As the angled stairway switched directions at each landing, their silhouettes etched the sky, then disappeared behind intervening columns until the procession emerged at the top.

There was an extended pause as the guards and priests conferred. When they drew back, the great shaggy figure of James stood alone, like a hairy reincarnation of John the Baptist, that wild man who had emerged from the desert decades before.

* * *

The crowd, sixty feet below, had swelled to thousands; a sea of upturned, white faces filling the Court. Among them, stark with fear, James' sisters, Assia and Lydia, stared at the scene above. Other family members kept arriving and crowded around them.

"James, be careful," Assia shouted, her delicate features twisted with tension, her unusually white skin blanched even whiter by anxiety. She dropped her face into her hands. "Oh, do be careful," she moaned, tears in her eyes.

Lydia, larger and more stoutly built, gazed at the unfolding drama above, her mouth pulled into a tight line, her face grim. She placed a muscular arm around Assia's shoulders. "Be calm, sister. Have faith. God will help him."

Her words were lost in the rising babble of voices from the crowd. "Why do they have the Just One up there?" someone shouted. "What has he done?"

* * *

One of the priests on the Pinnacle stepped forward and raised his right arm. The noise subsided.

"Hear me, oh citizens of Jerusalem," he shouted. "The Just One, whom many of you know, has something to tell you. He wants to correct the behavior of those of you who think Jesus was the Messiah. Listen well. He speaks on orders of the High Priest, Ananus."

The priest stepped back. Two guards, spears lowered, prodded James forward. Upon a signal from above, a priest disguised as a pilgrim raised his voice from below. "Speak, Just One."

James advanced, raised his arms, palms turned upward, and lifted his eyes toward a sky piled high with white clouds. He seemed frozen in place. His silence spread to the murmuring throng below until only a faint rustle of voices remained.

Slowly, deliberately, James lowered his arms and looked down at the crowd.

"Hear me, oh citizens of Jerusalem -- "

His voice had a new, ringing clarity, carrying throughout the Temple compound, even to the Roman soldiers watching from towers of Fortress Antonia, abutting the north side. James stabbed a finger toward heaven.

"Hear me as I pass on the word of the man God sent to save you, and whom the Temple priests rejected and crucified."

The priests moved toward him. James gave one a shove and edged forward, almost to the edge of the platform.

"Hear me, oh citizens of Jerusalem..." There was total, frozen silence below now. "...These same men who sent the Lord Jesus to his death on the cross would have me say that you must not believe in him, that his is not the true way."

James balled his right hand into a fist and hammered the air above his head. "They lie! He has fulfilled the scriptures. He was crucified, rose on the third day and for forty days thereafter was with those of us who knew him, and then ascended into heaven. He will return soon. On that day, there will be a reckoning. You must rid yourselves of sin or suffer eternal damnation when that day arrives."

Many in the crowd dropped to their knees and prayed. Others tore their clothes, moaning and rocking with fear. Still others stood transfixed, their eyes riveted on the massive, robed figure set against the firmament above.

"Hosanna to the son of David!" The cry began with a lone voice. It was repeated by other scattered voices. More and more voices joined in. It grew into a thunderous chant, swelling, reverberating, echoing in the countryside beyond the walls of the city.

Lydia saw two guards rush toward James. He shoved them again, moved even further out on the platform, teetering precariously, smiling triumphantly. He held up his right arm, palm open.

"I have not finished. I warn you. The day of judgment is near for false prophets and desecrators of the law." He turned and glared at the priests, then resumed.

"So you and Ananus ask me about the Son of Man and his way. I say to you that at this very moment he is in heaven, sitting next to God, and from there will depart soon and return on a golden cloud to stand in judgment over all of you."

This apparently was more than the priests could permit. Assia and Lydia saw the guards rush at James from both sides. He struggled in their arms as they dragged him back from the precipice.

James hurled one guard to the surface of the platform and shoved another. The man stumbled, dropping to his hands and knees. James, carried forward by those around him, tripped over him, lost his balance and careened toward the outer edge. A guard rushed him; spear held athwart his body, hurled himself at James. The shaft caught the teetering giant across the chest and sent his huge body hurtling over the edge into space.

Women screamed in horror. James, twisting and kicking, plunged toward a stream threading depths of the Kidron Valley, a hundred feet below.

The crowd went berserk, shouting in fear, hate and rage, surging toward the Golden Gate where it would be possible to peer over the edge and determine what had happened to James.

Lydia was among the first to sight the prostrate, crumpled figure flattened in the muddy bank of the stream. A few startled men and women who had been washing clothes there stared in astonishment, first at the body that had come hurtling down upon them, then at the crowd above, pounding down the steps leading into the valley.

As many tore their clothes and beat their chests, the body began to move. First, it was a twitching in one leg. Then an arm came up. Then James raised his head and gazed around. He heaved his muddy body upward and drew his knees under him.

"He lives! He lives!" The cry came from the Temple compound above.

"Kill him! Kill him!" a priest screamed. "He has desecrated the Temple!" The priest started down the steps. Other priests joined him, pausing to pick up rocks as they descended.

James knelt, began to pray.

A stone arched through the air, struck him on a shoulder. Another hit him in the back. James cried out in pain, but continued praying, shouting the words, "Forgive them, Father, for they -- "

Scores of stones rained down. A huge missile glanced off James' head, another hit him in the side, a third crashed into the base of his spine. He collapsed, lay still momentarily, then struggled back to his knees, resuming his prayer, "-- know not -- "

The priests swarmed around him, shouting, hurling rocks, screaming, "Kill him! Kill him.!" More stones battered his hairy body. He collapsed again, then lifted his head. His lips formed his final words, "...what they do."

A man who had been washing clothes in the stream, approached, carrying a club used to beat dirt from his garments. "What are you doing?" another launderer shouted. "Can't you see he is praying for you?" It was too late. The club came down with crushing force on James' head. He pitched forward into the mud, never to rise again.

* * *

Tom, back in his hotel room, looked up as he read these lines, searching his memory for corroborating information he knew was buried somewhere in his files. He rose, extracted a folder of research notes from a box, and returned to his chair. He ran a finger down page after page then stopped. There it was, a notation he had underlined: "A shrine to the memory of James the

Just was erected at the spot where he fell and was stoned and beaten to death."

Tom looked further. His notes didn't say what happened to the body. Was James buried at the site? Were his bones later placed in a stone burial box, as was the local custom? Why were there persistent rumors that bone box still existed, was secretly held by some unidentified collector? One note stated that James' remains were sealed under the altar of the nearby Cathedral of Saint James in Jerusalem -- named for a different man, James the Elder, but Tom could find no documentation to support that belief.

Suddenly the telephone rang. At first Tom, his thoughts elsewhere, couldn't grasp what had happened. He looked up, gazed at the pale square of light cast by the moon through the hotel room window, then at a thermos of unopened coffee on the table. Finally, he focused on the phone, jangling on the stand next to his bed. He picked up the receiver.

"Hello." His voice seemed to come from outside his body.

"Tom?" There was a long pause.

"Sharon, what can I do for you?"

"You sound different."

"My mind was on something else. Is something wrong?"

She explained she had failed to include a reworked section of the Samuel tapes in the transcript she had brought to him earlier in the evening. "What should I do about it?"

Tom pondered a moment. "I do need it tonight, Sharon, despite the hour. Could you catch a cab and bring it here? I'll pay for the trip."

"I think so. It'll take a while. I'll have to walk to the cab stand near the marketplace. I'll get there as quickly as I can."

"I'll be here."

Tom returned to his chair and picked up the transcript. What had he been reading? Oh, yes, that Symeon, the first cousin of Jesus, succeeded James as the Christian Bishop of Jerusalem. Symeon, the transcript said, immediately resumed the warnings James had voiced that a great catastrophe would overtake the

Jewish people if they did not rid themselves of sin. It did. Five years later tension between Jews and Romans burst into flames. The long expected revolt began -- and Tom was there too, reading, seeing, and visualizing the story as it unfolded.

Chapter XVI

A fiery spear of lightning hurtled out of the heavens and shattered into flaming particles against the mountaintop. A simultaneous clap of thunder swept outward, battering the hills of Galilee with the artillery of a spring storm rushing in from the sea. In that moment of illumination, as the forest and coastal plain were lighted by the power of a million candles, a Roman encampment stood etched against trees near the outskirts of Ptolemais. The tents, precisely aligned, leather sides shedding the drenching rain, sent water gushing toward lower levels of the camp and out into a nearby stream.

In a large tent near the center of the third row, where the two main camp streets crossed at right angles, a stocky, square-built man watched this display from the entrance of his tent, then, scowling, stomped over to a map spread on a tabletop lighted by a flickering candle.

"Where are they," he shouted, banging his fist on the table. "They should have been here weeks ago. By Jupiter, I'll instill some discipline in this army if it's the last thing I do!"

He began to pace. Flavius Vespasian, fifty-eight, hero of the Roman campaign in Britain, was angry.

In the summer of 66 A.D. Jewish Zealots had captured an abundance of arms in a surprise assault on Roman units atop the mountain fortress, Masada. Using these weapons, they overwhelmed the Roman garrison in Jerusalem in mid-August, then ambushed and mauled the Twelfth Legion when it moved south from Syria under Cestius Gallus to recapture the city. Nero, the Roman emperor, in Greece when informed of this disaster, summoned Vespasian and ordered him to crush the revolt.

Vespasian sent his son, Titus, to Alexandria to pick up the Fifteenth Legion, and rushed to Antioch to alert the Fifth Macedonian, the famous Tenth Fretensis or "Free Legion," and what was left of the decimated Twelfth. He ordered them to Ptolemais, then traveled on in advance to establish his headquarters. That was three months ago and they still hadn't arrived.

"They're coming, sire. You can count on them," said an aide, standing well back from Vespasian's circling course around the table. "We've had messages from the Fifth and from Trajan, commander of the Tenth. They are en route. And Titus will get the Fifteenth here as rapidly as possible."

Vespasian stopped, his body projected in huge outline against walls of the tent.

"I know I can count on them," he growled, "but when? And what about that miserable Twelfth. If Cestius Gallus hadn't been so hesitant, this revolt would have been crushed before it got started. Can you imagine a Roman commander allowing himself to be ambushed by these ragtag Jews?"

Vespasian resumed his pacing, his short Roman sword banging against the armor on his right thigh. He was worried. He had little information about what was happening in Jerusalem, where leaders of the uprising had concentrated their forces. And he had few troops to protect his headquarters if the Jews should attack before the approaching legions arrived. He did know the Jews were preparing to defend the countryside north and south of Jerusalem, and had sent a man named Joseph to command their forces in Galilee to the east.

"Damn these Jews," Vespasian muttered.

A sudden commotion outside brought a shouted challenge from a sentry, a babble of voices, then the thud of spear butts slammed into the packed gravel platform in salute. The tent flap swept open and a tall, lean soldier, dripping rain, stepped inside. The newcomer drew himself to rigid attention, right arm thrust outward in salute.

"Hail, Sire! The Tenth Legion awaits your orders. We are closing into camp now."

"Trajan!" Vespasian shouted in surprise. "What a welcome sight. I feared you wouldn't arrive for another week or so." He threw his arms around his comrade.

Trajan, although pleased, protested. "Sire, I'm soaking wet. I'll get you wet too."

"Never mind. Any word on the Fifth Macedonians? And where is Gallus? Here, get out of those wet clothes and dry off." Vespasian tossed a drying cloth and spare robe to Trajan. "Servant, in here immediately! Hot food and wine for this man."

A smile unfurled across Trajan's face. "I was afraid you were in an exposed position, so I drove the men without rest. The Macedonians should be in by dawn. And Gallus -- he'll be ten days or more."

Trajan removed his helmet and dripping cloak, toweled off head and shoulders, then slipped into the robe. With his left hand he accepted a goblet of wine thrust at him by a servant and took a long draught, sighing as he lowered the container. A trickle of red, dribbling from a corner of his mouth, was wiped away with the back of a wrist.

"Thank you, sire. I didn't realize how famished I am."

"Sit down, sit down," Vespasian said, "and get some food into your belly. After you've eaten I want to tell you my plan of attack."

Vespasian waited until Trajan had assuaged his hunger, then summoned him to the map table and began. Vespasian pointed, talked, made thrusting motions with his right hand, fingers extended, then a sweep with an arm, symbolizing a military envelopment. Finished, he stood back, awaiting Trajan's comment.

The Fretensis commander studied the map. "I gather that initially you will use all of your forces to crush resistance in

Galilee, and most of Judea., then you want me to sweep south of Jerusalem. I'm to destroy any Jewish forces I encounter there, explore what is going on at the outpost of the Essenes at Qumran, then move into Jericho in time to participate in an all-out attack on Jerusalem?"

"Precisely. That way we will isolate the resistance, with the exception of diehards in fortresses like Masada, Herodium and Machaerus, and can concentrate on crushing the enemy in Jerusalem. And while we're cleaning up the countryside, we will be allowing time for the Jews to reduce their strength there by fighting among themselves."

"But why the interest in Qumran? I've never heard of the place."

Vespasian's perpetually strained expression -- some said he looked like he was having a difficult bowel movement -- changed to one of deep thought. He paced, hands behind his back..

"I don't have a precise answer for that. I'm pursuing a hunch. What intelligence I have indicates the Jews there believe in a godlike figure they call the 'Teacher of Righteousness.' They have prepared books of discourse about him and their beliefs.

"I know they also oppose the priests who run the Temple and harbor a dream of replacing them one day. My concern is that after we crush resistance in Jerusalem, we might leave the seeds of a new Jewish nation intact at Qumran if we don't determine what is going on there, and, if necessary, eliminate it. I want to know more about this 'Teacher of Righteousness' and the creed they have laid down in their books. I'm hoping you can bring both the Teacher and their main writings to me."

Trajan studied Vespasian. He spoke softly. "I gather you find this subject fascinating, Sire."

"In truth, I do. The Jews are the most exasperating people I've ever encountered. But something in their writings intrigues me. I suspect some principles are emerging here, something we Romans do not understand. We had better know what it is if we are to deal with it. Perhaps you can help me determine if there is a threat to Rome in all this."

In the weeks that followed Vespasian had Trajan study intelligence reports on the Essenes and some of their manuscripts that had fallen into Roman hands. Trajan was fascinated with what he read, but inevitably, research had to give way to military duty.

On a spring morning in 67 A.D. the Romans, seven legions strong, broke camp, hoisted packs and standards and marched away to the east, pennants flying.

They defeated the Jews at Gabae, Sepphoris and Jotapata, where, after a forty-seven day siege, they captured Joseph, the theater commander. More victories followed at Seythopolis, Tiberius, Tracheae, Gamala and Gischala, ending all organized resistance in Galilee.

Vespasian rested his troops that winter then struck east of the Jordan river, captured Gadara and split off columns that took Coreae and Jericho west of the river. Other forces conquered Antipatris, Thamna, Lydda, Joppa, Jamnia and Azotus on the coastal plan west of Jerusalem.

It was at this time the Tenth Legion began its march to Qumran.

Trajan stood in his stirrups, studying the column struggling across the desert. Heat waves shimmered before his eyes. Dust stirred by moving feet made visibility difficult, but as far as he could see his men were plodding forward in good order.

The lean Roman raised his arm, signaling the trumpeter to sound the call for a rest stop. As the staccato notes floated in the air, preparatory commands echoed down the line. Trajan dropped his arm. More commands halted the column.

Water carriers rushed forward in each century, a unit of one hundred men. Every legionnaire gulped a few swallows, their centurions cautioning against drinking too much.

Trajan peered toward a rocky outcropping beyond the head of the column. As he watched a black speck popped over the ridge. It expanded into a horse and rider, shrunken by distance but approaching rapidly. The drumbeat of the horse's hooves could be heard now. It grew louder, then the rider was upon them in a clatter of sound and swirling cloud of dust. The horse, reined in hard, came down with stiffened legs. The rider hit the ground simultaneously, delivering a quick salute.

"Sire, the settlement is in sight, and I believe they have spotted us. Men working in fields directly ahead were looking in our direction when I rode into their line of sight. They must have seen the dust from our column."

"Are they still under observation?"

"Yes. The advance patrol remains just below the ridge."

Trajan turned to his senior tribune.

"I don't expect a fight, Sextus, but we can't take chances. I'll ride forward and look for myself. Start the column in approach formation, and order the catapults to move up front."

Trajan spurred his horse, cape flying out behind, as the trumpet sounded again. The resting men heaved upward. Files straightened, grew rigid. Segments broke away, double-timing to positions left and right of the former column head. More shouted commands and a ringing peal of the trumpet, moved the Romans, into a front of ten cohorts -- a unit of four hundred men.

Trajan dismounted at the rocky rise where the patrol lay peering into a shallow valley below. In the distance, he could see a leaden glint of water. That's the Salt Sea, he decided. To the right, an outcropping of hills, pockmarked with caves, rose against the sky, while to his front; forty to fifty men were gathered in a green field, looking in his direction. Other groups clustered around a watchtower atop a large, stone building, surrounded by palm trees, in the background.

Trajan shaded his eyes. He could see sunlight glancing off shields and swords in a ragged line of men forming between the field hands and the building. Their arms appeared primitive, and the raggedness of the formation indicated they were poorly trained.

Momentarily his thoughts focused on the Essene documents he had studied at Ptolemais. *Who are these people? Why have they moved into this forbidding desert? What did they mean when they spoke of establishing a brotherhood of mankind? Why am I so fascinated with such an idea?*

Trajan shook his head, cleared his mind. He rode back, wheeled around, and positioned himself in front of the advancing legionnaires. He topped the rocky ground first, a lone rider on the horizon. His staff of six tribunes followed, riding abreast. A second line of tribunes came next, then the column fronts of the cohorts, emerging from the cloud of dust, a moving forest of javelins stabbing the sky. As one, the array of human, rectangular blocks moved forward, the sound of their tramping feet filling the air. There was no other sound.

Trajan raised his hand, then dropped it, shouting, "Legion! Cohorts! Halt!" Trumpets pealed, then a new command echoed, "Execute!"

Trajan rode forward, halting fifty paces from four men waiting at the edge of the cultivated field. He raised his right hand, palm open, a symbolic gesture to show it held no weapon. "We come in peace to talk to your leaders and find a camp site for our legionnaires."

A white-robed, old man approached, stopping some ten steps away. "Many times you Romans have said you come in peace. It isn't always so." He spoke in perfect Latin.

"You are hopelessly outnumbered. Your weapons are no match for ours, so let us talk. We have no quarrel with you."

"True. We will talk to avoid conflict, but we will fight if we have to."

"Put your arms aside," Trajan ordered.

"We will stack them, but keep them close by. My men will lead your legionnaires to a campsite beside the Salt Sea. We can spare you a small amount of water from our cisterns if need be. I will send a delegation to your encampment at sundown to bring you to our conference room. We can talk then."

Trajan nodded agreement.

Trajan bathed in his tent, donned a fresh tunic and was waiting with two staff aides at the entrance to the emerging Roman camp when the Essene guides arrived.

Their leader, a large, bearded man in a white robe, bowed. "Good evening Sire. Please follow me." He motioned toward the Essene building.

They passed through the grove of palms, then between two freshly lighted torches flaming at the building entrance. The old man Trajan had talked to in the field, and three others, were waiting there to receive them. All wore white robes.

"My name is Mordecai," he said, his wrinkled, prune-like face wreathed in smiles. "I am the senior elder. These are my Council members, Abraham, Menachem and Michael." Each nodded as his name was pronounced.

Trajan studied each face. Only Michael, sullen and scowling, with a mop of tangled brown hair, aroused suspicion. His eyes locked momentarily with Trajan's, but were quickly averted.

Surveillance completed, Trajan introduced his aides, Sextus and Cerolinus, then positioned himself beside Mordecai as the elder motioned for them to follow.

"We thought you might like a tour of our settlement," Mordecai said. "Perhaps that will convince you we are no threat to you or your higher commanders." He led them down a dim hallway, torches set in wall holders, lighting the way. Mordecai turned left up a smaller corridor then stepped through a narrow entrance.

"This is our scriptorium," he said, gesturing toward stone desks arrayed along one wall. "In this room our scholars transcribe documents, then store them in the library over there." He pointed toward an adjoining room.

The tour continued. Mordecai showed them a kitchen, storerooms, rooms filled with cooking utensils, a washroom, a well-kept latrine, a bakery, cisterns, inner and outer courtyards, then led them to a conference room.

Trajan sat on the far side of a long table, across from Mordecai and positioned so he could watch Michael at one end. Trajan's aides sat beside him. There, in the flickering light of more torches, they heard Mordecai tell the story of the Essenes.

"We consider ourselves the chosen people of God," he began, his voice echoing in the otherwise silent chamber. "More than two hundred years ago we attempted to correct the religious mistakes imposed on Judea by the Pharisees and the Sadducees. A struggle for supremacy followed. We lost and were shut out of Temple life. To practice our religion without interference, and fulfill our obligation to establish a brotherhood of man, we moved into this desert near the Dead Sea, built a headquarters and established satellite groups in smaller villages."

Mordecai paused to see if Trajan had any questions.

Trajan did but remained silent, his eyes on Michael who was staring contemptuously at Mordecai. This underscored a thought growing in Trajan's mind. Michael was a Zealot, and probably some of the tougher-looking guardsmen Trajan had noticed were too. He didn't know how this could be, but was convinced he was correct. *What's going on here? There is an undercurrent of tension between Mordecai and Michael. Who is the real leader of this community?*

Mordecai continued his discourse.

"Here at Qumran we have reached the pinnacle of our development. Our numbers have grown to two thousand. We raise crops and irrigate them by hand from six cisterns that capture our sparse rainfall. We have skilled farmers, shepherds, cowherds, beekeepers, scholars, scribes, and carpenters. They constructed this building from gray stone and earth mortar, roofed it with beams from palm trunks, overlaid by interwoven reeds from the banks of the salt sea that have been smeared with clay. The walls have been plastered with a lime mix, and, as you can see, the floors are paved with pebbles."

Mordecai droned on. Some of the elders began to nod, but not Trajan nor Michael. They continued their duel of silent observation.

Trajan learned only Mordecai and a small group of leaders lived in the building. The others resided in caves in the nearby cliffs and visited the headquarters only when they had business to transact. They lived a monastic life without women. There were strict levels of rank, also great concern with ritual and physical cleanliness.

"Our members begin work at dawn," Mordecai continued. "They come in from the fields an hour before midday to wash, eat and pray. There are two baptismal and swimming pools in this building and a third south of the building. They return to the fields in mid-afternoon then work until sundown."

Mordecai cleared his throat. "You will note we dress in white for official occasions." He nodded toward his elders. "We do not offer animal sacrifices like the Temple priests. We believe the body is corruptible, but the soul imperishable. When one dies, the soul escapes to dwell in heaven, if the person has led a virtuous life, or to rot in a murky dungeon if not."

Mordecai stopped, looked at Trajan, expecting a response.

Trajan pondered what he had heard. To him, Mordecai's description of Essene beliefs sounded much like those of that new, Jewish sect that called themselves Christians. They also believed in universal brotherhood, ritual washing, baptism, that amassing treasures of gold and silver should be avoided, and that chastity was a high form of virtue. But one thing troubled him.

"Elder Mordecai, I thank you for the description of your life here. You have made a remarkable adaptation to harsh surroundings. But you have said nothing about your great prophet, the Teacher of Righteousness. Where is he? We have heard he is a messiah-like figure who leads the community."

Mordecai eyebrows rose.

"Sire, the Teacher of Righteousness died in the eighth decade after Qumran was established. He is buried in an unmarked grave in our cemetery east of here. His memory is revered and his teachings studied. But he is no longer with us."

"Then there is no new Teacher to take his place?"

"No one. Our loss is great. The void cannot be filled."

Trajan stroked his chin. "I see. I assumed he was alive, or if he had died you would have either assigned his role to someone else or expect his return in a new body and person."

The deep lines around Mordecai's mouth tightened. He

seemed worried. The other elders, now fully awake, listened intently, their eyes darting around the table.

"Sire, it is true we do believe the dead can come back in the form of a new person, and we do expect our Teacher to return someday, but so far that has not happened. There was one period -- " He stopped abruptly, looking flustered, coughed and cleared his throat then broke off the sentence without completing it.

Trajan showed immediate interest. "You were about to say -- ?"

"It is not important." Mordecai glanced at the other elders. Their eyes, filled with alarm, were riveted on him.

Trajan had another question. "There was a man from Galilee, a carpenter who appeared in Jerusalem some thirty years ago. He too preached penitence, humility, chastity, a brotherhood and love of mankind. He was hated and feared by the Temple priests and was crucified. His followers expected him to rise from the dead. Indeed his body did disappear on the third day after he was taken from the cross. His beliefs have become the foundation for what may become a new religion. Does not this sound like your Teacher of Righteousness?"

Now Mordecai was visibly disturbed. He swallowed, took a deep breath.

"Sire, you must not make such comparisons. We, of course know about the Galilean and have studied the sayings attributed to him. And it is true many of his concepts were, and are, our concepts. I am amazed you, Roman, know this. Obviously, you have done a great deal of studying. But I must point out differences also. Our Teacher did not love his enemies. He thirsted for revenge, and expected divine help in achieving it and correcting the ritual abuses in the Temple. The Galilean preached that one should love his enemies that if someone strikes you, turn the other cheek. That is a fundamental difference."

Trajan waved his right arm in front of him, as if brushing aside what Mordecai had said. "Couldn't that have been merely a refinement of an Essene belief without altering substantially the agreement that exists in other areas? And I have another question.

Is it not true that your Teacher was crucified by a Temple leader known as the 'Wicked Priest,' another startling similarity?"

The elders erupted in loud conversations, shouting at each other and Mordecai in Hebrew. It took Mordecai several minutes to restore order.

"I don't know where you heard that, honored Trajan. The truth is we are not certain how the Teacher met his death. He was captured. There was one report he was crucified with about eight hundred others who had opposed the Wicked Priest. We did not recover his body immediately. When we did it was so broken, so deteriorated, we could not determine what had happened to him. As for your other suspicions, it is true we did note the similarities between the Galilean and the Teacher of Righteousness. It created excitement here for a time, but we decided the differences were too fundamental for him to be our great leader, reborn and returned in a new body. We could not accept his idea of forgiveness. We still want revenge. Besides, the Galilean was crucified thirty-eight years ago. We are no longer as interested in him as we once were."

The elders squirmed in their chairs. The tense lines around Mordecai's mouth deepened. Trajan doubted the elder was telling the truth, but realized the conversation had come to an end. He rose.

"I realize you have had a long day." Mordecai said. "However, let me offer you our humble hospitality. My chief executive, Michael" -- he paused, nodding toward the elder at the end of the table -- "has suggested you might find a swim in our baptismal pool refreshing. He will take you there if you desire."

Trajan turned to Sextus. "Leave two guards at the entrance of the headquarters building. I'll pick them up when I'm finished." The meaning was clear. If Trajan didn't appear within a reasonable time, the guards could summon help.

Michael, now smiling, approached. "Please follow me."

They walked along a short, broad corridor, then down a stairway, opening onto an open-air patio paved with stone. Moonlight glinted off a sunken pool. "This way, sire," Michael said, starting down fourteen steps to the water's edge. There they stripped. Michael dived in, Trajan right behind him.

The Roman, a remarkable athlete, stroked up the pool and back, paused to catch his breath, then up and back again and again, until he felt tension draining from his body. He crawled out and sank onto a couch near the bottom of the steps, breathing heavily.

Trajan closed his eyes. When he opened them moments later, he thought he was dreaming. A figure, obscured in shadow, glided silently down the steps and shed a cape just as the moon came out from behind a cloud, flooding the scene with light. A beautiful woman stood there naked, poised on the rim of stones around the pool. The moonlight bathed her body in silvery brilliance, accentuating the curve of young, protruding breasts, the concave dip of her waist, and the long, sensuous line of muscular thighs, brushed by tresses of hair cascading down her back.

Trajan gasped. The girl dove into the water and swam slowly to the end and back. When she clambered out, body iridescent in the moonlight, she stripped water from hips and legs, then twisted it from her hair, picked up her cape on the crook of a finger, draped it behind one shoulder and strolled over to Trajan's couch. Her eyes were round and luminous, her red lips half open.

Before she could speak, Michael approached. "I will leave you now, Sire." He turned and disappeared up the stairway.

The girl lay down beside Trajan, dropping her cape beside the couch, her body damp and chilled by the water.

"What is you name, fair one?" Trajan asked in a choked voice.

She smiled. "Mostly they call me Sin."

Chapter XVII

The knock brought Tom back to his immediate surroundings. He crossed the hotel room in three strides and opened the door. Sharon stood framed against the light of the hallway, looking pensive, uncertain, bundled in a worn cloth coat against the chill of the night. A tentative smile plucked corners of her mouth.

"Sorry to disturb you," she said, shifting the package she was carrying. "Got here as soon as I could."

Tom was disturbed. She looked unusually attractive, strong, muscular, emanating vitality and toughness. She was a sabra, the succulent, fruit-bearing cactus used as a metaphor in describing Israeli women -- tough and prickly on the outside, sweet and flowing inside. But Sharon was tough and sweet both inside and out.

"Come in, Sharon. Thanks for coming. Let's see what you have."

She placed the package on the table, laid the coat on the bed then unwrapped the bundle. "These pages belong at the end of the last section. They replace the last forty pages. I retyped them, and inadvertently put the old pages into the manuscript instead of the new ones." She averted her eyes, then stole a quick glance at Tom.

He examined the first of the retyped pages, showing no indication of being suspicious, found the right place, lifted out the old section and put in the new.

"Thank you very much," he said, turning, not certain how to end the encounter. He stood there awkwardly, then, remembering, opened a bureau drawer and removed a bill from his wallet. "To cover the cab fare," he said, extending the money. He knew he was being abrupt, but thought that the safest course. The setting was too provocative.

"Tom, I was -- "

"Oh, sorry. I didn't mean to rush you. I was afraid you might lose your cab. They won't wait too long, you know."

"I let the cab go. I was hoping we could talk for a while."

"Oh? Oh, okay. Would you like some coffee?" He gestured toward the thermos on the table.

"Yes, thank you." Sharon took the extended cup, steam curling up from the black liquid, then sat on the edge of the bed, the closest place to him. She looked down at the cup then up at Tom. He was staring at her.

"Tom, I've been wanting...I need to talk to you, and I don't know how to begin."

Tom said nothing. He found the fact she was sitting on his bed very suggestive.

"I want you to know how much I've enjoyed working for you. It has done a great deal for me, financially and emotionally. It was satisfying to put my language training and typing through such a test...and I've enjoyed getting to know you."

Tom re-crossed his legs, suddenly aware changes were taking place in his body.

"I know that's coming to an end." Sharon looked down at the cup again. "We still have to take photos of the fingerprints on the Isaiah scroll and the tile, and I guess we'll talk to Samuel a final time or two. Then it's over."

"You've done an outstanding job, Sharon, I'd be happy to recommend you -- "

"I know," she sighed, sounding wistful. "But suddenly I feel lost. My life has been so devoid of human contact. Working with you and Dr. Nizer filled that gap. Now it's being taken away."

"Oh, Sharon, I'm sorry. I wish you wouldn't feel that way. I'm going to miss you, but -- " He realized immediately it was the worst thing he could have said.

Sharon looked up, her eyes filled with yearning. "Oh, Tom, I'm going to miss you so. You've meant so much to me." She was off the bed and moving toward him. He rose too, emotions aflame. He folded his arms around her, crushing her body against his. They kissed passionately. Tom pulled her toward the bed.

"Oh, Tom," she gasped.

He stopped abruptly. "What am I doing?" He slapped his forehead. "I can't let this happen!"

"Don't stop now." Sharon tugged on his arm, trying to pull him back against her.

He resisted firmly. "Sharon, I can't do this to you. I want to make love to you. You're a warm, beautiful woman. You give so much of yourself. I need that. My God, how I need it, but I would just be using you. There is no future for us."

"Don't talk like that, Think about now. You need me and I need -- "

Tom took her back in his arms. He kissed her upturned lips, her cheeks, her neck. He pulled at her blouse, popping a button loose. She removed the blouse and her bra, and he kissed her breasts.

They moved to the bed. She pulled at Tom's belt. He slipped off his shoes, then his pants, shirt and underwear. Sharon quickly took off the remainder of her clothes and pressed against him.

She was soft and moist as he entered. She clamped down hard and he groaned. Tom thrust very slowly, lingered, paused, then slowly again, penetrating deeper, then repeated this slow rhythm, each time moving a little faster, pushing a little harder.

Sharon, breathing heavily, made strange, high-pitched, increasingly frantic noises. Tom lost control, now in full voice too, pounded her body. They climaxed in a crescendo of motion and sound, Sharon screaming, Tom gasping and grunting, then collapsing against her. They lay still.

It was over. They both knew it. Sharon, huddled against his body, whispering broken, fragmented sentences.

"I love you, Tom...I know...can't have you...Don't understand...hope Fran realizes what...getting. She's...not much of a woman...Afraid to be.... I'm more woman than she is...for some reason...not enough."

Tom pulled his head away to look at her, then at the wall.

"You *are* one hell of a woman, Sharon." His voice was almost inaudible. "And I suppose it's true Fran isn't all she should be right now, but she's in my blood...I can't remove her. She has jarred me out of my predatory ways, made me realize there are obligations that come with love."

Tom stopped. "I know that sounds melodramatic, but I don't know any other way to say it. I found I couldn't have her for my passing pleasure. That forced me to weigh how much I wanted her, whether I was willing to accept the responsibilities imposed by a lasting relationship."

He sucked in a long, shuddering breath. "I discovered I loved her deeply, and that despite my frustration over her refusal to give in to me, I needed for her to remain the way she was, and is."

Tom paused. "Oh, I know she's paralyzed as much by fear and guilt as guided by moral principle, but her adherence to an unchanging moral standard was something I needed to encounter and deal with. I had so little of that in my childhood. My parents were constantly shifting the rules that governed my life. One day lax, another day tough. Then they would change again and give me everything I wanted. I learned I could manipulate them, and most other people too. I was a person who exploited other people's weaknesses. But with Fran it didn't work. There is a constant there. It's difficult for me to accept that I need something I thought I detested, but I'm afraid that's the way it is."

Tom's response had become a soliloquy, addressed as much to himself as Sharon. He sat up in bed, cross-legged. His eyes found Sharon's as she turned toward him, probing the sadness he saw there.

"You say Fran's not much of a woman, but I suspect you know she's going to be quite a woman, too, one day. She has to start doing her own thinking. She needs to become more like me in some ways, and I need to become more like her, more concerned with moral principle."

Tom looked directly at Sharon. "Please don't ask me to make more sense of it than that. It's just the way things are. I love Fran for her beauty, and for what she is and can become."

He was struggling and knew it, but continued.

"I think I love you, too, in my own inadequate way, but life won't let me have both of you."

Sharon pulled him down next to her and wept silently, her head against his chest.

"Actually, I'm grateful to you." Tom's voice had become hoarse and strained. "You've given of yourself without asking much in return. You've taught me what a woman can be. I'll remember that always, but if we continue, you'll end up hating me. I don't want that to happen. I know it sounds corny, but you'll meet a guy someday who deserves you. As for me, I'll just have to hope I can find a way to work out my problems with Fran, if it's not too late. God help me if it is."

There was finality in what he was saying, in everything they had done. It was a type of farewell. They would see each other many times in days to come, but never again as lusting, seeking, passionately aroused man and woman.

Sharon dried her eyes and blew her nose, blinking away the final tears. She dressed quietly. Tom did too. He called a cab for her, then helped her put on her coat and kissed her tenderly on the cheek. She turned at the door.

"Goodbye, Tom...I hope you find whatever it is you're looking for." The door closed and she was gone.

Tom slumped in his chair, thinking. He got up, poured more coffee, then picked up the transcript of the Samuel tapings. With difficulty, he forced his mind back to his reading. It took a while, but eventually the words came up around him, enfolded him, recreating that strange and vital time when the Tenth Legion was trying to determine what was really going on at Qumran.

Chapter XVIII

Michael and Mordecai glared at each other in the Qumran conference room.

"I tell you, we must hide it now!" Michael slammed his fist on the worn, wood table between them. "The Romans have been here a week and show every indication they will stay longer. Sooner or later they'll discover we have gold and silver, and when they do they'll take it."

Mordecai shook his head, scattering scraggly white locks across his wrinkled brow. "I see no indication they know about our treasury."

"You know very little, old man. Trajan has his spies out. He's learning more every day. Yesterday my agent, Sin, informed me that he had read your War Scroll. Because of that silly document, he thinks you Essenes are plotting a new revolt. He's suspicious. We must move both the gold I brought with me from the Temple and what you already had here."

"That's another thing," Mordecai flared. "That woman! That whore! You had no right to bring her and her companions into this community. You know women are not allowed, especially a woman who flaunts her whoredom in her very name. Even worse, you let her defile our baptismal pool. You must remove her immediately."

"Oh shut up." Michael said, disgusted. "That would be stupid. She's our best source of information on what the Romans are doing, so stop arguing. Your tongue just keeps wagging in your empty head. Actually, you're lucky to have a head. I could have had you executed, you know."

"I'm aware of that. You Zealots have worked your will ever since you arrived. And now you want to take away the gold we need to overthrow the Temple priests, and put it Jehovah knows where. You might even lose part of it. Besides I'm already removing our library documents and storing them in the caves. That's difficult enough without also having to transport the gold and silver to a new location."

"Don't worry, old man. You're not going to lose anything. We'll divide the gold into small amounts and bury it in unlikely locations. The sites will be recorded on two copper plates in language no stranger can understand. Then we'll roll up the plates and hide them. After we've defeated the Romans you can recover your precious gold -- if we don't beat you to it." He laughed.

"What about our library?"

"Oh, Satan can take your library." Michael, exasperated, jammed a hand through his tangled hair. "Just pack it off and hide it as best you can, but don't make Trajan any more suspicious than he is already."

Michael rose, adjusted the dagger belt under his robe, and spat into the corner of the room, to Mordecai's horror. "I'll let you know when all the gold and silver have been moved." He turned and walked out.

* * *

Michael was correct. Trajan was planning an extended stay. He enlarged the Roman camp and ordered more supplies. He also stayed on friendly terms with Mordecai, and continued to enjoy Sin's nightly visits to his tent. He knew she was Michael's agent, so gave her only information he wanted passed on to the suspicious Zealot.

What he didn't tell her was his belief the Essenes were concealing a leader who could carry out the type of revolt envisioned in the War Scroll, one of the sect's principal documents. It forecast a coming struggle between the "Children of

Light"-- the tribes of Levi, Judah and Benjamin -- and the "Children of Darkness" -- the Edomites, Moabites and Ammonites, all old enemies, plus the "Kittim" of Assyria and Egypt, meaning the Romans.

He told himself: *Mordecai is a frail old man. He couldn't possibly lead such an uprising, and Michael is too crude. The Essenes must be concealing a more dynamic leader somewhere. a new Teacher of Righteousness, or someone capable of filling that role.*

His suspicions began the night of his tour of the headquarters building. Mordecai avoided one part of it. When asked why, he'd said: "That's a sacred, religious sector. It's barred to all but the Council of Elders." Trajan immediately ordered his best agent, a tough, dark-skinned, little man, known as "Julius the Sly," to investigate. Three days later Julius reported his findings.

"That area contains a chamber of rooms behind locked and guarded double doors. Two sentries, on duty at all times, are changed every four hours. Only Mordecai and members of his Council entered while I was watching. One or more of them appeared daily and passed through after the doors were opened."

"Did you see inside?"

"Got only a quick look, Sire. There are rich carpets on the floor and tapestries on the walls. Looked like there might be two or three rooms."

"Did anyone come out other than the Council members?"

"No, Sire. Only those who entered.."

Trajan, dissatisfied with the meager information, eyed his agent, drumming his fingers on the camp desk where he was working. "All right, get your miserable body back there and keep watching. I want to know everything you learn."

Two days later Julius reported again: "Last night I saw two of the chamber's nighttime guards outside the headquarters building. They had a goatskin of wine, apparently stolen from the Essene's storeroom, and were swilling it down. It was almost empty. It's a good thing, too. The way they were going at it, they would have been drunk very soon."

Trajan stared at Julius, mind racing.

"Could you place a jug of wine where they would find it right after they go on guard duty?"

"I think so, Sire."

"Good. Let me know when you have a workable plan."

Julius returned the next day. He explained his proposal and Trajan approved. Two nights later, they were ready. Trajan took wine from his own supply, laced it with poppy juice, and gave it to Julius, who concealed it in his robe and returned to his tent.

At midnight, Julius emerged and slipped quietly down the camp's main street. He glided between two tents, waited in the darkness there until certain he had not been followed, then scrambled over an unguarded sector of the earthen barricade encircling the camp.

Julius studied the dark mass of the Essenes' headquarters building ahead, two torches lighting the main entrance. Seeing no sign of danger, he followed his usual route, entering through a basement opening. He reached a back staircase and tiptoed up to the main floor. Moments later he dropped to his haunches in a dark hallway. The secret chamber, fronted by a rectangular court, was to his right. Another hallway entered the court to his left. He settled down to wait.

An hour later the silence was broken by the sound of marching feet. A column of guards stomped into the court, short Roman swords slapping against plates of leg armor. "Detail Halt!" The soldiers stopped. Two men fell out and the old guards fell in at the end of the column. Another command and the column marched off down the hallway.

As always, the two new guards -- the same two Julius had seen drinking from the goatskin -- made a dash to the nearby latrine. When they disappeared through the door, Julius sprinted across the court and deposited the jug of wine in open sight within the armory closet next to the double doors. Another dash and he melted back into the darkness of his own hallway, just as the first guard returned, walking with legs far apart, lifting one foot, then the other, as he scratched his crotch. His companion was a few strides behind.

Yawning and grumbling, they strode over to the closet. The first guard opened the door, leaned in and handed a spear to his companion, then turned and grasped one for himself. The weapon caught in its holding slot. "Balls of Satan," he grumbled, jerking on it. The spear came free and struck the wine jug, tipping it on its side. Wine seeped onto the floor.

"What's this?" The guard reached down and dipped a finger in the red liquid.

"Now you've done it, Saul," the other guard said. "The commander will have our hides for this."

"Wine," Saul said, standing there, finger in his mouth, an expression of amazement on his face, eyes staring.

Julius, in his hallway, began to sweat. He had not considered the possibility the wine might spill and drain away. If that happened he knew Trajan would have him flogged. He watched anxiously as the second guard reached down and picked up the jug, also testing the spilled wine with a dipped finger.

"What are we going to do?" Saul asked. "They'll never believe we didn't put that jug there, Joshua. We've got to get rid of it."

Joshua pulled out the partly dislodged stopper and took a hefty swig.

"Hold on there," Saul growled. "I found it. Some of it's mine. He grabbed the jug, took a long draught. "But what are we going to do about it?" he persisted, wiping his mouth with the back of a wrist.. "We can't leave the wine here."

"We're going to drink it and throw the jug in the latrine," Joshua retorted, grabbing the wine again. He took a long drink.

"My turn," Saul shouted.. "Don't drink it all."

The two guards passed the jug back and forth until the last drop trickled down Saul's throat. Then, laughing and feeling better, they assumed their posts in front of the bolted doors, forgetting the jug, tossed carelessly to one side.

Julius sighed, relieved. All he had to do now was wait until he was certain the drug had taken effect, then report to Trajan.

* * *

Trajan, seated at his camp table, looked up from the papers he had been reading as Sextus entered his tent. On a stand nearby, candles flickered in a seven-stem holder he had borrowed from the Essenes.

"Sit down, Sextus." He motioned toward a stool. "Sorry I had to summon you at this hour, but I have an important project to discuss with you."

"I was up and working also, Sire," Sextus said. "A number of matters require your approval."

"Your business first, then."

Sextus laid a sheaf of papers in front of Trajan -- requisitions for supplies needed from Joppa, for more horses and a status report on strength of the legion. "And, oh yes. Here is a miniature of the Tenth Legion tile the engineers have designed to be placed at the base of the new storage building. Does it have your approval?"

Trajan turned the small, ceramic plate over, examining the outline in green of a galley and a boar on the facing side, and a black Roman number X superimposed over the image.

"Our engineers designed this? It's more decorative than usual."

"Yes, several of them are artistic, Sire. It differs a bit from the corner plates we've used before on legion buildings. They're usually stamped 'Leg X Fre' for Tenth Fretensis Legion."

"I'll take a closer look, later, Sextus, and let you know." He tucked the tile into his sword belt. "Right now I want to tell you about an intelligence problem we're trying to solve."

He explained his suspicions about the sealed chamber in the Essenes' building, told Sextus of the drugged wine and the expectation he and Julius could enter the chamber within the hour.

"If I'm not back by cock's crow, come looking for me,"

Trajan said, tightening the sword belt around his waist. He was standing in the center of the tent.

"I'm coming with you, Sire, and I think we ought to take at least two members of your personal guard. This could be dangerous."

"No," Trajan said emphatically. "We have to do this quietly. Slip in and get back before new guards are posted about dawn. It's a job for as few men as possible. Julius and I can handle it. I'll let you know tomorrow what we find." Sextus departed, still protesting.

Julius arrived moments later. Trajan followed him into the darkness outside, two swiftly moving shadows, darting from concealment to concealment until they reached the rectangular court inside the Essenes' building.

They found the guards, Joshua and Saul, collapsed, one on each side of the door. Trajan smiled. They would sleep several more hours from the opium he had put in the wine -- but he wished they wouldn't snore so loudly.

He motioned Julius to follow. They dashed across the court to the double doors, flames from wall torches projecting their elongated shadows onto the opposite wall.

Trajan placed his shoulder under the cross-beam locking the door and lifted. It moved. Gathering his legs under him, he shoved again with Julius assisting. The beam moved up, clearing the two L-shaped bronze clasps holding it in place. Julius and Trajan laid the timber on the floor, then pushed against the double doors, swinging them into the chamber.

Trajan gasped. Before him was a torch-lit reception area. Red wine-colored carpets covered the floor. Tapestries from Parthia draped the walls. In one corner, atop a cedarwood table, lay a leather-bound register, apparently to be signed by all who had entered. Just beyond this book was a smaller chamber, set off from the reception area by partitions extending partway across the room from both walls. The opening was draped with a floor-to-ceiling, gossamer curtain, its golden strands flashing in the torchlight.

Trajan, his heart pounding, pulled the curtain aside. A large marble altar, topped by a white marble cross loomed there, bathed in the flickering light.

"The symbol of the Christians," Julius whispered, his voice barely audible.

Trajan nodded. He didn't understand a cross being displayed in an area controlled by Hebrews, but was impressed by the setting. Hammered gold ornaments glittered from the walls. A silver chalice rested in front of the cross. Candles in gold-inlaid holders flickered on both sides of it. The marble seemed alive, pulsating with internal fire that rose and receded with the intensity of the light that fell upon it.

Trajan stood transfixed, then noticed a heavy, red velvet curtain in one corner of the altar room, concealing what appeared to be an entrance to another chamber.

He approached the curtain warily. For some reason he was afraid. He stopped, gulped, edged forward. Holding a torch in his left hand, away from the curtain, he reached over with his right, grasped the drape and swept it aside.

There was a blinding flash. Trajan reeled back. Heat engulfed his body. He dropped the torch, fell next to it, felt the flames on his head. His right hand came up to shield his eyes from a dazzling light, then fell back in spasmodic, jerking motions, catching on his sword belt, and depositing the Xth Legion tile he had concealed there, on the carpeted floor.

Trajan retained one further memory. He sensed an overwhelming presence in the room, standing near the velvet curtain. There were strange vibrations in the air, a humming sound that seemed about to burst its bounds. Then an aged, wrinkled hand reached down, moved the sputtering torch and laved water over his seared head. His last impression was of the hand picking up the tile. Then the presence was gone. The vibrations gone. Darkness closed in.

Sextus was not certain when a sense of impending crisis took control of his mind. He had been uneasy ever since learning of Trajan's plan to enter the Essenes' secret religious area, but returned to his tent and fell into a fitful sleep. He awakened with a start, his heart pounding. There was a strange humming noise outside. He stumbled to his feet, groping for the entrance.

"What's happening?" he asked a sentry.

"I don't know, Tribune," the guard replied. "A moment ago there was a flash that lighted the sky near the Essenes' building, then this strange sound."

At that moment the humming stopped. Silence returned, broken only by the renewed chirping of crickets in the distance.

Something was wrong. Sextus sensed it. Knew it. Badly wrong. He dressed, slipped into his sandals and buckled on his sword,.then sent a hastily scribbled message to the commander of Trajan's personal guard: "Meet me immediately at Trajan's tent."

All was quiet when he arrived there. Maybe he was over reacting, but maybe not. He paced nervously, uncertain what to do. What could have happened? Should I try to find out? Trajan had said I should take no action before cock's crow, more than an hour away.

Sextus turned over an hour glass on Trajan's desk and watched the sand sift slowly -- ever so slowly --downward. But what if Trajan is injured, or apprehended in an area that's sensitive to the Essenes?"

The senior centurion of the guard detachment arrived suddenly, ducking through the tent's entrance, pulling up to rigid attention and saluting.   Sextus returned the salute, snapped off an order: "Ready a force of two hundred men immediately and have them stand by outside." Now he felt better, so also summoned the Xth Legion quaestor, Trajan's administrative officer, and issued instructions to mobilize all troops at sunrise unless he, Sextus, personally canceled the order.

Now he was functioning, in charge, but continued his pacing.   Anxiety finally overcame caution. When half the sand in the hourglass had slipped from top to bottom, Sextus burst through the tent flap and shouted for the guard centurion.

"Have your men follow me, double pace. Destroy anyone who attempts to stop us."

With sword drawn, Sextus led the legionnaires down the camp's main street into the darkness beyond. In the distance, he could see the flaming torches at the entrance to the Essenes's building.

The two guards there, apparently hearing the approaching, rhythmic pounding of Roman boots, stepped in front of the entrance, spears ready, in a throwing stance.

The Romans, six abreast, burst into the circle of torchlight at the front of the building and were upon them before the sentries knew what was happening. Two sword thrusts and both fell. The legionnaires kicked them aside and rushed through the entrance.

Sextus led the clattering column -- its pace reduced to a half-walk, half-run -- to the assembly area where the Essenes' guard detachments formed. He rounded up the startled, off-duty men there, locked them in a nearby room, then sent patrols charging down the corridors. "Find that sealed chamber," he ordered.

Shouts and clashes of steel on steel echoed from one hall then subsided. The legionnaires who had gone that way returned, elated with the way they had dispatched the Essenes who challenged them. But they found no sign of Trajan.

A second patrol returned, also without results.

More shouting and sounds of fighting came from other areas of the building. Almost simultaneously, a highly agitated Mordecai appeared at Sextus' side.

"What is the meaning of this?" he demanded. "Why are your soldiers running amok? What in the name of Jehovah is going on?"

""Where is Trajan?" Sextus demanded. "What have you done with him?"

"How would I know where your commander is? Why would we -- "

A centurion leading another patrol burst out of a hallway to the left. "Come quickly, Tribune. We've found him...and I think we'll need more men."

Ignoring Mordecai, Sextus signaled the three returned

patrols to follow him. They charged down the hall after Sextus and the centurion, now running ahead, holding a torch aloft.

The column, boots crunching the pebbled floor, turned left into the rectangular area outside the sealed-off chamber. The Romans kicked aside the two snoring guards in front of the open double doors. Sextus entered first, took in the scene -- the lifeless, huddled form of Julius near one wall, and Trajan lying face down to the right of the altar, hair on the upturned side of his head singed away. Only tiny curlicues remained. Welts and rising blisters, intermingled with ridges burned the color of charcoal, covered the upper half of his body.

Sextus dropped to a knee, placed an ear on Trajan's chest. "He's alive, but just barely. Quickly now," he ordered, motioning to the centurion, "make a litter from spears and cloaks and rush the commander to his tent. You," -- he pointed at a messenger -- "run ahead and alert the physicians. Tell them what you have seen here. Order the physicians, in my name, to prepare unguents for severe burns. And you, centurion, as soon as the litter bearers are on their way, send a messenger to the quaestor, ordering the legion to fall out in full battle gear immediately."

The room exploded into action. Men rushed back and forth, colliding, sliding by, disentangling, then dashing on. The centurion bawled commands as Sextus resumed his inspection.

He noted the altar, the chalice, the candles flickering weakly in their gold-inlaid holders and the hammered gold wall ornaments. Then he saw the red drapes off to the right. They were pulled back, torn and scorched as if burned by a burst of fire.

He sidled through into an empty room. The floor was covered with the same red wine-colored carpet used elsewhere in the chamber. There was a large bed, a table, a small sunken bath off to one side and a wall lined with shelves holding hundreds of scrolls.

He felt the bed. It was warm, had been occupied recently. There was a partly opened scroll on the table. A small candle flickered there. Near the bath he found several fresh robes, neatly folded, on shelves, and four pairs of leather sandals. Whoever had lived here had not wanted for much -- except perhaps his, or her, freedom.

Sextus strode back into the altar room. Activity there had subsided. The litter bearing Trajan had disappeared down the hall. The remaining legionnaires stood along one wall, awaiting orders. The centurion commanding them gave Sextus an anxious look, his mouth pulled into a tense line.

Sextus ignored him. His eyes moved from the scorched velvet drapes to a burned area in the thin, lace-like curtain between the altar and reception area. Some searing force had passed from the inner room, past the velvet drape, past where Trajan had been found, through the lace curtain and out the door -- where the two Essene guards still snored loudly. What could it have been? Suddenly Sextus' mind snapped back to the present.

"Let's get out of here," he shouted. "Double pace back to the camp. If there is opposition fight only to get through."

He turned and ran toward the guard assembly area and the outer doors where they had entered. The guard detail caught up quickly, boots crunching against the floor.

Sextus heard sounds of great activity in the building now, men running through nearby halls. A distraught Essene, obviously coming from the library, burst from a side entrance into the hallway, his arms loaded with scrolls. Spotting the Romans, he wheeled quickly and dashed back the way he had come.

The legionnaires surged out the main gate. Sextus heard shouting, a rustling of many bodies moving in the darkness. Suddenly a shower of spears and arrows arced down on the Roman column. A legionnaire went down, gurgling, a spear driven cleanly through his neck. Another shouted an oath, grabbing at the spear protruding from his side. He stumbled and collapsed. Arrows glanced off bronze helmets and shoulder armor, and appeared as if by magic, protruding from pumping arms and legs.

"Keep going! Keep going!" Sextus shouted.

The column disappeared into the night, but soon reappeared, thudding down the torch-lit main street of the Roman camp. Sextus halted the soldiers at Trajan's tent, where he mounted a platform and addressed his waiting commanders.

"Tribunes! Marcus! Rufus! Constancius! We attack immediately.The Jews have almost killed our commander. You, Marcus, assemble the legion in a front of ten cohorts at the edge of the camp, spaced for battle. When we attack, the two cohorts on each end of the line are to swing wide and envelop the building. The six center cohorts will storm the building. Destroy everything in your path. The auxiliary cavalry will stand by ready to pursue. My guess is the Essenes will evacuate key personnel and documents to those caves near the Salt Sea. Run them down and bring the documents to me. Now form up and await my command."

Sextus entered the tent where the physicians were working over Trajan. The leader of the team looked up, perspiration dotting his forehead.

"He's going to make it, Tribune. His pulse is stronger. He's delirious, but he's talking. rambling about a burst of light, a ghostly hand, cold water gushing over his head. I can't make sense of it."

"Keep working on him. I'll be back as soon as we clean out the Essenes. I'll need to know how soon he can travel." Sextus strode out of the tent, mounted his horse, saddled and waiting for him, and signaled the guard detachment to follow. The sun rose, spreading light across the desert as he galloped down the street.

Sextus pulled up in front of the legion and raised his sword. "Cohorts forward! Battle readiness!"

A roar of approval erupted from the serried ranks.

Sextus brought his sword down. "Execute!"

The legionnaires raised their shields chest high and drew their swords. . Trumpets sounded. The columns stepped out boldly.

Sextus signaled the commanders striding at the front of each cohort. A line of scouts raced forward, forming a screening force a hundred strides in front of the main body. Sextus' bodyguard also dashed ahead, deploying in a line between him and the scouts. Behind him the legionnaires, sweating and stinking in the early morning heat, advanced in a ground-pounding cadence.

Sextus could see a thin line of Essene guardsmen forming across the front of the headquarters building as the Romans advanced.

"Battle line!" he shouted. "Double Pace!" His sword aloft again. "Execute!" His horse reared and plunged. The trumpets blared again. The columns writhed and uncoiled, sending units jogging out to both sides. Three parallel lines emerged.

The scouts now were within range. Spears arced through the air in both directions as the scouts surged up into and beyond the Essenes' line. The battle was joined.

The three-deep Roman formation swept over the defenders and burst into and around the headquarters building. Sextus rode up to the entrance. Legionnaire detachments rushed by, racing up the many halls, killing as they went.

Screams and sounds of battle rose to a crescendo, then receded. Sextus turned to the cavalry commander. "After them! Quickly now! Cut off anyone fleeing toward the caves."

The legionnaires killed every Essene they could find in the building and the horsemen rode down and slaughtered most of those fleeing on foot.

In a final inspection of the battle scene, Sextus came across Mordecai's body, sprawled in a bloody heap, inside the sacred chamber where Trajan had been found. The other elders, Abraham, Menachem and Michael, lay dead nearby, in blood-drenched robes. Three dead Romans around Michael indicated he had made the Romans pay for his life. Sin's body was not found.

Sextus shuddered. The still, waxen forms of people he had known, the terrible butchery of war. He would never get used to it.

He continued his inspection. The library had been stripped clean. Not a scroll remained. Likewise the scriptorium -- one desk there was overturned -- the kitchen and storerooms. Sextus decided the Essenes had carried out a carefully prepared plan to transfer all valuables and key personnel to the cliff caves by the Salt Sea, where it would be difficult to dislodge them.

In the following days the Romans attacked and cleared some caves, but did not find the main cache of missing scrolls. Their efforts became less and less productive. Finally, the day arrived when Trajan was well enough to travel. There was nothing more to keep the legion at Qumran. Whatever threat the Essenes posed had been removed. Their leaders were dead, their ranks devastated, their gold and storehouse of key documents sealed away in unknown, hidden locations.

So the great Xth Fretensis legionnaires broke camp and began the long march north toward Jericho, their column stretched across the desert with the ruins of Qumran, engulfed in flames, receding behind them.

Chapter XIX

Derek awoke with a start. At first he could see nothing in the darkness, then, as his eyes adjusted, he made out two large men standing beside his bed, and Four-fingers Guzik a few feet away.

Cold fear swept over him. He sat up, heart pounding, right hand reaching for the revolver in his nightstand.

A backhand blow caught him across his right cheek.

"No cute stuff, professor," one of the large men said. He pointed at a chair by the kitchen table. "Get up and sit over there." Both seemed massive in the poor light, heavily muscled, bodies crammed into tight-fitting wrinkled suits.

Derek, shaking, near panic, moved cautiously, eyes riveted on the intruders. He swung his legs to the floor, toes feeling for his slippers.

"I said move," the man shouted. He grabbed the front of Derek's pajama top, jerked him to his feet and hurled him across the room. Derek crashed into the kitchen chair and slid to the floor, stunned, and now fully awake. He was amazed at the man's strength.

"Take it easy, Jack," Guzik said as Derek rose and sat down, eyes, wide with fear, staring at Jack. "We just want to talk to the professor, make him understand a few things." He snapped on a light over the kitchen sink, dimly illuminating the room.

"He don't understand nothing," Jack said, "but he will.

What did you think you was doing, professor, making a two hundred dollar payment on your gambling debt? That'll hardly pay the interest for a couple of days."

Guzik lit a cigar and strolled closer, the tip glowing in the gloom, a trickle of smoke drifting out of his nose.

"You're going to have to do a lot better, professor." He swung a chair around and straddled it, facing Derek. "That's why me and the boys are here. Now tell us how you're going to pay off this debt of yours. Never occurred to me you might be a deadbeat."

Derek, trembling, voice quavering, shook his head. "But I don't have any money. I've given you what I have. I -- "

The sudden slap caught him on the left cheek, knocking him to the floor again. He sat there, shocked, trying to struggle back into the chair. He slipped and fell, but finally sat down.

"Now try again," Jack suggested. "I'm sure you wouldn't want my friend here" -- he nodded toward the other hulking figure, now moving closer -- "to get into this. He's a lot meaner than I am."

"But I tell you I don't -- " He was barely audible.

The other man grabbed Derek's right arm, twisted it behind his back, forced it up, then released it. Derek screamed in agony. A follow up slap caught him again on the left cheek.

"Shut up man," Jack said. "Let's start all over again. Now tell us how you're going to pay off your debt. We didn't ask you to borrow the money, you know."

"Oh, my God," Derek moaned, "oh...oh...oh..."

Crying, gasping, completely terrorized, he bent forward, holding his aching arm in his lap. "Oh, God. No more...please. I'll do anything you say." He rocked back and forth, struggling for control, trying to think of something, anything that would prevent further pain.

He stopped sobbing, swallowed. "I do...have a plan," he managed. .

"We're waiting," Jack said.

"I've asked my girlfriend, Fran Brown, to marry me..."

He was still rocking, wincing, clutching his arm, breathing hard. "She has some savings. If she accepts...and I expect her to...I can get money from her."

Jack and the other big man looked at Guzik.

Guzik stared at him. "How much?"

"Several thousand." He didn't want to commit himself to a specific amount. His voice was a little stronger now.

Guzik thought a moment. "That won't work. I've seen her, She don't look that prosperous to me. Far as I can tell, all she's got is a couple of boobs that'd knock your eyes out. Man, how I'd like to get into her pants."

Blood rushed to Derek's head. Before he could control himself, he lunged at Guzik, shouting, "You filthy bastard, don't talk about her like that. I'll -- "

The bigger, unnamed man caught Derek, slammed him back into the chair, grabbed his right thumb and twisted. Derek's scream set off a flurry of action. Guzik stripped the case from a pillow and Jack stuffed one end in Derek's mouth.

"Cut out the noise, professor," he snarled.

Derek, rendered mute, sat there, eyes streaming, body jerking as he gasped for air, afraid to move.

"Now let's start over again," Jack said. "Doesn't seem there's much prospect of us getting our money back from that dame of yours."

Derek, quaking, glanced wildly from tormentor to tormentor, seeking some sign of compassion, trying to think.

"Well, professor --." Guzik flicked cigar ashes in Derek's lap. The other two eyed him, ominously. The silence lengthened. Suddenly Derek grunted and motioned toward the gag.

"Okay, but no more hollering," Jack said. "Now what do you have in mind?" He removed the pillowcase.

Derek coughed, worked his mouth, drew several deep breaths, wiped his nose with a pajama sleeve.

"There's another possibility." He swallowed. "I'll need some time. It's not as far fetched as it might sound." He gulped again, aware he was grasping at a straw.

"What are you talking about?" Jack asked.

"I have a friend who is conducting historical research here. He has uncovered information about some buried gold."

"Yeah?" Jack said, standing up straighter, moving closer.

Guzik stopped puffing, removed the cigar from his mouth and stared at Derek, waiting.

"This friend has interviewed a man who knows what went on here in the first century when the Romans were tearing up the place."

"Yeah?"

"He told my friend he knows the location of King Solomon's mines, or some other old Jewish treasure just as valuable."

Jack raised his hand, ready to strike. "That old turkey! King Solomon's mines are a myth."

Derek ran a hand through his hair, trying to remember what Fran had told him. "It was the part about the Jewish treasure I was referring to," he added.

"That doesn't sound much better," Jack said, "but get on with it. Where's all this buried gold?"

"Information about the location is in a report my friend and two other people are preparing, and it's recorded on an old scroll."

Jack rose angrily; his hand rose again, "You're feeding us a lot of bullshit."

"Wait a minute," Guzik said. "What was that about a scroll?"

Derek answered quickly, head bobbing up and down. "The scroll is made of copper, and that doesn't deteriorate, so the writing is clear." He filled in as many details as he could recall.

"I still think it's a lot of bullshit," Jack said, "but maybe we ought to run it by the chief. Let him decide if he wants us to check it out."

"That scroll business grabs me," Guzik said. "I know the council's interested in them old, antiquities things. Some people will pay a fortune for them." He eyed Derek. "Okay professor.

You bought yourself some time. Do whatever you have to, to find out about that gold and keep me informed. Then we'll decide what we should do."

The three men rose and left quietly.

Derek, perspiring, chest heaving, right arm and thumb aching, sat still on the kitchen chair several minutes, trying to grasp the enormity of what had happened. He rose, staggered to the nearby cupboard and removed a bottle of brandy. He filled a glass tumbler, gulped it down then carried the bottle and tumbler with him to his writing desk. He sat there trembling, downing more and more of the liquor. Within a few minutes, he felt better. The alcohol warmed his body and eased the pain, but his mind was not functioning.

He got up, lurched into the bathroom to examine his beaten face. To his surprise, the only marks were a distinct redness. Guzik's enforcers had done a skillful job, leaving little evidence he had been beaten and tortured other than a mangled thumb.

Derek returned to the desk, sat there gazing into space, waiting for an idea to come. Soon he had a starting point. I have to find out whatever it is Tom that professor and Sharon know about that gold. I've also got to press Fran to accept my marriage proposal. I may have to make a partial payment to those bloodsuckers, or even attempt a fast getaway, and I'll need her for that."

He continued thinking.

How can I push her for an answer when I've got to concentrate on getting information about the gold? And how can I get her to break with Tom? I have to get him out of the picture.

He thought some more. Finally, all the parts fell into place. Derek poured the rest of the brandy into his glass. He picked up a pen and wrote a note to Fran in sprawling letters, made almost grotesque by his stiff, swollen thumb:

> Fran, my dear,
> Just a note, old girl, to let you know
> I'll be out of town several days. Hope

to see you later in the week. Meantime,
I insist you have it out with Tom. Tell
him you are going to marry me.
Get him out of your life. I think you
owe me that much. Ta Ta for now.
Derek

As he picked up the note, his hand hit the tumbler, spilling the last of the brandy over a corner of the paper.

"Damn," he said, blotting it as best he could with another sheet of paper. He folded the note and rose, holding onto the desk to gain his balance. "Well, at least I know where to begin," he muttered. He dressed and left immediately.

Chapter XX

That overwhelming sense of loneliness had returned. Once again Sharon felt abandoned, alone in the world, as she left Tom's room and the King David. The empty, deserted streets of Jerusalem, rushing by outside the taxi window, reinforced that mood. They were dark, desolate, devoid of life, swept by occasional gusts of wind that whirled dirt and paper into and beyond the amber light surrounding lampposts at each corner.

She was mired in these feelings when the taxi pulled up before her apartment building. The driver had to speak to her twice. "Miss. Miss? We're here. Are you all right?"

She turned and looked at him. "Oh...Yes, thank you."

She paid the fare, entered the building and started up the dimly lighted stairway, her feet scraping on the gritty, un-swept steps. She paused at the top and started down the hall toward her room, fumbling in her purse for the key.

Not until she turned to insert it in the lock did she realize something was wrong. The door was ajar.

Sharon suddenly felt cold. Her hand trembled. She dropped the key.

Summoning all her courage, she pushed the door. It swung inward, squeaking loudly, then stopped. She pushed again. This time, squeaking even more, it opened all the way.

An odor of tobacco smoke assailed her nostrils. Simultaneously she saw the outline of a man's head against the square of light cast by the moon through the window.

Sharon gasped, shoved her right hand into her mouth to stifle a scream and turned to run. Then she heard the voice.

"Don't be frightened, my dear. I wanted to talk to you. The door wasn't locked. I felt certain you would return soon, so I decided to wait here in the darkness. I didn't want to attract undue attention."

Sharon flipped the wall switch, her heart still pounding. She recognized the voice. It belonged to the professor who had approached her in the school hallway about doing some typing for him.

"I don't understand, Doctor, coming here at this hour. If it's about that typing I'd rather talk another time."

The professor stood up and re-lighted his pipe. She noticed his right hand seemed badly swollen.

"I realize this is a bit unusual," he said, puffing vigorously, a cloud of smoke swirling around his head, "but I'm a night person. It never seems that different to me to conduct business at any hour, and I do need to settle this typing matter." He looked at her over the bowl of the lighted pipe, eyebrows raised.

Sharon hesitated. The situation was strange. He seemed tense, but not threatening. After a long pause, while she weighed all the factors, she finally said, "All right. We can talk, I guess. Would you like some coffee?"

"That would be nice." He seemed relieved.

"I'll get a can from my locker down the hall. Be right back."

Sharon turned left at the first hallway and stopped before a row of compartments lining one wall. She inserted a key in the one with her apartment number, pulled the door open and removed the coffee, a luxury made possible by the income she had received from Tom. Her mind snapped back to her visitor. Why was she so uneasy about him?

She started back without finding an answer. He could have contacted her at school. That wouldn't have delayed his typing more than a few hours. Sharon shrugged. There was no accounting for the reasoning of some persons.

She had been gone about five minutes when she approached her room again. Light was seeping out over the threshold. She pushed on the door and entered.

The professor was hunched over the table. The papers she had been working from, the notes and false starts, plus a few pages she had decided to type over, were spread in front of him. He jumped back, startled, a cigarette lighter in his hand, as she walked in.

"Oh, I didn't hear you," he said, visibly surprised. "I was examining your typing. It's very good." He backed away, looking very large in the glare of the lone, overhead, light bulb.

Sharon stood still. What had he been doing? He didn't have any business looking at her draft copies and notes. There was a long pause. Now she knew something was wrong.

"I think you had better go, professor," she said slowly. "Suddenly this seems more than just odd. I'm really not certain now why you're here. If you still want me to do some typing for you, you can reach me through the school employment office."

Derek remained silent a moment. "Perhaps you're right. I should have called. I apologize if I've upset you. But I do want you to type an article I've prepared for a London magazine. Why don't you drop by my office in the Liberal Arts building tomorrow and we'll discuss it."

Sharon nodded stiffly.

He buttoned his jacket and moved unsteadily toward the door. For the first time she realized he reeked of liquor. He turned.

"Good night, my dear. I'll see you tomorrow."

Sharon stood frozen in place as the door closed. She could hear her visitor's steps fading down the hall and on the stairs to the first floor. Then there was silence.

She recovered her key, locked the door and looked around the room. Something was wrong. She walked over to the table and examined the papers there. Some contained notes so jumbled only she could decipher them. Then she spotted three pages of rough draft typing and one or two more finished sheets she had discarded. He had arranged them neatly in one pile. They all dealt with the elliptical language in the copper scroll describing sites where the Zealots had buried gold and silver.

Could that be what he was after?

Cold fingers marched up her spine. The professor had something in his hand when she returned to the room. What was it? Oh, yes, a cigarette lighter. Could the lighter have been a camera? Had she permitted him to gain information he had no right to? Had he looked at the papers on the table before she came home to find him in the room? And did he photograph them? She felt certain he had. Yet, examining each page, she could find nothing she thought would make much sense to him.

Should she call Tom? She looked at the alarm clock on the nightstand by her bed. It was three a.m. She didn't want to disrupt his reading again, and actually had nothing to report other than a hunch. Finally, she dialed his number from the pay phone on the first floor.

"Hello?"

"Tom, it's Sharon. I apologize for disturbing you again, but something strange just happened."

She related the details of Derek's visit.

Tom remained silent after she finished, then said: "I don't know what to make of it, Sharon, but I'm glad you let me know. I'll keep it in mind in the event there are other developments that fit the same pattern."

Tom hung up. Sharon slowly returned the phone to its hook on the wall. Was Tom taking this too lightly? It seemed that way to her, but she knew why. He was impatient to get back to his reading. She could almost picture him picking up the Samuel transcript, dropping into his chair, then, with that intense concentration she knew he was capable of, returning to the world of Biblical times when the fate of Jerusalem was being decided.

Chapter XXI

The sky drifted low over Jerusalem. An eerie silence blanketed the city. Behind the north wall, Eleazor, son of Simon, wearily lifted his grimy head, straining to detect sound or movement in the surrounding countryside. His eyes were bloodshot, his face eroded by a lack of food. He heard nothing.

South of him, inside the Temple, John of Gischala and his band of brigands likewise waited in filthy rooms filled with debris accumulated during constant fighting with their neighbors. They, too, strained unsuccessfully to detect some audible signal in the enveloping stillness.

Further south, Simon, son of Gioras, stood on the roof of a partly burned grain storehouse, torched only days before by John's marauding forces. He scanned hills to the east, north and west and saw nothing. He and his followers also drifted in the void.

Each sensed a new, massive presence approaching. They could neither hear nor see it, but felt it, a dangerous force out there, moving toward them like a monster in a nightmare.

Others besides these three Zealot leaders sensed it, too. Thousands of half-starved Jews huddled in the ruins of their homes, in filthy inns and dilapidated buildings, aware great danger hovered just over the horizon. Some were residents. Some were pilgrims. Most were refugees. All were victims of the three bands of Zealot fanatics, thieves and highwaymen who had poured into Jerusalem from ravaged, war-torn Galilee, Samaria and Judea, and then fought savagely to exploit the city's rotting carcass.

Jerusalem's small band of Christians, among those who had fled into the Jewish capital, huddled in the basement of a partly destroyed home in the Lower City. They too listened to no avail.

The silence continued.

Then there was something, not sound, perhaps a vibration, a tremor in the ground.

Eleazor rose to peer through the crenelated battlements of the north wall. John lifted his bearded, dirt-encrusted face, all senses aquiver. Simon again searched the hills. And Symeon, bishop and leader of the Christians, first cousin of Jesus of Nazareth, placed an ear to the ground.

It was there again. A rhythmic beat made by pounding boots, movements of thousands of bodies, rolling wheels, animals straining, hooves striking rocky ground.

Now it was sound, a mixture of many sounds -- of shouted oaths, raucous laughter, a meaningless "Te Dum, Te Dum" chant of marching soldiers, and creaking, groaning noises from scaffold-like towers and terrible instruments of war -- ballistas, with their long, powerful throwing arms; and smaller catapults, including a launcher called the onager or "wild ass" because it leaped off the ground with a terrible kick when it hurled a missile at the enemy..

This faraway clamor of an army on the move emerged as three areas of sound, approaching Jerusalem in a great concave arc. From Emmaus to the west came the Vth Legion. From Jericho to the northeast came the Xth Fretensis Legion under its new commander, Sextus, replacing Trajan, who had been rushed to Ptolemais to recover from his burns. And from Caesarea to the north came the XVth and rebuilt XIIth.

Each advanced in combat march formation: A screen of horsemen in front. Then the archers and the engineers who would prepare the battlefield, Then the advance guard, the command staff, the baggage trains, siege engines and main force -- a forest of undulating bodies and vertical lances, glinting dully in weak April sunlight filtering through low clouds.

Inside Jerusalem the Zealot defenders rushed to the walls, listening to this pounding of marching feet, a sound rolling in louder and louder, engulfing the city, and spilling into the land beyond, each straining to sight the first enemy soldier.

"There!" one finally shouted, pointing --a lone horseman on the horizon to the northwest, transfixed in a momentary shaft of sunlight, glancing off breastplate and javelin.

"And there!" another proclaimed. He extended an arm toward the north, where a group of mounted men suddenly topped the line of hills.

"Over here, too!" another yelled. This time cavalrymen came over the rim of high ground to the northeast.

From his Temple compound headquarters, John of Gischala set aside his pangs of hunger and watched these harbingers. Spasms of fear dread and hate surged through his filthy, hairy body. Anger took over. He scribbled two notes, handed each to a runner, then shouted, "Commanders into the sanctuary!" The order was repeated down the line, growing fainter as the distance increased. Ten minutes later John, armed with quick answers to his two messages, entered the first of the two sacred areas, the Holy, and addressed his lieutenants, their bearded faces peering at him out of the gloom.

"I've offered a truce to Eleazor and Simon and recommended they join us in striking the Romans as they are making camp. They've accepted. Select units from their forces are en route here now. Prepare for battle."

* * *

A group of mounted Roman officers, freshly-polished armor flashing under the weak sun, topped Lookout Hill, the highest point opposite the north wall. A slim young officer, riding a prancing white stallion, led them. This was Titus, the new Roman commander succeeding his father, Vespasian, who only weeks before had been called to Rome to become emperor after

Nero's death.

Barely thirty, Titus was known as a daring and courageous leader, a reputation earned through his service in Germany and Britain, and as commander of the XVth Legion in Palestine. He was in the forefront of every battle, easily recognizable by his chiseled features, waved, closely cropped blond hair and strong chin.

Now, as he reined in his horse and looked out over the city of Jerusalem, his mind churned. *What a sight, the beating heart of the Jewish nation, a white-walled fortress. Conquer it and the war is over. Can I do it? Yes. And now I must begin.* He pulled in a deep breath, turned toward his legion commanders, waiting nearby, and pointed with his sword.

"Study the terrain, then I will give you your orders."

Before them they saw the first of three successive walls surrounding the city. The nearest and northernmost loomed ominously, thirty feet high, fifteen feet thick. Built by Agrippa II, grandson of Herod, it had been completed only a few years before. South of it, inside the city, and almost as formidable, stood a second older wall, and still further south a less visible, very ancient wall. Each had been constructed to protect Jerusalem as it expanded over the ages.

"Let us begin," Titus said. "Note that steep valleys protect the city on three sides. That's why Jerusalem has been virtually invulnerable over the ages. We can attack only from the north and down a limited arc on the east and west. "So you, Silaneous" -- Titus pointed with his sword -- "deploy the Fifth Legion on those hills northwest of the city. Bring your siege engines into range and prepare the ground to move battering rams forward."

He paused, pointed again. "You, Sextus, move the Tenth Legion onto the Mount of Olives, the high ground to the east and make similar preparations.

"And you, Larcius and Cestius, place the Fifteenth and Twelfth Legions in the area where we are now. I will set up a temporary headquarters here also and displace forward as preparations advance. Now move out."

* * *

The Jews surged along battlements of the northern and eastern walls as the three columns veered toward their destinations an hour later.

"Bastard Romans," one huge warrior bellowed, "you will reap death and disgrace here! You cannot conquer us! You will never know the joys of fornicating with our Jewish women. They won't submit to filthy beasts. The new Kingdom of David is being born. His power and glory will destroy you."

A cheer went up as he finished, accompanied by whistling, catcalls, clapping and jeering.

The Jews of John's force, among those shouting, settled back to watch. Then, with Simon and Eleazer's soldiers finally beside them, began slipping into the Kidron Valley, between them and the Tenth Legion. They formed a triple line, descended the slope, then advanced up the far side. So absorbed were the Xth legionnaires in making camp, the Jews were almost upon them before being discovered.

A bloodcurdling cry pierced the air: "Death to the unbelievers!"

They charged. Romans dashed for arms laid aside while they worked. Others fled up the hill toward the main body of the Xth. The Jews came howling after them, while more warriors poured out of the city to join the fight.

Titus, a half mile away on Lookout Hill, heard the shouting, cursing and clash of metal to the southeast. He looked up, saw the faraway Jewish lines advancing with no sign of a Roman counterthrust.

He leaped on his horse, spun the animal around, shouted to his executive officer standing nearby, "Have all cavalry units join me and send a cohort of foot troops after us!"

Titus, sword aloft, thundered down the hill. Single horsemen, then groups of horsemen, finally whole units, raced after him, closing the gap as trumpets blared and officers shouted commands. The still-forming column of Roman horsemen crashed into the Jewish flank and knifed through, scattering the attackers.

Titus wheeled his horse, faced the direction from which he had come. "Again!"

This time the Jews were ready. They slashed the horses' legs, thrust spears into their bellies, brought down mount after mount. Titus, shoved into an isolated pocket with two subordinate commanders, fought for his life. A huge warrior clad in wolf skins rushed him, spear raised, screaming, "You die, Roman, you die!"

A sweep of Titus' sword sent the man's head, gushing blood, spinning off to one side. A quick thrust stopped another attacking Jew.

"Fall back! Fall back!" Titus ordered.

A new sound came from up the hill -- shouted commands, a rustling of spears and arrows cleaving the air. At last, the Tenth was counterattacking.

Just then, the cohort of infantry hurtled down from the north, cutting, battering, ramming the Jewish flank, while more Jews plunged into the fray from the valley below.

For almost an hour the two armies swayed in an agony of death, then slowly the Jews gave ground, retreating into the city. Titus, gasping for breath, turned to his trumpeter.

"Sound assembly, then retreat."

He looked up to see the sun sinking into the western hills, lighting a scene of carnage. The date was April 23, 70 A.D. The first day of the battle for Jerusalem was over.

The following four days the Jews stayed within the city, shouting and cursing as the Romans leveled ground approaches on the west, north and east. On the fifth day the Vth Legion brought up a ballista, their most powerful siege engine, capable of hurling huge stones several hundred yards into massed enemy formations. It consisted of a basic, horizontal frame below two huge throwing arms.

"Take it away! It won't work!" the defenders shouted as legionnaires swarmed over the weapon and a sweating Roman struggled forward, carrying a sixty-pound rock. Suddenly he tripped, careened forward and fell on his face.

The Jews on the parapets collapsed in each other's arms,

laughing.

Another Roman recovered the rock, loaded it, then, joining other crewmembers, inserted a pole, and wrenched the two horizontal throwing arms backward under great tension. The pole broke and three of the Romans fell to the ground.

Now the Jews were ecstatic, again collapsing in laughter as the Romans started all over again. Finally, all was ready.

The throwing arms swept forward, leaping, crashing. The huge stone arced into the sky, cleared the wall and slammed into the massed Jewish defenders. For a moment there was stunned silence, then anguished cries for assistance.

At first the cries were faint, whispered by torn and mangled men, some with a broken arm, some with shattered legs, some ripped open. The appeals grew louder, more frantic, intermingled with screams of agony and new appeals for aid.

The Romans trundled a battery of smaller catapults forward, and reloaded the ballista. Again, the huge arms crashed forward. A new missile swept into the sky.

"Baby on the way!" a Jew shouted, a warning that became standard for incoming artillery. The descending stone smashed into the Jewish ranks again, repeating the savage toll.

"Pull back! Reduce wall units to half strength!" The command thinned forces on the battlements, presenting a less vulnerable target, exactly what the Romans wanted.

"Towers forward!"

The Jews heard the order ring out up and down the line. Whips cracked. Teams of oxen leaned into their harnesses. The ungainly structures, seventy-five-feet tall, braced with crossbeams and scores of vertical supports, advanced, creaking and groaning, on huge wooden wheels.

More catapults rolled ahead of them. More and more missiles whistled through the air. A shout went up as the first tower banged into the wall. Its crew wedged it into place. Roman soldiers swarmed over the scaffolding, grabbed ropes. They hauled back a huge, suspended beam, capped with a metal ram's head, then released it. It swung down and crashed into the stone wall.

The dull boom echoed through the city. People stopped and listened. The sound came again. A few moments of silence then a third boom. Like a slowly-cadenced drum, the sound took up a steady beat. Boom! Silence. Boom! Silence. Boom! The first of the great rams was in place.

* * *

Symeon spoke, weariness in his voice. Flickering light from the candle in the center of the room, accentuated the age and physical strain etched in his face. "I assume everyone understands the gravity of our situation. We must make decisions. There will be danger in any course, but greater danger if we remain here." His eyes scanned the encircling faces. The haunted expressions told him they did understand.

"Very well, we will hear from our two youngest members, who have just returned from a food gathering mission outside the city."

All eyes focused on James and Sokker, grandsons of Jude, one of the brothers of Jesus. James spoke first. He swallowed. Tension lines appeared around his mouth. Perspiration dotted his forehead..

"We must leave the city or we'll starve," he finally managed. "We can escape to the south. The Romans are patrolling there, but their main forces are in the north. With two persons leading who know the ground, we should be able to get through at night. On our last trip we could purchase only one sack of grain, enough to feed us another few days, but we can't be certain of even such meager rations in the future."

"That's right," Sokker chimed in. "While James bargained at one of the farms I stood guard. I saw Romans rob two Jews carrying gold to buy food. Legionnaires are swarming into the area now on their own time, hoping to intercept such gold bearers."

"But you think we can escape?" Symeon asked.

"In small groups, yes," James replied. "I suggest Sokker and I evacuate the church elders first, take them across the

Hinnom Valley into the hills beyond. From there they can strike out for the Jordan River, cross over and assemble in Pella, where the others can join them later."

"Any comments?" Symeon asked. No one spoke. "All right, the elders first. The Mother Mary, sisters Assia and Lydia, and the two brothers, Joseph and Simon next. The remaining disciples and I will wait until the final trip."

Everyone turned toward the group around a serene, gray-haired woman in a corner of the room. She nodded in acknowledgment, a faint smile on her deeply lined face, then all eyes shifted back to Symeon. He cleared his throat.

"Brethren, before we part, I must pass on sorrowful news. This morning I received confirmation of earlier reports that our friend Simon Peter was crucified in Nero's Circus on Vatican Field near Rome six years ago and buried there. The confirming message was brought by a Jew who slipped through Roman lines last night. He said he had been in Rome when the execution took place, and had been en route to Palestine ever since. Peter was forced to watch the Romans kill his wife before he died. Likewise, he said Paul, who made a flaming torch of the Christian message, was crucified in the same area later that year. Let us pray for their salvation."

As Symeon extended his hands to clasp those of the men next to him, a voice from the corner asked, "What news is there of Jude, honored Symeon." The brother Joseph was asking.

Symeon sighed. "As you know he preached in Judea, Samaria, Idumea, Syria and Mesopotamia. When last heard from he had entered Persia. It is my understanding he was killed on Mount Ararat and the Christians there have elevated him to sainthood."

Total silence enveloped the room, then Symeon began the traditional prayer. "Our Father who art in Heaven -- "

* * *

Jerusalem drifted into chaos. A great stench enveloped the city. Drunken soldiers staggered through the streets. Starving Jews fell in the gutters, unable to rise. Their bodies were left for roaming dogs to consume, or were thrown over the wall to rot in the valleys below. John's brigands returned to raiding the northern and southern areas controlled by Eleazor and Simon. They burned and looted, stole food, raised a din of shouted oaths and screams of rage and pain.

Amid this bedlam, the thunder of the battering rams continued day and night. The Jews named the largest of them "Victor" -- and with good reason. On May 7, after fifteen days of pounding, a portion of the west wall crumbled. Jewish forces fought savagely, defending the opening, but the Romans crashed through in a night assault, forcing the defenders back behind the second wall.

"Victor" advanced until wedged against a northwest corner tower of that barrier. This time he did his job in four days. The wall and tower were there one moment, crammed with shouting, spear-throwing Jews, then a block under assault shattered. The tower teetered, swayed, pitched forward.

The Jewish faces and bodies hurtled outward in a still intact tower and seemed to hang there momentarily. Then the tower disintegrated into individual blocks and human forms, raining down on the Romans below. The legionnaires attacked immediately, driving the Jews back into Fortress Antonia and other areas behind the oldest city wall.

For two days after that Titus rested his forces. The Romans washed clothes and cleaned and polished equipment, preparing a psychological assault to convince the Jews they should surrender. On the third day, half the Xth Legion marched around the northern end of the city to level ground opposite Herod's tomb on the west side. They joined units from the other legions waiting there.

Titus, a scarlet cloak flying from his shoulders, polished armor and plumed helmet flashing in the sun, galloped up with his commanders, halting just beyond archery range. He faced the sharply etched legion ranks. With a scraping sound, he unsheathed his sword, raised it aloft and shouted, "Prepare the parade!" Trumpets blared. Orders sounded. Ranks snapped to attention.

Titus swept his sword downward. "Execute!"

Trumpets pealed a new martial call as the left foot of every soldier struck the ground simultaneously. Drums rolled and pounded. A deep-voiced, male chorus thundered a marching hymn, praising the glories of Rome. The legionnaires surged forward, arms pumping, heads erect. Once again the hypnotic beat of marching men battered the walls of Jerusalem.

For an hour, the soldiers surged by, turned left opposite the northern wall, then curled back to halt in a column front facing the western battlements, just out of range of Jewish arrows and spears. The Jews watched in silence. They had never seen such a mighty army.

Tables suddenly appeared before every century as the last cohort swung into line. Men struggled forward with clanking sacks of coins. Each man answered as his name was called and received his pay.

Then wagons rattled up. Carcasses of oxen, lamb and pig were hoisted on spits over newly lighted fires. Succulent odors of cooking meat drifted toward the starved Jews lining the city walls. Groans of anguish arose and mounted in volume. Finally, envy burst into flames.

"Bastard Romans," John of Gischala shouted, "choke on your filthy food!" He brandished a sword. Others joined the outcry, raging and screaming.

Finally, Titus deployed his last weapon. Joseph, the former Jewish commander in Galilee captured at Jotapata, moved forward and faced the wall.

He eyed his countrymen there. They stared back, recognizing him immediately, aware he had changed his name to Josephus Flavius, was cooperating with the Romans, and was writing a history of the war. Reports that he was trying to stop the fighting had circulated widely in Jerusalem.

"Traitor! Coward!"

The epithets began as isolated shouts, then rained down, increasing in volume to a thunderous chant. Stones, hurled from the battlements, battered the ground in front of him, all falling short. Joseph, thirty-three, pulled his short, slender body erect, raised his right arm, palm outward, and shouted back:

"You obdurate fools! Can't you see what you're doing? Throw away your weapons. Take pity on your birthplace. Turn around and gaze at the beauty of what you are betraying."

The shouts from the wall grew louder and more insulting." Cowardly bastard! Your mother was a whore! You lick women!"

Joseph persisted, undeterred.

"What a city! What a Temple! Against these will any man direct the flames? What deserves to be kept safer than all this. Pity your families. Let each man set before his eyes his wife and children and parents, so soon to perish...if you don't lay down your arms."

Derisive laughter greeted him. Another shower of stones descended. Josephus finally gave up. Despondent, he shrugged, shook his head in despair and returned to the Roman lines. He knew now the situation was hopeless. His beloved Jerusalem would be destroyed. The Jews would not surrender.

* * *

The next day the final battle began. The half-crazed Jews stormed out of the city daily to attack the Romans. They set fire to the assault towers, seized and tortured prisoners, captured supplies. The surcease once afforded by darkness ended. Every night, before the moon came up, hundreds of darting figures appeared outside the Roman encampments. They seized sentries, scaled the encampment barricade, ripped open tents, took whatever they could find, tossed oil and flaming torches atop the leather enclosures, then dashed away, shrieking and cackling with laughter.

Titus, enraged by these forays and by reports that Jews were escaping through Roman lines at night, raised an earthen barricade around the city. This *circumvallatio*, manned and fortified, shut off further flights.

Now Jerusalem truly starved. Jews tried to escape in mass rushes. In a single night in July, two thousand were captured. Many were ripped open by

Romans who believed they had swallowed gold coins. Others were hoisted on crosses within sight of the city walls to terrify the Jews inside into submission.

It did no good. The battle continued.

On July 22 battering rams broke through into Fortress Antonia. The Romans overran the exhausted defenders and advanced to the northern edge of the Temple wall. A few days later, they reached the Temple itself.

* * *

At first, the dimly lighted room seemed deserted. An oil lamp flickered on a table in the corner, but there was no sound, no movement in the early morning darkness. James and Sokker edged down the steps, fearing the worst. They paused in the doorway, searching the shadows for some sign of those they had left there two weeks before. As their eyes adjusted they saw a bony hand grasp the looped handle of the lamp and lift it. A bearded, wrinkled face appeared in the elevated globe of light and a querulous voice asked, "Who's there? Who disturbs this sacred hour of sleep?"

"Symeon?" said Sokker. "Where are the others? What has happened?"

The aged figure shuffled forward, holding the lamp above his head. "God be praised!" he said softly. "It is you, James, Sokker. We had given you up for dead. The three remaining members of our group are close by."

He advanced again, then stopped as the lamp's pale light revealed the two haggard faces. "You look terrible. How long since you've eaten? Come quickly. We have a little gruel and some bread crusts. Eat first. Then we'll talk."

Symeon shuffled to a darkened corner of the room, felt along the wall, pushed back a concealed door. In the fetid, inner chamber, James and Sokker saw three lumpy forms on the floor, a cold stone hearth and grimy bowls on a table. James and Sokker tore savagely at the shards of bread Symeon thrust at them and tilted the bowls of gruel to their lips, licking the last remnants from the splintered wooden interior.

James ran the back of a dirty hand across his mouth, looking intently at Symeon. In the corner of the room, he could hear the lumpy forms beginning to stir. "We must get you out of here."

"How?"

"We've made arrangements. The city will fall in a few days. If you're caught you'll be killed or enslaved, and right now the Romans are not interested in slaves."

"How soon must we leave?"

"It will be daylight soon. We cannot go now, but tonight, before the moon rises, we must go. As we entered Jerusalem last night, the Romans were setting fire to the double doors into the inner Temple. In a few hours, the Temple will be captured and the Romans will overrun the Lower City where we are now.

"Outside the situation is equally bad. The Romans have encircled Jerusalem with a fortified earthen wall. That's why we were without food for a time and so long in getting back. We couldn't find a way through. Then Sokker noticed something familiar about the commander of Roman forces along the southern part of the barricade, and finally recognized him. He is Cornelius, the Roman that Peter baptized at Caesarea. We met him later that year. He was the first Gentile brought into the faith."

James scrubbed grimy knuckles into his bloodshot eyes, sighed wearily. "Once we were certain, we approached him while he was walking outside Roman lines one day. 'Peace be with you,' I said, moving my right hand in the sign of the cross. He was startled. 'Every day is a good day for peace,' he replied. I kept talking while Sokker drew the outline of a fish in the dirt. Cornelius recognized the symbol of Peter the fisherman."

"'Do I know you?'" he asked.

"'We have met, Sire,' I said. We identified ourselves. He allowed us to pass through the Roman lines, and arranged for us to slip back through again tonight, under the pretext we are Roman spies. We must reach his Outpost Number Four before dawn. Sentries there will expect us, but one wrong move and we could be killed."

James and Sokker discussed their plan with Symeon another hour, then fell into exhausted sleep.

* * *

All day the battle raged. The Romans charged through the charred ruins of the double doors into the inner Temple. The Jews fought back ferociously. Missiles from three captured catapults on top of the Temple rained down on the Roman formations. A deafening din filled the air -- Roman swords clanging against Jewish shields, shouted oaths and commands, screams of pain and anger, and the pounding of the battering rams against unbreached parts of the Temple walls.

By midday the Romans controlled the Court of the Women and assaulted the steps leading to the Court of the Israelites and the blood-stained altar beyond. This too fell and legionnaires advanced into the Priests Court and down the outer walls of the sanctuaries.

Midway in the battle a Roman soldier, riding the shoulders of a colleague, hurled a torch into the Holy of Holies where the Zealots stored supplies, including olive oil. Flames exploded through the window and out the doors, casting an eerie glow over the shattered city as night descended.

* * *

James and Sokker saw this illuminated northern sky as they led their group from the basement room into the darkened street. Sokker paused, the others clustering around him, gazing at the distant flames on the highest point in Jerusalem. The fire formed a halo around a clearly etched Temple, its white, columned front, shrunken by distance, standing out against the fiery background.

"It's the end," Sokker said quietly.

"What have we done?" Symeon muttered. "The Zealots have led us to disaster."

James tugged on Symeon's robe. "We must go. There is nothing we can do. Jerusalem is doomed." He led them down the narrow, twisting street. In single file they entered an alley, then edged down circular stone steps to a rocky cavern below. James moved into a tunnel descending into a channel of waist-deep water, obscured in darkness. For an hour they stumbled forward, holding the garment of the person in front, at times tripping and falling, rising, calling out until contact was reestablished.

Just as it seemed they could bear the ordeal no longer, the stone floor rose and water dropped to ankle depth. They stumbled out onto dry ground, a hillside bathed in pale starlight two hundred yards outside the city walls. Before them the ground dropped into the Hinnom Valley. Beyond that black pit, torches flared along the Roman's earthen barricade.

"Outpost Number Four is that cluster of lights to our right front," James said. "We must go directly there. A misstep will bring a Roman patrol down on us, so be careful. If you're rested, let's move out."

The column of six dark figures wound down the hillside. Symeon, stumbling, fell and mumbled an oath. Sokker grinned. "Remember, you are the bishop." Symeon glared at him. The descent continued until the ground leveled off, then began to ascend. Suddenly a human voice wailed in anguish above Sokker's head.

"My God! My God! Save me!" The voice subsided into incoherent mumblings and groans of pain.

Sokker, heart pounding, looked up. A naked man hung from a cross directly above him, head rolled back, eyes gazing at the dark sky. The outcry set off shrieks of despair further up the slope. Sokker, peering into the darkness, could make out crosses as far as he could see in every direction, each with its contorted figure nailed in place.

"Let's get out of here," Symeon whispered, his voice edged with fear.

With great difficulty, they climbed the valley's ascending slope. At one point, a Roman patrol, just off duty, crossed in front of them, the men talking and laughing en route to their quarters. James froze in place, raising a warning hand. The danger passed.

The moon rose, casting dim light over the ground. Slowly, the earthen barricade became visible. The guard tower of Outpost

Number Four rose in stark silhouette against the sky to their right. James edged closer, a finger to his lips. He raised his head and howled, imitating a wolf. He waited. No response. Once more his mournful wail floated in the night air. This time a responding wail echoed back. He motioned the others to follow and crawled forward. A Roman command shattered the stillness.

"Halt! Identify yourself!"

"The ways of Jupiter are strange and just," James responded.

"Just indeed," the voice replied. "Advance and state your mission."

James stood and walked boldly forward. He conferred with the sentry then returned to his companions.

"We can proceed now, but let me do the talking." The group advanced wearily. They were led to the commander's tent, where James entered while the others waited. A half hour later, he reappeared with a pass in his hand.

"We can go now."

The tent flaps opened behind him. A stocky, grizzled man appeared in the triangular fragment of light that spilled into the night. He stared at the pitiful group of Christians.

"Peace be with you," he said softly.

"And unto you, peace," James replied. "Your kindness will be remembered in heaven."

The Roman nodded. James turned and led his group up a tortuous, hillside path. By the time they reached the summit, they were exhausted.

"We are safe here," Sokker said, gazing toward the brightening sky in the east. "We'll rest until the sun comes up."

They sat in silence, watching as dawn bathed Jerusalem's domes, towers and walls in searing white light. The city looked stark and naked, surrounded by hills stripped of trees by the Romans. In their place, a ghastly forest of crosses studded the slopes, each with its crucified Jew.

To Sokker, the spectacle dramatized the foolishness of the Zealots, the brutality of the Romans and the horror of a world in which man inflicted suffering on his fellow man in a never-ending cycle of violence.

James and Sokker rose wearily and motioned the others to follow. They struggled up to the top of the ridge. Sokker looked back one more time at the sunlit, smoking ruins of Jerusalem. The tragedy was complete. The Temple had been captured the day before, August 29, 70 A.D. Three days later the Romans overran the Lower City and Herod's Palace, then the Upper City on September 26.

The battle for Jerusalem was over.

Chapter XXII

Week after week the candle burned in the darkness, casting an amber glow over the interior of the cave. It revealed a battered bench next to a smoke-blackened hearth and fireplace oven. Nearby, chairs, piled one upon the other, loomed in the darkness. A rude bed stood next to the earthen wall, and timbers of pine and cedar rose in neat stacks near the entrance. Opposite the ledge where the candle flickered, tools of the carpenter's trade hung from a rack -- iron saws, chisels, an axe, rasp, hammers and an adze. A deep coating of dust covered it all.

The candle burned lower as time drifted by until only a stump sputtered in the gloom. Then one day that too died, projecting a final flicker of light over the small tile under it, resting on a fragment of inscribed parchment. Darkness closed in, encasing the room in the black silence of a tomb.

Months later the exterior door was thrown open. Brilliant light swept into the outer room and seeped into the attached chamber. Just as suddenly it was blotted out as Sokker edged through the entrance, carrying bundles under each arm, and dropped them on the floor. He stepped back through the open door. Once again light flooded the long-sealed residence as Sokker's voice was heard in muted conversation with others outside. His words became distinct and clear when the door opened again and people pushed through, then receded as they left.

"Put the grain over there," Sokker said, "and see if you can get a fire going."

The pulse of life returned to the home.

Assia walked up the hill to Mary's Well and returned balancing a jug of water on her head. The brothers Joseph and Simon chopped wood, and Lydia and Susanna, Symeon's sister, attacked the dust on the furnishings with straw brooms and rags. By nightfall warmth coursed through the Nazareth home and gruel bubbled in the oven.

James, seated atop a low stool, surveyed the faces assembled around the slab of rock in the center of the room, used as a table. He could see a veneer of well-being there, overlying privations of the recent past. His eyes locked onto the steady gaze of Symeon, the ancient patriarch seated next to the aged, serene Mother Mary, resting in the best chair in the room. Symeon's snow-white hair spilled down his head to mingle with the tangled mass of his beard. Across his face, the lines of time had collapsed into a mass of wrinkles, but the piercing blue eyes flashed with life, purpose and determination.

"We have much to be grateful for," James said, his voice tight with emotion. "We have come through a difficult time. I suggest our bishop lead us in prayer."

Symeon's ancient, cracked voice filled the cave with a paean of gratitude for deliverance from the hell of a dying Jerusalem, and concluded with the traditional "Amen"--so be it.

James smiled. "Now I propose a toast of thanksgiving." He extracted a bottle of wine from the bag beside his stool.

"In the name of Jehovah," Symeon asked, "where did you get that?"

"Sokker found it at the bottom of the larder pit over in the corner. How it survived undiscovered I'll never know."

A filled cup passed from person to person. James continued:

"Now we must make plans. Our leadership of the numerous Christian communities has dwindled to the group in this cave. We have to reestablish communications with our followers in Pella, Antioch, Caesaria, Damascus and Alexandria, and more distant groups in Greece. But first we must find a way to survive. Without that, everything dies. We have only a small amount of grain left, and no way to replenish it once it's gone."

"What do you suggest?" Symeon's croaking voice broke the silence that followed. "Your judgment, and Sokker's, was eminently correct in getting us out of Jerusalem."

"There is the farm."

"That's right," Sokker added. "James and I lived there three years ago, then fled when the Romans marched across Galilee. I don't think it was damaged much in that campaign. The servants left with us, but we lost contact with them during the ensuing confusion."

"What's there?" Lydia asked. "I've heard about the farm since I was a child but I've never seen it."

Sokker turned to face her. "The accommodations are poor. The house is crude. James and I lived there with our great uncle James, our first bishop, before he was killed eight years ago, and again afterward. We spent most of our time tending crops and clearing land. But an adequate house can be built, and the soil is deep and rich.

"There's a stream of fresh water nearby," James added. "And in the evening, when the sun drops behind Carmel, the hills turn to fire and the grain fields are brushed with gold. There we can heal our wounds, rebuild our numbers and construct a church. Some of us will have to live in a tent for a time, but it is a solution to our dilemma."

Symeon closed his eyes, thinking. When he opened them he looked at James. "You agree this is possible."

"I agree."

"How should we proceed?"

"I think Sokker and I should leave for the farm tomorrow. We'll scout the place, reestablish our claim and take possession. Some grain may still be growing wild in the fields. If so, there will be dove and other game nearby. We can harvest those seeds and set traps, then one of us will return and begin transferring everyone here to the farm. Sokker and I will concentrate on getting a new crop in the ground. Everyone else will have to help build a new house. It's already fall so it won't be easy. But with good fortune, we can harvest some grain in the spring and will have a roof over our heads."

Symeon sighed, grimacing as he rubbed a knee. "These old bones of mine have grown quite ancient. They can't withstand any more long marches, but the rest of you should go. Susanna and I will remain here. Nazareth is our home."

James frowned. "I hate to see the family divided."

"I know, but as bishop of the church I must try to restore cohesion to our movement, and I can do that better here than from an isolated farm. But I agree we should build a new base. You and Sokker will have to carry on from there after I'm gone. How far is it?"

"Two days to the west, in the heart of the Plain of Esdraelon."

"Then we'll do as you and Sokker suggest. And now I recommend we retire. You'll need strength for your trip tomorrow."

James and Sokker rose at dawn, hoisted packs and were into the hills west of Nazareth by the time the sun rose. On the second day, they topped a low rise. There before them lay fields of the farm they had abandoned in 67 A.D., a tangle of weeds and stalks of wild grain. James pointed. "Look, Brother, the house is intact."

"And smoke's coming from the chimney."

They studied the two-room structure, then cautiously approached. At that moment the door opened. Three men emerged, talking animatedly as they walked toward a nearby shed. James and Sokker halted, studying them.

"I believe -- " James began.

"It's them!" Sokker broke into a run.

The three men turned, staring at the two figures racing toward them, shouting. "David, Solomon, Jonah!"

"Master James -- " one of them said, then also shouted,

"And Sokker. I can't believe -- "

The two owners and their former servants embraced in a frenzy of back pounding and tears of joy. "Where did you come from?" Jonah kept asking. "We thought you were dead."

Over cups of gruel, James and Sokker recalled how they had fled toward Nazareth ahead of the Roman advance. The servants said they were scattered by a cavalry charge, but returned to the house individually months later to live off the grain still growing in the trampled fields.

James and Sokker settled in. They worked from before dawn until after dark. Under their healing hands, two fields were cleared and planted, a small reserve of grain collected and stored, and part of it taken to Nazareth. The house was cleaned, the roof repaired and a tent erected to shelter family members when they arrived. At the end of the month Sokker returned to Nazareth and brought back the Mother Mary, Joseph, Simon, Lydia and Assia, while James stayed at the farm, clearing and planting a third field.

The day after their arrival Sokker addressed the brothers, Joseph and Simon. "Why don't you dig a pit, pour in clay, water and straw, trample the mixture with your feet, and make the sun-dried, earthen bricks we will need to build our new home."

He turned to the sisters. "And you, Assia and Lydia, might take those stones over there" -- he nodded toward a pile collected in clearing fields for planting -- "and lay a foundation and floor, following a plan I will draw on the ground. You can chip and fit them together as you go."

They all accepted their assigned tasks.

Every day after that, James and Sokker looked up from their labors in the fields to see the house slowly rising from the ground. In the late fall, Sokker returned to Nazareth and piled unused timbers in Joseph's workshop on the backs of three braying, protesting donkeys, borrowed from neighbors. He hauled the lumber to the farm where he and James used the wood to frame the roof and make furniture.

By January, with freezing winds sweeping down from the Galilean hills, the house was complete, strong and well-built, smoke spiraling from a newly finished chimney. James' heart swelled with pride as he noted all this one morning from the nearest field. *We've done it. The crops are planted. We have shelter, a small grain reserve and hunting and trapping this winter will provide extra food. We'll survive.*

They did, and when the days grew warmer and green sprouts appeared in the fields, he knew bountiful relief was on the way.

In this fashion the weeks slipped by. Six months later they constructed a church. The Christians in Pella and Antioch came to visit, help with the construction and to worship. All this activity seemed strange to their Jewish neighbors, but no one interfered. Indeed, gradually, the Jews accepted them, particularly after they donated grain to help nearby farmers survive an unexpected dry period.

The Romans also left them alone, although patrols occasionally stopped to note what they were doing. Then one day in the spring of 81 A.D., James and Sokker were clearing a new field when two riders appeared on the trail from Nazareth. James rose up from his stooped position and watched them approach.

"Romans," Sokker said. He also was watching.

"Maybe they'll pass," James replied. "We must go on with our work as if we see Romans every day."

Both returned to their labors, but were aware the horsemen were riding across the fields toward them.

James stood erect again, spooned a gourdful of water into his mouth from a clay vessel then laved more water over his hands and face. He had rinsed off the worst of the grime when the leading Roman, a centurion, halted his horse a few feet away and leaned across his saddle.

"We are looking for the Ben Joseph family," he said. "Can you direct us to their farm?"

"We are of that name." James replied.

"And what is your given name?"

"James. This is my brother, Sokker."

Sokker nodded.

The Roman eyed them carefully. "Perhaps you can answer my questions. I am informed your family is of the House of David, that you are descended from the Hebrew king of that name. Is that correct?"

"Yes," James said.

"It is also reported you teach the strange, new doctrines of Christianity, and a central belief is that a new kingdom will be established in this part of the province of Syria. Is that also correct?"

"The kingdom is emerging now," James replied, "but it is not of this world. Its beliefs and rewards are spiritual. They will come to each Christian only upon his death."

"You teach this?"

"When we can, but as you can see we are farmers. We have only a few persons to teach at any given time. We must sow and must reap. Our days are full and exhausting. We have little time for more."

"You farm only?" the centurion asked.

"Throughout the planting, growing and harvesting seasons. During the winter months we do visit Christian friends and they visit us."

"You do not advocate resistance to Roman rule with your belief in this new kingdom?"

"What we teach and believe does not concern this world or Caesar. We are not fomenting rebellion."

"Are you expecting a Messiah to lead you to this new kingdom?"

"The only true Messiah, our great uncle, Jesus, was crucified, rose from the dead and ascended into Heaven. He will return one day. But again, what he taught, and what we teach, is no challenge to Roman rule. We are concerned not with this world but the next, when you Romans, too, shall be judged." There was an edge in James' voice.

"You are leaders in this faith, yet you say you are farmers," the centurion said. "Let me see your hands. They will tell me whether you spend your days in toil, or are traveling the countryside exhorting the Jews to rise against the Emperor Domitian, under a new leader from your House of David."

James thrust his hands forward, palms up. Sokker did likewise.

The centurion swung down from his horse. He examined their rough, horny calluses, then prodded and probed the arms, shoulders and legs of each man.

Satisfied, he mounted again.

"I believe you are farmers. Make certain that is what you remain. We will be watching. Also I must inform you we have arrested your relative Symeon in Nazareth. He has been taken to Antioch for trial on charges of inciting the populace with his incessant talk of your coming new kingdom. If found guilty he will be crucified. Let this be a warning to you. We will not tolerate subversion from members of the House of David, or any other Christians or Jews." The Romans rode off in the direction from which they had come.

James and Sokker stood frozen in place, watching, stricken.

"My God," Sokker whispered. "Symeon arrested?"

"We have to help him, Brother."

Both men sprinted toward the house. By nightfall they were far down the trail to Nazareth. They hiked through the night. When they reached Joseph's Cave the next day, they found a tearful Susanna, Symeon's sister, packed and waiting. She rushed into Sokker's arms.

"They have taken Symeon. I tried to stop them, but they wouldn't listen."

Sokker tried to comfort her. "We must get you to the farm for better protection, but first we must free Symeon."

"It's no use," Susanna said. "He is already in Antioch. He left orders you were not to follow. He kept repeating the future of the church now is in your hands. You must not risk getting entangled with the Romans. He made me swear I would convince you not to come after him because that would imperil the future of our movement."

"But we must help," James said. "We cannot stand idly by. He is the bishop of our church."

"It is for that very reason you must follow orders. He is your superior."

"It would be cowardly not to help him," Sokker argued. "Surely there is something we can do."

Susanna broke down, sobbing, shoulders heaving, head bowed. "I tried to change his mind, but he was adamant. Finally, I came to understand the wisdom of what he was saying. He has no fear of death. He has had a long and fruitful life. He wants others to have as much fulfillment.They can if they have our faith to believe in. But if you go after Symeon and endanger the chances of that faith surviving, you will have destroyed the very essence of our being."

James and Sokker looked at her in silence.

James swallowed. There was a long pause. "I guess we have no alternative," he muttered. His voice was almost inaudible.

Sokker shouldered Susanna's bundles, and started down the trail leading east, Susanna following. James stayed behind to close their Nazareth home.

He walked into the outer room and gazed at the scene he knew so well -- the glowing embers in the fireplace, the iron cooking vessels, the jug of water in a corner, the chairs, once again stacked neatly.

James wandered into the attached chamber. Memories arose, crowding his mind. He heard voices whispering there. The voice of Jesus. The voice of Joseph, father of Jesus. Voice of the mother, Mary. The voices of Bishops James the Just and Symeon.

James walked slowly to the back wall, turned and studied the scene, burning it into his memory. He knew he would never live here again. Then, overcome with emotion, tears coursing his face, he walked quickly outside, past the still-unnoticed, burned-out candle in the wall niche, above eye level, and the tile and enscribed parchment beneath it. He closed the door, turned up the street and struck out with steady strides toward the western hills, the unknown future of the Christian religion going with him.

Part Three

Reaping

Chapter XXIII

Daybreak. Tom put down the last page of the manuscript. His eyes were bloodshot and burning from reading through the night. He felt stiff and drained, but his thoughts were racing. Question after question tumbled through his mind, propelled by a rising sense of excitement. Why did this hastily assembled information have such an aura of authenticity? His research methods had been rudimentary, yet the story had fidelity and unity, and implications so astounding he was almost afraid to put them into words.

Tom rose, began to pace. Three times he started toward the phone, then, glancing at his watch, thought better of it. It was only six o'clock. He stepped to the window, gazed down at the hotel veranda below, trying to deal with the turmoil in his mind.

Who or what had been in the secret, guarded chamber at Qumran? Had that person transported the tile, picked up near Trajan's burned and unconscious body, to Joseph's cave in Nazareth? What was all this about the tile being atop a piece of inscribed parchment? Was the parchment still there? He did not recall feeling anything in the niche other than the tile when he had discovered it after striking the cave wall.

But if it was there he felt certain now that it was a message. The tile was used to hold the message in place, and the candle on top of the tile was there to attract attention to the message, although it failed to do so.

Finally, he had a whole series of questions about the family farm in the Plain of Esdraelon. Did Samuel know its location? He hadn't said he did. Did he have any idea what happened to the descendants of James and Sokker and other members of Christ's family? Did they go on living there? Could anyone from the Ben Joseph family still be in the area?

This time Tom didn't stop, He walked to the phone and dialed.

The answering voice was foggy with sleep.

"Hello."

"Fran? Fran, this is Tom. Please don't hang up. I must talk to you. It's important. Very important. Please hear me out."

There was no answer, but the line stayed open.

"First of all I apologize for calling so early, but I need your help, and I want very much to regain your friendship. Life is pretty grim without at least that much."

Her silence continued, then: "I'm listening." Her voice was strained.

"As for what you saw at the camp, I want you to know I was not the instigator."

"That's pretty crummy, Tom, blaming it on the girl." She sounded far away, remote.

"I guess...well, maybe it is at that. I'll leave explanations for another time." He paused, hoping she would respond, but heard only labored breathing so continued.

"I've just finished reading the final compilation of everything we got from Samuel. The implications are more than I dare trust to my judgment alone. I'd like very much for you and Dr. Abe to read it, and give me your thoughts. Do you suppose --"

"Tom," Fran broke in, still speaking with difficulty, "I think it only fair to tell you I've decided to marry Derek. Obviously our relationship can never be the same because of that, and because of your involvement with Sharon."

Now it was Tom's turn to be silent. Despair gnawed his stomach.

"I guess I should have expected that," he managed in a cramped voice. "I had hoped it wouldn't happen, but it doesn't change my need to regain your friendship and get your help. I was wondering -- "

"What is it you want, Tom?"

"I was wondering if you and Dr. Abe could come over here. I'll order breakfast for us, then perhaps the two of you could read through this manuscript and give me your thoughts. Once we've sorted out the most important points, perhaps I'll have a clearer idea what to do next."

Silence again. Tom assumed Fran was weighing his request.

"Okay," she finally said, this time with more force. "I assume you'll call Dr. Abe. I wouldn't want to tangle with him this early in the morning."

Tom assured her he would.

An hour later Dr. Abe, Fran and the room service breakfast arrived together. Tom arranged the dishes on a table by the window, got the waiter on his way, and poured three cups of coffee.

"Help yourself," he said, gesturing toward the scrambled eggs and oven-warmed sweet rolls. "And while you're eating, perhaps you both can begin reading the transcript. I guess Fran should go first. She's a speed reader. Dr. Abe, you follow."

Silence fell over the room, broken only by Dr. Abe's loud slurping of his coffee, and the rustling sound of Fran rapidly turning page after page.

Tom gulped down some food, then, although anxious for their reaction, went into the bathroom to shave, shower and dress, while the reading continued. When he emerged, feeling refreshed, he saw Fran turning the pages even faster than before. She'd read well into the first half of the report.

She looked up. "Tom, this is amazing."

Tom sorted his laundry, went downstairs to buy toilet articles and jotted notes on a pad. Two hours later Fran put down the last page, and shortly after that Dr. Abe, having skipped sections he had digested at the camp, completed reading also. He rose, took off his glasses and walked to the window. "There are a lot of unanswered questions -- "

"There certainly are," Fran echoed.

"Okay, ladies first." Tom poured more coffee.

"My first question is what was Samuel trying to say happened in that secret chamber at Qumran? And is it correct that the Tenth Legion destroyed Qumran?"

"That's historically correct, although the date is uncertain. And I have the same feeling about your other point." He repeated the questions that had formed in his mind earlier.

"I'd like to know where on the Plain of Esdraelon the family farm was located," Dr. Abe said.

"Samuel said it was two days walk west of Nazareth." Tom pointed at the manuscript. "With the hills they had to go through, I would say that couldn't have been much more than thirty to thirty-five miles, and I doubt it was that far. One passage talks about residents of the farm watching the sun set behind Mt. Carmel. That places the farm east of Carmel. Still another passage says the farm was in the heart of the plain. That gives us *something* to go on. But what about this business of buried gold and silver?"

"I've checked that," Dr. Abe said, putting down his coffee cup. "Everything Samuel told us at the camp about the document he and other members of his family compiled is correct. A copper scroll, with information about the burial sites, has been found, is being translated in London and copies of the translation as it progresses are being sent to the University here.

"This has been done under tight security. Even I did not know about it, even though it was going on virtually under my nose.. When I took the information to my superior he admitted it was true. I guess I shouldn't have been surprised. Since the first scrolls were found, about two hundred caves have been explored in the same area, some by organized scientific teams, but more often by Bedouins who have sold what they found to anyone who would pay them. At least seven of the caves have produced major caches of manuscript fragments. The copper scroll was found in the seventh cave opened."

Dr. Abe slurped more coffee.

"It's strange, though, that Samuel knew all this. I suppose he could have heard of the copper scroll through his knowledge of the oral tradition, and then learned it had been found through some unofficial channel, perhaps a member of one of the cave exploration teams. But it's disturbing that he knew the scroll was being translated in London and copies sent here. That information is still classified."

The three of them talked for another hour, comparing notes on what each thought was important in other parts of the transcript. Tom attempted to sum up his conclusions.

"I think I should go back to Joseph's Cave and try to recover that inscribed parchment from the niche where I found the tile, and I think you, Dr. Abe, should interview Samuel again and get more information on the location of the family farm, plus anything he can provide on identifying descendants of the Ben Joseph family."

He turned toward Fran. "And Fran, I'd like very much for you to come with me. I'll need your help. The trip will take several days."

Fran bit down on her lower lip. "I can't do that, Tom. I'm engaged to Derek. It wouldn't be proper, although I would like to help."

Dr. Abe's eyebrows shot up. "I didn't know you were engaged. When did that happen?"

Fran bit harder on that lip, turned toward him. "Dr. Abe, could I talk to you for a moment. . . . privately?"

Before the professor could answer, Tom stood up. "I need to buy some more things downstairs. I'll be back in ten minutes." He glanced at his watch and left.

* * *

Fran folded her arms and stared out the window. "Dr. Abe, I need some advice. I'm terribly confused." She reached into her purse and extracted the note from Derek she had found under her door that morning, and handed it to the professor.

"I don't know what to make of this," she said. "The handwriting is almost illegible, and the paper reeks of liquor. Then there's the demanding nature of what he says, virtually ordering me to break with Tom. I wouldn't be so concerned if this were an isolated incident, but he's been on edge lately, very strident, flares up at the least little thing. I think something's wrong -- and just when I'm considering marrying him."

"Considering? I thought you just said you were engaged?"

Fran looked sheepish. "I know. Actually, I haven't accepted. I guess I said that to hurt Tom, retaliate for some of the pain he's caused me. Now I don't know what to do."

The professor stroked his beard, looked away, then back at Fran. "I don't think you should rush into any firm commitment to Derek when you have such doubts. And if you're so uncertain about Tom, you should talk to him, try to clarify your feelings."

Fran looked relieved. "Derek is out of town, heaven knows where, and I'd like to go with Tom. That would give us an opportunity to talk things over."

The professor hunched his shoulders; spread his arms, palms up. "Well then, that's what you should do."

Decision made, Fran felt better and informed Tom when he returned to the room, then called her office and asked for two weeks off.

Chapter XXIV

Tom gazed at the road ahead. Fran sat stiffly at his side, talking little, answering with only a few words whenever he attempted conversation. It had been that way since they left Jerusalem an hour ago in his rented car.

Tom stole a quick look at her then concentrated on his driving, trying to blot out the image -- reddish brown hair, cascading down to her shoulders, the almost perfect profile, full lips, rounded curve of her breasts.

"We do need to talk, Fran. I don't know what we'll encounter at Joseph's Cave, but it's important we time our visit carefully."

She looked at him, listening.

"I think we should make our move late in the afternoon when the crowds have thinned and before they turn on all the lights."

He paused, but she didn't respond.

"When I give the signal, I'd like you to speak to the attendant, keep him talking with his back to me. I'll need at least three or four minutes. If I find the parchment, I'll leave. You can follow and meet me back at the inn where we'll be staying. That sounds okay?"

Fran bit her lower lip. "I guess so," she said, voice quavering "but wouldn't it be better to ask permission to inspect the ledge legally?"

"No way. That would take forever and involve a lot of paperwork. They would find out I had taken the tile the first time I visited the cave, and would want to know why. There is no way of knowing how long it would be after that before we could check on what else is in that hole."

"Maybe so." Fran looked away, "But it does seem dishonest."

Tom smiled. "No, just sneaky. I don't think we'll have any problem. The attendant is not the most observant person I've ever encountered. Besides, you'll charm the pants off him."

"I certainly hope not." Fran fixed her eyes on the passing countryside, but brightened when Tom pulled into the courtyard of the inn where they had reservations. "I'll see you in an hour," she said.

"Make that a half hour." Tom glanced at his watch. "We ought to go to Joseph's Cave right away, look things over, then do it. We don't have much time."

Thirty minutes later they hiked up the street to the Church of St. Joseph and descended the stone steps to the cavern below, Tom carrying a well-padded shopping bag. Everything seemed the same. Tourists were strolling in and out, taking flash photographs. The attendant was near his table, answering questions when asked, selling pamphlets and picture postcards, and occasionally glancing around.

Tom moved toward the left wall, while Fran, face drawn, waited near the entrance. He tried to be casual, pausing at several display cases, but continued on until he reached the dimly-lighted area where he had found the tile. He raised his eyes. The hole was still there, apparently unnoticed, above the normal line of sight. Tom rejoined Fran.

"Let's do it," he whispered. "The crowd is drifting away and the attendant seems bored." He feared Fran would lose her nerve if they waited longer.

She blanched. "Now?" she said querulously.

"Now. Conditions will never be better."

Fran stood up straighter, took a deep breath. "Okay. I'll

move over near the attendant and wait for your signal, but do it soon. I've never been so frightened in my life. I feel like I'm about to rob a bank."

Tom squeezed her hand and slipped away before she could change her mind. He watched her as he drifted toward the wall. Finally she was in position, looking in his direction. Tom ran a hand through his hair. Fran stepped toward the attendant.

"I beg your pardon," he heard her say. "I wonder if you could help me?"

The attendant turned toward her, his back to Tom.

Tom moved quickly. No tourists were near or looking in his direction. He thrust two fingers of his left hand into the hole, groping for the bottom of the recess. Nothing. He could feel soft dirt, but nothing flat and rigid like paper or parchment.

He shot a glance at Fran. She seemed to have calmed down. The attendant was talking to her, obviously pleased by attention from a pretty girl.

Tom tried again, this time with his right hand. Again nothing.

He began to sweat, although the cave was damp and cool. He studied the room. He hadn't attracted attention yet but had to do something quickly. The whole purpose in coming to Nazareth was at stake.

Tom visually measured the distance to the hole. He raised his right fist, brought the fleshy part down hard against the hole. The wall crumbled. A gaping aperture opened, six inches across, and silt cascaded onto the floor.

Astounded by the damage, he gasped, wanted to run, but didn't dare. Again his eyes swept the room. Still no one watching, but a noisy group of tourists, apparently Americans judging from their clothes, had entered the chamber and were moving in his direction.

He couldn't wait. Tom thrust his left hand into the hole, and sifted the silt in the bottom. Suddenly he encountered something. It felt like a small piece of thick paper. He felt another piece. Tom pulled both free; dropping them into the shopping bag, then inserted his right hand. Two of the Americans, a very loud talking man and woman, had moved closer.

Again, Tom found more fragments and extracted them. A third, fourth and fifth try were equally successful, but further sifting produced nothing.

Tom headed for the stairs. Behind him he heard a loud voice exclaiming, "Honey, look at this big, old hole in the wall. What do you suppose that's there for?"

"Well, I declare," the woman said, "you'd think they would keep this place clean, being a holy place and everything. Look at this dirt on the floor."

Other tourists, attracted by the comments, sauntered over and began talking too.

"There was a young guy standing here a moment ago" the man continued. "Wonder if he knows anything about this. Honey, see if you can spot him."

Tom strode toward the stone steps as fast as he dared without attracting attention. He sensed the attendant had turned and was heading toward the gathering group around the two loud talkers. He dashed up the stairway just as he heard the voice behind him. "Oh there he is. Hey, mister!"

Tom pretended not to hear. He raced through the crowd in the church above, burst out the entrance, cut right, wheeled right again at the first intersection, then doubled back and headed up a parallel street to the left. He could hear faint sounds of commotion behind him.

Tom kept changing directions, moving along side streets then reversing again to travel toward the inn where they were staying. He felt certain Fran could extricate herself without difficulty. There was nothing to link her to him and the hole in the wall. Finally, Tom slipped back into his room and waited. Ten minutes later there was a tap on the door.

"Tom? Are you there? Let me in." It was Fran.

Tom cracked the door, then swung it open when he saw she was alone.

Fran burst into the room, bubbling with excitement.

"Wasn't that something! You should have seen the confusion after you left. The attendant kept looking at that hole and shaking his head. I don't think he ever connected it with you, but that loud tourist kept talking about getting you to come back and take a look. He actually ran to the top of the steps but by that time you were gone. I waited a few minutes then left."

Fran, almost out of breath, gulped, swallowed. "Oh, Tom, I didn't know crime could be so stimulating! Really, I didn't! And, oh, what did you find? Did you get the parchment?" Tom had never seen her so radiant, eyes sparkling, face aglow.

He laughed. "Slow down. I did get some fragments, but haven't examined them. I don't know what we've got. I do know I got everything in that hole. If there were any more pieces they were so small they felt like silt going through my fingers."

Tom set the shopping bag on a table and peered in. He could see seven pieces of parchment clinging to the cotton wadding he had placed across the bottom and up the sides.

"If you've got a pair of tweezers, Fran, maybe I should use them. I don't know how brittle this stuff is."

Slowly, ever so carefully, he extracted the fragments and assembled them on top of the table, fitting them together like parts of a jigsaw puzzle. There were several gaps, but they formed about seventy percent of a single sheet of parchment.

"You speak and read a little Hebrew, Fran. Can you make out the writing?"

Fran studied it then used a small magnifying glass to take a closer look. "It's very faint and very dirty. There's apparently some tallow on it too, which would support Samuel's report the parchment was under a burning candle. But I can't make out the writing. I see characters I think I recognize, but they differ from the ones I know. Still, I guess this isn't in worse shape than other old manuscripts that have been found."

"Good." Tom looked at his watch. "I'd like to work on this, but let's go eat. Then we can discuss the second part of our plan when we come back."

Fran nodded in agreement.

* * *

Two hours later, in the room next to Tom's, a dark complexioned man dialed a number on his cell phone, then waited. "Guzik? It's me. Yeah, I caught the duty today. Emma and I were assigned to the cave and we hit pay dirt. Guess who walked in about four o'clock? Yeah, that's right. I spotted him soon as he came in. Looked just like the photos you provided."

The man paused, listened. "Yeah, yeah, that's right. I watched him. He knew right where to go, over to the left wall. Hadn't occurred to us to look again in the same place. I saw him take six or seven pieces of something -- it looked like parchment -- out of the hole. It has to be that scroll we been looking for. And considering where it was found, and its age, it should be worth a bundle."

Again, he stopped, nodded his head impatiently. "That's what I'm trying to tell you. Just about that time a bunch of loud-talking Americans arrived and messed up everything.

"They swarmed all over the place. One fat guy spotted the hole and raised a ruckus commenting on it, attracting a lot of attention. He tried to follow Shannon out of the chamber, got in my way and I lost contact, but we spotted him in a restaurant later, and followed him back here. Had a girl with him. I slipped into the adjoining room and listened on a wall mike while Emma signed us in at the office."

A third time the man stopped, listened. "I'm getting to that. Just let me finish. I learned plenty. They said they was going to hike west through the hills into the Esdraelon Valley tomorrow. Damned if I know why, but the way I see it that plays right into our hands. We can't take them here. Would make too much of a fuss and get the police involved, so I've alerted Morrie. He will follow and do a job on them somewhere out in the countryside, then bring the scroll back here."

He stopped still again, apparently listening to instructions from the other end of the line. "Yeah, Morrie knows you want it done with as little mess as possible, leaving nothing that can be traced back to us. And ...yeah...yeah...I'll warn him. But Shannon doesn't look that tough to me. Shalom."

Chapter XXV

Dawn was lighting the eastern horizon as Tom and Fran strapped on their backpacks and left the inn the next morning. They hiked westward into the hills bordering Nazareth, picking up a well-traveled path at the end of the last meandering street of the old city. For the first hour, it was tough going. The trail ascended steeply, threading around huge boulders and sharp precipices, then leveled off, rising more gently as they approached the top.

At that elevation, the houses shrank in numbers and dwindled in exterior dimensions and trappings of affluence, changing from modern buildings to mountain shacks. Likewise, the walkers they passed -- at first men in western attire -- became people right out of the Bible, their lean, brown bodies draped in sour-smelling robes, dusty feet encased in sandals. But each greeted them with a smile, a nod and often a warm, *"Salaam,"* or *Shalom aleichem,"* to which Tom always replied, *"Aleichem shalom."* -- Peace... peace unto you, and unto you, peace.

An hour after departure they reached the top of the first line of hills. Ahead they could see the trail dropping into shallow, hanging valleys, and ascending to top other hills in the distance, a pattern repeated over and over, each summit revealing more hills to the west.

Tom and Fran walked through this spectacular scenery in silence, saving their breath for the climb, communicating by exchanging glances, muttering brief comments, or pointing when they found a panorama of unusual beauty before them. Neither noticed a small muscular man in dark clothing following about a mile behind them.

At midday they rested and munched on cheese sandwiches, washed down with water from Tom's canteen. By mid-afternoon both were tiring, and by five o'clock, with the sun descending, Tom called a halt. Amid scraggly Mediterranean pines, he pitched their pup tents side by side in a clearing notched into a steep precipice, and hauled water from a nearby stream to prepare their evening meal. By dusk, Tom had a fire blazing and stew bubbling in a frying pan. Some crackers, a little cheese and cups of fresh water completed their repast.

* * *

Morrie, the man tailing them, likewise settled down on an outcropping above their camp. He watched them through binoculars as he nibbled a piece of hard cheese, chewed a strip of dried beef and drank from his canteen. Finished, he wiped his mouth, adjusted his shoulder holster and tested the action of the Mauser pistol he kept there. That accomplished, he made certain the knife and blackjack suspended from his waist were riding securely, then leaned against a rock to watch Fran and Tom beside their campfire below.

He saw Fran, boots off, knees drawn under her chin, studying Tom as he washed their utensils and put them away. He could even hear their conversation, carried on the increasingly chill night air.

* * *

"I didn't realize you were so good at this sort of thing," Fran said, her large brown eyes following Tom's every move.

"Something I learned as a boy scout. Haven't used it much since." He studied her. "How are you feeling? I'm surprised how well you kept up."

"I'm tired, but I'm in fairly good shape. Been jogging regularly. How about you? The way you set up this camp and put our meal together, you don't seem tired at all."

"I'm showing off." Tom smiled as he finished drying the

last cup. "I'm certain I'll sleep well tonight." He tossed more wood on the fire before settling down in front of his tent, legs crossed in front of him. The fire blazed, driving back the shadows now enveloping the hillside.

Fran, silent a few moments, stared at the flames. "I'm glad we decided to do this. I'm still not sure it will produce any useful information, but it's good to get out and walk, away from people, close to nature. There's something healing about it."

"We had to do it, Fran. If you hadn't come I would have hiked it alone. We can't be certain this is the same trail used by James and Sokker to walk from Nazareth to the Plain of Esdraelon, but it follows a natural passage through the hills and there aren't many other ways to get through. We also know it's been used for centuries, so we may well be on the same path."

"You think it will bring us out near the Ben Joseph farm?"

"It should take us to the general vicinity," Tom said. "We don't know what James and Sokker meant when they said it was a two-day walk. Did they mean they arrived at the end of the second day, or sometime during the second day? They probably also were faster hikers than we are. They did

hard manual labor and must have been very strong, so would have covered more ground than we will in two days. Nevertheless, by following the trail we'll determine where it emerges on the plain. If that happens tomorrow, we can assume the farm is within a day's walk from that point in some direction."

Fran nodded. "That makes sense, even though we won't know the exact location or what's there now."

"Right. I'm hoping Dr.Abe will get more specific information from Samuel that will solve that problem."

"By the way," Fran said. "What did you do with the parchment fragments? I meant to ask before we left."

"They're in my pack over there, pressed securely between two rigid pieces of cardboard so they can't move or disintegrate further." Tom pointed toward his tent, some twenty yards away. "They're riding okay. I checked them."

* * *

In the rocks above them, Morrie sat up straight when he heard this. He had been planning to kill the man and woman after they went to sleep. Now there was an alternative. If he could sneak in, steal the pack and get out, it would be a nice clean job like the council always preferred. In the darkness that should be possible. Then it would be only a simple robbery, and if he were discovered while stealing the pack, he could still eliminate the man and his girl friend.

He began visually exploring a way down the mountain to the back of Tom's tent. Shouldn't be too difficult, he decided. He'd negotiated worse terrain many times. He rose, took a deep breath and began a slow descent.

* * *

Fran shifted her eyes from the fire to Tom, now lounging on his side, gazing into the flames.

"Tom, who do you think was in the Essenes' secret chamber at Qumran?"

Tom turned toward her, studied her.

"Do you really want to get into that?"

"Yes."

He searched her face, saw determination there.

"You've got to understand what I think is only a theory, Fran."

"I understand."

"You've also got to understand, if I tell you what I think, it could conflict with your religious beliefs, and, whether you realize it, I don't want to make you angry, or hurt you, particularly after our most recent difficulties. This trip, the two of us together, means a lot to me. I want it to bring us closer, not drive us apart." His voice rasped with emotion..

"I understand."

Tom cleared his throat. "Well, let me present the evidence as I see it, then suggest a conclusion. Maybe it won't sound so preposterous if I get the reasons out front first."

He paused, aware of her unusual beauty in the flickering firelight, hair pushed back, face slightly flushed, lips parted.

Aware also that they were alone in an isolated, rural setting. He shook his head, tried to eliminate such thoughts. "Let's begin with the crucifixion."

"The crucifixion?" Fran's voice and eyebrows rose.

"Yes. Christ was raised on the cross at the third hour, meaning nine o'clock in the morning. He was pronounced dead at the ninth hour, or three in the afternoon."

Fran covered her eyes and swallowed hard. The story of the crucifixion always affected her emotionally.

"He was on the cross only six hours, yet most deaths from crucifixion took one to three days."

Fran stared at him, hanging on every word, wondering what point he was trying to make. Tom tried to concentrate on the facts he was mustering, not the curve of her breasts, visible through her partly open blouse.

"Crucifixion is a form of strangulation," he continued. "Blood sinks into the lower body. Too little blood with too little oxygen reaches the brain and heart. Faintness follows. By pushing down on the support under the feet, the victim can relieve this faintness and bring blood back to the upper body. For this reason the Romans often-hurried death by breaking the legs below the knee with a blow from a club, a practice called *crurifragium*. This was done to the two robbers crucified with Christ, but not to him. He was pronounced dead after being tested with a spear thrust in his side. That's item number one."

"What's next?"

"A passage from the Bible, Mark, Chapter Five, verses twenty-five to thirty-four."

Again Fran looked surprised but said nothing. Tom quoted:

"'And there was a woman who for twelve years had a hemorrhage and had suffered much at the hands of many physicians, and had spent all she had, and found no benefit, but rather grew worse. Hearing about Jesus, she came up behind him in the crowd and touched his cloak. For she said, 'If I touch but his cloak I shall be saved,' and at once the flow of her blood was dried up, and she felt in her body that she was healed...And Jesus...perceiving in himself that power had gone forth from him, turned to the crowd and said, 'Who touched my cloak?'"

Tom paused. "It's the words about power passing from Jesus to the woman -- 'power had gone forth from him' -- that I want to deal with."

"Why?"

"Because I think Christ was a man of great psychic energy and force that could erupt unexpectedly, especially during times of stress."

"Hmm. Sounds like you're over on my side of our religious argument." Fran moved slightly, lifted and repositioned her body to a more comfortable position. Tom tried to ignore the jiggling under her blouse. He took a deep breath.

"A few years ago, at this point, I would have brought up the Holy Shroud, the Shroud of Turin. It once was thought to be the cloth in which Christ was buried because it bears the image of a man who died under conditions almost identical with those suffered by Christ. But carbon dating of samples of the cloth, at two universities in 1998, determined the shroud originated in the Middle Ages, between 1250 A.D. and 1390 A.D, most probably about 1350, so it couldn't have been Christ's burial cloth."

"What has that got to do with identifying the person in that room at Qumran?"

"I'll get to that." Tom sat up. "Originally I thought the image on the cloth came from a great burst of energy, that it was imprinted by heat, and was proof that Christ, recovering from the trauma of crucifixion, released the type of psychic force that dried up the hemorrhage of the woman mentioned in Mark."

Tom tossed another piece of wood on the fire, watching as the flames leaped higher.

"And I still feel I have to bring it up because there are many unanswered questions about the shroud. We don't know how the image got on the cloth. One scientist who participated in earlier tests, Walter McCrone of the McCrone Research Institute in Chicago, concluded it was a watercolor painting done about

1356 A.D., an amazingly accurate estimate made before the carbon dating took place. But personally, I -- "

A small rock came rolling down the hill behind them. Tom looked up, startled, rose to his feet. Cold chills raced up his spine.

"What was that?" Fran asked breathlessly, leaping up.

Tom studied the rocky incline behind their tents, only partly visible in the darkness. Hair on his neck felt prickly and his palms were sweaty. He walked a few steps toward the hill, stopped to listen, stood rigidly in place. He heard nothing, finally shrugged.

"Some animal, I guess. Nothing to worry about." He walked back and sat down. Fran also resumed her place. "Let's see, where was I? Oh, yes. We were talking about the image on the shroud. Personally, I doubt it's a painting. It's entirely on the surface. The coloring matter did not penetrate the fibers. Furthermore, the image refracts in a manner consistent with a reproduction produced by heat. McCrone also doesn't explain how an artist could have painted the equivalent of a photographic negative five hundred years before the discovery of photography."

Fran looked puzzled. "A photographic -- ?"

"Negative. Yes. That means the image is reversed. Left is right and right is left, and there is no gradation of shade. But when you photograph it the image emerges as a positive with considerable detail. There is shading and the sides are not reversed."

"Wouldn't that rule out any possibility the image was painted?"

"It does for me. There's only one way a negative could have been placed on that cloth. It had to be imprinted directly from a body or a reproduction of a body, probably by heat. It had to be produced by contact, or near contact."

Tom hurried on.

"It is also strange the image has no thumbs on the hands. That was a puzzler until experiments on corpses demonstrated that nailing a body to a cross with spikes through the wrists -- and that is the way it was done in the first century, not through the palms --

strikes a nerve that pulls the thumbs into the palms, obscuring them from sight. So, if the image were a painting, it seems unlikely the artist would have known he should include that particular detail."

Fran shifted position again. "As I recall there was another image of Christ..."

"Yes, called the Image of Edessa, a cloth found inside a wall over the city gate of a Syrian border town in 544 A.D. Edessa, now known as Urfa, is in southern Turkey. For a time there was speculation the Shroud of Turin was the Image of Edessa, brought to Europe after one of the Crusades, and there's some evidence to support that belief, but the Edessa Image dates back to at least the Sixth Century, and the cloth of the shroud originated in the fourteenth century." Tom looked away, gathering his thoughts.

"I wish you would tie all this together," Fran said. "I don't understand what you're getting at."

"I will, but first let's talk about links between the Essenes, the group that produced and buried the Dead Sea Scrolls, and the early Christians."

"I'm listening." She was. Intently. Hanging on his every word.

"The place in the Jordan River where John the Baptist baptized Christ was only about ten miles from Qumran, the main Essene base."

"What about it?"

"John was Christ's teacher and very likely an Essene. He wandered in the desert where Qumran is located. That's one possible connection between the two groups."

"Not much of one."

"Then there are conceptual similarities -- their mutual belief in duality, light against darkness, good against evil, spirit against flesh -- and similarities in the ceremony the Essenes went through at their main meal and the Christian communion. For example, the Essenes initiated that meal with what can be called a ritual ceremony. They were not allowed to break and eat their bread until a priest broke his bread and touched his wine.

Fran took a deep breath, expanding her chest, and again moved to get more comfortable. Tom noticed, but plunged ahead.

"Now we have even more compelling evidence of contact. The Temple Scroll, the longest and most recent of the Dead Sea Scrolls, has been translated. And just as in fundamentalist Christian doctrine, it forbids divorce and polygamy, for example, and lays down strict codes of behavior in sexual relations -- the same codes that governed both the Essenes and the Christians."

"So what precisely are you saying?"

"I'm saying there could have been close association between early Christians and the Essenes through John the Baptist and Christ himself."

"That's ridiculous," Fran said. "There's nothing in the Bible to indicate Jesus was ever at Qumran or dealt with people there."

"The Bible says Christ wandered in the wilderness for forty days and forty nights after his baptism by John. The wilderness is the Dead Sea area where Qumran is located, close to the baptismal site. Later we have Christ preaching many of the ethical and moral beliefs of the Essenes."

"Again, what point are you trying to make?"

"I'm arguing that Christ could have spent at least part of those forty days at Qumran, that he knew the area and perhaps some of the people. There also is a theory advanced by a few theologians, that as a young man he may have been educated at Qumran during the missing years before his ministry began. The Reverend Charles Francis Potter, in his book, *The Lost Years of Jesus Revealed*, says Jesus was familiar with the books of the Qumran library and patterned his life after the Essenes' Teacher of Righteousness.

"Indeed, the European scholar, Dr. Ernst Dupont-Sommer, has written that Jesus in many ways was an astonishing reincarnation of the Teacher of Righteousness. He points out both preached penitence, poverty, love of one's neighbors, chastity and humility. Both were hated by the priests of the Temple and both were condemned and crucified.

"What I'm leading up to is that during a time of travail, when Christ would have needed help, shelter and sustenance, he might have gone to Qumran to be with people he knew and respected and who respected him."

"Okay," Fran said. "For the sake of my sanity please tell me what all this is supposed to mean."

Tom looked into the dying embers of the fire, almost afraid to proceed.

* * *

On the slope above, Morrie resumed his cautious descent; relieved the rock he had loosened had not caused undue alarm below. He was halfway down and approaching a hazardous area on his left -- the edge of the precipice. Dark, yawning space just beyond. And he had to move that way to reach Tom's tent..

He studied the chasm of blackness. The rocks along its edge were bathed in moonlight. Good visibility, and the footing looked solid. He looked to the right. Could he detour that way? His eyes searched the jumble of stones rising precipitously there. Impossible. He would have to move along the edge of the abyss to reach the clearing and the tents beyond.

Slowly, he lowered his body from one large boulder to another, moving ever closer to that dark emptiness that seemed to beckon.

* * *

"What I'm saying, Fran," Tom said softly, "is there is a possibility Christ survived the crucifixion, he was on the cross such a short time; that he regained consciousness in the tomb, left the tomb and went to Qumran seeking assistance, was kept as a virtual prisoner there, although treated regally because the Essenes couldn't make up their minds whether he was their Teacher of Righteousness reincarnated. So it's possible he was the man in that secret chamber when Trajan and his agent, Julius, slipped in; that it was the force of his great and probably uncontrollable psychic energy when they broke into his living quarters that seared the curtains and all those in its path, and that he was the one who picked up the tile that fell from Trajan's belt. Then he carried it to his boyhood home in Nazareth, lit a candle and left the tile there, as a type of paperweight, atop a message to his family. After that who knows where he went. That will have to remain one of the great mysteries of all time."

Fran looked ashen. She stared at him in frozen, shocked, disbelief.

Tom avoided her eyes, keeping his gaze focused on the fire, then chanced a quick look as the silence lengthened. Some color had returned to her face, and the rigid tension lines around her mouth had eased.

"Tom," she began wearily, "just when I think you might accept Christian values you come up with another preposterous theory."

She lowered her head, moving it slowly from side to side. "Let's see now. First you cast doubt on the virgin birth of Christ and the perpetual virginity of Mary, saying she probably had children in a normal, biological way. Then you tried to take away the Christmas story, saying the birth of Jesus at Bethlehem might have been contrived to make the story conform to Jewish requirements for the Messiah. You said he was probably born at Nazareth and lived there much of his life.

"Now you're attacking the whole basis of Christianity, saying there was no resurrection, that Jesus was not a god and did not rise from the dead."

Her words stabbed his soul. What he had wanted most to avoid had happened. He had added to the religious barrier between them, perhaps had lost her forever. Maybe now she would indeed marry Derek as she had said she would.

Tom spoke quietly, slowly. "You're right about some of those things, Fran, but not all. I do question Christ's virgin birth, Mary's perpetual virginity, that Bethlehem was Christ's birthplace and to some extent that he was a god, although he may have been the next best thing -- a man imbued with a godly purpose, a man on a mission of great value to mankind, to teach concern for others as a way of life.

"To state it in the crudest terms, I think some of these Christian beliefs are nonsense, and I don't see how they strengthen Christianity. Why should modern Christians, with all the historical and scientific evidence available to them, accept such doctrines? But on the resurrection, you do me an injustice."

The moon suddenly slipped behind a cloud, plunging the area into darkness. The only light came from the flickering flames of the campfire.

Tom looked up, startled by the sudden, almost total, blackout. He was even more startled when a small avalanche of rocks came rattling down the mountainside into the clearing where they were camped. He leaped to his feet, picked up a piece of wood from the pile by the fire, and moved cautiously in the direction of the noise.

* * *

Fifteen feet above him Morrie clung desperately to a large rock, trying to get his feet under him, terrorized by the black void to his left and the advancing figure of Tom below, partly visible in the glow of the fire.

Finally, one foot struck solid ground, then the other. He drew them under him, breathing heavily as he pulled the knife from his belt and waited, crouching. Tom was only ten feet away.

Tom stopped, listened, peering into the darkness. He moved forward again then halted. Behind him Fran called anxiously. "What is it Tom?"

Morrie held his breath.

Tom stood frozen in place, club half raised, then edged forward, taking small half steps.

Morrie rose to a half-crouch, knife hand up, ready to strike.

Tom was only five feet away now.

Morrie lunged. As he drove his body forward, the rocky debris under his feet suddenly shifted to the right. He was propelled abruptly to his left, careening off balance toward the edge of the cliff.

He teetered there; arms wind milling, then plunged over.

His screams echoed eerily through the mountains, growing fainter as he plummeted deeper and deeper into the canyon below, then stopped abruptly. An ominous, empty silence followed.

Tom scrambled back to the fire.

"My God! What was that?" Fran said, leaping to her feet, her eyes large and staring.

"I'm not sure," Tom gasped, swallowing. "Think it may have been a mountain lion, a large cat of some kind. Screamed like one. Sounded almost human. Scared the daylights out of me."

He sat down, gulping air, staring into space, clasping his hands to keep them from shaking. It took a while, but five minutes later, the moon came out again and bathed the camp in silvery light. Tom stood up, still upset, heart racing, but feeling better. He put more wood on the fire, drew in a long, shuddering breath and let it out slowly.

"Wouldn't want to go through that every night. Let's see, where were we? Oh, yes. I was about to say you had done me an injustice, saying I had attacked the basis of Christianity by maintaining there was no resurrection."

"Well?" Fran stared at him.

"What I said was Christ may have -- may have, mind you -- survived the crucifixion. And that needs explaining. It doesn't necessarily contradict everything you believe."

He paused, waiting for her to comment, but she remained silent, glaring at him.

"It's true, the fact that Christ was on the cross such a short time raises questions. The Romans, even Pontius Pilate, when Joseph of Arimathea asked permission to bury the body, expressed surprise Jesus could be dead so soon. It is also true the burial was hurried to beat an approaching deadline -- sundown of the eve of the Jewish Sabbath. Burial would not have been permitted during the Sabbath. But it is equally correct that all available evidence indicates Christ was dead. The Romans had tested him, stabbed him in the side, and he did not respond. You can be sure they would not have released the body unless they were convinced he was dead.

"Then we have the time in the tomb. Some important things may have occurred there. Let me cite some parallel examples. It is not unheard of for persons who give every appearance of being dead to return to life. You have probably read of cases in which a hasty judgment sends a body to a mortuary. Then some attendant discovers the person is breathing and signs of life are returning.

"There are also many cases of what might be called 'temporary death,' or near death. Those who have these experiences report being overcome by a sense of peace. Others say they saw a glare of light at the end of a tunnel, with a figure of a long dead loved one waiting for them. Still others have said they left their bodies and looked down on their own death scene, then suddenly they returned to this world."

"Are you saying there is a moribund state in which life has left the body, but the final, irrevocable decision for death to take over has not been made?" Fran asked.

"Exactly. Death has occurred, but is not final. Jesus could have been dead when taken from the cross, and could very well have come back to life in the tomb."

Tom stared at the dying fire before continuing.

"Let's assume Christ was a mortal man. The words of his disciples indicate that's what they thought during his lifetime. So did members of his family, although many of them came to believe he was anointed by the spirit of God at his baptism and thus became the Messiah. Even Paul said Jesus was 'made of the seed of David according to the flesh.'"

"What is that supposed to mean?"

"I think that if Christ did emerge alive from the tomb -- and I think he did, after all a number of people saw him -- it really makes little difference whether you think of him as God, the son of God, or only as a man anointed with the spirit of God. The same distinction split the early Christian movement into two groups, those thinking Christ was God and those who thought he was *of* God. To me, this is a distinction without a difference. His impact on history is the same under either version. So is his influence on human conduct."

"Are you saying you believe there was...resurrection?"

"I'm saying I think it is possible something very special took place in that tomb. If you want to call it resurrection, go ahead. He apparently did come back to life. Whether that was the result of natural forces, or caused by divine intervention, I'll leave up to you, and every other person according to his or her beliefs. And whether that made him a god, or *of God,* I'll also leave for you, and others, to decide. At least there is evidence to support the belief he returned to life, unlike some assumptions in the bible that have no factual base."

Fran leaped to her feet, her face radiant in the light of the dying fire. "Tom, oh, Tom. I've misjudged you so."

Instinctively she moved closer, reached out, placed a hand on his arm. "Tom I -- "

Tom, aflame, swept her into his arms, kissed her passionately on the lips. For a moment she responded, then pushed away.

"I'll see you in the morning,," she said hoarsely and turned and entered her tent.

Tom stood there alone in the night, his blood pounding, every instinct in him yearning for this elusive woman. He heard the wind rising, moaning through the pines. The fire had subsided to a few glowing embers. He kicked them, sending a shower of sparks flying into the darkness, then retreated to his tent.

Inside the warmth of his sleeping bag, he tossed fitfully. Thinking, trying to make sense of what had just happened. Gradually he came to realize he and Fran had confronted issues that had damaged their relationship in the past, and, somehow, that relationship had been strengthened this time. By discussing, even arguing bitterly at times, they had come away feeling better, each about the other. And Tom, by accepting the possibility that Jesus had, indeed, been resurrected from the dead, had partly restored his former status with Fran. Finally, he slept.

Chapter XXVI

Tom rose at dawn and prepared a breakfast of coffee, toast and canned corned beef. Fran washed the dishes while he packed their gear, then they struck out down the dew-spangled mountainside, feeling a new camaraderie from their discussion of the night before. Two hours later the path dropped precipitously and surrounding hills dwindled to gently rolling elevations covered with grass waving in a warm, morning breeze.

By mid-morning they were out of the high country, hiking on a broad dirt road bordering cultivated fields. From this main artery, access roads led to farmhouses dotting the countryside.

Tom glanced at the sun. As nearly as he could tell, they had emerged further south than he had anticipated. If so, the buildings he could see to the northwest probably were Kiriyat Tiv'on, but he was not certain.

"Where are we, Tom?" Fran asked. "I don't recognize anything but Mount Carmel over there." She pointed to the west.

"I'm not sure. We'll have to ask for directions."

They turned in at the next farmhouse. A woman in a soiled dress, her hair a tangled uncombed mess, emerged and met them at a sagging gate, a shaggy, nondescript dog barking furiously at her side.

Tom bowed slightly. "Shalom. Could you help us? We seem to be lost." Eyebrows elevated, his face asking a question, he poked a finger at the map and handed it to her.

She examined it, coarse, dark features constricted in a scowl. Suddenly they relaxed.

"Here." She pointed toward the ground, then at the map midway between Ramat David and Kfar Yehoshua. "Kfar Yehoshua," she said, pointing to the southwest. She held up four fingers of her right hand. "Kilometer."

"Four kilometers?"

She nodded and smiled, then signaled for them to wait. She returned bearing a ladle brimming with cool water.

Tom passed it to Fran. She gulped down several swallows, then he took a long drink while the farm woman stroked the dog, now quietly nuzzling her leg.

"English?" she asked.

"Americans," Tom replied. "Thank you very much. Must go now."

"Americans!" the woman said, voice rising. "Americans!" Again she turned and disappeared. This time she rushed back with two bunches of freshly washed grapes. They thanked her, and again headed south down the main road.

The grapes were delicious. The morning bright and clear. The road ahead level and unfolding to the horizon. Life was succulent as a melon, dripping with goodness. Tom, pervaded with a sense of well-being, his lust of the night before tamped down, grasped Fran's hand as they walked side by side. She pulled it away abruptly, suddenly remembering they were not supposed to be so friendly.

"Isn't this morning and the countryside magnificent." She swept an arm in front of her, gesturing, eyes sparkling below perspiration-dampened hair. "Isn't this just absolutely magnificent."

Tom laughed. "That it is, Fran. But it may not be so magnificent if we can't catch a bus out of Kfar Yehoshua back to Jerusalem. I'd like to have that rented car I turned in before leaving Nazareth. We've accomplished all we can for the moment. We've got the parchment fragments, and determined the trail from Nazareth enters the Esdraelon Valley further south than we thought.

"Now, I'd like to obtain a map blowup of this area, with every farm and village plotted. Then, using our emergence point between Ramat David and Kfar Yehoshua as the center, draw concentric, half-circles five miles apart, extending out say twenty miles, a good day's walk. Then we could divide the area inside the circles into sections and canvass every house, asking for information on the oldest residents of the area, specifically whether a Ben Joseph family ever lived in that vicinity.

"But we can't organize such a search here. We must get back to Jerusalem and find out what Dr. Abe learned from Samuel. That will help determine how we proceed."

"Sounds like a big job."

"It will be time-consuming, but much of the area is sparsely populated, and we wouldn't have to talk to everyone, just one knowledgeable person in each home. To do that we will need bodies. Perhaps Sharon can roundup some students. They're always eager to earn extra cash, and I guess we could pay them something."

An hour later the buildings of Kfar Yehoshua came into sight. They headed for a rickety bus-stop shelter near the center of town, where Fran, with her basic knowledge of Hebrew, determined an attached sign stated a bus passed twice daily going south. One was due in two hours.

They sat in the shelter and munched crackers and cheese. Fran fell into a sound sleep, her head on Tom's shoulder. Tom was dozing, too, when the bus awoke him with a great squealing of brakes. Tom jostled Fran awake. They were the last to board, after passengers who had gathered while they napped.

"Jerusalem?" Tom asked.

The bus driver nodded. They paid their fare then edged sideways down the aisle, through foreign tourists seated around a uniformed girl guide standing at the front of the bus.

"This is a typical Israeli rural village," the guide was saying in monotonous, memorized English. "It was founded some thirty years ago..."

Tom and Fran slid out of their packs. Tom stowed them under a seat in the rear then sat beside Fran, who was next to the window. They dozed again, but Tom kept awakening, each time hearing the Girl Guide droning on and on.

"To our left," she was saying, "is the dome of a Nazarean church in a settlement called Cochaba. The Nazareans are a religious sect that goes back to Biblical times."

Tom closed his eyes. He remembered waking briefly when they passed through Megiddo and again at Nablus, but didn't come fully awake until they arrived in Ramallah Bira. Fran was gazing out the window into the rapidly descending darkness, and in the distance, he could see the lights of Jerusalem. The air coming through the window was much cooler.

Ten minutes later, they arrived at the Jerusalem bus depot. Both took cabs, Fran to her apartment, Tom to the King David. Tom immediately called Dr. Abe to report on his trip, and schedule a meeting with the professor for the next day. Then he listened as Dr. Abe told him about a new development.

"While you were gone, there was a break-in at the archaeological lab. Copies of the copper scroll translations were found outside their locked drawers. I didn't know what to make of this, so I called my friend Inspector Kahane. You remember him, the officer who caught the masked bandit at the Hump of the Camel restaurant. I told him about our project, since it involves the copper scroll, and suggested he join us. His investigative skills might be a great help."

Tom agreed, then called Fran.

* * *

Tom arrived at Dr. Abe's cluttered office at ten o'clock. Fran and Sharon were already there, looking uncomfortable in each other's presence. It was their first encounter since Fran had come upon Sharon, half naked, in Tom's tent at Samuel's farm. Dr. Abe and Inspector Kahane were off to one side, using a magnifying glass to examine photographs scattered across the professor's desk.

"Morning, Tom," Dr. Abe said, looking up. "You know

Inspector Kahane, I believe."

Kahane nodded, smiled. "Good to see you again." They shook hands.

Dr. Abe motioned toward the photos. "These are the shots Sharon took of the fingerprints on the Isaiah Scroll and the Tenth Legion tile. The inspector says there are several matches."

Tom froze. "Some are identical? Made by the same person?"

"That is a reasonable probability," Kahane said. "The prints on the scroll are far less distinct than the one on the tile. But where the lines can be made out, or are suggested, there are many similarities. I would say there is better than an eighty percent probability, enough to provide supporting evidence in a criminal case."

Tom sat down, stunned, his head reeling. He had located two objects he believed had been handled by Jesus, both bearing identical, or near identical, fingerprints. Had those prints been made by the Christian messiah? He thought so. The evidence was persuasive.

"So much for that," Dr. Abe said, trying to appear very much in charge, despite being perched atop two chair cushions to raise himself to normal height above his desk. "Tom. You have something for me, do you not?"

Tom took two pieces of cardboard, taped together, from his briefcase. Dr. Abe cut them apart and, using tweezers, removed the parchment fragments, pressed between the two flat surfaces. He examined each with a magnifying glass, placed them in an envelope, then summoned a girl from the outer office. "Take this to Dr. Leiberman in the archaeological laboratory. Tell him I'll check with him later."

Dr. Abe turned back to the group.

"I've taken the liberty of asking Inspector Kahane, who volunteered his services, and Sharon, to join us in the next phase of our research." He nodded toward the policeman. "Shlomo is a top investigator. He can help us, since what we will be attempting is a type of detective work. I've briefed him and Sharon on everything we've been doing, including our most recent travels.

"I've also asked Sharon to round up two dozen students to work for us, as per your request last night, Tom. Now, I believe you have some questions for Shlomo."

"Indeed I do." Tom turned toward the inspector. "I need to determine whether family relationships can be established through similarities in fingerprint patterns."

Kahane shifted to face Tom. "A number of experts have attempted to determine whether there is an inherited similarity in fingerprints. Some have theorized identical prints should turn up in a mathematically determined sequence, like dominent and recessive characteristics do, according to the Mendalian law. The same sort of thing. I haven't followed these theories and will have to ask our research staff to work up a summary of the latest information before I can give you a better answer."

"But in your opinion there is a detectable relationship in the fingerprints of relatives?" Tom asked.

"Let's say I was impressed with their arguments. I'm inclined to believe them."

Tom sank back in his chair, feeling triumphant. He nodded to Dr. Abe, indicating he was satisfied.

"Let's move to another subject," the professor said. "Tom filled me in last night on what he and Fran accomplished at Nazareth and on the exit point of the trail from Nazareth to the Plain of Esdraelon. Now I'm sure you're waiting to hear about my conversation with Samuel."

Dr. Abe sighed. "I wish I could tell you it went well." He tented his fingers, looking off into space. "Samuel has had several recent respiratory attacks and is in a weakened and disoriented condition. He seemed to understand what I asked him, but I got almost gibberish in reply. He is showing signs of senility, too, and isn't eating properly. Indeed, I fear he may not have much longer to live. I located a relative, who promised to look in on him. In any event, I questioned Samuel a number of times and taped his replies. Sharon, I would like you particularly to listen and see if you can translate what he said."

Dr. Abe turned on the recorder. After some preliminary static Dr. Abe's voice came through asking Samuel in English if any of the descendants of Jesus' family still lived in Israel. If so, where, and how they could be identified.

There was a long pause punctuated by heavy breathing and sounds Tom recognized as coming from Samuel's habit of opening and closing his mouth before speaking. Then the ancient, cracked voice began, firing Hebrew in bursts, followed by gasping for air, a few coughs, then more words. Tom could make out several proper names, including Jude and Joseph, but little else. The recording ended as abruptly as it began.

Sharon frowned, looked puzzled. "Play it again. I'm not sure I'm hearing what I think I'm hearing."

Dr. Abe reversed the tape, found the beginning, hit the button.. The words were repeated, Samuel's cackling voice again filled the room. Sharon asked for a third replay. Both Dr. Abe and Kahane took notes. Without saying anything Sharon walked over and looked down at the translation Dr. Abe had scribbled on a pad in front of him, then did the same with Kahane.

"As best I can make out, he is saying something like, 'Jude, Joseph, James and Sokker every other time,' then something about a Nazareth church, some mutterings about 'He lied!' and a sentence that uses words I translate as 'place of the stars,' 'star place,' 'find the star,' 'search out the star,' or even 'follow the star,' whatever that means."

"Oh great," Tom said. "Does he think we're the three wise men? He told me he knew everybody whoever lived in this area. Now he gives us mish-mash like this!"

"Don't be too hard on him, Tom," Dr. Abe said. "He's terribly confused. He tried to answer, but had trouble expressing himself. What we're getting is only an approximation of what he's trying to say. Shlomo, how should we proceed?"

Kahane cleared his throat. "I think the important thing is to fill as many blanks as we can and look at the pattern that develops. Your idea, Tom, of a canvass of every house within a reasonable day's walk from the point where you emerged into the

Esdraelon Valley is a good one. I can get the maps we'll need, by tomorrow if necessary. I suggest we set up a base camp near the exit point, organize teams to interview people in assigned areas, and have them use prepared questions that will identify the oldest families. We can go back to those families, hoping we'll hit what we're looking for."

Sharon raised a hand to get Dr. Abe's attention. "I'd like to take that tape with me and play it several more times. There's got to be something more there. It doesn't make sense. Is this the only recording? You said you questioned him several times."

"It's by far the best," Dr. Abe said. "I have an earlier cassette or two with false starts but they're less distinct. As far as I can determine, he said the same thing each time."

Sharon nodded. "I'd like to listen to them anyway. They might provide a hint, an inflection on a word or two, that could be helpful."

"I'll get them for you," Dr. Abe promised. "I suggest we meet here tomorrow at the same time to plan our move into the Esdraelon Valley." Everyone agreed. "And Tom," Dr. Abe added, "would you stay a few minutes? There's something I need to discuss with you."

After the others had gone, the professor waved Tom to a chair.

"I didn't bring up one part of my conversation with Samuel while the whole group was here. On a separate tape, I asked him about the buried gold and silver, trying to get more specific information. The replies were not much better than his other answers with one exception." Dr. Abe stopped, glanced down at notes he had made on a pad. "He kept insisting the treasure involves three thousand, two hundred eighty-two talents of silver and one thousand, two hundred eighty talents of gold, apparently in some loose form, plus sixty-five gold bars, six hundred eight pitchers containing silver coins and six hundred nineteen vessels made of silver or gold.

"The damnable thing about that is the numbers are exactly the same as those in London's translations of the copper scroll.

It's too accurate to be an accident, and it's about the only thing he said that was precise and clear. I'm concerned the police will discover Samuel has such information and try to connect him with the break-in at the archaeology lab. What do you think we should do?"

Tom was unsure. "Right now, nothing," he decided. "It's a real puzzler. Let's wait and see what develops."

Dr. Abe agreed. Tom went back to his room to pack.

Chapter XXVII

The searchers pitched their tents in the shade of scraggly pines on the farm where Tom and Fran had obtained directions the week before. From that encampment every morning, shortly after dawn, two-member student teams traveled by jeep to the area each was assigned to canvass. And every evening, as shadows lengthened, they returned to fill their campsite with laughter and boisterous talk about what they had encountered that day.

"At last, we're on our way. We're making progress," Tom kept telling Fran and Dr. Abe. He was swept up in the spirit of the enterprise.

His enthusiasm carried over into the social gatherings they had with the students around a campfire every night. Accompanied by plaintive pluckings on a guitar he raised his off-key baritone in an attempt to sing an American folksong:

"Oh Shenandoah, I long to see you. We've gone away..."

He joined in the good natured shouts of derision and laughter that followed. But after a week of reading the reports each team brought in doubts began to build. Would this information ever lead him to the Ben Joseph family? And after ten days without a breakthrough he was so concerned he asked Fran, Dr. Abe. Shlomo and Sharon to join him in his tent after supper.

Conversations died when he dropped onto a campstool in front of them.

"We're about halfway through our survey," he began, "but

aren't obtaining what we need. I thought it might help if we took stock.

"Sharon," he said, turning toward her, "you've read the reports our teams have produced and reviewed the tapes of Dr. Abe's conversations with Samuel. Have you discovered anything new?"

"Not really." Sharon sounded depressed. "If there's a key hidden there, I haven't found it. I'm not even certain now Samuel's talking about a church in Nazareth in one of the taped passage. He repeats words that sound like Nazareth, but they're not always the same. And that business about 'find the starry place,' or 'place of the stars,' I can't fit that into any context."

"What about you, Dr. Abe? Have you any suggestions? And did you ever locate the false-start tapes you had?"

"Yes. I found all the tapes and have them here except -- " He caught himself. He was about to mention the separate recording of Samuel's answers to his questions about the buried gold, then remembered he and Tom had not shared that information with the others. He coughed and blew his nose to cover his bobble.

"As I was saying I found all the tapes. Sharon and I have gone over them. We're as mystified as ever."

"Shlomo, do you have any suggestions?" Tom asked.

Kahane was studying Dr. Abe intently, then realized Tom was speaking to him. "Oh, excuse me." He removed his pipe from his mouth and tapped the bowl against his right shoe. The ashes spilled onto the dirt floor. "My mind was wandering. No -- " He paused to suck on the pipe stem. "No, I don't think I can offer any suggestions." He tested the pipe again. "I think probably we're too close to our information. There very likely are important clues in what we've already found. We just don't recognize them.

"I've been in similar situations in criminal cases. Each time progress began when we recognized the importance of a fact we had overlooked. I suggest we pound away at what we're doing. Something should turn up." He sucked on the pipe one more time before dropping it into his jacket pocket.

The meeting broke up ten minutes later with Tom remaining where he was, turning pages of his notebook as the others departed. Fran and Dr. Abe found him there when they returned a half hour later.

"Are you all right, Tom?" Fran asked.

He looked up. "I'm worried. I've been going over the books. We're running out of money and our chances of finding workable leads are diminishing rapidly."

Fran bit down on her lower lip. "I've saved a few thousand dollars. Would that help?"

Tom's eyebrows arched. Dr. Abe also looked surprised.

"That's very generous of you, Fran, but I couldn't risk your savings on an effort that has so little prospect of success at this time. Besides, I wouldn't feel right unless I used my money first. I've been trying to get my father's permission to sell the stock he gave me when I graduated six years ago, but he has the final say and won't budge."

Fran pushed back a reddish brown lock that had strayed across her eyes. "Actually, I came about something else, Tom. I must get back to Jerusalem. I haven't been able to raise Derek on my pocket phone. I'm worried. He's been acting strangely. He should have returned from a trip but hasn't, and apparently has missed several of his classes. I'm afraid he's been drinking, too. I have to find out what's going on. It's not normal for him to be away so long."

Tom smiled wanly. "That's okay. I've about decided to close the camp anyway. You can take one of the jeeps and a student to drive you. Dr. Abe can decide which one."

"Why don't we put the camp on a standby basis," Dr. Abe suggested. "If we don't have a compelling reason for continuing by, say, the day after tomorrow, we'll cut back to one working team, then return to Jerusalem to raise more funds. We've come so far, I hate to fold the operation completely."

Two days later Tom followed Dr. Abe's suggestion. The camp was reduced to two students. The others packed and headed back in a convoy of heavily loaded jeeps. Fran's early departure and the breakdown of a second vehicle left them so short of transport Tom and Shlomo had to hike to Kfar Yehoshua and catch the same bus to Jerusalem Tom and Fran had taken before.

Tom was surprised to find the same uniformed Girl Guide reciting her memorized lecture to another group of tourists in the front seats. He slipped by, followed by the stocky policeman, and sat in the rear while she went on, almost word for word, with what he had heard before. Tom wished she would shut up. He wasn't interested in stories about Kfar Yehoshua, Nazarean churches, some obscure settlement called Cochaba, or the battle of Armageddon.

Shlomo fell into a fitful sleep. Tom wasn't so fortunate. Sitting by an open window, with the hot, dusty air streaming in, he thought of the progress they had made in tracing Christ's descendants -- the fingerprint on the tile, the apparent same print on the Isaiah Scroll, the many clues from the recorded narrative provided by Samuel, and the possibility of more clues in the parchment fragments taken from Joseph's Cave.

Now, it was mid-August, two months after his arrival and he should be on the threshold of success. Instead, the project had stalled. He was nearly out of money, maybe out of luck. He knew Dr. Abe had no realistic chance of raising more school funds, and he had no prospect of convincing his father he should sell his stock.

There *is* that buried gold and silver, he reminded himself, but...well...that's ridiculous...

Tom's dejection deepened. He wasn't equipped to handle failure. The prospect left him with a gnawing, queasy feeling. *What if I have to go back to teaching in Detroit, without Fran, and my project in ruins. God, what a prospect!*

He was in a black mood when the bus bumped and jolted down the final block of its journey and pulled to a stop at the depot in Jerusalem. He mumbled a goodbye to Shlomo who, aware of his companion's low spirits, looked after him with concern as Tom shouldered his pack and hiked to the King David.

The desk clerk hesitated when Tom, unshaven, unkempt

and clad in dungarees, asked for his key, then recognized him and nodded a belated greeting. "We've kept everything just as you left it, Mr. Shannon. It's good to have you back."

Tom was only vaguely aware something was wrong when he stepped off the elevator. The hallway was dark. A short circuit must have knocked out the lights.

Then he saw the door to his room was ajar. He stood there, startled, key in hand, undecided whether to summon help. Suddenly, a man burst out, drove a shoulder into Tom's stomach, bowled him over, and sprinted down the hall to the stairwell.

Tom scrambled to his feet and raced after him. He heard pounding footsteps echoing up the stairs as he started down. The intruder was about two levels below and moving fast. Tom exited at the next floor and punched for the elevator. One stopped immediately. He jumped in, startling an old lady and her granddaughter. The child, thoughtfully licking a sucker, gazed at him with big, brown eyes.

The elevator reached the ground floor without further stops. Tom dashed into the lobby, scanned the area. No one was running for the entrance. Everything appeared normal. He ran to the stairwell and opened the door, listening intently. There was no sound of anyone descending.

Suddenly it struck him. The intruder could be sitting in one of the chairs watching him and he wouldn't know it. He hadn't seen his face, gained a clear impression of his size, or gotten a look at his clothing. Furthermore, the intruder could have left the stairs at any floor. He might even have a room and be in it now. The guy had escaped.

Tom returned to his room. It was a shambles. His suitcase had been opened and thrown on the floor. Clothes had been pulled out of drawers. Papers from the translation of the Samuel tapings were scattered everywhere.

Tom began assembling them in numerical order. It wasn't until he finished that he realized what was missing -- one entire, new photocopy of the Samuel tape transcripts, and Sharon's translation of the document prepared by Samuel and his ancestors, dealing with the buried gold and silver.

Tom, his depression forgotten, phoned Dr. Abe. The phone rang several times before the agitated voice of the professor came on, shouting, "Shalom! Shalom!"

"Dr. Abe I've got some disturbing news."

"You've got disturbing news? You ought to see the mess I've got here. Someone broke into my house while I was gone and ransacked my study. I've called the police. As far as I can determine the only thing missing is the tape with Samuel's comments about the buried treasure from the Temple and Qumran."

Tom was stunned. It took a while to calm Dr. Abe sufficiently to tell him information on the gold also had been stolen from his room.

"That means someone else knows about the gold and silver," Dr. Abe said, shouting again, "and may have been tracking it for some time. Just look at the evidence. First Sharon had a visit from a man apparently seeking information on the gold and silver. She told me about it. Then there was that break-in at the archaeological lab, where some of the copper scroll translations on the gold and silver were found out of place, and may have been photographed. Now intruders have taken records from both you and me that deal with the same thing. My guess is whoever it is will use the information to find that buried treasure. So call Fran and Shlomo and I'll be right over. We've got to beat them to it."

* * *

At that moment in another part of Jerusalem, Meyer Bernstein paced behind his desk in the Club Tomcat, the four members of the syndicate's council standing rigidly in front of him. He was livid from the top of his baldpate to his neck. Even his ears had taken on a reddish-purple tinge.

"Son of a god-damn bitch!" he raged, slamming a fist on his desk. "You mean they found his body. He's dead?"

"Yes," Doc Steiner said cautiously.

"Where was it? What happened?"

"We don't know exactly, Boss. He was found at the bottom of a canyon. We searched for almost a week. He apparently fell from a cliff two hundred feet above."

"That shlump. How could he be so damn incompetent? He was supposed to be a skilled hit man. All he had to do was take the scroll fragments from an unarmed man and woman and he falls off a cliff trying to do it. What a klutz."

Bernstein again pounded his fist on the desk. The pen and papers there jumped to one side. "Sometimes I feel like this whole operation is jinxed. First we lose Schwartz, now Morrie. We can't stand any more losses, so forget the scroll for now. Let's concentrate on the gold. Where do we stand on that?"

"The professor's cased the operation pretty well. Says the gold is located somewhere near the Dead Sea. He doesn't know exactly where, but is convinced Shannon and his crew know and will try to dig it up soon."

Bernstein stopped his pacing, glaring, waiting.

"So we're watching both Nizer and Shannon. If they make a move, we'll follow. We've got a team ready to go."

"The professor's is going to lead them?"

"Yeah. He's scared shitless. He'll do anything we say to get out from under the money he owes."

"Do you trust him?"

"For this operation I do. It's his only way out of the mess he's in. He'll do okay."

Bernstein glared at the group, jabbed a finger at them. "Now get this. There can't be any more screw-ups. That gold could put this organization on easy street for years to come, so make absolutely certain every one of your guys knows what he's supposed to do. They'll catch hell from me if they mess up this time!"

Again the four men got out of the room as fast as they could.

Chapter XXVIII

The car raced through the night toward the Dead Sea, Schlomo Kahane driving, Dr. Abe seated next to him. Tom, in the back seat with Fran, leaned forward and repeated the question. "So how did you pinpoint this site?"

Dr. Abe turned to face him. "It wasn't too difficult. Samuel uncovered clues to a number of places where the gold and silver might be buried. It took only a little more research for me to pick an exact location."

Schlomo glanced toward the professor, inclining his head to hear better.

"I concentrated on two locations singled out by Samuel. One was described in the Copper Scroll as: 'Sixty cubits from Solomon's trench toward the great watchtower, buried at three cubits, thirteen talents of silver.' The other was said to be: 'In the fortress which is in the Vale of Achor...under the steps entering to the east, a money chest and its contents, of a weight of seventeen talents.'"

Fran shook her head. "What's a talent? What's a cubit? I know they are measurements but other than that my memory fails me."

"I'll get to that." Dr. Abe continued. "Samuel surmised, and I agree, that the first location is within the ruins of Qumran. The word 'watchtower' indicates it is. So does 'Solomon's trench.' One of the catch basins for water at Qumran is known as

Solomon's cistern. It is fed by a trench that brings in runoff after rainstorms."

Dr. Abe paused, swallowed. "The other citation was almost as easy to decipher. The term 'Vale of Achor' appears in many Hebrew compositions. In Hosea, for example: 'Therefore, behold, I will allure her and bring her into the wilderness, and speak tenderly to her. And there, I will give her vineyards and make the Vale of Achor a Gate of Hope -- '

"Other references indicate the Vale is the plateau running parallel to the Qumran cliffs. The Essenes used it as farmland and looked upon it as a gateway to their settlement."

Dr. Abe shifted position to face Tom more directly. "There are a number of ancient fortifications in the area, but it seems clear the one referred to is a great, castle-fortress on the Vale's western edge, built on a hill by the Jewish priest-king John Hyrcanus in the second century B.C. The ruins and the steps are still there. I decided this site was best for our purposes because it's isolated, not patrolled, and the amount of buried treasure seems to be larger."

"Honestly, I'm out of it," Fran said. "How much gold or silver are we talking about?"

"Okay, okay," Dr. Abe said huffily. "A cubit originally was the distance from a man's elbow to the end of his middle finger, a measurement obviously not the same for all men. For modern purposes, it has been standardized at eighteen inches. A talent is a much more erratic measurement, of weight, not distance. It has ranged from forty-five pounds in rabbinical literature to a more likely twelve ounces in more recent writings.

"At forty-five pounds the total amount of the treasure mentioned in the copper scroll would come to more than seventy-three tons of silver and twenty-eight tons of gold, far more than the Essenes and the Zealots at Qumran could have handled. So something closer to twelve ounces seems likely. But that's still a lot. If what is buried under the fortress steps is all gold it would total two hundred ounces or more, and at today's prices would be worth eighty thousand to a hundred thousand dollars -- enough to finance the rest of our project and give Samuel an excellent reward for his detective work."

The conversation ceased momentarily, the sound of the car's motor filling the void. Then Dr. Abe began again.

"In working through material on the Vale of Achor, I came across references to the Zealots being at the fortress ruins early in the uprising against the Romans. They probably moved into Qumran from there about three months before the Tenth Legion arrived. That would have been logical. Qumran had both the Essene's gold, and stores of food and water the Zealots would have wanted access to. The fortress guarded the approaches to it.

"I believe the Zealots placed their soldiers among the Qumran guards, and brought in women, too. That would explain why the Essenes, normally a passive group, resisted when the Romans attacked. It would also explain why Michael was able to offer Trajan the services of Sin, and why modern-day archaeologists have found female skeletons in the cemetery at Qumran, a male, celibate establishment."

"I wondered about that," Tom said.

Shlomo slowed the car, studying the road ahead, then abruptly turned right onto a narrower, dirt road. After a few minutes, he wheeled right again onto a rutted trail. Ten minutes later the moon rose, flooding the desert with pale, silvery light, as a dark hill-like mass loomed in front of them, its jagged edges silhouetted against the sky. Shlomo eased the car to a halt and switched off the motor. "This is it," he said.

Tom opened the car door and helped distribute picks, shovels and spades from the trunk, then they headed up the slope, single file, Dr. Abe leading.

"Watch out for snakes," he warned." In the fifth century A.D. when Saint Sabas came here, he reported the ruins were infested with snakes, ravens and wild beasts. He decided they were demons in disguise and killed most of them, but some of their descendants could remain."

"Snakes!" said Fran from the end of the column. She dashed forward, leaving Schlomo to bring up the rear.

"There's no real danger," Dr. Abe assured her. "If any are here they won't be out at night. They are cold-blooded animals and prefer to hunt and bask in warmer daytime air."

They halted at the top of the hill, breathing heavily, sweating in the warm summer night. Dr. Abe switched on a flashlight, revealing steps descending the other side, partly hidden under accumulated debris.

Tom and Shlomo started down, unreeling a long, metal tape measure, marking the distance on the ground, while Dr.Abe jotted figures on a scrap of paper. When they reached the bottom, the professor began to add and divide.

"Eighteen into this goes...let's see...eight times, leaving four...Aha! Just as I thought. The steps are eighty cubits from top to bottom, so we'll dig at the midpoint, forty cubits down or up, and see what's there."

They measured from both directions and marked the center. Tom sank his shovel into the ground at the mid-point and dumped the spade to one side. He repeated this several times, then placed the tip of the blade under the steps and pried upward. The steps didn't move.

On the other side, Dr. Abe hacked futilely at the ground. Each time he stepped on the spade he was propelled backward instead of forcing the blade into the dirt. Shlomo mercifully took over. He dug slowly, steadily, throwing the earth behind him.

Tom and Kahane worked in silence, pausing periodically to mop perspiration from face and hands. Twice Tom thought he heard cars approaching and even the distant sound of voices. Dr. Abe said it probably was noise from the highway and a tourist hotel close to the turnoff to Qumran.

"We're only six miles away. Sound carries in the desert at night."

Some time later Tom heard faint sounds again, much closer this time, but Shlomo said he heard nothing. Tom paused several more times to listen but the sounds were not repeated.

They kept digging. After two hours Tom and Shlomo had cleared a trench five feet deep, three feet across and eight feet long, extending under the steps from one side to the other. As he was removing the last, loosened dirt, Tom's spade hit a hard object. He thrust the spade in the ground again. Again, it struck what appeared to be a rigid framework.

"I've got something," he shouted.

Shlomo joined him. They scraped the dirt away, revealing the top of a metal chest. Tom, working frantically, cleared dirt along one side, then shoved the chest with his right foot. It moved. He spaded around the other side and shoved again. More movement.

Shlomo and Tom dug deeper, pried, dug some more and pried again. The chest shifted abruptly to one side. Fran and Dr. Abe dropped into the hole to help. Tom and Shlomo each took an end, Fran and Dr. Abe the two sides. All four lifted. Slowly, the box rose out of the ground, leaving a rectangular cavity.

They set it down, pausing to mop their dripping faces and catch their breath. Then, with Tom and Shlomo doing most of the work, they hoisted the box, again staggered over to the side of the pit, and deposited it on the soft dirt at the edge. Tom and Shlomo helped Dr. Abe and Fran out of the hole, then scrambled out themselves. Grasping the chest, each on an end, they dragged it to more open ground.

Dr. Abe switched on his flashlight. The bright, yellow glare illuminated what appeared to be a metal box, about a foot deep, two feet long and one and a half feet wide. The metal was rusted and encrusted with dirt. A heavy bolt, bent at one end, ran through a hasp, locking the lid in place. Tom used a wire brush to rasp dirt and rust off the latch, then struck the open end of the bolt with a hammer. It didn't move. He pounded it again, and again. Ten minutes later, with the aid of penetrating oil and more pounding, the bolt gradually moved backward, then out the other side.

Tom reached down and lifted the lid. It rotated upward and fell to the ground. The yellow beam of the flashlight probed the interior, revealing a heavy layer of dust over rectangular objects.

Tom dropped to his knees and swept the dirt away with the

cupped edge of his hand.

The moon suddenly flooded the scene with light. From inside the chest, a pale golden refulgence drifted upward in an expanding misty cloud, traveling up the beams of the flashlight and rays of the moon, then diffusing in all directions. There, arrayed before them in neat rows, were bars of gold, stacked loosely, one atop the other, each about three inches wide, four inches long and a half-inch thick, filling more than half the chest.

For a moment, there was complete silence.

"My God," Tom breathed.

Shlomo picked up a bar and hefted it, first in one hand, then the other. "Each of these is going to be several pounds and there must be a hundred or more. We've got a lot more than the two hundred ounces you mentioned, Dr. Abe."

Fran stood there, mouth open, looking down at more wealth than she had ever seen. "To think that's been here all these centuries and we found it."

Tom was uncetain what happened next.

There was a sudden pounding of running feet. A dozen black-clad, hooded figures came hurtling out of the darkness from three directions. Dr. Abe retreated backward and fell into the pit. Tom, equally startled, saw one of the figures closing on him, a raised club descending. He ducked. The blow caught him across a shoulder. A sharp pain shot down his right arm. He heard Fran scream then saw a hand clamp her mouth. She was jerked to one side.

Tom, going down, saw Shlomo charge another attacker. The detective slipped under a swinging club and drove his head into his assailant's stomach. The man gasped and both fell. Shlomo, rising quickly, dug something from his pocket. The shrill blast of his police whistle pierced the darkness, then halted abruptly. Another hooded figure crashed a club down on Kahane's head.

The fight was over. Tom saw a large man, machine pistol in hand and a knapsack on his back, rush forward and shout, "Bring them over here." His voice was muffled by the dark cloth over his head, but Tom thought it sounded familiar. "Drag them if necessary. Tie and gag them. And get that truck up here. Let's load this gold and get out."

    A truck thundered out of the darkness and squealed to a stop. Four of the black-clad figures staggered toward it, carrying the chest of gold bars.

    Then, suddenly, the desert was flooded with light. A loud voice speaking over a bullhorn shouted, first in Hebrew, then English: "This is the police! Stop where you are! Drop your weapons and raise your hands! I repeat, this is the police!! You are under arrest! Do not move!"

    A ring of officers advanced into the blazing headlights of more than a dozen, encircling, police cars. The policemen advanced slowly, Uzi machine pistols at the ready.

    The big man directing the hooded attackers turned; apparently saw the advancing officers and his men raising their arms. He raced down the elongated shadow of the truck, and bolted into the police headlights beyond, machine pistol blazing, raking the area.

    Two officers, twenty feet away, went down, grunting in pain. A third grasped an arm and dropped his weapon.

    The black-clad figure sprinted. A dozen more steps and he would be out of the illuminated area. A police gun stuttered, then jammed. The big man, now only a few steps from the enveloping night and freedom, lunged, his long right leg extended in front of him, left arm holding the machine pistol, out behind. Then he was gone. Bullets stitched the ground where he disappeared, then stopped.

    Whistles shrilled. The voice on the bullhorn bellowed: "After him. Get those nearest jeeps moving. Sergeant Cohen,, take ten men and follow him. Sweep the area. The rest of you secure these prisoners, and bring the medics up to help the wounded officers."

    The confusion slowly subsided. The probing headlights and gunning engines of the search patrol faded in the distance. The captured, black-clad men were herded together, manacled, and their hoods removed. A team of officers helped the three wounded policemen reach a nearby ambulance. As the chaos of shouted commands diminished, a police lieutenant marched up to Kahane, now sitting up, gazing around. The lieutenant saluted smartly.

"You all right, Inspector?"

"What took you so long?" Kahane ruefully rubbed the back of his head. His hand came away sticky with blood.

"We got here as fast as we could," the lieutenant said, beckoning for a medic. "As soon as we heard your whistle."

"Seemed like ages." Kahane stopped talking as the medic knelt beside him and took a bottle of medicine from his aid kit, daubed the broken tissue and matted hair. Kahane winced.

"I'm going to clean this up, sprinkle it with sulfa and put on a bandage," the medic said. "I'm afraid if I cut away the hair I'll increase the risk of infection. Hair has lots of bacteria and will get in the wound. We'll also have to get you to a hospital for x-rays."

Kahane growled, "I don't want any damn x-rays. Here, help me up."

Tom suddenly became aware of Fran, sobbing nearby. He put an arm around her. She wept some more, head on his shoulder, moaning. "Oh, Tom. Oh, Tom."

At that moment, a muffled voice behind them began shouting. "Get me out of here! Where is everybody? What's going on?"

Tom turned. In the pale light, he could see the top of Dr. Abe's homburg racing back and forth in the pit under the steps. The officer who had spoken to Kahane looked in that direction, too. Tom released Fran, telling her, "I'll be back in a minute. Lieutenant, will you help me?"

They walked to the edge of the pit. Dr. Abe's face peered up at them from the gloom.

"It's about time you got here," he sputtered. "What in the world happened? What was all that shooting and shouting? Why did you leave me in this hole?"

"Sorry, Dr. Abe." Tom reached down to grasp one of the professor's hands. "I'm not certain what happened myself."

The officer took the other hand. Together they hauled the little man up and deposited him on the edge of the excavation, where he stood blinking at the strange scene before him -- policemen milling around the handcuffed prisoners, others loading the box of gold bars into an armored car, and medics lifting stretchers, bearing the wounded officers, into an ambulance.

"We'll leave the patrol to search for the escapee through the night," the lieutenant told Kahane, "but there's no reason the rest of us can't return to Jerusalem."

He directed Tom and Fran into one police car, Dr. Abe into another. Shlomo Kahane, a white bandage around his head, rode in the lead car. "You'll have to come to headquarters with us," the lieutenant said. "We should be able to release you quickly, but I'm sure there will be questions to answer later. We'll bring your car along too."

At the station Tom, Fran and Dr. Abe provided identification and answered questions for a preliminary report. Then, at the insistence of Shlomo, were released with the understanding they would return the next day to help the police complete the report. The bedraggled group left immediately, uncertain exactly what had happened to them, and why, but hoping they would learn more tomorrow.

Chapter XXIX

Derek sprinted into the enveloping darkness, gasping for air, eyes wild and searching, mind racing. He cut left, then dove into a gully as the bouncing headlights of a pursuing jeep swung his way.

The glare swept over his hiding place and faded in the distance. He leaped up, dashed up the shallow trench and again hit the ground, this time behind a copse of bushes when he heard shouted commands close by.

Again and again this was repeated. The short run, dive for cover, and him hugging the ground with the machine pistol still clasped firmly in his left hand. Not until he had run a mile or more did he realize the search had moved away from him, toward the main Jerusalem-Jericho highway to the north.

Derek tore the black hood from his head, mopped his face with it and threw it on the ground. "Now what?" he muttered, gulping air. He felt terribly alone and frightened, one man in a dark, menacing desert, desperate and without hope.

He tried to think, control his fear, stop the trembling in his hands, the shaky, queasy feeling in his stomach. He was headed west. The searchers were going north. He should get as far from them as possible, but where could he go? He couldn't just wander. Daytime heat in this biblical wilderness was a killer, reaching one hundred twenty degrees or higher -- and he had no water.

Still pondering, he turned south.

Suddenly it came to him. Despite his desperation, he almost smiled thinking about it. What a brilliant idea. That's the last place the police would look, he told himself.

Derek glanced at the moon, made a calculation, and struck out boldly to the southeast. After hiking an hour, he crossed the north-south highway traversing the western shore of the Dead Sea.

He kept going, a lone man seeking shelter. The ground began to rise, then immediately in front of him loomed a mass of earth and stone, dimly outlined against the night sky.

Derek slung the machine pistol around his neck and began to climb, hand over hand, foothold-by-foothold, gasping for air, directly up the face of a cliff.

A black opening loomed above him. A last heave of his body and he was there, breathing hard, drenched in perspiration, but safe for the moment -- in a cave overlooking the ruins of Qumran.

He laid down, head on his knapsack, aware it had begun to rain outside. Good. That will wash out any trail I left behind. Now I have to devise a plan, find a way to safety and freedom -- but how, where? That was his last thought. Exhaustion took over and he slept.

Chapter XXX

Tom picked Fran up at her apartment the next morning. Her eyes looked glazed, her face pale. She kept shaking her head and repeating, "I don't understand what happened to us last night."

"I'm uncertain about part of it, too, Fran, but we should know more soon."

They checked in at the police station and were escorted to an interrogation room where Dr.Abe and Sharon sat waiting. Shlomo Kahane, his head swathed in white bandages, walked in moments later and closed the door. He gazed around, his eyes finally resting on Tom and Dr. Abe.

"I hope we can still be friends," he said. They nodded stiffly.

Kahane, frowning, leaned against a desk. "There's no way I can easily explain what happened last night, but hear me out." Every eye in the room was on him. No one spoke.

"Several weeks ago we received a call from Hebrew University reporting a break-in at the laboratory in the archaeological department. We investigated but could find nothing of value missing and no motive for the break-in. We were convinced, however, it was done by someone who knew the room layout and exactly what drawers and areas to explore.

"We had more pressing cases to look into, but the apparent lack of motivation in the lab case intrigued me. Through persistent questioning,, I learned about the copper scroll, that it was being translated in London with drop copies being sent to the lab, and that those translations listed sites where gold and silver had been buried in the first century A.D. This, plus the fact that those translation copies had been moved and apparently examined during the break-in, and perhaps photographed, raised interesting possibilities."

Kahane sat on the edge of the desk, one leg swinging.

"One, of course, was that the burglar could have been seeking information about the gold and silver. On checking further, I found an unusual entry in an old laboratory record book. A man named Samuel Ben Ashod had come to the lab that day, trying to sell a document dealing in part with the buried gold and silver. This led to the discovery that Samuel was still alive and had provided tape-recorded information to you, Tom, and to Dr. Nizer, and that Sharon Ausch, your student friend here, had translated that information into English.

"Sharon was questioned and ordered not to tell anyone we had talked to her. That's why I asked her to come here today. I want to be certain you do not blame her for not informing you." The detective glanced at Sharon. She blanched, looked embarrassed.

"She said that as far as she knew only the four of you here, plus Samuel, knew there was information in the Samuel document about the gold and silver. But she also told us of an unusual visit by a university professor, who she suspected was trying to get such information from the notes and translations she made during and after the tape recordings at Samuel's farm.

Kahane, still frowning, took out his pipe, pressed tobacco into the bowl but did not light it. He gestured, his pipe in hand. "I started dropping in on Dr. Nizer whom I had met previously, every time I was at the University, hoping to pick up additional information.

"This led to Dr. Nizer's invitation to join your project, since I had some knowledge of fingerprints and knew how to conduct an investigation. I didn't know where this would lead, but felt that eventually I would understand the relationship between the lab break-in and what you were doing with Samuel's information.

"The real breakthrough came quite by accident. One of our deep cover men in Jerusalem's underworld reported that word was circulating there about a big heist that would take place soon. It was supposed to involve a man who was into the syndicate for quite a sum of money and was trying to get out from under his debt. A closer look focused suspicion on one Professor Frost. A little more checking revealed Frost had access to the lab, that he was deeply in debt to the syndicate, so had monetary motivation for the break-in, and had frequent contacts with bagmen from the syndicate.

"By tailing Frost we established that he knew Tom and Dr. Nizer had knowledge of the gold and silver, was spying on their movements and probably was responsible for the break-ins at Tom's hotel room and Dr. Abe's house. The fact that he was also the man who tried to get information from Sharon confirmed his involvement.

"The break-ins, of course, precipitated your decision to try to find the gold and silver. You can pretty well piece together the rest of what happened. I had to tell my superiors about your plans. We felt certain Frost and his underworld associates would follow you since they didn't know where to dig. They hadn't cracked the code to the extent you had. So we made plans accordingly. I went with you, Frost and his gang followed and the police followed them."

Kahane lit his pipe and puffed several times, wreathing his face in smoke. "Of course we thought we could disarm Frost and his men before any shooting started. Unfortunately we were wrong."

Kahane paused, gazed around the room, obviously expecting some comment. No one spoke so he resumed. "One more thing. I don't like deceiving friends. I have come to know and like all of you. I hope you will allow me to continue working with you on your project. My acting in secret, and as a double agent so to speak, was required by my job. It is standard policy to share information on a developing case with as few people as possible. I hope you will see I had no choice."

Dr. Abe cleared his throat. "I think we understand, Shlomo, although it will take a while to recover from so many surprises. And I do wonder what would have happened to us if your police hadn't followed Derek last night."

The little professor suddenly sat upright. "Heavens, I might still be in that hole!"

Everyone smiled except Fran. She had a question. "You mean that awful man out there, the one who ordered those thugs to bind and gag me, was Derek?"

"We're reasonably certain it was."

"I don't understand," Fran said, shaking her head. "Why did Derek get involved with criminals? Why didn't he ask me or some of his friends for help? And what will happen to him now?"

"Professor Frost was, and is, a compulsive gambler. I've seen that sickness break the best of men. As for the rest of it, with his credit record, it was impossible for him to borrow from conventional sources, and he probably had too much pride to ask friends for help. I trust I'm not revealing any secret when I say our investigation revealed he had asked you to marry him. Since you had some savings we presumed he was after that money, too. Still, in his own twisted way, I think he loved you, Fran. His actions weren't just an effort to get some cash. That's what our psychologists think anyway."

Fran's face turned white.

Tom, seeing she was shaken and embarrassed, tried to reassure her. "I think he did too, Fran, love you that is. I'm certain his relationship involved far more than an effort to get money. I hate to admit it, but he was a formidable rival. What a tragedy."

Kahane, puffing his pipe, gazed out the window. "We'll continue to search for him, of course. He can't go far. We put bloodhounds on his trail this morning. They found his ski mask, but I fear a heavy rainfall last night reduced our chances of catching him immediately."

"What happens to the gold now?" Tom asked.

Kahane looked down at his pipe. "There was never any chance you could have used that gold, even if Derek hadn't tried to take it, and even if we hadn't taken it from him. It is the property of the state, an historical treasure, worth more than its monetary value. You couldn't have spent it without violating Israeli law. I'm surprised you weren't aware of that."

Dr. Abe replied immediately. "Tom and I both knew that, but we were presented with a crisis situation. We didn't want the gold to fall into criminal hands. We had to act. I felt certain that if we found it, the state would give us a substantial reward that could be split with Samuel and permit us to go on with our research."

"Where's the gold now?" Tom asked.

Kahane pointed toward a side door. "In there. You can see it if you want." He stood up, moved in that direction. Tom and the others followed.

The gold bars were stacked on a heavy table, a pile about two-thirds the size of the chest they had been found in. There was also a clay jug filled with coins.

"We found this at the bottom of the chest," Kahane said, emptying the coins onto the table. He held out the jug. "It's an ordinary ceramic of no archaeological value. You might as well keep it as a souvenir, Tom. That way you will have realized something from the evening."

Tom accepted the vessel in silence. His thoughts were elsewhere. He suddenly realized his quest to find the descendants of Christ was tottering, about to fall over the brink into total failure. He had only a small amount of money to continue his research, and no hope of gaining new financing. What could he do? He didn't know. He was in a black mood when he returned home.

Chapter XXXI

Derek opened his eyes, gazing first at the machine pistol lying in front of him, then at the entrance to the cave, outlined by the rising sun. He sat up, slowly turned his head, taking in the earthen walls and darker shadows in the cave's interior. Where was he? Why wasn't he home in bed? Then full recall swept away the fog of sleep. "Oh God," he moaned. "What have I done? What have I done?"

He sat there frozen, head resting in his hands, cool morning air washing over him as he tried to grasp the enormity of the disaster he had brought on himself. Twice he opened his eyes, looked around, and twice he closed them, wanting to crawl back into an inner world where the pain of reality didn't exist.

Finally, silently, tears came, coursing down his face, dripping off his chin, drenching his hands and shirtfront. He wept uncontrollably, sobbing, shuddering in total despair. He'd lost everything. He was a fugitive. The police would be looking for him, out there in the desert, and everywhere he went. They obviously knew his identity or would not have been so aware of his movements last night.

A new, shattering realization suddenly stabbed his soul. He had lost his job, too. The University would never keep a felon on its faculty. Then an even more devastating understanding of his predicament flooded his mind. He couldn't even return to his apartment to pick up his belongings. If the police weren't

watching there, enforcers from the syndicate would be.
   Derek began to wail openly, great sobs wracking his body. Slowly his sorrow turned to rage. Long-suppressed anger surged within him, overwhelmed him. He grabbed the machine pistol and hurled it to the ground, shouting, "Everything...everyone is against me!" He kicked the cave floor and slammed his fist into the wall. "They all hate me."
   For a full five minutes he stormed around the cave, screaming, kicking the dirt, hurling his knapsack, beating his fists on the powdery dust where he had slept. Then he sat down and cried again until the tears ebbed, dying amid heaving, shuddering body spasms, spaced at increasingly long intervals. Finally, he was quiet.
   Emotionally spent, he sat with his back against the cave entrance, trying to make his mind function. He stared at the ruins of Qumran below. He could see the crumbled walls where the watchtower had been, and the stones outlining the courtyard, kitchen and main building. Employees of the National Parks Authority, the Israeli agency operating the site, were moving around the premises, preparing for the day's influx of tourists. One of them emerged from a building, sipping a cup of coffee, talking to a companion. Derek slapped a hand to his forehead. What about food? How am I to survive?
   He walked over to his knapsack, lying in a heap against one wall. Was that sandwich and thermos of coffee still there? In the excitement of waiting to begin the raid last night he couldn't remember whether he had eaten the lunch he had prepared. He pawed through the bag, pushing aside the transcript of the Samuel tapings, stolen from Tom's room, then sighed, relieved. The sandwich was there. So was the coffee. Although now lukewarm, it would get him through the day.
   Feeling somewhat better, he sat down to eat and think. What could he do to ease his problems? Was his situation hopeless? Was there any way he could rebuild a normal life?
   He closed his eyes, hoping to begin his usual systematic reasoning process, and quickly reached one conclusion. He could

take no action before nightfall. He would be caught immediately if he ventured out in daylight while the police were searching for him.

Then he made a second decision. He not only couldn't return to his apartment, he didn't dare return to any part of Jerusalem. He might encounter a friend who would recognize him, and intentionally or otherwise, disclose his presence to authorities. Could he eliminate that danger? Perhaps change his appearance? What if he let his hair and beard grow? That might do it. Yes, it was worth a try.

Derek felt even better now. His mind was beginning to function. Then he pondered a new question. How long would it take to grow sufficient head and facial hair to make him look different? A minimum of four to five weeks, he decided. Oh God, that long? And where could he hide during that time? He had no idea.

Then he remembered, or almost remembered, his mind groping for an elusive memory. Something he had read a few weeks before. Suddenly it came to him, a magazine article explaining why so many wanderers had survived in the Dead Sea area of the biblical wilderness. He struggled, trying to recall the details.

It came in a rush. The area wasn't entirely arid, despite its desolation. There was a fresh water spring two miles south of Qumran on the highway bordering the western edge of the Dead Sea, the highway he had crossed in getting to the cave last night. It fed a dense stand of reeds in a nature reserve.

There also was an isolated *kibbutz*, a collective farm named *Ein Gedi* nine miles further south. It had a guesthouse, cafeteria, commissary and campground. He could hike to the spring after dark, clean up, drink his fill, then continue on to the *kibbutz* and hopefully rent camping equipment. With food purchased at the commissary, he could survive in relative comfort -- if he had sufficient funds.

Derek pulled a battered wallet from his hip pocket and counted the bills. He had enough if he was careful. He had cashed a school expense check just before leaving Jerusalem. He smiled. Some certainty was returning to his life. Only a few details to tie up now.

Where would he go and what would he do once he resurfaced in Jerusalem with a beard and long hair? That was easy. He would ask Fran for help, persuade her to flee to Jaffa with him, where hopefully, using her money, they could board a tramp steamer to America, and he could take that MIT job.

After all, she should be willing. She would be getting an excellent husband. And she did love him -- or did she? Momentary doubt crowded his mind. At their last meeting she had been hesitant about committing herself to marriage. Derek swept that aside. She would help him -- or else.

Satisfied, he settled back to eat the other half of his sandwich and pass the time perusing the photo-copy of the Samuel transcript. He wanted to read it in full, rather than just those parts dealing with the buried gold and silver.

Slowly, page-by-page, he progressed, feeling first shock, then disbelief, then horror. He read on, at times turning the pages diagonally to read marginal notes made by Tom. Anger and resentment grew. Finally, he put the transcript down and stared at the ruins of Qumran below, now sweltering under a midday sun.

Could Christ have been educated there as a youth?

Could he have survived the crucifixion and returned to Qumran to recover among old friends?

Was it true that many of his ideas were similar to those of the Essenes? *Was* he, in many ways, amazingly like the Essenes' Teacher of Righteousness?

Was it true that Mary had other sons and daughters and therefore could not have been a virgin all her life?

Was the virgin birth, purportedly in Bethlehem, a hoax created by early Christians to make Jesus' life conform to the biblical requirements for being the messiah?

Was Christ a man on a godly mission, or a god on a mission for man?

Was modern Christianity actually created by the Apostle

Paul, who introduced his own ideas and those of the Greek mystery religions until it became a faith to some unknown extent different from what it had been during Christ's time?

Did James and the other leaders of the primitive Christian Church have serious differences with Paul over these changes he made in their creed?

Did James, Symeon and Jesus' other relatives actually exist?

Could their descendants be with us somewhere in the world today?

The transcript and Tom's marginal notes implied the answer was "Yes!" to all of these questions.

"No!" Derek shouted, jumping to his feet. He hurled the offending pages to the ground and stomped on them. "That's not the way it was. That's blasphemy. What right has that pagan, Tom Shannon, to stir up issues settled centuries ago by patriarchs of the Church? How could he know more than they did?" Derek stormed around the cave, arms waving. Suddenly he stopped, thinking.

There was one passage he liked -- the speech by James from the Pinnacle of the Temple. He didn't think James ever existed, but he agreed with the words James spoke.. He wondered if that part of the story could be true, even if the rest was not. It sounded so right.

His interest aroused, Derek picked up the pages scattered on the ground and reassembled them in proper order. Over and over during the day he read and reread James speech, while studying the ruins of Qumran below and drifting off into extended periods of sleep to overcome his exhaustion from the night before.

During one of those naps, he heard that voice again. Always before it had come from inside him, urged him on, encouraged him to take risks when he gambled. Now suddenly it was different, sly and cunning, perhaps even evil, coming from somewhere outside his being. It was just a whisper but he clearly heard: the voice say: "You must warn the people."

Derek awoke, terrified. He looked around, wild-eyed,

expecting to see someone in the cave. He saw only shadows, and fiery light from the setting sun, pouring through the cave entrance.. He stood up, trembling, but mustered enough courage to explore the back of the cavern. No one there.

"But I *didn't* imagine it," he said aloud. "I *did* hear a voice."

Fearing the voice might speak again, he stayed awake until night descended on the desert, then repacked the Samuel papers, picked up the machine pistol and climbed slowly down the cliff to begin a star-lit journey to *kibbutz Ein Gedi.*

Chapter XXXII

Tom circled his hotel room for the umpteenth time. He was angry and worried, keenly aware his project to find the descendants of Christ was drifting and endangered. He was almost out of money, had only enough funds to continue the camp another week or so, and no prospect of new financing now that the gold venture in the desert had failed.

"Damn!" He rammed fingers through his tangled hair, slammed a fist into the palm of his hand, told himself, *I can't give up now. There's not much time left. I've got to keep trying.*

He dropped into a chair.

Tom wanted to discuss his problems with someone, get those problems out in the open, relieve his internal tension. But Dr. Abe was consumed with university work neglected while he was at Samuel's farm. Tom felt alienated from Shlomo Kahane because of the dual role the inspector had played in digging up those gold bars in the desert. He didn't want to call Sharon, knowing that could lead to complications both wanted to avoid. And Fran, the one in whom he wanted most to confide, was at a church conference in Tel Aviv, although due back sometime today.

He glanced at the clock. Noon. Worth a try. He dialed her number, listened. Her phone rang and rang. He slammed down the receiver in exasperation. The impact caused the ceramic jug on the table -- the artifact Inspector Kahane had given him -- to teeter precariously. Tom grabbed it as it was about to fall.

"And this God damned thing." He raised his arm, ready to hurl it to the floor. He looked with disgust at the dusty imprint it had left on the table and the dirt that had sloughed off on his hands. He had been so preoccupied he hadn't noticed how badly it needed cleaning.

He held the jug under the tap in the bathroom lavatory, rubbing off lumps of dried earth as he turned it slowly. A crack appeared, running diagonally across one side of the receptacle. Tom looked closer. Another crack came into view, taking off at an angle from the first, then several more, branching in different directions.

Tom dried the jug and examined it at the hotel room window. His eyebrows went up. "I'll be damned." He suddenly realized the lines that had emerged were not cracks but an incised design. He studied the jug more closely, noting there was a single word in Hebrew script and a round dot at each intersection of the converging lines.

Tom turned the jug slowly, his amazement growing. *Why, it's a geographical sketch of Judea as it once existed! There's Jerusalem. And that has to be Megiddo. But what are these other three sites, particularly the one with the strange marking? It has a place name in script under it and a cluster of three stars above.*

Tom stared, not certain what he was seeing, then telephoned Dr. Abe. The professor responded grumpily.

"Really, Tom, I hope this is important. I've got work to do. I should have known better than to go off on some wild adventure in the country with you. Now I'm paying for it"

"Okay, Dr. Abe but I've discovered something that could be important." He described the map on the jug and the place name he couldn't make out.

"Probably doesn't mean anything," Dr. Abe snorted, "but come on anyway. I'll be in the office all day."

Tom arrived to find the professor barely visible behind huge stacks of examination booklets on his desk. Dr. Abe peered at him over this barrier, through spectacles hanging on the tip of his nose.

"Okay, let's see this thing you've got." He shot out an arm, knocking a pile of the booklets to the floor. His face flushed. "Now see what you made me do. Look at that mess."

"Sorry." Tom handed the jug to Dr. Abe, then began picking up. The professor held the receptacle in the light of his desk lamp and kept turning it, studying the design from various angles. Suddenly he scrambled off his built-up chair seat, fished a magnifying glass from a desk drawer and scurried over to the window.

"Ha!" he said, turning the jug. "Ha! For once, you're right. That definitely is Jerusalem and Megiddo." He picked up a pencil to point at the words on the jug. Tom moved closer.

"As you probably know our ancestors didn't use vowels in writing the Hebrew language, only consonants. To decipher a word you have to find a logical combination of vowels and insert them between the consonants. Thus silver" -- he reached down to write letters on a piece of paper -- "was written KSP, but the full version is *Kesaph* in Aramaic or *Keseph* in Hebrew. If you use this procedure on three of these locations you come out with Jerusalem, Megiddo and what apparently is Nazareth. At least the words are close and the geographical positions are correct.

"For the same reason I'm reasonably certain this place near the southern end of the Dead Sea is Masada. Both the consonants and the location fit. But I'm not sure about this one, west and south of Nazareth. The three stars above it are confusing. None of the others have any such symbol. As nearly as I can tell the inscribed name may be some form of the word Kochba, as in the name of the leader of a revolt in 130 A.D., Bar Kochba. His name meant 'Son of the Star.'"

Tom's mouth dropped open. "Kochba...star...could it be Cochaba? Is that a form of Kochba, the word meaning star?"

Dr. Abe's eyebrows went up. He picked up the magnifying glass and looked again. He was silent a full two minutes, then a strange expression spread across his face. "Why I believe it just might be. The words are related. Cochaba would mean Place of the Stars, Starsville, or -- "

"Suddenly Tom realized what the professor was saying. "My God!" he shouted, dropping the booklets he had collected. "That's it. That's what Samuel was trying to tell us. Cochaba, place of the stars. That's where he was telling us to look."

He told Dr. Abe about the tour guide on the bus at Kfar Yehoshua, recounting how she had talked about Cochaba and the Nazarean church there. Abruptly, he stopped, gulped, almost swallowing his words as a new thought flashed in his mind. "And that explains something else Samuel said. He wasn't talking about a church in Nazareth in those incoherent phrases he used on your last tape. He was talking about a Nazarean church."

Dr. Abe nodded vigorously. "That fits. The Nazareans were a distinct group in Jewish history. I've got something on them here some place." He stepped over to his floor-to-ceiling, wall-to-wall, bookcase, studied the volumes a moment, then jumped up and tipped a book off the seventh shelf, catching it as it fell.

"As I recall the name Nazarean was applied to most of the first Christians, that is members of the church headed by James and Symeon. Let's see now -- " Dr. Abe flipped pages back and forth.

"Ah, here, listen to this: 'Nazarean is a loose term applied to early followers of Christ, including those called Ebionite Christians. By the end of the first century Nazareans were established in some forty communities, and by the fourth century had more than five hundred settlements extending across what is now northern Israel and part of Syria into areas east of the Jordan River.'"

Dr. Abe looked up. "That sounds like what you learned about Conon, the descendant of Christ who supposedly built 'synagogues of a special type' in Galilee."

Tom agreed. "It does at that. Interesting. Maybe Nazarean settlements were built around those synagogues."

Dr. Abe read on: "'The amount of source information on such groups is limited, but Eusebius of Caesarea' -- one of your sources, Tom -- 'in his *Ecclesiastical History*, cited a letter written by Julius Africanus, a Roman leader. That letter mentioned the family of Jesus and said those members who survived the 67-70 A.D. Jewish War against the Romans fled Jerusalem and went to Pella -- '"

Dr. Abe stopped, looked up. "That's what Samuel told us in our taping sessions. Tom." He continued. "'Many other Christians went to Pella about the same time, while members of Christ's family moved on to villages called Nazara and Cochaba and were living there at the end of the First Century.'"

Dr. Abe glanced ahead through succeeding passages. "This says there is one additional historical reference. Epiphanius, a Jew who became a Christian and established a monastery at Thebes in the fourth century -- again one of your sources -- also mentioned Cochaba in one of his writings, but he placed it in Batanea, which is east of the Sea of Galilee, that is east of the Jordan River and not on the Plain of Esdraelon."

Tom, who had been frozen in place, suddenly sat down in a straight-backed chair by the professor's littered desk. He felt giddy, stunned, speechless.

"You all right?" Dr. Abe asked without looking up. "Oh, here's some more. It says Nazareans also were known to live west of the Jordan at that time -- that would take in the area where Cochaba is located -- and that some of their writings were found in the library at the rabbinical college at Tiberias, the seat of the Jewish patriarch in those days."

Dr. Abe closed the book slowly, and removed his spectacles. He polished them with a handkerchief, then looked directly at Tom.

"By Jove," he said softly, reverting to some long forgotten British conditioning, "I do believe we've got it."

Tom was equally enthused but trying to control his emotions. He almost stuttered, when he converted his thoughts into words. "What...what...we've stumbled onto indicates members of Jesus' family went to two places, called Nazara and Cochaba, shortly before or after the fall of Jerusalem in the first century A.D. That basically conforms with what Samuel told us. We think we know where Cochaba is now, but what about Nazara? Could that be Nazareth?"

Dr. Abe stared fixedly at Tom. "That is a strong possibility. This is the breakthrough. Shlomo Kahane was right. The clue we needed was right under our noses and we couldn't see it. I think we should ask Sharon to reassemble our teams and alert the two students back at the camp that we're returning to make a survey of Cochaba."

Tom agreed. "This will be our last shot, Dr. Abe. If we don't find what we're looking for within a few days we'll be broke."

There was a moment of silence. Dr. Abe: placed a hand on Tom's shoulder. "Any doubts? You certain this is what you want?"

Tom grinned. "No doubts whatsoever. Let's do it!"

Chapter XXXIII

Tom led them back with spirits soaring. The students were enthusiastic, whooping and shouting cowboy yells they had heard in American movies as they turned off the road into the grassy meadow of their encampment.

This brought the two students left behind running from their tent, creating an emotional scene, everyone embracing and milling from group to group in celebration of their revived fraternity.

Tom, smiling and watching, waited until the excitement subsided and tents were pitched, then convened a meeting to outline the procedures they would follow in their new survey..

"That's how we'll do it," he concluded. "Now I insist everyone get to bed right after you eat. We've got a long and arduous day ahead tomorrow."

The next morning, in rainy, drizzly weather, he set up his headquarters in a curtained jeep on the outskirts of Cochaba, and sent the student teams into the town, despite concern over occasional flashes of lightning on the horizon. He hoped they didn't signal the approach of a major storm.

"Report back no later than mid-afternoon," he told the leaders, glancing again at dark clouds now rushing in, propelled by a cold wind.

Then came the interminable waiting. To pass the time Tom studied the villagers hurrying by, some in business clothes moving toward the center of town, others in denims, carrying hoes and rakes, en route to nearby fields. All stared at the vehicle that had not been there the day before. Finally, one man approached. When Tom opened the curtain the man asked in good English, "I don't mean to be rude, sir, but may I ask what you are doing here?"

"Conducting a population study." Tom smiled. "Should be completed in a day or two."

The man seemed satisfied. He passed on Tom's answer to others who had gathered during the conversation.

Tom read, munched a sandwich, and drew up charts to use in recording the teams' findings. He had just completed the last one when the first group reported in, followed quickly by a second. He was surprised how consistent their findings were. By four o'clock there was such a confluence of information he was certain of his next move. One family was repeatedly singled out as having lived there longer than any other, possibly since biblical times.

With mounting excitement, Tom arrived at the Nazarean church the next day to keep a hastily made appointment with the Reverend Jacob David, bishop of the diocese.

He was escorted into an austere anteroom with stark white walls and a window at one end. It was bare of furnishings save a black, upholstered chair and an ancient sofa with a coffee table in between. A small crucifix rested against a bowl of fresh-cut flowers there. An old pendulum clock ticked loudly from a position halfway up the far wall.

Tom dropped into the chair. He became increasingly nervous as the minutes slipped by. His hands were clammy. He could feel perspiration beading his forehead. Had he finally come to the end of his long search? Was he about to meet a direct descendant of Jesus of Nazareth, the God-man whose ethical and religious beliefs had conquered the western world? Was this the culmination of a quest that had eluded mankind for centuries -- living, verifiable proof Jesus Christ had indeed come and gone in this little corner of the world?

The clock ticked loudly. Thunder grumbled and complained in the distance, and Tom mopped his brow with a soiled handkerchief. He tried to swallow and couldn't.

Suddenly the door on the far side opened and a tall, slender man in denim work clothes entered. He was about six foot three, a little taller than Tom, and appeared to be in his fifties. His dark hair was brushed with snow at the temples. A closely cropped beard circled his jaw, below regular features set off by prominent cheekbones. But it was the eyes, large and luminous, that commanded Tom's attention. They flashed like signal fires atop his slightly stooped body. Tom was struck dumb. Icy fingers danced up his spine.

"Mr. Shannon, I apologize for being late. Your request to see me reached me at the farm this morning. I came as soon as I could get away."

The words, in a rumbling bass, were spoken in precise, European English as the man advanced toward Tom, right hand extended.

Tom stumbled to his feet. "I...I...," he began while managing to grasp the proffered hand.

"Sit down, sit down," the Reverend David said, waving Tom back to the chair as he moved to the sofa. "Perhaps you will join me in a cup of tea. It will help us shake off the chill of this beastly weather."

Tom nodded, gulped, as the door opened and an aide brought in a steaming pot and two cups.

"Reverend David," Tom began after a few swallows of the fragrant brew, "I hope you won't think me too presumptuous, but I'm here on a rather unusual mission."

The luminous eyes peered at him over the rim of a raised cup. "Actually, Mr. Shannon -- " He lowered the cup. " -- I know why you're here. I've been expecting you."

"You have?" Tom stiffened, even more nervous than before.

"Of course. Word was brought to me shortly after your first students arrived in town. Parishioners told me strangers were here, under the direction of a young American, who was trying to locate the family with the oldest roots in the village, one whose ancestry dated back to the first century A.D. Since it's possible my family meets those requirements I assumed you would eventually ask to see me."

"Oh." Tom felt better, "I hope this didn't -- "

"But actually," the Reverend continued, "I was expecting you long before that. I knew that one day, you, or someone very much like you, would come here making inquiries."

Tom could feel goose bumps prickling his arms, and was acutely aware of the descending gloom of the day outside, partly visible through the far window. "How could you possibly know I would come here?" He could hear the tension in his own voice.

The Reverend smiled. "How do you Americans say it? It was in the cards...a stacked deck." He looked pleased, having found the expression he wanted.

"I still don't understand," Tom said, haltingly.

The Reverend nodded. "I realize it may sound like I'm jumping to a conclusion, but I can tell from the questions your students have been asking what your purpose is in coming here. So perhaps it will save time if I provide some background. It's a long story. Please bear with me."

The tall clergyman set his cup down, leaned back on the sofa, eyes fixed on the clock's swinging pendulum.

"As you know by now my family has lived in this area for centuries, quite possibly since biblical times. There is no absolute proof, but from time to time my ancestors have mentioned in letters and other extant writings that they believe our family sprang from the House of David. Indeed our name indicates that. At one time it might have been Ben David, or perhaps Bar David. Both versions mean son of David, in Hebrew and Aramaic. But since you have studied Jewish history, I'm certain you know that."

Tom felt those goose bumps again. *How could he know what I have studied?*

The Reverend picked up the crucifix from the table..

"You may not be quite so familiar, however, with a

particular naming practice followed by many Jewish families. The firstborn son is named after the paternal grandfather, the second after the maternal grandfather, and daughters, likewise, after paternal and maternal grandmothers. Later children are given the names of aunts and uncles."

The Reverend began turning the crucifix over and over in his hand. "I mention this because it plays a part in what I want to tell you."

There was a knock on the door. The portal flew open and a little girl, about three years old, burst into the room, followed by a more sedate boy of perhaps eleven. A pretty, dark-haired woman followed.

"Papa we're ready to leave," the little girl said, crawling into the clergyman's lap and throwing her arms around his neck.

He hugged her as she bussed him on the cheek and then reached out with one arm to draw the boy close. The Reverend's face beamed with pride.

"Mr. Shannon, this is my wife, Mary, and these are two of our children, James and Lydia. They are going to join their brother and sister, Joseph and Assia, who are visiting in Nazareth. All of them are bilingual, in Hebrew and English," he added proudly. "We've raised them that way."

Tom rose, bowed slightly to Mrs. David, patted the little girl on the head and gravely shook the boy's hand. Lydia, nestled in her father's lap, stared at Tom with large, brown eyes.

"This is my papa," she announced. "Have you met him?"

"Yes, indeed I have, young lady. Thank you." More pleasantries followed, then the three departed as quickly as they had appeared.

"Sorry for the interruption." The Reverend gazed off into space. "Let's see now. I had just mentioned the repeated sequence of names." He paused.

"Quite a number of years ago -- " His voice sounded strained. "--Twenty years to be exact, I had a caller. What he had to say totally disrupted my life. Until that moment I had lived quietly as a pastor and part-time farmer, head of a congregation of Nazarean Christians here and in satellite churches scattered across Galilee. Actually, these congregations are largely a closely-knit, extended family of cousins, nephews, nieces, uncles and aunts, and other relatives. Then that caller, that infernal man, almost destroyed all of that."

Tom edged forward in his chair.

The Reverend David's hypnotic eyes fixed on the clock's swinging pendulum across the room. The crucifix rotated rapidly in his hand. Then he resumed.

"That man . . . he introduced himself as Samuel Ben Ashod -- "

The name hit Tom like a thunderbolt. His head jerked up. He stared at Reverend David and grabbed at the arms of the chair for support. Tom's mind reeled. He felt giddy. But he realized some perplexing questions were about to be answered.

"He was a professor," the Reverend continued, "a teacher of Middle Eastern archaeology and anthropology, also an authority on Jewish genealogy and the oral tradition in Jewish history. He told me his research indicated that of all the families with historical roots in Galilee, mine was the oldest. To prove his point, he spread an elaborate chart before me. He pointed out the repetition of various underlined names -- James, Joseph, Simon, Jude, Sokker, Assia and Lydia, or variations of those names, in generation after generation of my family -- but did not say why he considered that important. He just wanted me to be aware of that recurring pattern."

"I noticed your son's name is James," Tom said, "and your daughter's, Lydia."

"I know, I know." The Reverend hurried on. "As I was saying, this professor talked for a time about Cochaba and a village I had never heard of named Nazara. He said, and I have since learned, Nazara was an early name for Nazareth. He also talked about the history of the Nazarean church.

"Basically what he said conformed with what I had been taught -- that the Nazareans were the first Christians, and that our church was the original, the so-called Apostolic Church, the church closest to Christ and his teachings, indeed the first authentic Christian community.

"Then he told me something I had heard before but never fully accepted as the truth. He said the church actually was founded by the family of Christ, not by the apostles, but by Christ's brother, James, and the other brothers -- Joseph, Simon and Jude -- two great nephews named James and Sokker, and a cousin named Symeon."

Reverend David suddenly seemed nervous, sipping his tea hurriedly. He almost slammed his cup into the saucer. The cup rolled off the table and crashed to the floor. "Sorry. Clumsy of me." He pushed the shattered fragments under the table with a foot, then gestured toward Tom with the crucifix.

"By this time, as you can well imagine, the professor's remarks were making me uneasy. He kept returning to four main points: the deep historical roots of my family; the fact that the nucleus of the family lived in Cochaba and had close relatives in Nazareth; that we were leaders of this ancient, Christian church, and the repetition of names in our family tree.

"The last point -- naming sons and daughters after their grandfathers and grandmothers -- he said is an excellent genealogical tool. It helps in tracing family relationships from one generation to another. The same names keep reappearing every other generation.

Something clicked in Tom's mind. Those strange words Samuel had given Dr. Abe: "Jude, Joseph, James and Sokker every other time." The same names occurring every other generation.

"Furthermore," the Reverend continued, "available records suggest my family used the name of Ben Joseph until the Middle Ages, then switched to Ben David and finally just David."

He raked a hand through his dark hair, and spun the crucifix in his hand.before continuing.

"As I said before, I was upset by my visitor. The associations he was making were becoming more and more explicit. Finally he told me the family of Christ had settled in

Cochaba and Nazara not long after the destruction of the Second Temple, and then -- I can recall it now as if it were yesterday -- he turned to me and said: 'Reverend David, my research indicates that you and your family are the closest living descendants of Jesus of Nazareth.'"

Tom came halfway out of his chair. The room swayed. He grabbed the chair for support and sat back down, swallowing, trying to regain stability. The Reverend David was talking again, the crucifix spinning in his hand. "You can imagine the impact of this. For a short time I was elated. I had always been devoutly religious. Now I was being told I was even closer to Christ than I believed possible. But slowly I came to understand the massive change Samuel had injected into my life.

"My relatives, on hearing the news, began to expect things of me I couldn't produce. One cousin sarcastically demanded I perform a miracle or two just to prove the relationship. I began to have difficulty working. Samuel wanted to bring in scholars to meet and talk with me, wanted to probe into the most intimate details of my past, before they made a public disclosure of their findings. Indeed, against my wishes, he did bring some of his colleagues here to plead his case. They even offered me money if I would answer their questions in a series of recorded interviews.

"Under this pressure my personality disintegrated. I drank heavily. I argued with my relatives, some of whom wanted me to take the money and give them part of it. More and more of them came here and stayed to watch the comings and goings of Samuel and his colleagues and to enjoy their new status as potential celebrities. Some of them used the situation to get out of working in the fields, where my people had always labored industriously."

Reverend David paused. The clock on the wall ticked loudly, the pendulum traversing its arc monotonously as he settled back on the sofa again, the crucifix still in his hand.

"You can understand how all this could destroy our family structure and the simple agrarian Christian morality that had held it together. I was being asked to assume the role of a virtual Godman and I was not equipped to do so."

Again a long pause.

"I don't know when the thought first struck me," he finally continued, "but gradually I came to understand I had to remove this cross, had to find proof Samuel was wrong, that there was no direct, physical relationship between my family and Christ. I went into the hills to think. No one knew where I was. When I returned a week later I was tracking the right answer. I had recalled seeing a certain entry in one of our ancient family bibles. I found it, made notes, told my wife I had to take a trip and would return as soon as I could.

"I left the next day for Antalya in Turkey, an ancient city known as Pamphylia during Biblical times. When I returned two months later, I had certified copies of records there that proved two of my ancestors left that city on a trading mission early in the Christian era. They came to what is now Israel, sold their cargo and were preparing to return when a storm dashed their vessel against coastal rocks. It was destroyed and the crew marooned here.

"The vessel's captain paid the men and told them to make their way home as best they could, as he intended to do. He and a small group from the ship traveled together and en route visited Galilee. They fell in love with the land and decided to settle here in Cochaba."

"I'm afraid I don't understand the point you're making, Reverend David."

"The point is, Mr. Shannon, those shipwrecked sailors and their captain were Greek, not Jewish. They did intermarry with local inhabitants, but my branch of the family is partly Greek in origin, not one hundred percent Jewish. That destroyed Samuel's theory."

The clock on the wall suddenly began to chime loudly. Reverend David's mouth dropped open. He stared at the moving pendulum. "The voice of God," he said, half under his breath.

Tom felt a sudden chill. What did you say?" He was uncertain he had heard correctly.

"The voice of God," the Reverend repeated. "That's what I

call it. That clock is always surprising me. It chimes at the most unexpected times, almost as if it were rebuking me."

Tom sat very still; stunned by the Reverend's statement he was not entirely Jewish. Reverend David paused, then continued.

"Let's see. I was telling you about my Greek ancestors. Of course, Samuel didn't believe me. He kept examining the documents I had brought back. He kept asking questions. He even sent an emissary to Antalya to see if the records there showed what I claimed. The man never returned. Then Samuel became angry and accused me of lying, of having faked the documents. I assured him they were authentic and he was unable to prove otherwise.

"In any event doubts were raised. His colleagues decided Samuel's conclusions were in error. He lost face, was discredited in the academic world and eventually became so embittered he stopped teaching and became a virtual hermit on his farm near Beit Shean. Samuel has lived there with his private demons ever since."

The Reverend got up, summoned his aide again and ordered another pot of tea. With a new cup in hand, and Tom's cup refilled, he continued.

"So perhaps you can see, Mr. Shannon, why I was expecting you. Although Samuel's study and erroneous conclusions were never publicized, I assumed that someday someone would pull together much of the same information he did -- so many clues had been left down through the centuries -- and when that someone did so, I knew the trail would lead him or her to my door. I was quite certain from the questions your students were asking that you had done just that."

Tom studied the Reverend, much of his earlier apprehension gone. He was vaguely aware the wind had risen and was whistling down the village street outside.

"Did you lie to Samuel, Reverend David?" Tom asked. "Were the documents faked?" Tom could hear thunder rumbling louder in the distance , was aware of the growing darkness outside as he waited for an answer.

Wind-whipped rain rattled across the roof of the building and flooded the window.

The silence lengthened.

The clock ticked loudly on the far wall.

Suddenly the Reverend David realized he was holding the crucifix in his hand. He set it down abruptly, as if it were hot and might burn. During the ensuing, strained seconds not a single, telltale sign reached his remarkable face to indicate an inner struggle over moral principle might be underway in his mind.

Finally an eyelid fluttered. There was a slight, almost imperceptible tightening around his mouth. Then even these tiny reactions disappeared.

"Of course not," he said firmly, his great, hypnotic eyes boring into Tom's. "Furthermore, I think you should understand just how ridiculous it would be to attach great importance to Samuel's findings, even if they were true."

"Why so?"

"Think for a moment. You had two parents. Your parents, collectively, had four parents. Your parents' parents had eight. Another generation back there were sixteen. You double the number of direct ancestors every generation. By the tenth generation, going back in time you would have had one thousand twenty four direct ancestors. If one of those one thousand twenty four happened to be a member of Christ's family you can see how greatly the original family strain would have been diluted. But in this instance, of course, we are not talking about ten generations. Nearly two thousand years have elapsed since the Second Temple was destroyed and the family of Christ left Jerusalem. That comes to more than sixty-three generations, allowing the normal thirty years for each.

"I can't even calculate the number of direct ancestors a single person, standing at the bottom of that inverted pyramid, would have. Obviously it would be in the tens of millions or more. After so much dilution, how could anyone believe that any detectable human inheritance could remain from a few ancestors among those millions?"

Tom shook his head. "What you say is only partly correct, Reverend David. You are overlooking the fact that in many births in Christ's family both parents were related to Christ, since many of Christ's descendants and their offspring intermarried. Every time this happened the physical inheritance from Christ's family was doubled. So while there was dilution there also was enhancement. Besides, physical, and perhaps mental, characteristics never totally disappear. They can crop up at any time."

"I suppose I can't dispute that, Mr. Shannon. Even I sometimes feel that -- " He caught himself, casting a worried look at Tom. "Rather in my case I don't feel any such association."

Outside the church the skies opened and rain came down in torrents. Inside the conversation obviously was nearing an end.

Tom felt sick. He had walked to the brink of Paradise, peered over the edge, then suddenly the vision had been swept away. His long odyssey, his carefully nurtured dream, was ending in failure, or, like Samuel's before him, in fatal, terminal doubt.

The storm, punctuated by crashing bolts of lightning, lashed the building, rattling windows and doors.

The Reverend David didn't pause. "There are one or two more points I would like to make, Mr. Shannon. You must understand one thing about me, and a very important thing about yourself." He drew in a long breath, his luminous eyes staring directly at Tom. Tom felt like he was looking into a fiery pit. The Reverend's voice seemed to come from far away, calm, measured, yet rumbling with inner force.

"I am not Christ. I cannot and will not play that role. One crucifixion in our fam -- " Again he caught himself. "One crucifixion is enough," he finished awkwardly.

"As for yourself, you must understand why you are here. Why you have gone to such lengths to track me down in this humble, farming village. You haven't expended all that effort to find a family of human beings. You are after something greater than that."

"What might that be?" Tom asked. His voice sounded

weak, distant, detached from his body.

"You have been searching for God. Surely by now you know you cannot find him in other, fallible, human beings, and that is all we have here. You must find him within yourself and within your own experience, just as have so many others before you. Go home, Mr. Shannon. Go home and let me live in peace."

The words were spoken gently, softly, but with shattering force.

Tom felt like he was sleepwalking, that he was outside himself, watching his own movements. He knew he rose, shook hands with Reverend David, thanked him in a strained voice.

As he stumbled out into the storm he heard the clock tolling loudly behind him.

With the rain gushing over his head and face, he stood beside his jeep and looked up at the roiling heavens. Dark angry clouds rushed by. The wind rose to a maniacal shriek, driving the rain against his soaked clothing. Lightning danced along the horizon, then a huge bolt streaked down from the sky and crashed into a tall tree on a nearby hill, shattering the wood, hurling fiery fragments in all directions. Thunder shook the ground under him.

Tom was like that tree -- torn asunder, his inner self broken into fragments. Slowly, mechanically, he got into the jeep and drove back to the encampment.

Chapter XXXIV

Derek came down the cafeteria line at *Kibbutz Ain Gedi* with only a glass of ice tea on his tray -- a treat he allowed himself every afternoon. He was dirty, unkempt, his face covered with stubble sprouting in several directions. He paid for the tea with coins from his pocket, carefully counted out, then shuffled over to a long rectangular table occupied only by a young Jewish couple he had seen at the nearby campground.

He sat at the far end and stirred his ice tea loudly, almost violently, beating his spoon into the bottom of the glass, sending a racket throughout the dining area. He glared around the room, wondering if anyone was watching him. Several were. He could sense it. Talking about him, too, particularly that young couple. He heard them whispering.

Derek spun around to stare at them, catch them in the act. The young man looked away and the girl looked down at her food. Face flushed, anger mounting, Derek continued to stare. Finally certain they would bother him no more, he returned to perusing the room and thinking about his stay.

Things had gone about as he expected. He had arrived at the *kibbutz* the morning after leaving the cave at Qumran three weeks ago, rented a tent and cooking equipment and set up housekeeping. He was able to purchase groceries at the commissary, had free run of the area and far too much idle time.

That was his problem, plus the slow growth of his beard --

and that voice. Derek winced at the thought of it, shrank back in fear even where he was sitting, his eyes searching the room, hoping the voice wasn't lurking nearby. It was never inside him any more. Always outside, and frightening. He never knew when it would speak, or in what manner.

Sometimes it was soft and seductive, almost sensual.

"You must warn the people," it crooned. "Only you can save them. You are their only hope. Christianity is in danger."

Other times it assaulted him, shouting, screaming, pounding him in loud, cymbal crashes inside his head, forcing him to clamp his hands over his ears, even grovel on the ground, begging, "No! No! Please!" while the voice thundered, "Do it now! Stop wasting time! Deliver the warning!"

At first this happened only at night. Derek would spring from his cot, look wildly around the tent, even check outside. Always he found nothing. Then the attacks started occurring during daylight hours also, so frequently he could never be certain he was safe, or that he had sufficient will to resist.

"I can't do that," he would shout in reply to this tormentor, startling anyone within ear shot, "I must wait. My beard and hair must be longer. My disguise more complete."

During calmer periods, Derek toured the *kibbutz*, studied its many functions from growing crops to sponsoring an orchestra, checked on the daily habits of his camping neighbors and noted the cars they drove, particularly the new Fiat used by the young couple now giving him trouble at the end of the table.

They were exchanging comments about him again, nodding and glancing his way. He could tell. Smirking too. Laughing at him.

Derek rose, eyes blazing, face red, and walked slowly, menacingly, to their end of the table. He stopped and jabbed a finger in the young man's face.

"Keep your God damned eyes off me and your opinions to yourself. You understand!" He shouted the last two words, thrust his upper body forward, pushing his livid face close to the startled countenance of the young man. Heads throughout the cafeteria turned to see who was causing the commotion.

"You understand!" Derek shouted one more time. He banged his fist on the tabletop, then stalked angrily out of the room, leaving a wave of whispered comments behind him.

CHAPTER XXXV

The failure of Tom's project left him with a deep wound in his sense of personal worth and mission in life. The damage emerged as a resurgence of the depression he had been fighting in recent months. He was psychologically drained of content and purpose. He spoke to those around him in as few words as possible. He acknowledged their kindness and concern, but lapsed into periods of contemplation, usually seated at the desk in his hotel room, gazing out the window.

He was there when Shlomo Kahane knocked on his door ten days after Tom returned from Cochaba. The Inspector sat down, got right to the point.

"We have the final report from our research department on attempting to use fingerprints to trace biological relationships, Tom. It can't be done. There is no predictable pattern of similarities."

Tom thanked him, closed the door after him and resumed his contemplation. This eliminated a last possible method of proving, no matter what Reverend David said, that he had found the descendants of Christ. His depression deepened.

He was also at the desk when Dr. Abe informed him Meyer Bernstein, Four-fingers Guzik and several of their henchmen had been arrested and deported from the country.

"They're gone, Tom. And good riddance. The government acted swiftly, viewing it as a situation that couldn't be tolerated."

None of this made an impression on him. He took to wandering the streets at night, walking aimlessly down one dim corridor after another. He stopped in at bars, sitting huddled in a corner, vacantly staring at the babble of sounds that came at him from the constantly moving mouths and scrunched up bodies in the room. Then he would walk some more.

Twice he was picked up by police and returned to his hotel in a semi-dazed condition. Fran and Dr. Abe were summoned by the hotel night clerk on both occasions and asked to take charge of him. Their anxiety increased as weeks slipped by with no visible change.

Two days after the second of these occasions Dr. Abe and Fran checked on him again. There was no response when they knocked on his hotel room door. When they pushed it open they found Tom seated at the desk, a half-empty bottle of scotch beside his right hand.

He looked up, waved them to nearby chairs.

"Tom, I don't think you should be drinking in your present condition," Fran said. "And you've got to get some sleep."

"I slept some. I'll be okay in a few days now, after I finish sorting out some things in my mind. Get my head on straight again."

"Where did you sleep?" Fran noted the bed was still made.

"Here." He patted the desk. "That's good enough for now."

"Tom, we brought you some news," Dr. Abe interjected. "We have the translation of the parchment fragments taken from Joseph's Cave. Not all of the sentences are complete. Some areas have eroded away, and there are a few missing pieces. But there is no doubt it is a well known passage from the Gospel of John. The citation is John, Chapter Eleven, verses twenty-five and twenty-six. Would you like me to read it?"

"No need. That's what I expected it to be." He took another gulp of scotch, then began to recite in a hoarse, half-whisper. "'I am the resurrection and the life -- '" He stopped, swallowed, took a deep breath, continued in a hoarse voice. "He who believes in me, though he were dead, yet shall he live -- '"

His voice drifted away. Tom took another drink. This time the words were stronger.

"'And whosoever liveth and believeth in me shall never die.'"

"You knew what was on the parchment?" Dr. Abe's mouth was open, his eyebrows elevated.

"Well, sort of. It fits with everything else I've learned."

"You're talking more than usual, Tom," Dr. Abe decided. "That's good, but how..."

"You look a little better, too," Fran interrupted. "Not quite as drained and tense as you have been."

"Tom smiled weakly, swallowed. "I am better, and suddenly I feel like I might be able to sleep for a while. "

"But what did you mean it fits?" Fran asked.

Dr. Abe placed a restraining hand on her arm. "I think we should go now. We'll look in on you again tomorrow, Tom."

Fran, looking back, saw him collapse on the bed before Dr. Abe pulled the door shut. She sighed wearily, worn down by worrying about Tom -- and Derek too. What could have happened to him? He had been swallowed up by the desert without a trace.

Chapter XXXVI

Derek crouched in the brush bordering the *kibbutz* campground. His face was covered by a dark beard, blending into a mat of tangled hair reaching down both sides of his head and over part of his brow. His clothes were filthy, his eyes blazing, as he watched the shadows of the young Jewish couple, cast against the side of their tent by a lone, overhead light bulb.

Derek was almost holding his breath, unable to believe his good fortune. The young man had driven up in his Fiat a half hour ago. As he picked up a bag of groceries purchased at the commissary, his wife urgently called him from inside the tent. He slammed the car door, rushed in, but forgot to remove his keys from the ignition. The wife's problem was apparently minor, since the commotion inside subsided, but serious enough to cause the husband to forget to return and lock the vehicle.

It wouldn't have mattered, Derek told himself. He could have forced the lock and hot-wired the ignition. This just made it easier.

He continued to watch. The shadow of the woman moved closer to her husband. She put her arms around his neck and kissed him. He cupped his hands under her buttocks, pulling her up tightly against him. The embrace continued several seconds, then the man's hand reached up and turned off the light.

Good, Derek thought. Sex would make both sleep well. He waited another half hour. All sound within the tent ceased.

Slowly, Derek rose from his crouch and crept forward. He opened the car door, rolled down the window, put the gearshift in neutral, and released the emergency brake. With his left shoulder against the windshield, and legs straining against the ground, he rolled the vehicle backward, steering with his right arm through the opened driver's-side window.

Twenty feet from the couple's tent he turned the car and pushed it toward the campground exit. Another 30 feet and he stopped, perspiring and breathing heavily. He crawled into the driver's seat, turned on the ignition. The motor caught immediately. At a very slow speed he drove the Fiat over to his tent, picked up his machine pistol and copy of the Samuel transcripts, then drove slowly out the exit gate. Not until he was a good two hundred feet beyond the camp did he hit the gas and move out quickly.

Derek grinned, happy for the first time in the five weeks he had spent at the kibbutz. This was a victory. His plan was working, even though a light rain had begun to fall. There would be no more insults from people at the camp talking about him, staring at him. No more sessions with the campground supervisor, passing on complaints from his neighbors and suggestions he should leave. Perhaps, soon, no more demands from that voice that kept screaming at him to warn the people about the blasphemy Tom Shannon was trying to spread.

"I'll warn them soon enough," he said, slamming a fist on the dashboard. "I'll take care of that, then it's you and me against the world, Fran, and on to America and a new life. Don't let me down, old girl."

He peered ahead through the increasingly heavy rainfall whipping across the highway, then pulled over to the side of the road. A quick check of the car's interior revealed what he was looking for -- a slicker wadded up in one corner of the back seat.

"Good," he muttered, putting it on. He stuffed the copy of the Samuel tapings into a large side pocket, then restarted the motor and drove on into the night.

Chapter XXXVII

It was a whisper in the night.

"Fran."

Fran, asleep, dreamed someone had called her.

"Fran."

She opened her eyes, lifted her head from the pillow. Had someone spoken her name? She heard it again.

"Fran!"

The summons was more insistent this time.

Fran sat up, cold with fear. She didn't dare move. Was someone in the apartment? She looked at the bedside clock -- five a.m.

"Fran, open up. It's urgent."

There was no mistaking now. Someone outside was calling to her.

Heart racing, she jumped up, pulled on a negligee, and pushed her feet into slippers beside the bed. She shuffled across the living room, heels slapping the floor, and peered through the peephole in her front door.

A large, lumpy figure loomed in the shadows.

"Damn it, Fran, let me in. We haven't got all night. Hurry it up now, girl." The voice was louder, more demanding -- and sounded familiar.

She swallowed, tried to speak.

"Who are you? What do you want?"

"It's me, Derek. Open up, I say. We can't afford to lose any more time."

Fran snapped on the porch light. The pale illumination revealed a huge man in a bulging slicker, a machine pistol slung over one shoulder. Rainwater dripped from his tangled brown hair, pasting it to a broad forehead, above two wild and glaring eyes. The face was covered with a heavy beard, sprouting in all directions.

"Who did you say you are?" she asked again, her voice quavering. She had heard the first time but didn't believe it.

"God damn it, Fran, it's me, Derek. Now open up. We've got a lot to accomplish."

"Derek? You don't look like Derek. Who are you?"

The man pounded the door with his fists.

"Open up, damn you, or I'll break this thing down! What the hell's the matter with you?"

She looked through the peephole again, saw lights come on in two neighboring apartments of the complex, a largely English-speaking enclave of foreigners, then backed away from the door, quaking with fear. Starting to turn, she tripped over a footstool and fell to the floor, but came up quickly and continued her retreat across the living room.

The battering at the door became more violent.

Fran stuffed a fist into her mouth. Could it actually be Derek? The voice did sound like his, with a harsh new edge, but that face, those eyes. No, it couldn't be.

There was a sudden shattering of wood and a foot appeared through one of the door's lower panels.

"What's going on over there?" a male voice shouted from next door.

Fran raced to the telephone, dialed, gave a room number and screamed, "Tom, help me! A man is breaking down my front door! Oh, come quickly, please!"

* * *

Tom, half asleep, came suddenly awake, his depression swept aside. He pulled the phone away from his ear, stared at it in disbelief, then clamped it back between his shoulder and head, shouting as he snapped on the bedside light. "Fran? Is that you? What's going on? Fran? Fran? Are you there?"

He heard loud, rending sounds, as if wood were splintering, then gunfire and what sounded like the crash of a door banging back against a wall. Somebody screamed and the line went dead.

Tom, aghast, hung up and dialed the police. After three, incomprehensible verbal exchanges in Hebrew a bored, sleepy voice came on and asked in English, "Yes, what can I do for you?"

"There's a break-in in progress at twenty-five Mocho Street in the Rehavia district. A woman's life is in danger. Please hurry."

Tom, in his haste, dropped the phone and grabbed his pants from the hotel room closet. As he jammed in first one leg then the other, and donned shoes without socks, he could hear the voice from the dangling receiver asking, "What was that? What did you say, sir? Was that address -- "

Tom ignored the phone, burst out the door and headed for the elevator, still tugging on a sport shirt over his head. Moments later he sprinted past the startled night clerk into the hotel parking lot, as the first signs of dawn brightened the eastern horizon.

The motor of his new rental car caught on the second try. With its headlights flooding the exit gate, he roared into the street, tires squealing. He whipped the car into a ninety-degree turn and raced away in the semi-darkness, eyes straining to see ahead. He was convinced now the voice he had heard was Fran's and she was caught up in some incredible emergency he couldn't begin to understand. He had to help.

Ten minutes later Tom's car skidded to a stop in front of her apartment building. He threw open the door and dashed up the walk toward people milling in front of Fran's shattered, ground-floor door. He grabbed the arm of a man in a faded blue bathrobe, and spun him around.

"What happened?" he asked breathlessly. "I got a call...she

sounded frantic."

"Better talk to him." The man motioning toward William Corman, a neighbor of Fran's Tom had met some weeks before. Corman, sighting Tom, broke away from a group he was talking to and approached.

"It's Mr. Shannon I believe. Are you here because of Miss Brown? We're trying to piece together what happened. I heard part of it, saw a little, too. I woke up when I heard someone shouting, calling her by name and pounding on her door. Then I heard gunfire. Whoever it was apparently shot out the lock. I looked through the window. Her porch light was on. I couldn't see much, other than her door was open. Then this big, hairy guy in a slicker rushed out, dragging Miss Brown. She was screaming, dressed only in a nightgown, robe and slippers. He kept hitting her and shouting something about going to the Pinnacle of the Temple to save Christianity. He forced her into the car and drove off."

Tom froze in place. "Pinnacle of the Temple!? There hasn't been any Pinnacle of the Temple since the Romans sacked Jerusalem. That makes no sense."

Suddenly he stopped, a thought flashing in his mind as he heard the wail of approaching sirens in the distance. He grabbed Corman's arm.

"Tell the police what you told me," he said. "Tell them to go to Temple Mount." He wheeled and ran toward his car with Corman calling after him: "Where on Temple Mount?"

"I don't know," Tom shouted back, slamming the car door. Moments later he sped up the street, tires squealing, horn blaring as he raced through early morning traffic toward the highest point in Jerusalem, the elevated platform where the Second Temple once reared against the sky, an area now called Temple Mount.

Chapter XXXVIII

Tom skidded to a stop outside Jaffa Gate. He bolted from the car into the walled city of Old Jerusalem, sprinted up David Street, turned right into the broad plaza fronting the Wailing Wall and halted, uncertain where to go next. His eyes swept the area. All was serene. Only a few, early worshipers stood there, chanting, nodding, praying, leaving folded messages in crevices of the huge stone blocks forming part of the western base on which the Second Temple once rested, now popularly called the Wailing Wall..

So where should he look for a huge, hairy man dragging a girl in a nightgown, robe and slippers? Tom, his fears mounting, had no idea. He tried to think logically, but felt panicky.

Think, mind! Help me! Give me some idea what to do!

His mind came up with nothing. He tried to think logically.

Fran's abductor had said he was going to the Pinnacle of the Temple, in biblical times a broad area atop the juncture of the former southern and eastern perimeter columns surrounding the Temple, a place that no longer existed.

So if the Pinnacle of the Temple was gone, where would the guy go now?

This time he got a glimmering.

Fran's abductor would substitute some other still-

identifiable site associated with the Temple. Why not the Wailing Wall, where Jews came to mourn the fate of their fallen house of worship?

That was it! Tom was convinced. And the Wailing Wall was right there in front of him, but where was Fran? He turned, looked around, saw only early morning strollers, shopkeepers nearby, pulling up squealing storefront shutters, and two early Bar Mitzvah processions approaching.

As the plaza gradually filled with people, he looked at the top of the Wall, sixty feet high, the equivalent of a five-story or six-story building. There were scores of places up there where the abductor, whoever he was, could hide. *Whoever he was --*

Tom slapped a hand against his forehead. Finally his mind was working. Of course, Fran's kidnaper was Derek. Derek knew Fran's name and address. So did the man who had kidnapped her. Derek was large. So was the abductor. And in a time of need, Derek very likely would seek help from Fran. He did not know why the Englishman had turned into a wild man, or had dragged Fran into the Old City in her nightgown, but was certain now he was looking for Derek. That helped.

Tom shook his head, trying again to think.

So where would Derek take Fran? He looked up, seeking a clue, just as the rising sun engulfed the Wall in a burst of blinding, golden light.

Tom raised a hand to shield his eyes. When he looked back again two figures emerged out of the glare at the top of the Wall, their bodies etched in fire against the sky.

One was a large man, his head a mass of tangled hair, his body swathed in a slicker, his right hand holding a bundle of papers aloft. The other was a struggling woman, clad only in a robe and nightgown, her body clamped against the man's side by his left arm around her neck. The man jerked his head up violently, sending his hair flying out in a sunlit nimbus around a bearded face. To Tom, he resembled a prophet out of the Old Testament as he held the pose, then looked down and began to speak.

"Hear me, oh citizens of Jerusalem -- "

Although faint, the voice was Derek's, different, but recognizable, and there was no question the woman was Fran.

God! What do I do now? Tom felt helpless.

Nearby, some of the worshipers also heard the voice and looked around, seeking the source. Then they heard it again.

"Hear me, oh citizens of Jerusalem, as I pass on the word of the man God sent to save you -- "

The voice was louder, more distinct now. Several more in the crowd looked up. One man pointed. Others raised their heads too.

"Hear me, oh citizens of Jerusalem -- " This time the words carried clearly in the fresh, rain-washed air -- "those who sent the Lord Jesus to his death would have me tell you that you must not believe in him -- "

The plaza below the Wailing Wall was jammed with upturned faces now, all eyes on the strange man and the struggling, scantily-clad woman who had materialized out of the sunrise atop the stone wall. Tom noticed that people in nearby streets also had halted and looked up, while far away he heard the mournful wail of approaching police sirens.

Thank god, Tom thought. The police will know what to do, how to rescue her.

On the wall above, Fran began to struggle. She screamed and kicked, trying to break free of Derek's arm. He jerked her head up against his side, choking her, and turned back to address the crowd below.

"Hear me, oh citizens of Jerusalem -- "

Tom knew now he couldn't wait. Fran's peril was too immediate, too great. He turned, dashed through the crowd, ran into people, knocked one old man down, murmured an apology, hurried on to the curved ramp leading to Temple Mount.

Up the incline he raced, through the brief tunnel of Moor's Gate, then onto the open platform above, panting and perspiring, looking around frantically, trying to plot his next move. The silver dome of the El Aqsa Mosque loomed to his right, the massive, golden super-structure of the Dome of the Rock Mosque to his left, set against the sky, partly screened by cypress trees. The top of the Wall, Derek and Fran, were to his left rear.

Tom sprinted toward the Wall, using the trees as cover, then slowed and approached cautiously. Thirty yards away, Derek was poised on the Wall's edge, his back to Tom. He was still waving the papers in his right hand and holding Fran tightly with his left arm. The machine pistol dangled from a sling around his neck. He was speaking again, his voice now resonant and clear.

"Hear me, oh citizens of Jerusalem, those who sent the Lord Jesus to his death would have me say you must not believe in him. I tell you they lie! He has fulfilled the scriptures. He was crucified, rose on the third day and for forty days -- "

Tom searched his mind. Where had he heard those words before?

As he stepped into the open from the shadow of the trees, a renewed screaming of police sirens suddenly filled the air, arriving and winding down, outside the Old City walls.

"Let her go, Derek!" Tom shouted.

The hairy figure spun around, eyes wild and glaring, body rigid. "You," he breathed. "You dare -- "

Fran, her head still held tightly against Derek's side, looked up enough to recognize Tom. She began struggling again, pushing, jerking, kicking frantically.

"Tom, help me!" she screamed. Her face was contorted with pain, her hair dangling, feet bare and bleeding, the bedroom slippers lost in fighting Derek. Torn fragments of her robe dangled from her shoulders.

"Shut up!" Derek shouted, jerking her tighter against his side. "I'll -- "

"Let her go, Derek!" Tom repeated, voice rising. "We can talk this out, get you some help. You've nothing to gain by continuing like this."

"Damn you, pagan," Derek snarled, waving the papers in his hand, "you're the one who caused all this with your blasphemous report. I'll settle with you in a moment."

He turned partway back toward the crowd below, but only far enough to permit continued surveillance of Tom, to his left rear. Derek's right hand stabbed the air again, waving his stolen copy of the Samuel transcripts.

"I have not finished. The day of judgment is near for false prophets and desecrators of the law!" He turned, pointed at Tom with his right hand, still holding the tapings, then turned back toward the crowd below.

"So you ask about the Son of Man and his way," he shouted. His voice was shrill. "I say to you at this very moment he is in heaven, sitting at the right hand of God, and from there he will depart soon and return on a golden cloud to stand in judgment on all of you, and particularly on this foul desecrator of Christianity."

As Derek again pointed at him, Tom suddenly realized where he had encountered those words -- reading James' address from the Pinnacle of the Temple.

"He deserves to die and he will!" Derek screamed.

He stepped back, face twisted, inadvertently loosening his grip on Fran's neck as he swung the machine pistol around in front of him to aim at Tom.

Fran, sensing the change, jerked her head free and swung a clenched fist. The blow hit Derek squarely on the nose.

Startled, Derek stepped back, brought up the gun. He fired at Tom just as Fran shoved him with both hands.

He reeled backward.

Tom hit the ground. The bullets ripped by over his head, stitching the dirt behind him.

Derek, off balance, lurched further back, face suddenly sick with fear. He back-pedaled, trying desperately to regain equilibrium.

Teetering on the brink of the Wall, he threw out both arms. One struck Fran across the chest as she turned to flee. The Englishman's clutching fingers grabbed her nightgown, as the other hand released an avalanche of the typewritten pages into the air.

For Tom, the scene shifted into slow motion.

Derek was falling.

Fran was staggering backward toward the abyss.

Tom, legs pumping, was sprinting toward her, but, as in a nightmare, at a paralyzingly slow pace.

Derek, eyes wide with terror, inch by inch, toppled backward into space, his raincoat filling with air, ballooning into bat-like wings around him, papers of the Samuel report forming a shower of white around his kicking, twisting body, falling in a manner strangely reminiscent of Tom's imagined image of James when pushed from the Temple wall so many centuries before.

"Help me!" Derek's terrorized scream echoed across the square as his body disappeared from sight.

Fran screamed too as she also went over the edge.

Normal speed returned.

Tom dived, landing flat on his stomach. He reached, desperately trying to grab Fran's arm, now disappearing below the rim of the Wall.

His fingers closed around her forearm, slipped, caught her wrist and held, as he was dragged across the ground.

Tom dug in his feet and clawed the dirt with his free left hand.

Suddenly those torn, bleeding fingers encountered an embedded stone. His forward motion stopped abruptly.

There was a jolt as Fran's falling body jerked to a stop, dangling down the face of the Wall.

A savage pain rocketed up Tom's right arm. He groaned, took several quick breaths, tried to pull.

He couldn't lift her.

He buried his face in the dirt, trying not to think, trying to ignore the pain and the screaming of Fran, twisting and kicking just below him, free hand clawing at the wall.

Minutes passed. He was in agony, the excruciating hurt in his arm and shoulder almost more than he could bear. He felt sick. Perspiration streamed down his face, dripped down his arm, reached the weakening fingers of his right hand, clinging desperately to Fran.

He looked down. Fran's face was ashen, contorted with fright. She looked up, her lips forming words without sound.

"Please help me."

Tom buried his face in the dirt again. He couldn't help her. He didn't have the strength to lift her and his fingers were slipping. Disaster was seconds away.

Suddenly the rock under his left hand shifted. Tom gasped, dug his fingers deeper. Again the rock moved, then held.

If the rock gives way will I release Fran and save myself, or fall six stories with her?

Tom groaned. He feared he would save himself.

Again the rock shifted.

Again Tom's grip on Fran slipped.

Now he saw the situation with terrifying clarity.

This was Fran's last moment on earth. Perhaps his too.

He looked over the edge into Fran's eyes. She looked up, somehow calmer and more resigned, no longer screaming. She seemed to read his mind.

"Let me go, Tom," she whispered. "Save yourself."

At that moment of agony, Tom did as man has always done when staring into the maw of approaching death --

Whether his God is called Yahweh, Jehovah, Jupiter, Buddha, Allah or Zeus --

Whether his God's messenger is Mohammed, Siddhartha Gautama, Lao-tze or Christ --

Whether his God is a white-haired, old man clutching a shepherd's hook, living somewhere up in the clouds, or he finds a divine, God-like pattern in the energy that permeates the universe, energy that gives life to all living things, including man and the germs that attack him --

Whether he thinks his God created man and the universe in six days, or lifted him up over eons of time in a form of creation called evolution --

Whether he believes God resides somewhere inside all of us and is responsible for those activities that uplift, ennoble and help us live more intelligent and humane lives --

Whether Tom believed any part, all, or none of this, he did as men before him have always done when faced with the certainty of death --

He lifted his head and prayed.

"Dear God, help me!"

It was a supplication torn from the soul of the great, irreconcilable agnostic -- and a demonstration that deep within him he knew that some force or process, above and beyond his control and understanding, had placed him and all other living creatures on earth, and that force was at the heart of the mystery of life, and therefore had to be God.

Almost simultaneously the rock under his left hand ripped loose, his body surged forward and he heard the pounding of running, approaching feet.

He was on the brink, going over, staring down at a sea of horrified, upturned, white faces below.

Suddenly two things happened.

Someone grabbed his feet.

And he felt a great surge of strength within him. Fire raced through his body, suffused his mind, engulfed his being.

He screamed, "Ahhhhhhhhhhhhhhh! Grunted. Gasped.. Gathered every resource of his agonized body, every ounce of strength within him. He Pulled! Pulled! Pulled!

Where there was no strength before, there was strength now. Where there was pain and desperation, there was searing heat, a furnace burning within him, a new power, still engulfed in overwhelming, agonizing pain. All this, mingled with desperation, anger and fear.

And where there was no hope before there was fierce determination.

He would not go over the brink! He pulled! pulled! And pulled some more.

Fran's body began to rise. Tom, agonized, screamed again, reached into the depths of his body and soul, mustered every scintilla of strength he had. His eyes protruded, head pounded, face twisted. He felt like his skull would explode, and the protruding, distended cords in his arm and neck would break. So he pulled harder.

Fran's body rose some more. Her head and tangled hair appeared above the rim of the wall, then her shoulders, high enough for many arms, clothed in police blue, to reach down and grab her.

Another blue-clad arm reached over Tom and grasped her shoulder. More arms grabbed her hair and nightgown.

Tom saw a vaguely familiar figure, speaking with the voice of Shlomo Kahane, drop down over the edge of the Wall, cling there by one hand and help lift her as she was deposited in a heap beside him.

He had done it! My God, he had done it!

Gasping with relief and exhaustion, Tom muttered, "Thank you, God." Slowly he slipped into a dark, peaceful world where there was no pain. His ordeal, and Fran's, was over.

Chapter XXXIX

Tom and Fran were placed in adjoining hospital rooms. Each was examined and told he, and she, would recover rapidly. Fran, particularly, although battered and bruised, felt better after a night's rest and went next door to visit the following morning..

Tom opened his eyes when she picked up his hand.

"How are you feeling?" Her voice was raspy with emotion.

Tom smiled weakly. "I'm okay. The doctor said I was exhausted from my recent bout with depression, and have torn ligaments in my right shoulder. But no incurable injuries."

Fran swallowed, struggling. "Tom, how can I express...how can I convey my gratitude...my admiration for what you did? You were incredibly brave. You saved my life."

Tom's smile was stronger this time. "Think nothing of it, Ma'am. All in the day's work. Besides, you were pretty brave yourself."

"Me?" Fran looked startled.

"Yes, you. You fought like a tiger. Even slugged him."

Fran looked even more startled. "I did?"

"Yes, right on the schnozola."

"On the -- ? You're kidding."

"No."

"Heavens! I remember struggling, but I don't remember that."

"You probably also saved my life."

Fran's eyebrows went up. She paled, swallowed, swallowed again. "I did? How?"

"You jerked loose, hit and shoved him, just as he fired that machine pistol. You threw his aim off. The bullets went over my head."

Fran stared at him. Never in her life had she done anything she considered courageous. Always she had run, crawled back into that box, tried to avoid pain and uncertainty. Now suddenly, she thought, perhaps, I'm no different from other people who do brave things. I acted despite my fear, and if I've done it once, just maybe, I can do it again.

Suddenly she felt better about herself than she had in a long time. She smiled, took a deep breath, savoring the moment, storing the memory, knowing she could revisit it whenever she needed to, draw strength from it. She was flooded with a budding sense of confidence and well-being.

"Tom, I know how disappointed you are over your project, how it turned out. I hope you won't let it demoralize you again."

Tom winced, looked out the window.

"I've done a lot of thinking about that. I'm still trying to understand the full meaning of everything that happened. Perhaps I'll have it straight in my mind soon."

Fran stared at the floor before continuing. "There is another matter. I hope you'll understand. I want to arrange a decent burial for Derek. He acted like a beast. I hate him for that, but we were close once, and I feel obligated. I also need to do some thinking about him and our relationship." She looked at Tom, almost pleadingly.

Tom sat up, grimacing as pain shot through his shoulder. He placed his bandaged left hand on the folded hands in her lap.

"Of course I understand. I wouldn't want you to do otherwise. I'll even come to the services, if they'll let me out of here." He paused, looked at her questioningly. "They recovered his..." He hated to say the word, body.

"Yes, Inspector Kahane was in earlier. You were asleep.

He said he had just returned to police headquarters from an all-night stakeout when you called to report the break-in at my apartment.

"He recognized the address and came racing over with the special assault team. They got to Temple Mount just in time to rescue both of us. He said Derek was killed instantly when he struck the pavement below."

Suddenly Fran looked even more serious. "And, Tom, I...we had a second visitor, actually two of them, while you were sleeping."

"Oh?"

"Yes. Sharon and her new friend, Nathan Green."

"Really -- "

"Yes. She came to see you, but because you were asleep, decided to make her peace with me. I'm certain she meant it for both of us. She expressed her regret over what had happened between us and Derek, said she understood what I had been through and admired the way I had endured and come out ready to face life again."

Tom's eyebrows went up. "Is that all she -- "

"No. She wanted to let us know she and Nathan -- and I gather he knows all about your previous relationship with her -- are going into business together, setting up a secretarial service."

Tom kept staring, anxious to hear the rest of the story.

"Obviously there's more to it than that. Sharon looked very happy. Actually beaming. I think she wanted to let us know she was going to be all right. I feel certain they're romantically involved or soon will be."

Tom exhaled. "That's a relief. I was worried."

They talked some more, then Fran returned to her room.

Tom found her dressed and packing when he visited her the next day. "They're releasing me, said I'll be okay," she reported. "I was coming to tell you. What are your prospects?"

"The doctor says at least two more days. He wants to build up my strength."

"Sounds like a good idea," Fran kissed him and departed,

promising to check with him later. She spent the rest of the morning locating an Anglican Church in the foothills of Jerusalem where she arranged services for Derek the next day. Fran, Dr. Abe, Shlomo Kahane and Sharon attended, with a number of professors from the University. Tom was still hospitalized.

The ceremony was brief and the eulogy -- by a Dr. Breckenridge from the English Department -- labored. But the sun shown down on the group, gathered at the graveside in the church cemetery. They heard the priest intone the final words: "Dust thou art, to dust returneth," thanked him, shook hands all around, then drove away.

For a time Fran returned to the grave daily after checking on Tom, now back in his hotel room. She sat on a bench beneath a tree near Derek's headstone, hardly moving, staring into space. At first she felt only grief over Derek's wasted life. Then she realized she was brooding over more than Derek. She was attempting to find meaning in the tragedy.

Why would a God who had given a man such talent sow within him the potential for his destruction; endow him with intelligence, knowledge and physical grace, yet cripple him with a compulsion he could not control, and with eventual madness?

She couldn't find an answer, but decided that what every person is given to work with at conception is a gamble, almost a crapshoot, in which thousands of genes in the parents' backgrounds are up for grabs and can come down in uncontrollable patterns. Perhaps God is too busy to be involved in arranging such happenings.

But why had her Christian standards failed her? She had seen in Derek all the virtues her religious father had taught her to believe in -- the divinity of Christ and his resurrection, the existence of good and evil, faith, belief in the power of prayer, in righteousness and rejection of sin.

She found an answer somewhat more obvious this time.

Derek was a sinner. He gambled, associated with thugs, lied and cheated, and almost killed her. She had erred. Her judgment of him was wrong, not her standards She had based her judgment of Derek's character on symbols, what she could see on the outside, not the reality of what was beneath the surface. Perhaps a little skepticism -- like Tom's -- was a good idea sometimes. Intelligence, knowledge of the world and a healthy wariness of human nature, were needed in living a Christian life.

The initial suspicion this could be so, then conviction that it was, came to her slowly, increment by increment, as she sat each day within a few feet of the mortal remains of this man she had known and almost accepted as a husband. And with the conviction came understanding that a certain part of her had died with Derek. She had lost a portion of the certainty that had held her life in a rigid mold from the day she was born.

That didn't surprise her. What did was the feeling of release that came with it. She suddenly felt free of a massive burden. She sighed, drew a deep breath, smiled. Her fear of life was being replaced by an awareness of the great feast life can be. She was beginning to feel like a woman reborn.

On the afternoon recognition of all this flooded her mind, dark, heavy clouds were casting shadows over the graveyard where she sat.

She looked up from her reverie to see the sun breaking through, bathing the church and the tree-shaded grounds in brilliant light. Off to one side she could see the Anglican priest who had conducted the services standing in the door of the church, looking in her direction.

She stood up, brushed wrinkles from her skirt, then walked slowly over to Derek's grave. Kneeling, she replaced the faded flowers there with the fresh ones in her hand.

"Goodbye, Derek," she said, choking back tears. "Perhaps we both were cheated by our imperfect understanding of God. Nobody warned us that could happen. Still I know he's out there, waiting, forgiving. May he finally give you as much peace as he has me."

She dabbed her eyes with a handkerchief as she turned and walked toward the priest, her face brightening into a smile.

"I want to thank you for all you've done," she said. "I

won't be coming back very often anymore. I'm going to start a new life, or try to. I've got a lot of thinking to do, but you've been a great help." She extended her hand, then turned and walked slowly to her car.

The priest stared after her. What a strange young woman, he thought. He hadn't the remotest idea what she was talking about.

Chapter XXXX

The morning after Fran ended her visits to Derek's grave, Tom awoke in his hotel room, feeling refreshed and back to normal. He bounced out of bed, walked to the phone and dialed.
"Fran? Tom. Could you come over? I'm finalizing some plans and need to discuss them with you." He completed a similar call to Dr. Abe and was standing by his bed, packing a suitcase, when they arrived.

"Sit down, have some coffee." He motioned toward a pot on the table. "Sorry to bother you, but I've decided to check out."

Fran froze, face suddenly pale. "Heavens, Tom, where will you...?" Her voice quavered. She sat down.

"You look better," Dr. Abe decided, Like you've come to terms with yourself." He remained standing, studying his former student, sipping his coffee.

Tom smiled. "I am better, a lot better. As for where I'm going I don't know yet. And yes, I've a new outlook. I've reached some conclusions about what happened to me here."

"Conclusions?" Fran was almost inaudible.

"Yes...all very personal stuff. I hesitate to burden you...but feel an obligation...." He swallowed, struggled for words. "I want to explain...my thinking... my feelings. It's not going to be easy so bear with me."

"Try us. Maybe we'll understand," Dr. Abe said. "What conclusions?"

Tom closed the suitcase, snapped the locks and poured a cup of coffee.

"For me, I guess the most important one is that, while I failed to find Christ's descendants -- or was unable to prove I had -- I found something I was looking for anyway. More on that in a minute."

Fran and Dr. Abe remained silent, listening.

Tom moved to the window, gazed out, turned and faced them." As you know I came here seeking the physical seeds of Christ -- his descendants -- and found seeds of a different kind."

"What do you mean -- *Seeds*?" Dr. Abe asked.

"Things he left behind, or you might even say 'planted.'"

"Such as?"

"Well, the tradition of compassion fostered by Christianity, for example. It would be stupid, even for an old agnostic like me, not to acknowledge that sentiment exists. It shapes our values, and at times makes us act more humanely than we might otherwise."

"There are others?" Fran said.

"Yes, and I found an important one through my experience here."

"You're losing me."

Tom took a deep breath, paused, glanced at them. "This is the tough part. Like I said it's all very personal, very private, and difficult to talk about. Sort of like undressing in public, to reveal all these inner thoughts, so be patient with me."

Again Dr. Abe mouthed the words, "Try us."

Tom looked out of the window again, hoping what he was about to say wouldn't sound too bizarre, too detached from every day reality. He spun around and began.

"While I was fighting my way out of my recent depression I kept mulling over three seemingly unrelated events. Didn't know why. Couldn't find a connection. One was some thoughts I had while driving through the desert the first time I went to Samuel's farm. Another was the crucifixion and resurrection. The third was a strange feeling I have whenever I'm near an important historical site or relic."

He cleared his throat.

"Then it all came together, and the moment it did I began to recover from the shattering experience of learning that my search for the descendants of Christ had ended in terminal doubt."

Tom walked back to the table and poured more coffee.

"I'll start with that ride through the desert to see Samuel. I drove by totally barren land. Death held it in a tight grip. Yet, nearby, the same kind of land was lush with crops, exploding with life. Water, fertilizer, intelligence, courage and labor had converted death into life. It was amazing.

"But I knew if the water, fertilizer, intelligence and labor were removed, death would return, so when life was in control there had to be a death potential in the land, And when death was in control, there had to be a life potential in the land. Seeds of life side by side with seeds of death. Otherwise there would be no way the land could yield crops when the necessary ingredients were supplied, or return to a moribund state when they were removed."

Tom studied his guests. "Are you still with me?"

Fran and Dr. Abe nodded.

"Then I had an epiphany." He laughed. "Boy, there's a high falutin' word. A brilliantly, enlightening moment and I had one. An idea burst in my head. I discovered a parallel between my thoughts about the desert land on the one hand, and the crucifixion and resurrection on the other, the same pattern imbedded in each.

"First I thought about the agony Christ suffered on the cross and possibly in the tomb.-- whether he was alive when placed there, whether he was dead when placed there, or whether his life hovered in between. At some point after his burial a powerful force took charge and life returned."

Tom rushed on.

"Just as in the desert land, there was in the tomb between that first Good Friday and Easter Sunday, a life potential and a death potential, and life emerged victorious, since available evidence indicates he did come out of that tomb. We should never forget that, because I think there is in each of us a similar life potential and death potential. Seeds of life that can be nurtured and made to grow, and seeds of death that also can be cultivated and set our lives on a downward course."

"Tom," Fran murmured, "I'm impressed."

Dr. Abe said nothing. He was seated now, still watching Tom closely.

"It was at this point I began to understand the third of the events -- the strange feeling I have when I stand close to some remnant or symbol of a great man, or great woman, or group of men and women, who have made extraordinary contributions to their larger communities and historical periods.

"I've experienced this feeling many times -- standing by the foundations of early homes built at Jamestown, Virginia, England's first successful colony in America; or discovering the crumbling walls of an old Butterfield stage station in Arizona; or walking at sunset through the ruins of the old Indian fighting post, Fort Bowie, before it was restored; or contemplating the brooding figure of Abraham Lincoln in his memorial in Washington, D.C.

"The last time this happened I was in Nazareth. I visited Mary's Well, looked down at those gushing, artesian waters. I felt goose bumps rising on my arms and neck. There seemed to be vibrations in the air. I was picking up something from the past. I didn't hear anything, but long dead voices were speaking to me. I was in a state of ultra-awareness. I was in communication with the past.

"Now it has dawned on me that what I sensed on each occasion was the legacy of these men and women. Their lives produced works of such value that when they died they lived on through the contributions they left behind.

"It was this after-life that I sensed and was in communication with. That also was what made me certain the message left in Joseph's Cave would be that quotation from the gospel of John, since the passage was about everlasting life. It fit into the context of the other things I was learning."

"Can you tie all this together for me, please?" Fran asked.

Tom, feeling more confident, sat in a chair, looked at her.

"Well, just as Christ in the tomb made a decision to live, each of these persons, or groups, at some point made decisions that propelled them along a course that produced their worthwhile accomplishments. They made decisions to contribute to the flow of those things we must have to live rich, fulfilled existences. They provided nourishment, mental and physical, to sustain life. Like Christ, they chose life.

"I think every person can make a similar choice, or vice versa he can devote his life to greed and self-gratification -- to taking from the life stream without contributing, or to taking more than he or she contributes. When that happens that person is moving toward a type of death. His life will contribute nothing, will be without meaning, as mine was when I came here..

"So each of us has a choice -- to live by producing a worthwhile, useful, beneficial moral, social or economic service or product, or suffer a kind of slow death by taking without contributing, or by taking more than he or she contributes. That choice is always there and can be exercised.

"So I repeat: Like the land in the desert, like Christ on the cross and in the tomb, there is always a life potential and a death potential side by side in each of us. Seeds of life and seeds of death. And we have to make a choice.

"We can cultivate either. At any time we can apply courage, energy, hard work and intelligence and convert death into life. Or we can remove those things and convert life into death. That's my interpretation of what happened to me here, flawed though it may be. It is something I can live by, an ethical structure that puts meaning into my life. To me, it is the most important seed left behind."

Tom stopped, smiled weakly, looked a little embarrassed. "God, I know that sounds corny, but I mean every word of it...and I'm glad I got it out in the open."

* * *

Fran looked at this stranger before her. Never before had

she seen him in full, unfurled dimension, his soul and character laid bare. For the first time she saw him as one of life's greatest creations -- a compassionate, mature, productive man.

Suddenly, the last remnants of the box that had encased her physical instincts and held her mind hostage, were torn asunder, never to be put together again. She felt an emotion she had never allowed herself to feel before -- a surge of sexual desire without guilt or shame, an unleashed yearning for life, a desire to participate, not to run and hide as she had in the past, to build and create, to contribute, swept over her. She swallowed, spoke in a strained voice.

"Tom, I wonder...could we go some place, spend some time together and really get to know each other better? I want you...rather I want to...oh, darn that doesn't sound right either."

She was embarrassed and confused, her face a deep pink.

* * *

Tom threw back his head and laughed. He looked at her and he saw another of life's greatest creations -- a compassionate, mature, productive woman.

"I was hoping you would say something like that, Fran, but I don't know. We've got to do this thing properly, you know, observe all the conventions. On the other hand I might be willing to make an exception. On second thought I can hardly wait. When do we leave?"

He came out of his chair, eyes devouring her.

The blush on Fran's face deepened, but she rose, too, afraid to say more.

Suddenly they embraced, kissing hungrily, bodies melded. Fran did not pull away.

* * *

Amen, Dr. Abe thought, sighing.

He felt like he had just turned the last page in a story he had been living a long time. Two of his favorite people had started from almost opposite poles and at last had found common ground. Each had cast aside his, and her, sterile past. Dr. Abe knew they would contribute enough to life to leave a worthwhile legacy behind after they died. They would enrich, not impoverish, the soil from which they sprang. Their lives would live on after them.

And in this way, the prophecy of Joseph's Cave -- "though he were dead, yet shall he live" -- would be fulfilled.

-0-

```
FIC
CARY
```

Cary, James

Seeds : search for
the descendents of
Christ

JUN 3 0 2006

Boynton Beach City Library
   Books may be kept two weeks and may be renewed up to six times, except if they have been reserved by another patron. Excluding new books, magazines and reserved items.
   A fine is charged for each day a book is not returned according to the above rule. No book will be issued to any person incurring such a fine until it has been paid.
   All damages to books beyond reasonable wear and all losses shall be made good to the satisfaction of the Librarian.
   Each borrower is held responsible for all items charged on his card and for all fines accruing on the same.